AUDINE'S STORY

A Sinful, Cursed, Malevolent, and

Deceptive Woman

Book One

Sondra J. Hardy

DEDICATION

Audine's Story is Dedicated to Valina Jackson

Sista Friend, I still can't believe that you're gone. I miss those times when you'd call me from a phone booth at the club you used to frequent, back in those days, to inform me that "so and so" just walked in. And like clockwork, first the pause, then hearing you howling in laughter, which put us both in laughter so hard that we could sense the tears rolling down our faces.

You were the one who introduced me to working

in and with the community. When you mentioned there was a job opening at eighty-eight Warren Street, you'd be perfect because I'll be your boss. That job lasted five years, through five galas, providing food on the table, paying bills, keeping a roof over my head, keeping the lights on, and sharpening my skills as a future leader.

Then you went somewhere where you were needed the most, and I went to many more places to not only learn more but to put what you taught me into use, opening bigger, better, and new doors.

Then, after many years of quiet, I heard the news that you left us; all of us.

It hurt, and made me cry, but through my tears, I managed a smile at those memories that will last a lifetime.

Rest on, my Sista friend, rest on peacefully.

ACKNOWLEDGMENT

"Writing my second novel about Audine and the characters in her story was at times a challenge. However, her story reflected what human behavior is like when things are so wrong; yet, when her true colors were brought to the surface, it was right. There are those who, from the beginning, were those "God-sends" whenever I needed them.

They say that people come into your life for a reason, a season, or a lifetime. You all are my lifeline. This project wouldn't have been possible without the unwavering support of my circle of friends and my mentor. Their belief in me has been my greatest inspiration.

I want to thank my mentor, Dr. Roland Gibson, who asked me the questions 'why,' 'who,' 'what,' and 'where.' When things didn't make sense, you and I had long conversations for hours to break things down, analyze them, and then rebuild them. There are more stories to tell, thanks to your advice and wise counsel.

Eric Scott Drummond: Whenever I sent those frantic emails asking which publishing house to work with, you were the one who advised on the ones that may have looked good on paper, but also advised me not to sign with them. Thank you for your advice and for asking me the questions of why, who, and when.

Cynthia Martin: Sister-friend, how many times have I called you frantic because something on my computer wasn't working or didn't seem right? You were the one who said, "Hold on, I'll be right over". After a simple fix and a few chats over coffee, you resolved everything, and I was able to complete the work without any further issues.

Wesley Gunn: Once again, you hit it out of the ballpark. When I visualized this book cover, you took the time to help me bring Audine's face to life. Your gift is organic as it is beautiful. I've more stories to tell, and you've more book covers to help me bring my vision to life. The world needs to know our creative gifts.

I thank the four of you for your continued presence to further encourage my gift of writing, creativity, and hard work that gave life to this vision."

Sondra J. Hardy, Author

ABOUT THE AUTHOR

Who is Sondra J. Hardy? Sondra was born and raised in West Haven, Connecticut, where she attended elementary school and graduated from West Haven High School in 1974. She attended Bay State College in Boston, Massachusetts, where she served as Senior Vice President and graduated with honors in 1977. She also received the Beatrice Ruderman Award for Fashion Merchandising and Design. Sondra has always had a love for reading novels, and as a result, she has a library of over five hundred books that she has read and collected over the years. She also has over two hundred cookbooks because of her love of baking desserts. Her favorite author is Walter Mosley, and her personal goal is to have one of her Easy Rawlins books signed by him. In 2023, Sondra published her first novel, Pieces. The novel was received with great success, winning the Book Fest Awards, the International Impact Book Award, and being a finalist for the Best Book Awards and Independent Author Awards. Sondra has completed her second novel, "Audine, A Sinful, Cursed, Malevolent, and Deceptive Woman," based on the character Audine Collins, who is in the first novel. Two more novels, "Extinguished," a novel about Kempton St. Laurent, the eldest son of Maria St. Laurent, who will serve in WWII, and whose mother, Maria St. Laurent, is a Hoodoo practitioner. The final installment will focus on the youngest son, Avid, who served as a doctor in the Korean War, and his time spent in Harlem in 1956. Sondra's personal goal is to see her novels appear as television series or movies

Page Blank Intentionally

CHAPTER ONE

New Orleans

"Get out of my sight!" Those were the last words I said to my soon-to-be ex-wife, Audine, as she left without even saying goodbye to our son, Mason. I watched her grab two worn-out suitcases, her coat, and her purse. Audine was still wearing the dress she had worn to church. During the ride home from church, she begged and screamed at me, pleading for another chance to save our marriage. Audine promised she'd never lie, steal, or gossip again. I didn't believe her for a second. That was a lie, because just before the service ended, she lied to several church members who asked about Violet's whereabouts.

"Oh, my daughter Violet decided not to go to that college because she's too smart to study there! Violet is heading to France to learn proper French, not that silly French Creole Maria and her daughters speak, hah! And when she's done, she said she'll teach French for a few years. So, who knows when she'll come back here, huh? My Violet is smart and beautiful, so I gave her my blessing to enjoy France! Wayne, Mason, and I plan to visit her in the Spring, just around the time Wayne and I have our first baby!" exclaimed Audine.

But the ride home was a completely different story. Audine broke down in tears again, pleading and screaming at me to give her another chance.

After explaining that our son, Mason, would stay with me, I told her that I didn't want him taken from one town to another just to end up in a rundown place with people likely to rob, steal, and get drunk. I also didn't want him around women who would flash themselves for a dollar or charge more if the man wanted to go all the way. After that, I asked Audine to leave, and we were done for good. She slammed the door, cursing and yelling.

It's eight o'clock and dark outside, so I've had time to think about her safety while she's walking alone.

"Mason, grab your coat and hat; we must find your mother. I have a bad feeling about her walking alone out there. If I see her, I'll let her know in the car and drive her the rest of the way to the train station. God only knows how horrible I'll feel if something were to happen to her", said Wayne in a distressed tone as he scooped up his coat and hurriedly buttoned it.

"Yes, sir," Mason replied, his voice flat.

Today's events had taken a toll on him. He could hear his mother screaming and crying, and overheard Wayne accusing Audine of being a gossip, a liar, and a thief! What hurt the most was the evidence: a torn, greasy envelope containing nearly a thousand dollars.

Mason thought bitterly *that my mother had everything: a husband, a new home, and a new life.*

Wayne stood frozen; his eyes locked on Mason. The weight on his face made him look like a completely different person, years older. Audine couldn't take Mason away from him.

Wayne muttered under his breath, "Over my dead body," thinking to himself.

Wayne strode over to where Mason was standing and put his hands on Mason's shoulders.

"You did nothing wrong, Mason," Wayne said.

"Your mother is mixed up. Stealing from me and telling me all those lies was completely unacceptable, especially since I was her husband. She also lied about our church friends. Deacon Brockelman pulled me aside and told me his wife left him just a few weeks ago because Audine spread rumors that he was spending hours at Mrs. Erma Beaks' house after work. Keep in mind, Mrs. Beaks is a widow who was engaged to Mr. Walter Donaldson."

"Wait, you mean Mr. Donaldson, one of the ushers at our church?" Mason asked, lifting an eyebrow.

"Yes, he and Mrs. Beaks had been secretly seeing one another for six months. It seems your mother overheard them conversing after church, and he had his arm around her waist. Whelp, that's when she saw them stealing a short kiss. Then the lies started, as well as accusations that weren't true. Honest to God, there were so many lies that I lost count," Wayne said disgustingly. "From what was told, your mother started a nasty rumor about Deacon Brockelman's wife, and she pitched a fit! She packed her suitcase and left on the next train to Atlanta. A week later, Mr. Donaldson requested the return of his engagement ring. Poor Mrs. Beaks cried so much that she refused to return to church. Humph, all this mess because of Audine's big mouth", said Wayne, shifting uneasily.

As memories of having a conversation with a tearful Vivian Beaks, who confided to Wayne that losing Mr. Donaldson was like reliving his death, a week later, Vivian moved to another town and joined another church.

"I still can't believe I put a gold wedding band on Audine's wicked ring finger," Wayne resentfully said.

"I never want to see her or Violet again," Mason said, his eyes welling up with tears that he didn't try to hide. "They both destroyed our family!" he shouted, grabbing his coat. "My mother turned out to be a terrible person; everything that comes out of her mouth is a lie, never the truth! And Violet? She's a common whore!" he bellowed, blinking back angry tears. Feeling exposed and vulnerable, he turned away from Wayne. Wayne saw Mason's shoulders slump, and his hand pressed against the wall for support. Wayne heard the unmistakable sounds of loud sniffling.

Wayne quietly approached his son and placed a protective arm around his shoulders. Mason broke down and wept. Then, pulling a handkerchief from his trouser pocket, Wayne handed it to Mason.

"Thanks," he whispered as he blew his nose.

"I know how you feel, son; your mother has caused much pain for our family. Audine's heart of wickedness has led you to despise her, and as for me, I no longer love her. Violet committed an unspeakable act that contributed to this mess. She knew what she was doing, and we all understand the consequences of what she and Clarence did. I don't hate Violet; I loathe what she did. And concerning Clarence, he's going straight to hell after what he's done," said Wayne.

"So why are we going out at night to look for my mother?" Mason frowned.

"Because even though Audine is no longer my wife, she's still your mother. If anything were to happen to her walking alone in the dark, whelp, it would be all my fault", said Wayne. "So, c'mon, let's go before it gets so dark that we'll see nothing."

Wayne and Mason grabbed their coats, with Mason stepping out the door first to start Wayne's car. Before Wayne left the house, he gazed into the kitchen, recalling the chaos that had erupted just a few hours earlier. He couldn't help but wince as he remembered Audine and Violent engaged in a fierce brawl.

There were still a few drops of Violet's dried blood on the floor that Audine refused to mop up. Still in shock, Wayne forgot to clean the remnants of the blood splatter. He couldn't shake the thought that part of that splatter was mixed with Violet's unborn child and Clarence.

Snapping off the lights, Wayne locked the door and hurried outside to the already running car. After getting in, he shifted the car into gear, turned on the headlights, and drove off into the night to search for the woman he once loved but now loathed.

CHAPTER TWO

After driving for forty-five minutes, Audine was nowhere to be found. The roads were eerily dark, with no one in sight. Even after Wayne pulled the car off the road and ventured into the darkest parts of the streets, which were treacherous and brutal to see, Audine was still missing. His heart racing, Wayne feared the worst - that Audine had been kidnapped or found dead, just like Jonathan. As he rushed back to the car, his panic growing, he couldn't help but notice Mason sitting alone. Out of breath, he hurried back to the car after a long, fast walk. Gripping the steering wheel, he leaned his forehead against it.

"Maybe she's still at the train station," Mason said.

"You may be right because it's getting late, and we must leave. Come on, let's go," Wayne said as he started the car.

Wayne drove for another twenty minutes until he reached the train station. He and Mason got out of the car and sprinted toward the platform. Nobody was there except for the dim lights that illuminated the area. Gazing into the darkness, all Wayne could see was the wooden awning bearing the name of the train stop, two sets of tracks running in opposite directions, and benches marked "Whites Only" and "Colored Only." The platform was littered with crumpled pieces of paper and one cigarette butt that was still lit but quickly smoldered.

Wayne's stomach churned with dread. He pulled out his pocket watch and flipped it open.

10:30. From the cigarette butt, it looks like the train just left.

"What the hell are you two boys doing here?" a male voice snapped.

Wayne and Mason both spun around at the same time to see who it was.

A white conductor wasn't alone; he was accompanied by a tall conductor whose face contorted with intense hatred. Both men occupied their space, standing with stiff postures, squared shoulders, and a lurching gait. The tall, menacing conductor with piercing green eyes seemed ready to throw the first punch. Wayne noticed that the conductor's hands were balled into tight fists.

"Evening, sir," Wayne said, nodding toward both men. Mason remained still, watching the conductors warily, particularly the one with his fists clenched.

"My son and I came here to make sure my wife got on the train safely, sir," Wayne said bluntly.

"As you can all see, there's nobody here. The last train left five minutes ago. Whoever you're looking for ain't here, especially some black woman you claim is your wife", said the shorter conductor, his voice matching the hardness of his gaze. He glanced over at Mason, eyeing him suspiciously.

"Yeah, I think you boys should move along," the tall conductor said, starting to edge closer to Wayne.

Mason's eyes were locked onto the tall conductor, and his hands were tightly clenched into fists. His only regret was that he hadn't landed a solid punch on Clarence's jaw when he shoved him up against the wall just a few days earlier.

"Dad, come on. Let's get out of here. Ma's on the train, at least we know that", said Mason, grabbing Wayne's coat sleeve and starting to back away.

"That's a good idea; both of you boys, get the fuck out of my station! Go on, get your black asses out of here!" the tall conductor bellowed. Then, out of nowhere, he shoved Wayne so hard that Wayne hit the concrete ground hard. The sudden shove made Wayne fall flat on his backside, trying to break the fall but scraping his elbows to avoid hitting his head.

"Shit!" he screamed in pain. Blood began to stain his shirt, which was torn at the elbows. The unexpected shove infuriated Wayne, leaving him to wonder why this brute of an asshole had pushed him for no apparent reason.

Mason charged at the tall conductor, smashing him square in the jaw. The conductor attempted to swing back but was too slow and missed. The shorter one wielded a quick blackjack.

"Leave us alone! We're not bothering you!" Wayne shouted angrily.

Before it was too late to prevent a potential brawl that could land Mason in jail or, worse, kill Wayne, he scrambled to his feet and tugged at Mason's coat sleeve.

"Mason, run!" Wayne yelled, and both took off from the station towards the car. The two conductors were running as fast as they could, but stopped to duck down and throw rocks at them while letting loose with curses.

"Get out and stay out of my goddamn train station, you good-for-nothing niggers!" screamed the tall conductor, who, after hurling a huge rock that narrowly missed Mason as he jumped into the car. Wayne started the engine and sped up, jerking the vehicle onto the road and heading back home.

As he sped away, gripping the steering wheel, Wayne felt a surge of relief that Audine was probably on the train that had just pulled out of the station and was headed somewhere, never to return to New Orleans. But he was also furious about how he and Mason had been spoken to and chased off the platform.

"Two-bit motherfuckers!" exploded Wayne,

enraged; the pain in his ass intensified, causing him to wince.

"I didn't even see that asshole push me until it was too late! Damn motherfuckers!" Wayne fumed.

Wayne never cursed, not even with Mason sitting right there. But the thought of Mason getting tangled up in a fight was unsettling.

Thanks to you, Audine! My son and I could have been seriously injured, arrested, or even beaten, all because of you, you heartless, deceitful woman! Wayne thought to himself as he sped up the car.

"You okay, Dad?" Mason asked, clearly furious after watching his father get assaulted.

"I was ready to fight that conductor! After what Clarence did to me, I'm pretty burned up about that! All I wanted was to hurt Clarence and that conductor!" seethed Mason, whose voice had risen almost to a scream, as he pounded the dashboard with his fist, which left a slight dent.

"Clarence did what to you?" said Wayne, eyeing Mason, whose face was looking distant.

"Look at me, Mason. What the hell did Clarence do to you?" Wayne demanded.

Memories from that day flashed back to Mason: Clarence's hand around his neck, slamming him against the wall, and leaving a bruise on his arm.

As Wayne accelerated the car to a higher speed, he listened to the sordid details of what Clarence did to Mason. The more Mason highlighted the particulars, the more Wayne shifted from agitation to rage, especially after seeing the large bruise left on Mason's arm when he unbuttoned the cuff of his shirt sleeve and pulled it up for Wayne to see.

As they pulled into the driveway, the silence was deafening. Mason gazed out the window, lost in thought, while Wayne clutched the steering wheel, his expression pensive.

"I'm glad he's dead, that low son-of-a-bitch. He gets Violet pregnant, then puts his filthy, greasy, farm-working hands on you! Fuck him, that low piece of shit! Glad he's gone, and I'm glad that snake bit him!" Wayne hissed, venom dripping from every word he spoke.

"I'm not only glad that Clarence's is gone, but he's gone for good, but we almost got into a fight with those two conductors. After the tall one pushed you, I wasn't going to stand by and watch him hurt you again, no, sir! I gave him one good smash to the jaw. I Betcha he won't be talking too much tomorrow morning when he goes to work!" he said, meeting Wayne's eye and giving off a nervous laugh.

"I'm proud of what you did this evening," Wayne said.

"You are?" Mason asked, staring into Wayne's eyes.

A sudden, unapologetic expression crossed Wayne's tired face.

"Yes, I am. I'm proud of you because you stood your ground, even with the possibility of getting beaten by that savage. You took the stance of bravery that saved us both from getting killed tonight, son. For that, I thank you," said Wayne, patting Mason's shoulder.

Earlier aggrieved while at home, Mason now felt safe. Audine and Violet were gone for good, but he had

Wayne, who stepped in as a father. The ride felt like it took forever, but they finally made it home. As they stepped out of the car, Wayne ensured the windows were rolled up, the doors locked, and the headlights off after turning off the ignition. Following a brief inspection, Wayne shoved the keys into his trouser pocket.

As he and Mason walked toward their house, they both stopped suddenly, a bubbling sensation rising in Wayne's throat at what he saw.

"Whose car is that in front of our place?" Mason asked, his voice shaking with fear.

Wayne stood motionless, his gaze fixed on the car parked in front of his house.

CHAPTER THREE

As the driver's side door of the car in front of Wayne's house opened, a woman in a dark blue dress stepped out slowly. Wayne took a closer look and recognized her, then got out of his car and rushed over, climbing the stairs to his house.

"Etta, what are you doing here at this time of the night?" Wayne asked, tapping her on the shoulder.

Etta flinched, not expecting the touch on her shoulder. She turned to face Wayne, and with open arms, he embraced her, holding her close to his heaving chest, where she buried her head. Wayne broke the embrace and exhaled.

"After all the commotion I witnessed outside the church between you and Audine, I had to come over here to make sure you and Mason were alright," she said, catching her breath. "Oh, is Audine even here? Because if she is, I'll leave right now."

Wayne glanced away and nodded to Mason that

it was safe to get out of the car and enter the house.

"It's all right, Mason. It's Etta! Come on, so we can all go inside. Hurry, son."

As Mason got out of the car, he scrambled toward Etta and hugged her warmly. In a surprising move, Mason embraced Wayne so tightly that Wayne clenched his teeth in pain, reminiscent of what happened after he fell on the concrete platform.

Etta watched this unfold in fascination. That's when she noticed the dried blood seeping through Wayne's shirt at the elbows.

"Oh, dear God!" she exclaimed. "What happened to you and Mason?"

Wayne studied Etta's face for a long moment and then spoke.

"A lot has happened to my family today," Wayne said, his voice wavering. "Mason and I could have gotten hurt really badly, or worse, killed tonight at the train station. But to answer your question, Audine is gone, and she's not coming back," he replied flatly. "Let's all go inside where it's safe, and I'll tell you what happened." Etta nodded, and they all headed into the house.

Emotionally drained, Mason left and headed straight to his room after saying goodnight to Etta.

"Have a seat, Etta," Wayne said as he helped her out of her coat, draping it across the couch.

"Thanks, Wayne," she said, settling into the easy chair across from the wood stove. The warmth of the fire filled the living room.

"Hungry? Given what happened today, I've got some leftover pie that never got served, plus some coffee. All I need to do is brew a fresh pot."

He examined the tears on his coat sleeves as he slowly took off his jacket. After removing his coat, he couldn't help but notice the crimson blood that had stained his shirt. The bleeding had stopped, but his back ached.

Seeing his painful expression, Etta lifted herself, walked over, and took his arm.

"Yes, I'm starving, but first, we need to talk about what just happened here," she said, nodding toward his injured arm. "You clean up, and I'll take care of the coffee and pie," Etta said.

Wayne looked into her eyes and realized that Etta, not Lena, and definitely not Audine, should have been his wife.

"I'll be back, and thank you for coming over here to look after Mason and me," he said in gratitude as he slipped away to use the bathroom to clean up and attend to his wounds.

Forty-five minutes later, Etta had made enough coffee for them and cut two thick slices of pie to last through what she thought would be a long conversation that might take all evening.

Etta thought to herself as she folded two napkins and loaded the tray, "I've so many questions to ask of my Wayne now that that malicious woman Audine is gone for good." She carried it into the parlor and carefully placed it on the low-wood table.

Sitting in the easy chair, Etta draped the napkin across her lap and poured a cup of steaming hot coffee for Wayne and herself. After taking a few sips of the rich, dark blend, she closed her eyes, losing herself in thought. She didn't notice Wayne walking a few steps away from her seat.

Wayne's eyes held her captive as he gazed at his friend of over twenty-five years. They had grown closer over the past several months after Lena ran off. Still, due to Audine's aggressive advances, Etta informed him that it would be best for her to stay away permanently, especially upon hearing of their upcoming nuptials.

Etta secretly wished for things between Audine and Wayne to fall apart, prompting Audine to pack her suitcases and leave New Orleans forever. After witnessing their heated argument and seeing Wayne stride into church alone, sitting beside a stoic Mason, it was clear that something was wrong since Audine never entered the church to attend the service.

Etta entered the fellowship hall earlier that morning, peered out the window, and saw Audine weeping hysterically in Wayne's car. At that moment, she knew it was over between Audine and Wayne.

"Thanks for the coffee and pie," Wayne said as he settled into the chair, easing his sore back and letting out a deep breath. He was wearing a clean shirt, slippers, and pants.

Etta was startled when he suddenly entered the room. She hoped he didn't notice her staring at the photos of him and Audine. One stood out, though: the one with Mason and Violet on Wayne's wedding day. Hushed tones circulated through the church, claiming that Violet had done something unspeakable and had been abruptly sent away.

"I'll be getting rid of the one with Audine and me," Wayne said as he took a bite of the flaky-crusted sweet potato pie.

"I'm sorry, I didn't mean to stare at those pictures. It's just that I remember that day so clearly, and now- "

"Etta, listen to me; it's fine," Wayne interrupted. "Audine's behavior as a wife was disgraceful."

Etta observed him looking down at his coffee, a disgusted expression on his face. She extended her hand across the small table. Placing his cup down, Wayne reached out and took her hand firmly.

"Tell me what happened in this house," she said,

her tone deliberate.

Wayne's face was twisted with anger.

"This all started and ended with Clarence Margaret not being able to keep his goddamn prick inside of his pants".

Wayne slumped heavily into the easy chair.

"I want to hear everything from you because the whole church heard the shouting between you and Audine. But the real surprise was when you stood up and announced that Violet would not attend college and that the award would be given to Carol Thompson. By the way, where is Violet?" Etta inquired as she took another bite of her pie.

"Violet had to be sent away to live in Harlem, New York. She's staying with Audine's sister, Cee-Cee, and her husband, Hubert," he answered.

"Why? I'm not sure I understand. Is she sick? Is she coming back?" Etta frowned, confused.

"Etta, Violet's not moving back here. She's having a baby," Wayne said, looking away from Etta.

Shocked by what she had just heard, Etta quickly set the steaming cup of coffee on the table to prevent it from spilling all over her lap.

"She's having a baby. Who's the father? Violet never had any suitors, and most of the boys she went to school with are now married or in the army! I don't understand this at all, Wayne, who- "

"It's Clarence Margaret's child," Wayne briskly interrupted. "Violet is having Clarence's child. When Audine lost our baby during our wedding trip to New York, she was devastated. So, when we returned home, Audine noticed her spare suitcases by the door. She asked why her suitcases were by the doorway and reminded Violet that she wasn't due to leave for Teacher's College for another two weeks. Before we could get an answer from her, Mason told us everything: how he caught Violet and Clarence naked in her bed," Wayne said, looking away, disgusted as he recounted the despicable details of Violet and Clarence and how Clarence put a baby inside Violet's belly.

"Oh, my goodness!" Etta exclaimed, covering her mouth and shutting her eyes tightly. "So you're saying that Clarence, who was married, did things to put a baby inside of Violet?"

"Yes, that is precisely what happened. I'm glad that he's never going to walk on this earth again; after everything he's done, he deserves his punishment in hell," said Wayne.

That's why Maria didn't want anyone at Clarence's funeral, and Violet wasn't with her family in the church. Etta thought to herself as she took another sip of coffee.

Etta pushed her coffee aside, rose from the chair, stood, and opened her arms.

"Come here," she beckoned to him.

Wayne stood and went straight into Etta's open arms, embracing her. This time, being in her arms felt right; Etta's heart pounded in her chest. Suddenly, Wayne lifted her chin and kissed her passionately. The quiet passion of years simmered between them. At that moment, they were more than best friends.

"I have to leave, Wayne. It's getting late, and I dare not call on Ricks and his men to escort me home,"

Etta said, pulling away.

"It's too dangerous for you to drive all the way home," said Wayne. I know this may not seem right in the eyes of most folks who know us, but I was hoping you could stay here with me and Mason. You can sleep in Violet's room. There are a few clean nightgowns in her room. I'll wake you up first thing in the morning. Please say yes to me, Etta, that you'll stay here with us because I won't take no for an answer from you."

"Yes," Etta said. A smile spread across her lips as Wayne lifted her into his arms again and kissed her deeply.

On cue, Wayne parted her lips with his tongue, and her mouth opened to meet his passionate kiss. Wayne tightened his grip on her until she began to moan softly.

"You have to know how much I want you," Wayne said, his deep voice barely above a whisper. His hands slid slowly down, cupping her generous backside.

Etta let out a soft gasp of surprise as a wave of wet heat surged between her legs, and the feel of Wayne's strong, masculine body made her want him.

"I want you, too, but if we went to your bed, it would be wrong. You're still married, and Mason is right next door – he'd hear us. I wouldn't do that to your son or us," she said, looking deep into his eyes.

"You're right; I don't want to put Mason through that ever again," Wayne nodded in agreement with Etta. "He's been through hell, especially with his mother showing us the kind of woman she is."

"No more talking about Audine," said Etta as she gently pressed her fingers on Wayne's lips to silence him. "From now on, it will only be about you, me, and Mason. I love both of you, and as we move toward the future, I'm not letting you go ever again."

Etta, I've wanted you for years, but I've made some unwise mistakes. First Lena, and now Audine. How can I make this right with you?" Wayne asked, speaking the words in a low, pained voice.

Etta met the heat in his gaze with her own, as the desire for Wayne flared in her eyes.

At last, he's all mine! Audine is gone forever, and

my best friend of twenty-five years made it clear that he wants me! I won't ever lose him again, never again! Etta thought to herself as she held onto Wayne tighter.

"You already started to make things right," she said, standing on her toes to caress his face.

"I know you made mistakes because, after all, you and I were just friends. After you married Audine, I thought I would lose you forever. All I could do was pretend that I was happy for you. But deep inside my heart, I was sad and miserable; my heart was broken," she admitted, her voice shaking, betraying her true feelings. "But that is over. Audine is gone, and we have a chance to be together. I'm not going to lose you to anyone ever again. I love you, Wayne," Etta admitted without hesitation or care whether it was right for a woman to confess her feelings first.

The admission surprised Wayne, but at the same time, he was pleased to hear those words from Etta.

Wayne leaned down to kiss Etta again; this time, she devoured his mouth with passionate kisses.

Where did she learn to kiss like that? Wayne

wondered. *He ran his fingers through her hair, smiling at her beauty and confidence.*

"What's got you smiling?" asked Etta.

"I'm just wondering where you learned how to kiss me like you did because, woman, you lit something inside of me that I thought was gone for good," admitted Wayne.

"I've dreamed about kissing and holding you for most of my life. I even prayed for it for years. But now I see that my prayers were answered, and now that I'm here, I will see that nobody stands in the way," said Etta, her voice shaking slightly, betraying her true feelings. "But we should be getting ready for bed because it's late. I plan to leave early tomorrow morning to go home and prepare for school. My second-grade pupils can't see me exhausted. So, I'm going to say goodnight. But before I do, would you call my aunt and uncle to let them know I am staying with you and Mason? They must be worried sick about where I am," conveyed Etta.

"Of course, I will; let's call them now," replied Wayne as he picked up the phone and dialed Etta's aunt and uncle's telephone numbers.

Standing behind Wayne with her arms wrapped around his waist, he told Etta's Uncle Cuff that it was too dangerous for her to drive alone and too late in the evening to wake Ricks and his men to follow her. She'd be safer sleeping at his house in Violet's room, and Etta would leave early the next morning.

Ricks would be called to escort her just in time for her to be present in class and ready to teach. Cuff gave his blessing, and Etta excitedly picked up the phone to say goodbye to Cuff and her aunt Evamae.

"I'll be sure to wake you as soon as I get up," said Wayne, pulling Etta close. "Violet's room is the last one on the right."

"Good night, Wayne," she murmured, embracing him.

"Good night, Etta," he whispered.

He watched as Etta removed her Oxford shoes, padded down the corridor, and slipped inside Violet's room, quietly closing the door. Wayne stared at the door, trying to process everything that had happened in the last twenty-four hours. He could not believe that his best friend —and now the woman he loved —was in the next room. Smiling, he strolled into the parlor, collected the dishes, and washed them in the kitchen sink, snapping off the lights and rechecking the front entry door to ensure it was locked.

Instead of going to his bedroom, Wayne wandered over to Violet's room and stood at the door. He listened for a moment but heard nothing except the rustling of the trees in the wind. He left and went to his room, shutting the door behind him. After undressing, he examined the scrapes on his elbows. The throbbing pain subsided, thanks to the salve that Maria gave him when Mason fell and cut his knee a year ago.

Wayne knelt by his bedside in prayer. He began by asking the Lord for Audine's safety and for patience in forgiving her.

That would take time. He thanked God that the woman he loved was asleep in the next room. When he finished, he climbed into bed and drifted into a deep sleep.

It was Monday morning, five o'clock, and the only sound in the house was the percolator. Wayne was already awake, and the smell of fresh, dark roast coffee filled the kitchen. Mason and Etta would be stirring soon.

He carried his Bible into the kitchen, placed it on the table, and stared at it for a moment. Letting out a deep sigh, he reached over and opened it up. He flipped through the pages of the book of Proverbs, where he found the marriage certificate tucked away in a sealed envelope. As he pulled it out and opened the envelope, his eyes fell on his and Audine's signatures. All the memories of their wedding day, the nightmare of their trip to New York, losing their unborn child, the shocking discovery of Violet and Clarence's affair, Violet's pregnancy, the arguments, and the expulsion from their home flooded back. For a moment, Wayne closed his eyes tight, trying to block out the pain that still lingered.

After opening his eyes, he realized what he had to do. He would call his supervisor to let him know he would report to work on Tuesday morning. A family emergency had arisen and needed to be resolved immediately.

At 1:00 p.m. on Monday, Wayne Collins finalized his annulment from Audine, looking ahead to a future with Etta.

CHAPTER FOUR

Audine

"Ouch! Shit, got-damned rock!" seethed Audine as she tumbled for the fourth time in the darkness of the roadway. This time, the fall left her sprawled on the dusty road, scraping her knee. Her stockings were ruined now, peppered with holes, and her once-shiny black oxfords were caked with dirt. Each time she fell, it felt like someone was behind her delivering a forceful shove. By the third tumble, she felt a powerful kick to her backside, sending her sprawling on the ground.

Terrified, Audine slowly stood up, brushed herself off, and sped up until she was running down the road. But then, her foot hit another huge rock, and she stumbled. Blood rushed to her hands, and at the same time, something wrapped tightly around her wrist, the grip sharp and fierce.

"Ahhgh!" she screamed in horror upon seeing the snake. Then, crying hysterically, Audine managed to pull the snake off her wrist and throw the creature into the woods.

"Fuck you, Wayne! I hate you, you son of a bitch!" Audine screamed.

"I hate you, Violet! That bastard child is growing inside you, and I hate you, Clarence, and your useless wife, Maria! I'm so glad you're dead, Clarence, hah! This is all your fault; all of you have caused me so much pain! Good for nothing—"

She was interrupted by a loud rumble in the distance, reminiscent of a car or truck. The noise crept closer, and Audine began to shake uncontrollably with fear.

"Oh my God, it's either evil white men or the Klan! Help me, Jesus, save me!" she yelled, again shielding her eyes from the intense headlight heading straight at her.

Out of nowhere, Audine felt a warm stream of pee running down her legs, followed by an overwhelming urge to relieve herself. The truck came to a sudden stop. Audine, crouched over in agony, cried uncontrollably, partly out of fear of who was inside the truck and partly from the humiliation of losing control of her bladder.

"Audine, is that you?" the driver asked.

Audine instantly recognized the voice. It was Turner Beckles.

"Yee-yes," stammered Audine, "It's me, Turner; how are you?"

"What in God's name are you doing out here in the middle of the night?" Turner asked, stepping out of the truck and approaching Audine. He was stunned to see Audine, who had looked stunning in her Sunday church clothes just hours before, now appear disheveled and wild-eyed. Her hair was a tangled mess, her stockings were in tatters, and the stench of urine mixed with the foul smell of Audine's flatulence was overwhelming. He had to pull his handkerchief from his pocket to cover his nose. Audine was embarrassed, trying to cover herself by crossing her arms.

"Where are you going? Are you okay? Where's your husband? For God's sake, why is he allowing you to walk out here in the dark at this hour all alone?" he asked in the most curious tone.

Audine stiffened at the curious note in his voice.

What gives Turner the right to ask me all these questions? He's got some nerve! And why is he covering his nose with a handkerchief like I stink? She fumed to herself.

"Well, if you really want to know, Wayne's car isn't working. At all. He was outside tinkering with it for hours! I told him I had to be in New York to see my sister, and the train was about to leave! So, I said I'd hurry to the train station as fast as I could and be there in no time. Humph!" she huffed.

Turner squinted in disbelief that Wayne would allow his wife to walk five miles through the pitch-black darkness of the night, especially in New Orleans, where no Black person felt safe when the sun went down.

Turner thought to himself, "Either Wayne is crazy to let his wife be out here alone, or Audine is an outright liar."

"I can't believe Wayne would let you walk out here alone if his car wasn't running. Why didn't he call Ricks or even me? One of us would've been able to come over and take you to the train station. I find this a bit strange, if you ask me," said Turner, eyeing Audine with suspicion.

"Think what you want!" Audine snapped. "I'm telling you the honest-to-God truth! Do I have any reason to lie about that?" she asked, her voice quivering with anger, making Turner even more suspicious.

She's a liar, plain and simple. She should be grateful that my wife Beryl isn't here, humph! Turner thought to himself, smirking, that the way she asked Audine questions would make Audine cry like a baby.

"Well, seeing that you're almost there, I'll give you a ride the rest of the way," Turner said, smiling at Audine's anxious face. "Thank you," said Audine, relieved there would be no more explanation.

"Let me help you with those suitcases. They look pretty heavy. I don't know how you managed to carry two without any help," said Turner, hoisting them and tossing them into the back of his truck, which was already loaded with trash and other debris.

"Watch out with those! I spent a lot on those

suitcases!" she yelled in a loud voice.

Turner's eyes narrowed at the words as his forehead set into a grim line, and he watched Audine climbing into the truck with difficulty. He noticed the two bloody scrapes on her knees, the holes in her stockings, and her tattered oxfords. The suitcases she claimed to have paid for were worn out and frayed, and the large one was held together with a rope.

There she goes, lying on her suitcases again, Turner thought, shaking his head in disgust.

"Are you ready yet? Come on, I don't want to miss the train to where I need to go!" Audine exclaimed, her voice filled with anxiety.

Angered by Audine's rude tone, Turner hurried to the passenger side of his truck and yanked the door open, startling Audine.

"Listen to me, Audine. Don't you dare speak to me like that. Do you understand? Ever since I saw you here alone, you've been rude to me when I'm just trying to help you out! Now I'll take you to the train station, and from now on, you'll be nicer and show some manners! I can see why Wayne let you go off alone!" Turner scolded.

Once inside, Turner slammed the door and started the truck. He lifted his foot off the clutch, looked in both directions, and then sped off, leaving Audine wide-eyed and speechless as she stared at him. His admonishment had rendered her unable to speak.

After half an hour of driving in silence, Turner made a sharp right and accelerated the truck. They finally arrived at the train station. Turner glided the truck to a stop and hurried out to retrieve Audine's suitcases. The stench of her urine-soaked undergarments was now noticeable, prompting Audine to quickly open the truck door and carefully slide out of the seat.

"Here," said Turner, lowering the suitcases to the ground with a thud.

"I thought I told you to be careful with my pricey suitcases! I paid good money for them, and now look what you've done to one of them! Thanks to your reckless driving, one of them's got a dent!" Her voice trembled with anger as she snatched up the two suitcases.

"Now I see what folks around here were talking about regarding you! And you know what? They're right about what they say: that you're mean, self-important, and a chinwag!" exploded Turner.

Before Audine could respond to Turner's verbal insults, he opened the door to his truck, hurried inside, and started the engine, which roared so loudly that it made Audine flinch. Turner carefully backed out, made a sharp left, and drove away.

Audine stood there in disbelief at the things Turner had no doubt said, leaving her numb.

Turner will go home to his fat, ugly wife and spill the whole story to her! She thought to herself, feeling deeply frustrated.

Audine snatched her suitcases and limped into the train station.

"Jackass!" Audine muttered, glancing behind her to make sure Turner was gone.

That moment marked a turning point for Audine Booker Collins, leading her to decide she would never return to New Orleans.

CHAPTER FIVE

Turner Beckles. As he drove away from the train station after leaving Audine, Turner's mind was racing.

This woman is not only a liar, but she's crazy! And what's odd, though, is that she never brought up Violet or Mason. Turner thought to himself as he sped up to get home to his wife of fifteen years, Beryl, whom he loved deeply.

They met when he was eighteen and she was sixteen. After she turned twenty-one, her parents gave their blessing for her to get married. He found a job at a local farm, where he slaughtered wild hogs and killed chickens every other Saturday for the community store that served Black residents, who couldn't visit Clarence Margret's farm, which had recently closed.

"Shame how Clarence died from a snake bite. I wonder how his wife and kids are managing now that he's gone," Turner thought out loud. He flinched at the thought of Beryl, worrying about what might happen to him, so he took the back roads leading home. He drove faster on those roads but stayed cautiously vigilant.

Home at last. Turner carefully parked the truck on a slight incline so he could see it clearly whenever he passed the window facing the yard. After turning off the ignition, Turner slid out of the driver's seat, rolled up the window, and locked the passenger and driver's doors.

"Hey there, Shorty!" The black-and-white mutt barked and bounded towards him, jumping on his legs, happy to see Turner.

Turner's front door swung open. His wife, Beryl, stood in the doorway, wearing an apron and a dish towel slung over her shoulder. She flashed a bright smile, revealing her white teeth.

Turner rushed toward his wife's open arms and enveloped her in his embrace. He leaned down to kiss her. Their kisses started softly and escalated in intensity.

"Where were you?" Beryl asked, staring straight into his eyes. "I was worried, then I got really scared, and every time I heard a car or saw headlights, I'd run to the window. When it got late, about an hour, I didn't know what to do! Did something happen to you?"

"Hey there, beautiful. I'm doing okay. Work was busy on the farm since two workers called in sick, so I had to handle their tasks on top of mine. But something did happen on my way home," Turner said, planting a kiss on Beryl's forehead. "Come on, let's head inside so I can fill you in on everything," Turner said, nibbling on his wife's rear and tightening his arm around her waist.

As soon as they stepped through the door, the scent of onions, tomatoes, garlic, navy beans, chicken, and dumplings wafted from the large iron cauldron simmering on the stove. Beryl had also picked up some apples from the market that morning that no one wanted. She peeled them, cut out the bruised parts, and added sugar and wild blackberries she'd gathered from the trees in the woods. With the leftover mixture, she made enough dumplings for a week from the baked hand pie. Turner closed his eyes, his full lips curving into a smile.

"Uh-huh, I thought you'd like what I made for you. No matter how long it took, I wasn't going to let this meal go to waste until I saw you walk through the door", said

Beryl as she led him into the kitchen.

Turner adored her completely.

"That's why I work every day. I work hard at my job to provide for us, and then I come home to you." Turner said, heading to the sink to wash up.

"Even though I couldn't hold onto the babies we lost, I lost five of them," said Beryl as she moved to the stove to ladle the soup into a bowl after he sat at the table.

"I love you no matter what; even if you did lose those babies, I love you more," he said.

After blessing the food, Turner folded his hands under his chin and gazed at Beryl. She took a spoonful of the steaming-hot soup, blew on it to cool it, then took a cautious sip. Turner placed his large hand on Beryl's forearm.

"Listen to me, sweetheart. I know what happened to us was heartbreaking, but that won't change how much I love you. We'll be blessed someday; I'm sure of it. And when it happens, I promise to dance all over our house," Turner said. "Oh, and by the way, I have so much to tell you – it'll explain why I was coming home so late."

"I'm ready to hear, and don't leave out anything," said Beryl, shoveling a spoonful of the savory soup.

Turner gave her a wink and a grin.

"Whelp, you won't believe who I saw walking in the dark on the old dirt road leading to the railroad station," said Turner.

"Who?" asked Beryl, focusing her full attention on her husband.

Audine Collins. As I was driving home, I almost hit her! You know as well as I do that the dirt road to the train station is dangerous at this time of night! So, I asked her again what she was doing, walking alone in the dark with two suitcases. That's when things got rather knotted. She told me Wayne's car wasn't working and that he said to walk to the train station.

"What? Audine was walking by herself in the dark. Has she lost her mind?" Beryl said, totally bewildered by her husband's explanation.

She wiped the corners of her mouth and put her spoon down in the empty soup bowl, listening carefully to him.

"Yep, that's the same thing I was thinking of, too!" he said as he ravenously attacked the soup, mopping the bowl corners with bread. "And then I asked her why she didn't call Ricks. So, she told me that she didn't need Ricks and that she could get to the railroad station by walking fast. And one more thing, she had two suitcases that she said she spent a lot of money on, but they were a tattered mess, humph! One of them was even tied up with a rope!"

"Turner, Audine is the biggest liar this side of New Orleans," said Beryl, disgusted by what Turner had revealed. Turner nodded as he took a sip of water. Audine is lying about everything because Etta and I watched and heard everything from the window in the small closet of the church. When I went to get my gloves and usher rosette from Etta, she was standing on a box by the window. I asked Etta what was going on. She put her finger to her lips for me to be quiet and waved me over to her. Shh, be very quiet! Wayne and Audine are having a big fight! Turn off the lights, lock the door, and come here with me! Oh, my goodness, Wayne just slammed the car door, and Audine is crying her eyes out! Etta said to me as we watched.

"So, what happened?" asked Turner as he stood to get a second helping of the soup.

"Etta and I stood at the window and heard much more. Audine was yelling at Wayne, and then he cut her off. He told her that he had caught her stealing money from him, but he had caught her in the middle of the night!" exclaimed Beryl as she sipped a cup of piping hot coffee and took a mouthful of the fruit concoction that had been on the table on a platter.

"Jesus! I always knew Audine was a liar, but a thief? Umph, umph, umph. Poor Wayne, I'm sure he's regretting marrying her," Turner said, finishing his soup and pouring himself a cup of coffee, along with two hand pies.

"Humph, that's not all! Wayne told Audine that after the church service was over, she would have to leave their house and never return! He informed Audine that their marriage was finished, that he would get it annulled on Monday, and that she wasn't taking Mason! She began screaming and hollering when Wayne said he was keeping Mason. Humph! At that point, she could barely leave the car because she was so broken up! Whelp, that was when Wayne got out of his car, hurried up the stairs to the church, and went straight inside. By then, Audine was wailing so loudly that you could hear her clearly through the car windows!" said Beryl.

"Damn, then what happened?" asked Turner, leaning in, shocked by the sordid details that Beryl was spilling out.

So, it appears Wayne and Audine's marriage was built on a complete lie. Wayne just learned the truth about his beast of a wife, Turner reflected, feeling sorry for both Wayne and Mason.

"Whelp, Audine opened the car window and began to talk with Sister Judith, who was passing by. Etta and I heard Audine tell Judith that she was very sad and crying because Violet had decided to leave for France to improve her French by attending school there so she could become a French teacher! Audine mentioned that she and Wayne were thrilled that Wayne got in his car and drove Violet to the train station to catch the next train to New York and, from there, take a boat to France to stay with some friends Maria St. Laurent had told her about".

"Wait a minute," said Turner, interrupting her in mid-sentence. "She told Judith that Violet was bound for France after Violet got all that money from her father and a scholarship to attend that Teacher's College for colored women in Virginia. What would she do in God's name with the scholarship award and the money Violet's father left for her?"

"Humph!" snorted Beryl as she took another quick sip of coffee. Audine told Judith that Violet said to give the scholarship to Carol Thomas, the girl who was beside herself over missing out on it. Audine told Judith she was so happy about that and that she and Carol's mother, Phyllis, would celebrate because they were best friends, hah! Now we all know that's a lie because Phyllis had to set Audine straight in front of the whole church when she told Phyllis that Carol could get a job as a toilet scrubber. The nerve of that woman telling Judith that they were friends, hah! Audine isn't anything but a liar! I'm so glad she is leaving New Orleans! Oh, and there's one more thing that I've gotta tell you," said Beryl, tilting her head back to drain her cup of coffee.

"What's that?" Turner asked, standing up to gather their dinner utensils and place them in the sink for washing.

"You have to promise me that you won't tell anyone what I'm about to tell you; it's just between us, Turner. Can you do that?"

"Yes, of course, tell me," He responded.

"Violet ain't going to France to be a French teacher, uh-uh. Violet left for New York to stay with her aunt and uncle," said Beryl.

"And why's that?" Turner asked, retaking his seat.

"Violet has a baby inside her belly," said Beryl.

Turner's eyes were huge with shock. He gaped at Beryl in disbelief, frozen in his seat.

"Did you just say that Violet has a baby in her belly? Who's the father?" Turner asked, baffled by this news.

"Clarence Margaret," she said, her face contorted with distaste.

"Oh my God, Beryl! I swear to you, I've just about heard everything tonight! First, about Audine and her lies, and now this! But how did you find this out?" he asked, mystified.

"Etta. She told me everything," said Beryl. "She only got a few bits of information from Mrs. Alice Wade, who said that Clarence and Violet were up to no good at Wayne and Audine's house while they were away. What makes it worse is that when Mason heard noises coming from Violet's room one night, the poor boy was terrified that someone had come in during the middle of the night. According to Alice, Mason snuck toward Violet's room, and the door was slightly open, just enough for him to peek inside and see them doing nasty things in bed together. He was so shocked by what he saw that he ran back to his room. Alice told Etta that he hated Violet and Clarence from that day on. But after seeing everything that happened today, Etta said she would check on Wayne and Mason and then ask Wayne more questions about what went on in that house," said Beryl.

"Oh my God," Turner said, repulsed. "What kind of man was Clarence? Humph! He had a beautiful wife, children, and that farm with a smokehouse! What more could he have wanted? Now that he's dead, I wonder who's going to take care of the baby he put inside Violet's belly, as well as his other children? What a mess, Beryl, what a got-damned mess!"

"Oh, I know," Beryl replied as she stood up to help Turner with the dishes. "I was just saying the same thing to Etta. She also mentioned that Wayne told her Audine hadn't kept the house clean. All the leftover food from the wedding reception went bad, and the mice ate boxes of vegetables that people had given away. Wayne was furious when Mason told him he had seen eight mice chowing down on those veggies, so they had to throw away almost all the food. Can you imagine throwing away all that food during a depression? I would have made all sorts of tasty dishes, and you wouldn't have to worry about lunch every day; humph! The nerve of Audine, wasting food like that! Good riddance to her, I say! I hope she never comes back!" Beryl declared.

"You know what?" said Turner, his eyes locked on her.

"What?" Beryl replied.

"I wanna show you how much I love you," he said, wrapping his arms around her ample waist and then playfully smacking her behind.

"I wouldn't say no to you, Turner. Are you ready to go?" she said, smiling.

"After you," he said, bowing from the waist. As Beryl walked past him, he smacked her behind a little harder than last time. She yelped and laughed as they both hurried into their bedroom.

"Before I take you, darlin', I'm going to take a quick bath because I've been in that bloody slaughterhouse all day, and I'm not about to get into our bed smelling like dead meat. Can you wait for me, okay, sweetheart?" he asked, unzipping his pants.

Beryl watched as he slowly pulled down his trousers and underwear, kicked off his shoes, removed his socks, and then his shirt. The flame of desire ignited between her thighs as she stared at his erection. It was enormous, and Beryl craved having it inside her.

"Before I go bathe, come here," he whispered.

Beryl's heart raced, and her pulse quickened as she walked toward her husband. Turner lifted her into his arms. They kissed passionately, panting as their bodies moved together.

"This is just the beginning," Turner said. "I had to get my head together before I could be ready for you. Can you wait a few more minutes, darlin?"

Her breathing was shallow, coming in soft pants; she felt a warmth spread between her legs.

"Of course, I'll wait for you, but please hurry, 'cause I'm about to burst if you're not inside me," she said, spreading her legs and taking his massive hand to guide him to her wet center.

"Give me just a few minutes to clean myself; I promise you; it'll be worth the wait," he said huskily. Kissing her forehead, he went to the bathroom, ran water for his bath, and took his time bathing. Ten minutes later, he returned to her; Beryl was beneath the covers, waiting for him.

"Shall I continue where I left off?" he asked, climbing into bed beside her. Without waiting for her to answer, he slid his fingers inside her and began work on her wet center. Squeezing her eyes shut and tilting her head back, Beryl let out a high-pitched moan, which made Turner penetrate her with three of his fingers. Going faster, Beryl's whole body was on fire with pleasure.

"Want more, darlin'?" he asked, smiling into her hazel eyes.

"Please don't stop!" she cried, gripping his shoulders. Now drenched in sweat, Turner kissed her deeply and, with his knees, parted her thighs further apart. The foreplay worked because he thrust his massive erection inside her so deep that she gasped, not expecting the surprise orgasms that followed. Beryl grasped his shoulders and wrapped her thighs around his waist. That was Turner's signal for him to pick up speed and penetrate Beryl deeper. He was working her into a frenzy, watching her writhe and cry out.

"Now Turner, NOW!" she cried out.

"Not yet, darlin'!" he replied.

He remained silent, but pulled himself out, sank to his knees, and buried his head between her legs. Then he slid his tongue deep inside her, savoring the warmth of her excitement.

"Turner!" she moaned and writhed wildly. "I need you inside me again, please, Turner, please!"

Just before Beryl orgasmed again, Turner instantly moved on top of her again and, using his knees, pushed apart her thighs as far as they would go. He took her breast, squeezed it, and caressed it gently. With her eyes squeezed shut, she was able to feel his tongue flicker and encircle the nipples of both breasts, causing her to release another intense orgasm.

"I can't wait another second, Turner; I need you inside me now!" she said through gritted teeth.

Turner's eyes burned with passion as he gave in to his wife's plea. He slowly pushed into her, the muscles in his neck standing out in sharp relief. His teeth clenched; his thrusts grew faster as she lifted her hips to match his intense pace. Beryl felt him fill her deeply, and she craved the feeling of his seed growing inside her, binding them together. As he thrust faster and deeper, the heavy oak headboard slammed against the wall with each move.

"Now, Beryl, NOW!" he cried out. Turner arched his neck back and came with a deep-throated cry. Beryl gripped his forearms, and with a loud, satisfied moan, she finally found her release.

Months of secretly preparing herself had led Beryl to realize that he had planted his seed inside her that night.

After their bath together, they made love twice more. As Beryl slept, she had a dream about two pink fish. In the same dream, a gold kitten jumped into her lap, curled up, and slept until Beryl woke up on Monday morning.

Turner was already out the door for work. Beryl rolled onto her back, placing her palm directly on her belly and smiling. After five days of enjoying a hot breakfast of oatmeal with honey, a finely chopped apple, and five chopped pecans, she decided to call Ricks and ask if one of his men could give her a ride so she could visit her friend, Maria St. Laurent.

CHAPTER SIX

"I just want Turner to stay home with me in our bed. I can't get enough of him, said Beryl. "It's like when we were first married – we couldn't keep our hands off each other. But you know what, Maria: last night was different."

Maria St. Laurent smiled at her friend of five years, Beryl. Beryl and Lena were Maria's only close friends, and both women had longed to have children soon after getting married. After Lena's passing, Maria and Beryl had grown closer, but even now, Maria still didn't know the whole story about Clarence and Violet. Today, their visit would be all about Beryl.

Midwife Alice Wade and Eucharista Birch sat at Maria's kitchen table, sipping steaming hot coffee and enjoying warm graham cakes with butter. The three women were thrilled by Beryl's dream revelation. Maria was convinced it was only a matter of time before her good friend's prediction came true.

"How did Turner like the coffee?" Maria asked with a smile. "Did you put cream and sugar in it?"

"He loved it!" exclaimed Beryl as she savored another forkful of cake. He kept asking me for more coffee, and each time he took a sip, he'd smile. He said the coffee made him feel warm all over!

"Whelp, that was the plan, honey, to get him feeling warm all over," said Eucharista. "You dusted cinnamon on top of the grounds, right?" Eucharista asked as she carefully poured cream into her second cup of coffee.

"And did you add a dash of nutmeg like I recommended?" Maria asked, lifting an eyebrow.

"Mmm, yes, I did! I even sneaked in a pinch of the cream! Turner's been rushing home from work every day for the past month just to have that coffee and a sip of me!" Beryl said with a sly grin, then burst out laughing.

Beryl's laughter was so contagious that everyone at the table fell under the spell of her joy. Maria clutched her belly while holding Beryl's hand; for Maria, it was the first spark of laughter since Clarence's death.

"Well, ladies, I hate to break up this lovely breakfast, but it's time for me to check on Maria," Alice said as she gently brushed the dust off her gold-rimmed glasses.

"We'll be back. By the way, Beryl, I have a special ingredient I'd like you to add to your oatmeal tomorrow morning. Please remind me before you head home so that I can give it to you," Maria said, wiping the corners of her mouth. She and Alice stepped away from the table to go into Maria's bedroom. Alice closed the door, leaving Beryl and Eucharista to chat in the kitchen.

"You seem so happy. I understand that you're also under Maria's wise and protective care," Eucharista said.

"Yes, ma'am. Maria has been taking care of me since August. I've been watching what I eat, sticking to the recommended foods, and adding some spices to our meals at home. I guess that's why Turner can't keep his hands off me! But you know what, Mrs. Birch?" Beryl whispered.

"Do tell me," Eucharista replied, leaning in closer to hear every word.

"I think Turner put a baby in me. I'm positive this time because we did it two or three more times last night, and then he had to wake up early this morning! Humph, I was so exhausted, but I wanted him inside me even more! I swear Maria put something extra in that cinnamon box she gave me!" said Beryl.

"Whelp, there's certainly one way to find out," said Eucharista.

She got up and strode to the extra chair where her bag was. Beryl watched as Eucharista pulled out a wooden box with her tarot card deck and a wooden teaspoon.

"So, dearest, are you ready to hear what will be said to you?" asked Eucharista as she cleared the table.

"Yes, ma'am, I'm ready," said Beryl, finishing her graham cake. Tilting her head back, she drained the remaining tepid tea until the loose leaves touched her lips before placing the teacup back onto the saucer.

"Okay, before we start, could you please wash your hands at the sink? Use cool water to rinse them off and then dry them."

"Yes, ma'am," answered Beryl.

She walked over to the sink, turned on the faucet, and let the water wet her hands. Picking up the soap bar that Maria had left on the edge of the sink, she couldn't help but notice the detailed specks of red and purple flecks scattered throughout it. Beryl scrunched her eyes shut, brought the soap bar to her nose, and inhaled the most beautiful scent she had ever smelled: lavender and strawberries! There was no doubt that Maria made the soap, but how could she make it lather into a creamy consistency? Beryl scrubbed her hands up to her elbows and rinsed them in cool water, following Eucharista's instructions. After patting her arms and hands dry, she shut her eyes and inhaled. Touching her arms, she felt soft and clean and smelled divine.

"I know. The soap Maria made smells wonderful. Come, sit down and face me."

Beryl pulled the chair away from the table and turned it to face Eucharista. She couldn't help but notice the dark beige, home-sewn apron with several pockets that Eucharista wore whenever she gave readings. Beryl settled into the chair. Drawing closer, Eucharista beckoned her to come nearer so that she could begin her reading.

"Beryl, roll up the sleeves of your dress to the elbow points so that I can begin my reading for you. I will prepare you, then spread my cards to hear what each one says. After we're finished, I will read your coffee grounds. Does that sound fine to you?" she asked soothingly.

"Yes, ma'am," she replied, lifted by the gentle, graceful tone of Eucharista's voice.

Eucharista reached over, took Beryl by the hand, and squeezed firmly.

"Gaze into my eyes; look deep into my soul. As I prepare you, you'll feel calm, but don't fall asleep, or you'll miss what the cards have to say to me", Eucharista said. "Now, place your hands here," she said, patting her lap.

She followed the instructions given.

On the table sat a beautifully detailed wooden box adorned with two hand-carved doves perched atop it. Clenched in their beaks were two gold coins, while the long talons gripped two hearts, which was most terrifying. As Eucharista opened the box, Beryl couldn't help but close her eyes and inhale the unmistakable fragrance of tuberose and honeysuckle wafting from within. Inside, a jar contained a creamy concoction. Eucharista opened the jar and, with two fingers, scooped out a mound of the billowy, jelly-like cream flecked with a kaleidoscope of iridescent colors never seen before. She smeared the creamy mixture onto Beryl's right arm, starting from her fingers and ending directly at her elbow.

Then, smearing a dollop of the mixture into the palm of her hand, massaged her palms together until they were warm, and then began to deeply massage Beryl's arm while reciting:

"Guardian Angels, I respectfully ask that Beryl and her husband, Turner, be protected. May she be the blessed vessel that carries the future and legacy long after they've grown old and gone to glory. Her heart is pure, and I ask that you please speak to me now through these cards, the visions you bless me with, and the grounds from the coffee created from the earth. For this, we are grateful."

Eucharista repeated the exact words on Beryl's left arm with conviction and truth. As instructed, Beryl kept her eyes on Eucharista until she finished.

"Now, let's sit at the table," she said as she capped the cream, put it back in the box, and carefully stowed it in her worn leather bag.

As Beryl pulled her chair up to the round table, Eucharista quickly rummaged through her sack, poking and prodding until she found what she was looking for. She pulled out a thick bundle of worn cards tied with twine and adorned with hand-drawn pictures. All the cards were made of sturdy cardstock, which kept them in good condition, without fraying at the edges. Beryl watched, captivated, as Eucharista carefully untied the twine. Then, she began shuffling the cards and stopped to arrange them in a perfect circle, covering the entire surface of the table.

"I want you to pull ten cards. You need to choose three from the top, two from the right, three from the base of the table, and the last two from the left. Do you understand?" asked Eucharista, adjusting her apron pockets.

"Yes, ma'am. I understand," Beryl replied, standing up from the chair. She moved slowly and deliberately to the head of the table, examining the cards closely.

"Take your time. You'll want to choose the card that draws you in," Eucharista said, still focused on the table. "Then pass them to me."

She picked up three cards that were below the window. Because the sun was shining brightly on them, she selected the first three.

"Very good; I liked how you chose those three cards where the sun shone on them! The sky is beautiful, and the clouds remind me of big puffs of cotton," said Eucharista as she took the first three cards that Beryl handed her. Strolling over to the right side, where the pantry was, she studied the cards intently. Suddenly, a rich mix of herbal and spicy aromas, especially cinnamon and nutmeg, enveloped her. Smiling, she selected two cards and handed them to a beaming Eucharista.

Glancing at the large stove, Beryl approached the cards nearest to the heat. Strangely, the wood stove was still radiating warmth. It felt as if Maria was cooking here; the heat was still palpable, Beryl thought. She selected two cards and handed them to Eucharista, who was delighted by how thoughtfully Beryl had chosen them.

She's going to love reading this! Today, the cards didn't bring any sad or disheartened messages, even though thoughts of her reading with Maria popped up. She quickly pushed that painful memory aside and refocused on Beryl.

"Just one more selection, and then we'll get started. Be very careful about choosing the three cards to pull. Once you've handed over the last three, we'll begin."

"Once I'm done, I'll take a few minutes to read the coffee grounds," Eucharista said, nodding and waving at the base of the table.

The table base is close to the parlor. Much occurred in that parlor as Beryl's thoughts returned to the evening of Clarence's demise: the wailing, weeping, and screeching of Maria's daughters and her youngest son. Then came the home departure of Maria's eldest son, Kempton, who was leaving for the army. Eucharista could sense the change in mood and noticed Beryl's stride, which was more hesitant than the confident stride she had shown just a few moments prior.

"What's the matter, dearest? Are you alright?" Eucharista asked.

"It's Maria's parlor. Just looking inside stirs up so many sad memories, especially after Turner and I heard about Clarence's death and then came back here to say our goodbyes to Kempton," Beryl said sadly.

"Listen to me, Clarence was not doing right by Maria or his children. The mere fact that not only did he leave Maria for that common whore Violet Booker, but he also left this place in a big mess. And between you and me, Maria has a lot to deal with. For now, let's think of that parlor as a room we can all share in our lives. So, I want you to pull the last three cards, and then we'll move forward with your reading. I have a good feeling that this reading will give you a lot of insight into your future. Go ahead and pull the last three," she said, giving

Beryl's shoulder a reassuring squeeze before stepping back to observe.

Beryl patted Eucharista's hand and let out a quiet sigh of relief. She confidently approached the table, selected the last three cards without hesitation, and settled into the chair.

With the last three cards in hand, she organized them with the other seven, arranging them precisely in the center of the table. She then gathered up the remaining cards, tapping them against the table to make sure they were straight, and placed them in a wooden box holder. Next, she went back to retrieve the ten cards from the center of the table. Taking them in her hands, she shuffled them ten times, ensuring the stack contained exactly ten cards. She then placed the cards on the table and, with deliberate speed, laid them face down in a circular shape, working clockwise.

"Are you ready?" Eucharista asked, her eyes fixed on the cards.

"Yes, ma'am, I'm ready," answered Beryl.

What if those cards tell me bad things? I'll never

forgive myself for agreeing to do this! Beryl thought to herself, panic-stricken.

Starting at the top, Eucharista flipped over the first card.

"Magnifique!" she exclaimed, clapping her hands together in delight.

Card number one was held up for Beryl to see. It featured a drawing of a large group of people gathered in a circle. At the center of the circle, a man and a woman faced each other, holding hands and appearing happy.

She let out a deep sigh of relief and beamed.

"So, what does this card mean?" she asked, leaning closer to see the details better.

Eucharista didn't answer immediately. Her eyes were glued to the card, and her lips moved as if she were speaking to someone who wasn't there.

"Thank you! I am truly grateful for such wonderful news! I'll tell her; tears of joy will fill her today!" Eucharista whispered. Finally, she spoke.

"The card that I hold is called protection. And what it speaks of is this: because you are so pure of heart, your home, property, your husband's job, and the money you both saved will be protected for the rest of your lives. Nobody will ever hurt or harm either one of you. You'll never get sick, and your life will continue until your hair turns white. How will you and Turner tell the stories of this time until the next? Then you both shall close your eyes until you soar towards the clouds."

Beryl couldn't stop smiling at what she heard.

So, Turner and I will grow very old together, Beryl thought, buoyed by such gratifying news.

She took a bite of a cookie that Eucharista had set on a small plate. The sweets were delicious.

Eucharista plucked out another card featuring even more people. The individuals in this card appeared optimistic, with several enjoying food and couples dancing closely together.

"Celebrations are coming to you and Turner next summer, just one month before September," said Eucharista. She squeezed her eyes shut and clasped her hands tightly together.

"Yes, again, I thank you. She has been a good wife and a wonderful woman, a helper to many. Rewards for her deeds; should I reveal everything to her? Yes, I shall tell her everything," said Eucharista reverently.

Beryl observed Eucharista swaying back and forth in her chair.

Who is she speaking to? Beryl wondered, feeling nervous prickles run up her spine.

"The celebration, which will be a huge one, will take place at the church. Lots of people who love you and Turner will be there. The card has spoken the truth, telling you that even when you and Turner face tough times, there'll always be something to celebrate. Being grateful for the basics, such as having food, a steady job, and clothes on your back, is something to celebrate. And then there's the biggest celebration of all, happening in August." She put the card with the first one she read face down.

Taking the next card, she examined it, and a more serious expression appeared on her face.

Eucharista kept staring at the card, her eyes fixed. Beryl watched her muttering to herself in a hushed tone, as if talking to someone not physically there. Beryl took another cookie and bit into it, feeling a sudden wave of warmth spread through her body.

This cookie is also delicious, but why do I suddenly feel warm and flushed? Beryl thought to herself. The heat radiated to a part of her that made her cross her ankles tightly. The sensation of warmth stirred feelings of arousal in Beryl, leaving her embarrassed to experience such emotions during a reading.

What's in this cookie that makes me crave more of them? She wondered. She took another bite, chased it with the cold glass of water in front of her, and grabbed another cookie.

"Beryl, I need you to listen carefully to what I am going to say to you because this card is important to you," said Eucharista as she held up the card. The card depicted four women engaged in various chores: one cultivating a garden, another caring for a child, another holding a pot, and the last one attending to a woman who appeared to be giving birth.

"This card speaks of coming together, and it's telling you that you, Maria, Alice, and I are to come together to help each other. We especially need to check in on our friend Maria. She may seem unbothered by things that have happened in her family, but believe me, she needs us. Alice and I will always travel together to help those women who are soon to give birth. However, tending to our flower and herb gardens is necessary, especially for me, so that I can make the salves and creams that heal. Etta, our friend, guides us about any of our church friends who may need our help and guidance. And then there is our friend Ricks and his men, who are always there to protect us if we need to travel anywhere. Now, take a closer look at the card. See that bird at the top of the card?" inquired Eucharista, tapping her finger on the card that bore a picture of a beautiful bird with a kaleidoscope of colors throughout its feathers. Its golden beak held two spools.

"The bird carries two spools, meaning it has two messages to share. May I share the first piece of news with you?" she whispered.

"Yes, ma'am, I understand, and I will not tell

anyone," nodded Beryl.

"It's about Ricks and his wife. A few days after Clarence's burial, Ricks called Alice. After he filled her in on what was happening, I told him to have his wife come over to see Alice. When Ricks and his wife arrived, Alice decided that she should be examined. Forty-five minutes later, Alice told Ricks' wife to get dressed and meet her in the kitchen," said Eucharista.

"Is she okay? Beryl asked with a concerned tone.

"Oh yes, she's better than all right. She and Ricks are expecting their first child to arrive in August! She was so shocked to hear the news because she didn't think she'd be able to have a child at her age, much less even knowing that she could have one. When Alice told them the news, Ricks was hollering and dancing all over Alice's house! Ricks said he wants to try for more after that one is born! Isn't that something!" she said, smiling, pleased with the news shared with Beryl, who seemed equally happy but wondered if Ricks and his wife were past the age of having any more children. After all, everyone knew that his wife was forty-two years old, and Ricks was fifty-six!

"The second spool is your news," Eucharista said directly.

Beryl turned around to see that Eucharista had risen from her chair. She gestured for Beryl to stand. Beryl stood and took a step towards Eucharista. She extended her hands to Beryl. Grasping them firmly, Eucharista's green eyes locked directly onto hers.

"You're having two babies! They'll be born on the same day, at the same time, just two minutes apart. Both girls will arrive in September. All I can say is, keep doing what you're doing, and try not to eat all those cookies, dear. Save some for Turner after dinner," Eucharista said with a chuckle.

Still holding Eucharista's hands, Beryl plopped down onto the chair and babbled words she couldn't comprehend. However, Eucharista seemed to understand every utterance until Beryl returned to herself.

"Did you say I'm going to have two babies, and they're coming in September?" Beryl stammered in disbelief.

"Yes, I did. You and Turner will conceive them around Christmastime. Alice will be seeing you just after the first of the year. But the remaining cards are calling me to give you more messages," said Eucharista as she released and patted Beryl's hands. Beryl trembled, overwhelmed by what she had just heard.

Not one, but two babies? How is this possible? I lost several babies, yet Turner stood by me, reassuring me that one day we'd be blessed with one, and now we're going to have two! Beryl thought to herself in disbelief.

Refocusing, Beryl concentrated fully on what Eucharista would say next.

Eucharista pulled three cards this time and turned them up. The first card depicted several women holding hands; in the background lay a bright roadway surrounded by flowers, a shining sun, and a perfect blue sky with feathery white clouds. The second card featured a woman with her arms outstretched as she faced outward. Beryl blinked several times; she could've sworn that one of the women was purposely staring straight at her. The woman wore a serene smile. The last card displayed several stunning illustrations of flowers in flowerpots at different stages of growth. Even the smaller flowers appeared healthy and strong, showing the potential for sprouting.

"This one stands out to me," Eucharista said, pointing to the card with the picture of several women holding hands.

"Friendship. The card says that we, meaning you, me, Alice, Maria, and Etta, will be bound to one another as friends for the rest of our lives. We aren't envious, nor would we ever hurt one another with gossip, unlike that woman who's gone from these parts forever. It's saying to you that we all need someone to trust to share our private thoughts and things that will come up in our lives. We are here for one another to offer advice that will provide us hope and wise guidance. The woman in the middle is me because of what I do and say for each of you," said Eucharista, pointing to the woman in the car who seemed slightly taller than the others pictured. Beryl nodded in agreement. Eucharista turned the card over and pointed to the card that featured the woman with outstretched arms.

"I knew this card here would be the one to tie

everything together, and it is meant for you," said Eucharista as she picked it up with the woman's outstretched arms.

"Hope. For you, it was always there, even after losing all those babies you and Turner tried to have. Don't worry about them because they've been carried upwards. You and Turner will see them until you're both very old." Eucharista smiled, grateful for such a card that seemed to soothe Beryl, whose eyes filled with tears. Eucharista reached out and patted Beryl's hand. She could feel Beryl's hand shaking after a moment of silence. Eucharista continued her reading.

As Eucharista said, this card reminds you to stay packed, full of hope, because that belief can change your future – not just for you, but for Turner, your kids, and the generations that follow. On this card, you can see the woman's eyes and her open arms, radiating love and hope." Then, Eucharista fell silent, closing her eyes.

"The message for you is that your hope will walk, holding the hand of peace in your household and several miracles," said Eucharista.

Taking the card, she placed it face down with the

others. The last of the three was the one with the flowers in their various stages of growth. Beryl's eyes were puzzled as Eucharista took hold of the card and hugged it tightly to her bosom, speaking in Creole.

"Merci, merci, thank you, thank you!" she exclaimed joyfully.

"What does the card say, Mrs. Birch? Will everything be all right with me?" asked Beryl, her concern evident.

"You've nothing to worry about at all because this card is telling me to tell you that your soon-to-be new family is going to flourish! The flowers in the flowerpots are different sizes, ranging from the smallest to the biggest, more colorful ones," she said, pointing to the two flowerpots that had two billowing flowers with sturdy stems.

"These two pink ones in the corner of the card are your daughters. And the smaller pot that has a shorter stalk is your other daughter! She's going to arrive in a year during the winter," said Eucharista, clapping her hands.

"What! I'm going to have another one a year after the first two. Are you sure about that, Mrs. Birch?" asked Beryl, who was now standing. She grasped the edge of the table to keep from falling. Her heart was racing from a mix of fear and excitement.

"Beryl, please sit down. I know this is such a surprise for you, and there's more to tell you!" said Eucharista as she helped Beryl back to her seat.

"You're going to have a daughter, a girl, a year after the twins, and you and Turner will find out in the spring of that year. Look closely at the flowerpot's dirt, because beautiful flowers will grow it once it's watered. Out of your pain from losing all those babies, growth will come. And because of that, you'll be blessed with three daughters. That's not all, though, because you'll meet many other women who've lost their babies and don't want to talk about it. After all, nobody will understand that, but you will," Eucharista said.

As Beryl was told she'd have another daughter and that her story would help women who lost babies, tears of joy welled up in her eyes. She felt hopeful, knowing she could share her own experience of losing several children.

"I can't believe this will happen to me, Mrs. Birch! I am overjoyed but also scared," she said, dabbing her nose with her handkerchief.

It took Eucharista a moment to respond, as she was still focused on the three cards remaining on the table. She flipped them over, and the first card she revealed showed a picture of an infant swaddled in a blanket. The mother, lovingly, cradled her child as she gazed down at it, a gentle smile spreading across her face.

"New beginnings. This card tells you that the woman holding the baby brings the happy news of a new addition to your family, for you and Turner to care for and love." Eucharista examined the card, her eyes welling up as she whispered to herself. A soft smile spread across her face as she pushed her gold-rimmed glasses up from her nose, a hint of warmth and love shining through.

"This child is going to be very special. It's what she'll do with her hands that will save many lives. There will be a life that she's going to save, a man who'll be left for dead, but she's the one who'll save him and many others like him. When she's born, there'll be a veil over her head. You're to bury it in a special place when Alice removes it. The following Saturday, you're to host a special gathering—serve only sweets and hot beverages because it will be a cold afternoon," she said.

Without a moment to spare, Eucharista pulled the next card. As she drew it, she tightened her wool shawl as if she were freezing. She then went to the stove and poured herself a cup of piping hot coffee from Maria's new coffee pot, which she had forgotten about for many years, buried in her wedding trunk. The mixture of coffee, cinnamon, sugar, and cream was delightful. Closing her eyes and inhaling deeply, Eucharista took two long sips; the warmth of the cinnamon enveloped her, warming her body.

"Hold off until winter, especially the three days leading up to Christmas. The card says that you and Turner will start your family on December 23rd. His seed will be planted, and your heartfelt wishes will all come true. The card only showed snow on the ground, trees with heavy snow drifts on their branches that still had ripe winterberries, even in the cold. Beryl's eyes lit up when she heard the dates.

"Those three days before Christmas will be the coldest New Orleans has ever seen. Nothing like this has ever happened! So, be prepared for food and have plenty of logs for your fireplace and stove. I must tell you that your dreams of birth are coming true. After that, the weather will return to normal," she said.

Grasping the final card, Eucharista examined it, and a smile creased her lips.

"What's making you smile?" Beryl asked.

"Hmm. Well, I want you to take a good look at this final card," said Eucharista.

Beryl rested her chin on both hands, leaning in to get a closer look. The card depicted a woman sitting at a table filled with all kinds of food. Beryl covered her mouth to stifle a loud laugh.

"Yes, that's right, dearest, you are at the table! It's perfectly fine because it will be a time of happiness, but the card also warns you to eat mindfully and carefully!

"The card advises you to continue eating the special breakfast Maria recommended. Five mornings out of every seven, eat a bowl of hot oats mixed with chopped apples and pecans or walnuts. You also need to make many stews with vegetables and sweet potatoes. Add cinnamon to just about everything, especially in Turner's coffee! Eat sparingly but enough to keep you full, and yes, you can have your share of cake now and then," offered Eucharista.

That marked the conclusion of the card reading. Beryl felt pleased, and the reading instilled in her a sense of fearlessness and confidence.

After all, I will be the mother of three beautiful daughters! Beryl thought to herself with excitement.

"I don't see the need for your tea leaves to be read today because the card reading told me more information than I expected. But remember a few things to pay attention to first: the dream you had about the kitten and two pink fish. The kitten represents motherhood. The two pink fish symbolize the twin daughters you will have, and the card speaks of new beginnings. You and Turner will shower your growing family with much love. He will work hard, but all his effort will keep a roof over your head. You married a wonderful man, a provider and protector," she said, scooping up the last card and tucking it into the deck. Then, she meticulously placed them inside her sack.

"So, when will I see everything happen, and is there anything I need to tell Turner?" Beryl asked, quickly slipping into her coat and bending down to tie her Oxford shoes.

"Let things unfold as they're meant to. If you start sharing everything you learned today with Turner, you'll start doubting everything, and if things don't happen right away, you'll become disappointed, and more questions will arise. So, no, don't say anything to him. Just keep doing things as you always have. Don't worry; those little surprises will happen when you least expect them", Eucharista said, giving Beryl's shoulders a reassuring squeeze.

"Thank you for everything, Mrs. Birch. I'll do anything you say to help give Turner the family he deserves because he's a wonderful man and husband. I'll do everything to keep him safe and happy, and keep him all to myself until our daughters arrive; then I'll have to share him," said Beryl, smiling.

Eucharista nodded and beamed.

"Ricks is on his way to take you home. Would you like to see Maria and Alice before you leave?" Eucharista asked.

"Oh yes, of course. Maria was so kind as to invite me over today, so you know I want to thank her before I leave," said Beryl.

Eucharista led the way to Maria's room, where whispers could be heard through the door.

"Maria, Alice? Is it okay for Beryl to come in?" Eucharista called from behind the door, knocking softly.

"Yes, please come in," Maria said.

Eucharista turned the doorknob and welcomed Beryl inside.

Maria, dressed in a loose, button-down robin's egg blue smock, sat on her bed, her back propped up by two pillows. She looked radiant, but her eyes were red and swollen as if she had been crying. She clutched a crumpled white handkerchief and cradled her belly with her free hand. Alice, sitting in a nearby chair, appeared nervous and concerned.

"Maria, I've come to say thank you for such a lovely time spent with you, Mrs. Birch, and Mrs. Wade. The tea was just what I needed, and those cookies were delicious! I ate three of them and wanted more! But what's in them?" Beryl asked as she bent down and nestled close to embrace Maria.

"Sit next to me, Ma chérie," said Maria, patting the soft bed. Beryl slipped off her shoes and settled in beside Maria.

"Ah, yes, those cookies. Did they warm you up and, you know, tickle you down there?" Maria asked, nodding at Beryl's private area.

"Oh my, how did you know?" Beryl asked, stunned by the gesture in question.

"I used to bake them after my children went to school. When the cookies cooled down to being warm to the touch, I would put them on a small plate and, with a cold glass of iced tea, bring them down to the barn for

Clarence," said Maria longingly. "While we'd eat them and talk, Clarence would always start sweating and then take off his shirt. I would start getting very warm, and before we knew it, Clarence would have his hands all over me, taking off my clothes, and well after a month, I'd miss my monthly flow and call Alice."

"And after her check-up, I'd confirm another baby is on the way!" quipped Alice.

Out of nowhere, a car horn started beeping.

"That's Ricks," interrupted Eucharista. "I'll go out and tell him that you're coming." Eucharista rushed out of the room.

"Before you leave, I've something for you and Turner," said Maria, pointing to a basket next to the small table with two burlap sacks. Carefully grasping the sacks from the basket, Alice walked over to Beryl, handed them to her, and embraced her.

"What's in here?" Beryle asked, surprised by the gift.

"Open it," Maria urged, waving her hand.

As she opened the first sack, the unmistakable

scent of strawberry, lavender, and mint wafted out. Beryl gasped and covered her mouth, clearly surprised by what was inside: large bars of soap, including the one she had washed her hands with earlier. Taking out another bar, she closed her eyes and inhaled deeply. The aroma of Angel's Trumpet, roses, and honeysuckle filled her senses, accompanied by another bar of soap that had a slight hint of nutmeg and coffee!

"How on earth did Maria do this?" Beryl wondered, captivated by the notion of a soap bar that smelled of coffee, nutmeg, vanilla, and cinnamon.

Eucharista suddenly burst into the room.

"Beryl, you must hurry, dearest, because Ricks has to pick up two more after he drives you home," she said.

"Yes, ma'am, I'm coming," said Beryl, scooting off Maria's bed and putting on her shoes.

"Thank you for this surprise, Maria! I can't wait to get home and take my time to open everything!" Beryl exclaimed.

"I wrote down some more important things for you to follow, so pay attention to everything that I wrote for you, okay, my love?" said Maria as she rolled out of bed, helped by Alice.

"Yes, I'll read everything carefully. I'm so excited to see what's in the other sack!" she said, hugging Maria.

"And I'll be hearing from you soon!" quipped Alice, her outstretched arms reaching to embrace Beryl. All three women hugged and exchanged their goodbyes, and then Beryl left with Ricks, who seemed cheerful and chatty as he drove Beryl home.

Eucharista returned to Maria's room. She took off her shoes and sprawled on the bed beside Maria.

"Today was wonderful. I was so happy to see Beryl. She's one of the few friends I have left," said Maria.

"Yes, she's a lovely woman with one of the kindest hearts I've ever seen," said Eucharista. She'll soon make a wonderful mother to the children, and her husband, Turner, is a good man. He's nothing like that scoundrel Clarence Margaret.

"Eucharista!" Alice exclaimed, her face twisted in disgust, as she shook her head violently back and forth.

"Oh, Maria, mon amour, je suis vraiment désolé

pour ce que je viens de dire au sujet de Clarence, oh, Maria, my love, I am very sorry for what I just said about Clarence. It's just that when I think back on what he did to you and this family, I get so damn mad!" remarked Eucharista bitterly. "If there is one thing I am going to say, and may the Lord forgive me, it is that I'm glad Clarence is dead."

"Ahem!" said Alice, clearing her throat several times rather loudly. "Maria, how have you been feeling? Please tell us the truth. I can see that you haven't been eating."

As Eucharista glanced over at Maria, she seemed to be staring down at her shaking hands, visibly upset about something.

"There are nights when I cry myself to sleep because I miss Clarence so much," she said, her voice barely above a whisper. "But then I remember what he did to me and our family: the lies, putting a baby in Violet's belly, watching them kiss each other right outside this house! I hate him even more now because Clarence has put our family in danger," Maria said.

"Danger?" said Alice, clearly alarmed by what

she had just heard.

"Yes, danger. I received a letter from the bank stating that Clarence had not paid off the house, the farm, or the smokehouse for over two months. We will lose everything if two thousand dollars isn't paid in the next six months! Where will the children and I go? Where will we live? How will we live?" Suddenly stopping mid-sentence, Maria's chest felt like it was going to explode as she let out a loud, sorrowful wail and cried hysterically.

"Oh no, no!" Alice cried as she flew into a rage. All she could think about was the day Clarence and Violet came to her home and the horrible confirmation that Violet was going to have Clarence's baby.

Good riddance, Violet. I hope you and Clarence both rot! Alice thought to herself, feeling scalding tears of anger streaming down her face. The more she wiped them away, the faster they came.

Eucharista held Maria tightly as she wept hysterically.

"Shh, it's going to be all right, Ma chérie. This is going to work out much better than you expected.

Remember what I told you when I gave you your reading and what the cards said to me? Your children aren't going anywhere," said Eucharista with conviction as she gazed out the window overlooking the barn. The life-saving answer and dark secrets that Clarence Margaret had held back from Maria for years were hidden in the deep crevices of that barn.

Four days before Christmas, New Orleans was hit with freezing temperatures and strong winds. The night was too cold for anyone to venture out, not even Ricks, who warned the community that he and his men wouldn't risk getting stuck in the cold. He advised everyone to stay indoors and keep warm. Many people who would typically work a night shift opted to stay home. What's more surprising is that their white employers told them not to come in, saying they wouldn't be responsible if they got hurt on their way home in the cold.

Every night, up until Christmas, Turner made love to Beryl. He couldn't keep his hands off her, his fingers ached to touch her, and his mouth craved her taste. Beryl was always on edge, desperate for him, pulling

Turner closer to her. Each morning for four days, she woke to Turner's strong fingers exploring between her thighs, driving her to a frenzy.

One day before Christmas Eve, Turner planted his seed inside Beryl, and just as Eucharista had predicted, it was confirmed that Beryl would glow and carry two new lives, arriving in September.

CHAPTER SEVEN

"Train bound for Chicago leaves in forty-five minutes!" blared the overhead speakers in the crowded train terminal.

The line of Black people was thirty, waiting in front of the only open ticket booth. Next to the Black people waiting to purchase were the White folks, who were attended to first. There were ten.

I've been standing here for over an hour now, and my feet hurt; I've got a headache and have to pee badly! Audine thought to herself, infuriated not only by the wait in line but by the conversation with Turner, Wayne ending their marriage, and standing in line holding two tattered, heavy suitcases, a thin wool coat, stockings now full of holes and snags, and held up by one garter. To make matters worse, a young mother directly behind her was holding her crying baby, whose cries gradually turned into high-pitched screams and occasional howling.

"Is our line ever going to move? I'm dead tired, and my baby needs a change", the young woman behind Audine complained.

Some white people in the other line shot the young woman holding her crying baby dirty looks, clearly annoyed by the baby's piercing screams. Audine squeezed her eyes shut to block out the baby's noise.

"Excuse me, miss?" said the young woman, tapping Audine's arm.

Audine acted like she hadn't heard her.

"Excuse me, miss? Can you help me?" she asked again, urgently tapping Audine on the shoulder.

"What do you want?" Audine spun around to face her. The woman was probably no more than twenty years old. She was underdressed, skinny, and had slumped shoulders. Her ring finger was bare, and her baby boy cried even louder. Every time he let out a wail, thick snot bubbled from his nose.

"Excuse me, ma'am, could you possibly hold my spot in line for me? I forgot to go to the toilet before I left home, and now I need to go badly. Could you help me out, please?" she asked in a soft, shaky voice.

"You want me to hold that crying baby of yours while you go all the way across the train station to use the toilet room, and then expect me to keep an eye on your suitcase too? No! I won't do it! I have enough things to do here than standing in this got-damn line waiting for you to get back! If you need to hear it now, my answer is no!" Audine snapped in a cold voice.

The unexpected and insensitive answer shocked the young woman so much that she silently bent down, gathered her belongings, and hurried out as quickly as possible to get to the toilet room with her baby, who was now screeching.

Humph! Who does she think I am, her mother? Who would take care of that bellyaching brat? She's like Violet, opening her legs to a married man, hah! Humph, it's just what New Orleans needs, another nasty whore! Audine thought to herself, disgusted, as she squared her shoulders, hearing the baby's cries fading in the distance.

Finally, the line of Black passengers began to move.

"At last!" Audine let out a sigh, clearly fed up, as she bent down to gather her suitcases from the dirty floor.

"Next!" shouted the ticket booth operator.

"I'd like to buy a ticket, please," Audine said with charm.

"A ticket to where?" asked the ticket booth operator with a flippant tone.

"I'm not sure, but I need to go somewhere really far from here, and I- "

"Listen, you need to decide now, or I'm taking the next person in line; now hurry up!" he interrupted rudely.

The announcement blared, "The last train leaving for Chicago boards in ten minutes! Get your tickets now!"

"Chicago, I'm headed to Chicago!" Audine blurted out.

"That'll cost you two dollars and fifty cents," the ticket booth operator snapped.

"I thought the ticket would only cost me two

dollars," Audine muttered as she handed the money to the operator with reluctance.

Snatching the bills and coins, he counted them twice and then flung the ticket to her, where it landed on the floor. Humiliated, she bent down and scooped up the beige-colored ticket.

"Thank you," she said, rising. "Where's the train?"

"Get the hell out of the line so these other niggers can get their tickets! Move!" he shouted, spittle flying from his cracked lips.

Bending down to grab her suitcases, she stepped out of line, which had grown to twenty more potential passengers. If they didn't board the train within the next ten minutes, they'd have to spend the night in the waiting area reserved for Black passengers, waiting twelve hours for the next train. This was one of the worst places to wait, with filthy bathrooms and toilets that didn't flush, leaving an unbearable stench. There were no places to get food or drinks, so Black passengers would bring their own, packed in shoeboxes, along with water in mason jars and the essential item: toilet paper. Unfortunately, Audine had forgotten to bring these essentials on her journey.

Feeling a desperate urge, Audine sprinted toward the sign that read: "Colored Bathrooms." As she drew nearer, she heard the high-pitched wails of the baby once more.

Damn it, not now! That screaming brat and whore are still here! Audine thought to herself, furious.

Upon arriving, to her horror, she found a line of ten women. The waiting room was even filthier than she had imagined and utterly miserable. The Black travelers waiting in the small, cramped room had an unavoidable view of passengers going in and out of the urinals and women's stalls. Passengers could see women's panties when they were pulled down to their ankles as they rushed to pee or squat over the toilet seat, sometimes missing the seat and leaving pee or old shit stains behind. Therefore, you didn't dare sit on a toilet seat. Of the three stalls in the ladies' restroom, only one could flush; the other two had broken toilet seats and week-old, fermenting pee, along with a bowlful of shit, causing the entire room to reek of a putrid odor. All the women held perfume-scented handkerchiefs to their noses.

There wasn't time to wash their hands because a sign on the faucet stated: "Wash Basin is Out of Order." Women brought along pre-soaked washcloths in their suitcases or separate bags to maintain some dignity when washing their hands after using the toilet.

The baby's high-pitched screams, which were almost unbearable, caused Audine to glance over to the left corner of the bathroom. The baby, still wrapped in a filthy blanket, was lying on the grimy floor, covered in dirt and soot. A note pinned to the child's blanket read, "I need a home."

"That young girl ought to be ashamed of herself for leaving that baby boy all alone!" complained one of the women in line.

"Humph, I watched her place that poor child on the floor, rush into a stall to do her toilet business, and then run outta here like the devil was chasing after her!" another woman, shaking her head in disgust, remarked.

"If I didn't have my five children, I'd take him," said another woman, who was balancing two sleeping toddlers on her hips while the other three clung to her coat.

"Whelp, I watched through the window, and you know what I saw? I saw her run across the way to a car driven by a white man! He took off so fast that she didn't even have time to shut the door!" said another female passenger with a look of repulsion. As the three women chatted loudly and quickly while waiting their turn to use the stall, Audine spotted a small wad of cash near the crying baby. As women finished using the stall, they rushed out, leaving a quarter or even a dollar near the baby so that any kind-hearted soul who wanted to take him in would have money to buy the essentials.

At this point, Audine had crossed her legs and desperately needed to use the bathroom. Keeping a close eye on the stall, she watched and listened as each woman went in, took care of her business, flushed, and pulled up her panties; that was the signal. Audine hurried ahead of the other women and burst into the stall, knocking down the woman standing behind her.

She hoisted up her dress and pulled down her panties. Audine squatted over the grimy, pee-stained toilet seat that hadn't been cleaned in months. The toilet rim and floor had noticeable dirt and fecal stains.

Audine ignored the cursing and yelling as the stream of urine sprayed all over the seat. She didn't think about the mess she was leaving for the next person, Audine finished, flushed, and rushed out of the stall.

"Sorry, but I had to go bad, and I couldn't wait for any of you!" she smirked.

"So did all of us, selfish bitch!" admonished the woman, whom Audine shoved aside to get into the bathroom stall, causing her to trip and fall onto the grimy floor. The woman's dress bore a ring of dirt and oil from where she had landed. Another older woman looked distraught and was being comforted by several women in line. Unable to hold it in any longer, she stood sobbing with humiliation as a small pool of urine spread down between her legs, soaking her dress and coat. As Audine walked by, everyone in line gave her a look of anger and disgust.

Ignoring them, Audine walked over to the shrieking baby. His hands were clenched into two tiny fists, as if he were fighting against the world of hate and prejudice to find his rightful place. Bending down, Audine scowled.

"Shh, shut up, you howling brat!" she whispered. "Your mother and my daughter have something in common: they're both whores. You're going to grow up to be a good-for-nothing, just like your mother. Bye now, and shut up that crying; you're giving me a headache!"

Before getting up, Audine acted like she was digging through her purse for some cash to leave with the child. But instead, she grabbed the money and slipped it into her purse.

Ignoring the women's rants, Audine grabbed her suitcases and ran past them, stumbling several times over her untied oxfords to reach the train platform before it pulled away. Waiting twelve hours wasn't an option.

"All Aboard!" Boomed overhead.

As she picked up speed, Audine was suddenly shoved, sending her sprawling to the ground.

"Who pushed me?" she cried out. Glancing back, she saw no one was there. Scrambling to her feet, looking down to see that her stockings were ripped and her knees were scraped and bleeding. Hobbled by pain, she limped to the line marked by the sign: "Colored Passengers Board Here."

The passengers in line moved quickly. The conductor, a tall, blue-eyed monster of a man who appeared to be angry, snatched tickets from the hands of the Black passengers boarding the Jim Crow section of the train. Several passengers asked him questions, but he either ignored them or told them bluntly, "Shut the hell up asking me stupid questions, or get off the train!" He ordered women holding their crying or fussy toddlers to get off the train because of the noisy children, took their paid tickets, and tore them up. If they protested, he gripped their arm hard enough for the woman to cry out in pain, shoving her and her child off the train, and tossed their suitcases to the ground, narrowly missing them.

"Excuse me, sir, but what time will this train get to Chicago?" inquired Audine.

"You should have asked when you bought your ticket!" he shouted, snatching the ticket from her hand.

"Move!" he shouted.

With a bit of awkwardness, Audine heaved her two suitcases onto her shoulder and followed the Black passengers to the Jim Crow car. Inside, the car was packed and dirty. Audine took the first empty seat she saw, removed her coat, and placed it on the seat to keep it from being taken. She shoved the first suitcase into the corner near her seat, took a deep breath, and counted to three before lifting the second one onto the luggage rack above her seat. Letting out a deep sigh, she put her coat back on and sat down.

As the train car filled up, a young couple sat down in the seat opposite her. Audine glanced up at the woman, a beautiful Creole who could easily pass for anything else, but her slightly broad nose gave her away. The man she was with, presumably her husband, was a six-foot-tall, well-built, pecan-complexioned guy. Audine noticed that they were indeed married, taking in their gold wedding bands and her garnet-stone engagement ring.

"Good evening. I'm Franklin Moreau, and this is my wife, Anais," he said, smiling. Audine couldn't help but notice his perfect smile, with a row of straight white teeth.

"Nice to meet you," Anais said, extending her hand to shake Audine's, who gave a brief handshake and looked away.

"My name is Mrs. Audine Collins," Audine said, smoothing out her hair to the side so the couple could see her wedding and engagement rings.

The Jim Crow car was crowded. All the seats were occupied, and the final passengers to board had to stand in the center aisle for the duration of the ride.

The train gradually gained speed after initially moving slowly. It was lively, with passengers chatting in the aisles and seats of the Jim Crown car. Audine nervously craned her neck to see if she recognized any women from the bathroom. Although she saw none, she overheard part of a conversation where a woman told her husband that the line to use the bathroom was so long that most people missed the train and would need to wait in line again to buy new tickets, facing another twelve-hour wait for the next train to Chicago. Audine discreetly reached into her coat pocket and retrieved the cash she had set aside for the baby. Ensuring no one was watching, she opened her purse, quickly counted the cash, then closed it, attempting to hide her crooked smile.

Five dollars! Thanks to that howling brat in the bathroom, I've got enough for food and maybe a treat, since I didn't get a chance to grab anything from my place. Thanks to that crying brat, I've got all the cash I need! She thought to herself, grinning with a touch of wickedness.

After about three hours, everyone was asleep. The passengers in the aisle sat in the middle and propped their suitcases on the floor against the outer edge of the passenger seats to support their backs. Others who knew each other sat back-to-back to lean on one another for support while sleeping.

Audine was fully awake.

She glared at Anias and Franklin with hatred as they held each other while they slept.

Wayne's thoughts overwhelmed her. She was haunted by the bitter memories of their wedding night, the passion they shared, and his reaction when he found out she was pregnant with their first child. The bitterness deepened into sorrow as tears welled up. The joyful celebration in New York turned tragic when she experienced a sharp pain at the nightclub, forcing her to push out a gelatinous, bloody sack — the remains of their unborn baby. The subsequent sorrowful journey back to New Orleans revealed that Violet had a child with Clarence Margaret, a married man.

And then my husband, Wayne, left me! Audine thought to herself, furious. "It's your got-damned fault, Violet, you ratchet bitch! What kind of daughter are you?" Audine hissed.

As Audine fell asleep, she was plagued by a string of nightmares. Meanwhile, the unseen tormentor who had pushed her at the train station looked on.

CHAPTER EIGHT

Voices echoed around her as the train raced toward Chicago. The smell of frying bacon, eggs, and dark roast coffee filled the air. Audine's nose twitched, and her eyes fluttered open. Her throat was dry. She slowly looked around and saw Black men sitting in the aisle, many with suitcases on their laps like makeshift tables. Closer inspection revealed many holding a biscuit with jam, a halved apple, and a mason jar with tepid sweet tea. Several shared and traded food items expected to last through the next two days.

"Good morning, Mrs. Collins. Did you sleep well?" Anais asked, looking and feeling vibrant.

Audine noticed that Anais and Franklin were once again holding hands, just as they had the night before. Franklin's gaze was intently fixed on Anais's face.

"Good morning," Audine replied, her voice chilly. "No, I didn't sleep well at all. My back hurts, my throat is dry, and I need to use the bathroom."

"Oh, I'm sorry you didn't sleep well. You were saying some things in your sleep, Mrs. Collins. Maybe that's why you're still tired. It woke me up and scared me. You kept calling out for a guy named Wayne. Is he your husband? Then you started calling out for a woman named, umm—"

"Violet," Franklin said, cutting her off. "You were talking about her and a man named Clarence, and how he put a baby inside Violet. Then you started crying, which woke everyone up. I was about to wake you, but Paul, who was sitting where you are now, told me not to because you were having a bad dream and to let it pass. We were all awake, watching you, Mrs. Collins. Is Violet your daughter?"

A cold shiver ran down Audine's spine, alarming her by what she had just heard.

What on earth had I just said? Everyone was staring at me, listening to every word that came out of my mouth. I was saying, and then they were all staring at me! Audine thought to herself, panicked and exposed.

"Mrs. Collins, is everything going to be all right?"

Anais whispered, leaning into Audine.

"Of course, everything is fine. My daughter is a schoolteacher who speaks perfect French! She's attending a college for Black women in Virginia. After she graduates, she'll teach in New York and marry a fine young man," Audine said, trying to sound genuine.

"So, who's Clarence? You kept saying how he's going to pay for what he did to Violet and- "

"Clarence? I don't know anyone by that name", interrupted Audine. "Uh, excuse me, where's the bathroom for us?"

"Over there, Mrs. Collins," Anais said, pointing at the sign that read: "Colored Bathroom."

Audine suddenly stood up and brushed by Anais, deliberately stepping on her toe.

"Ouch!" wailed Anais in pain as she bent over to care for her injured toe.

"Ma chérie, are you alright?" asked Franklin frantically.

"No, she mashed my toe badly! Oh my God, it

hurts so much, and I think it's broken!" Anais exclaimed, trying to hold back tears.

"What a vulgar woman she is! She didn't even say excuse me to any of us sitting here in the aisle; why she practically stepped on all of us, gheeze!" complained one of the passengers sitting there.

Everyone nodded in agreement.

"Hi, I'm Alberta. I'm a nurse, and I saw what she did to you. If you'd like, I can take a look at your toe", said the woman with a stylish appearance and a warm complexion.

"She stepped on my wife's foot on purpose!" Franklin said, enraged, his eyes now shining with anger.

"Franklin, please don't talk too loudly, or we'll get thrown off the train and miss your cousin's wedding. Miss Alberta is a nurse and will take care of me," Anais said.

Alberta nodded in agreement with Anais.

"I will slowly remove your shoe to examine your toe, okay?" Alberta said as she eased off Anais's Oxford shoe. Grasping Frankin's arm tightly, Anais squeezed her eyes shut.

"Oh, this hurts!" she muttered, her throat rasping. Alberta finally removed the shoe and looked at Anais's swollen toe, which appeared to be worsening. She reached into her nurse's bag and took out a large jar of salve. Opening it, she dipped two fingers and carefully massaged Anais's toe. The cooling, sweet-smelling salve was already easing the pain, bringing her relief.

"How are you feeling now?" Alberta asked as she placed the salve back in her bag.

"Oui! I feel so much better! The pain is going away, and the salve smells good!" she said.

"That's good to know. Here, I want you to put this sock on," she said, handing her a blue sock. "Keep your foot on top of your suitcase. If you need to get up for the bathroom, do so with your shoe untied and walk carefully. The swelling should be gone by tomorrow morning," said Alberta, snapping her bag shut.

"Thank you, Alberta. How much do I owe you?" asked Franklin, who was already reaching for his wallet to count out cash to pay for Anais's treatment.

"No, Franklin, you owe me nothing," said Alberta.

"Just make sure that she keeps her foot propped on top of her suitcase and does not walk unless she goes to the bathroom. By tomorrow morning, the swelling and pain will be gone."

Then she left, sitting a few seats away from where they sat.

"I forgot to bring toilet paper. Now, what am I going to do?" Audine muttered loudly as she finished peeing.

The restroom shared by Black men and women on the train was appalling.

As she searched her purse again, she found the only thing that could save her: a neatly folded handkerchief tucked at the bottom. Wayne had given it to her as a small gift during their wedding trip. The delicate handkerchief was scented with her favorite perfume. She pulled it out, closed her eyes, and took a deep breath.

"Wayne," she whispered, fighting back tears.

The abrupt knock on the bathroom door snapped her back to reality.

"What do you want?" she answered in a choked voice.

"I gotta use the bathroom! How long will you be in there?" the man with the gruff voice said from the other side of the door.

Taking the handkerchief, Audine quickly wiped herself and tossed it back into her purse. After fluffing her hair and smoothing down her dress, Audine took her time opening the door.

"Move, got-damn it! I need to use the bathroom right now! It took you long enough! Now get out of my way, move!" seethed the train's three-hundred-pound, barrel-shaped cook as he bulldozed past Audine, practically knocking her down.

"Can't you say excuse me!" she yelped.

"Not if your ass is slow as blackstrap molasses!" With mockery, he sneered as he slammed the door shut. A loud noise of him expelling gas could be heard.

Glancing at the line, several chefs, second chefs, and Pullman Porters stood. The train was traveling at a high speed, causing Audine to lose her footing and tumble onto the train's dirty floor, ripping another hole in her stocking.

"Help me, please, someone help me!" Audine wailed, humiliated that she'd fallen in front of the men. She tried to close her legs, which were still gaping, revealing her garters, but strong arms suddenly lifted her.

"Are you alright, miss?" the handsome Pullman porter asked, standing six feet two inches tall.

Gazing intensely into his eyes, he wore gold-rimmed spectacles like Wayne. Audine stood frozen, captivated by his striking, chiseled features. His skin tone was fascinating: bronze-tinted, and although the Pullman Porter's cap covered his head, a few gray hairs peeked through.

"Excuse me, ma'am, are you alright? Are you hurt? You took a tumble to the floor," he said, concerned.

"I-I guess I'm alright," Audine stammered. "I wasn't expecting the train to move so quickly! I'll be okay, anyway. I should get back to my seat before I fall again,"

"What's your name?" he inquired.

"Audine, I'm Audine Collins," she said, maintaining eye contact.

"Pleased to meet you, ma'am. I'm Walter Pickman, and I'd be honored to be your porter until we reach Chicago tomorrow afternoon. Have you eaten anything at all?" he asked.

Audine shook her head, looking down. She felt embarrassed that, despite the long journey, she hadn't brought any food to eat.

Wayne is the reason I have nothing to eat! For God's sake, the least he could've done was send me off with a sack of food! What kind of husband is he? she thought bitterly.

"Come here," he said, guiding her to a corner away from the cooking staff, waiting for the bathroom.

"I have some buttered toast and warm coffee in the mason jar," he whispered. Pulling out a small, wrapped slice of toast and a mason jar of warm coffee with a splash of cream, he patted her handbag to open it and quickly deposited the contents inside. Audine opened her purse, took the toast and the mason jar, nestled them inside, and snapped her purse shut.

"From now on, I'm going to serve only you. Come meet me here at noon during lunch. I'll grab you a quick lunch – a sandwich and some water. It won't be the best, but it'll be something to tide you over, okay?" he said.

Audine nodded.

"Thank you, Walter! I'm so grateful for this toast and warm coffee piece because I haven't eaten anything since last night! I'll be here at noon waiting for you. How can I ever repay you?" she coaxed, batting her eyelashes and smiling.

Walter leaned down to her ear, his arm securely wrapped around Audine's waist to prevent her from falling again.

"In due time, darlin. When we reach Chicago, you'll be satisfied with the favor. See you for lunch," he whispered. Surprisingly, he squeezed her hand, giving her a wink and a grin.

An amused smile danced across Audine's lips as

she spun around, making sure her hips swayed for him while she strolled back to her seat. Walter kept his gaze on her, licking his lips with feigned pleasure and intention.

"Humph, it looks like Walter got another one pegged," commented line cook Wardell Blue.

"Yeah, I see! Last month, he was fucking a gal so much on the train that it was a miracle his tall ass didn't get caught!" said Chef Ted Woods.

"He'd better watch out, though, 'cause I heard that girl he was messing around with is crazy, looking for him every day since we got off in Chicago. But I've got to give it to him; that guy knows how to fuck them and then vanish. He's like a magic man - one minute they see him, the next they don't, ever!" The two men burst out laughing.

Knowing exactly what they were laughing about, Walter smiled and chose to ignore them. He was preoccupied with thoughts about what to do with Audine.

As she returned to the Jim Crow car, she stepped

over passengers sitting on the floor in the aisle, deeply engaged in conversation. Anais sat with both legs on Franklin's lap and removed her sock, revealing a noticeably swollen toe with a cracked toenail. Audine received icy stares from the couple. She sank into a seat and opened her purse, releasing a foul odor that made Anais wrinkle her nose and cough several times. Unable to contain herself, Anais buried her face in Franklin's shoulder. Franklin's jaw clenched as he glared at Audine, who remained oblivious to what she had done to Anais and did not apologize.

Pulling out the toast and coffee, Audine opened the grease-spotted napkin, mortified to find the buttered toast soggy, falling apart, and burnt! When she uncapped the mason jar to examine the coffee, she looked closely and noticed several coffee grounds floating on the surface.

Walter needs to make my toast exactly how I like it: light and with plenty of butter. He should also prepare hot coffee with sugar and cream—at least that much! Audine thought as she reluctantly ate the burnt toast and took two quick sips of her coffee.

After finishing the awful-tasting breakfast, Audine listened to the conversations of the passengers sitting in the aisles. They were all teachers heading to Chicago. Thoughts of Violet crept into her mind, making her furious once more.

"So, how's your toe feeling? Does it still hurt? Audine asked Anais unapologetically.

Anais lifted her head from Franklin's shoulder.

"Reste loin de moi, espèce de chien grossier!" Anais hissed, venom dripping from her every word.

"And don't speak to us either! We'll be so happy to see you leave once we arrive in Chicago! How dare you step on her toe and not even apologize!" seethed Franklin.

"Don't talk to me like that! Where are your manners? If her foot weren't in my way, I wouldn't have stepped on it, hah! She should apologize to me! I could've tripped over her foot, hurt my head, and messed up my hair!" quipped Audine.

Anias and Franklin couldn't believe what they had just heard. They continued the journey in silence, saying nothing else to Audine. They spoke only in French Creole to one another.

Audine, feeling smug and finding the toe stomp hilarious, continued her journey, smiling as she looked out the window and thought of Walter Pickman.

CHAPTER NINE

One o'clock. *Where the hell is Walter? He was supposed to be here with my lunch! That piece of shit, where is he?* Audine thought angrily to herself as her stomach growled and churned.

Anias and Franklin engaged in a lively discussion while enjoying chicken sandwiches, apples, and pecans.

Humph! She must want to make up with me because now and then, she looks at me and says strange-sounding words like "chein sale," "putain puant," and "salope." Hah! Those words sound like compliments made especially for me, but why would she say them and smile at me? Audine thought to herself as she smiled back at Anais, who doubled over in laughter.

"As long as I'm alive, I'm never taking a train under these conditions ever again," remarked one of the passengers sitting in the aisle playing cards with his fellow riders.

"I understand because my wife said those waiting rooms are horrible. There's one for White ladies and white men, and one for neither men nor ladies, but for Black people, which means we were neither considered as men nor women! What makes this worse is the dirty waiting room, with more broken chairs than we can count, and the wooden benches are so broken they're completely lopsided. One side of the bench lies on the floor while the other is split in two," complained the card player, shuffling cards for the next round. "We always get the worst waiting rooms, and they're never well-lit or clean."

"If you think that's bad, just wait until you all hear about the toilet room for us colored women. As you know, we have no privacy because there is no door separating the toilet room. So, people can see when we have to use the toilet, even with a broken door that doesn't lock. People can see our underpants around our ankles in plain view when we're doing our toilet business. Why, I was in tears when I was done!" said a woman who sat two seats up. Upset, she took out her handkerchief and dabbed the tears spilling from the corner of her eyes. All the women nodded and murmured their agreement about the humiliation.

"I paid extra money for a compartment where my wife and I could sleep in the lower berth. It would be near the bathroom, but we didn't care. Well, as soon as we got on this train, we asked the conductor where the lower berth was. Humph! He told us there were no berths for us and to shut up and get on the train! And if we didn't like it, get off! So, here we are, after paying all that extra money. I tell you all now; this is the last time we'll ever take a Jim Crow train again!" an exasperated Black rider said as he tightly held onto his wife's hand.

Everyone nodded in agreement except Audine, who was craning her neck and searching for Walter, who had yet to arrive. Frustrated, Audine looked out the train's window and gazed into emptiness.

As Anais pulled out a paper bag of fragrant, soft, and chewy molasses cookies, she took one, broke it in half, and fed it to her husband. She ate the other half herself. The scent of the familiar treat caught Audine's attention, and she turned toward Anais, frowning. Anais winked at Audine as she took a bite of the tasty cookie and licked her fingers clean.

Next, Anais motioned for Audine to lean in with her finger, indicating she wanted to whisper something to her. Audine did so cautiously.

"Tu es un cochon grossier et méchant! Vous sentez la merde de porc par une chaude journée d'été!" she said, whispering and smiling.

Finally, Anais apologized to me! She seems to have seen the light and treats me like someone much more educated, even though I don't get that French Creole language. But I can tell just by the way she talks to me and smiles that she's finally admitted she was wrong. That stupid woman, Audine thought to herself, nodding and smiling slowly at Anais.

"Oh, mon Dieu, quelle idiote c'est, cette imbécile!" said Anaïs out loud, laughing with delight.

CHAPTER TEN

It's midnight, and everyone's asleep. The only sounds are the train and the occasional rustle of a passenger shifting around to get comfortable on these hard seats. It's a wonder that Black people hate riding the train. To make things worse, it's freezing.

"Where the hell are you, Walter? I had nothing to eat for lunch, and by dinner time, everyone else had something except me! Humph, you liar! I only got that burnt piece of toast, and that's all!" Audine thought bitterly before closing her eyes to fall asleep.

Initially, she felt a poke on her shoulder, making Audine flinch. Then she felt someone tapping and shaking her arm, waking her. It was Walter. A sudden shock appeared in Audine's eyes as she looked at his smiling face.

"Shh, don't talk. Get up slowly, pick up your suitcase, and hand it over," he whispered, extending his hand to take the suitcase from her.

Audine quickly shook off her sluggish state and sprang awake.

"Oh, oh, Walter! Where were you? I waited for you! I'm so—" Audine stuttered, but she was quickly silenced when Walter gave her a stern look to stay quiet. She handed the suitcase to Walter, and as he reached out, Audine took his large hand. Together, they quietly made their way down the aisle, carefully tiptoeing so as not to disturb anyone.

"This way," he whispered, his deep voice sending shivers down her spine. In that instant, Audine forgot her hunger as she took in Walter's towering six-foot-four frame, clad in his crisp navy blue Pullman Porter uniform, matching cap, perfectly pressed white shirt, and black shoes that gleamed with a spit-shine.

"Jesus!" Audine murmured, grasping Walter's hand tightly. "Where are we going?" she whispered.

"Where whitey ain't supposed to be. You'll see, we're almost there," he said in a low voice.

Gliding smoothly at top speed, the train started to sway from side to side. Frightened of falling again,

Audine clutched Walter's hand so tightly that her hand went numb temporarily. Walter didn't seem to mind, giving her hand a comforting squeeze, which made Audine smile with relief.

Walter approached an empty berth, lifted the suitcase from his shoulder, and set it down easily. He reached into his jacket pocket, pulled out a key on a chain, and inserted it, producing a loud click that startled Audine.

"It's all right, darlin', after you," he said, as he pushed the door open.

Audine stepped inside the berth.

"Oh, my goodness, what is this?" she exclaimed.

Inside, the berth had a bed big enough for two people, positioned against the window side. It was equipped with fresh white sheets, two pillows, a blue blanket, and a table where Walter carefully arranged his tools to ensure he could do his work effectively.

Audine approached the table and admired his tools: a hard-bristled clothes brush, an extra-blue Pullman Porter's blanket, his deep blue uniform cap, jacket, vest, trousers, tie pin, keys for all the berths, lockers, car, and a complicated item that she couldn't quite identify.

"What's this one?" inquired Audine, pointing to the odd-looking item.

"It's an essential tool I use to open an overhead bed. In the White-only section of the train, they have the privilege of sleeping on berths with overhead beds that I, as well as the other porters, must prepare for them, yet in the colored section, you all have to endure sitting in those terrible seats all night. That's why so many of us hate taking these damned trains. It's unfortunate, but sometimes there's no other choice," he affirmed. "That's why you didn't see me all day. I thought about you all day, though, Audine. You don't know how much I wanted to be near you," he said, gazing down into her eyes and licking his full lips.

"Really? How long did you think about holding me, Walter?" she asked.

As he pulled her in, he smiled as if he could read Audine's thoughts.

"Like I said, all day. You're a woman after my own heart, you know. The only thing holding me back is that you're married," he said.

Audine looked at her engagement ring and gold wedding band before covering them with her hand.

"So, darlin, what happened between you and your husband? Tell me the truth," he said, his voice firm.

Oh my God, why didn't I remove the rings? Audine *thought to herself, her panic growing.*

"Before I say anything, can I please have that steak and potatoes over there? It seems you forgot I haven't eaten since this morning, and you promised to look after me!" she hissed.

"Well, I was hoping to get some answers before we reach Chicago tomorrow night at nine o'clock, but because you haven't eaten, you win," he answered with a sensual, soft laugh. "But let's make this enjoyable. Put the plate on the bed so we can talk as you eat, because I want to watch you chew on that meat," he said, eyeing her.

"That sounds fine to me," purred Audine, hungrily

eyeing the steak, which looked well-done with a dollop of butter and a hefty scoop of mashed potatoes. A glass of water with a lemon slice on the side was also nearby. Walter stood up, grabbed the food, and placed it between himself and Audine on the bed.

Audine could have invested more effort into devouring the cold, tough steak. The potatoes resembled rocks, and the butter was outdated. Yet, none of that mattered to her. What truly mattered was that she had food before her. For the first time, she felt grateful just to have a meal.

Walter stared in disbelief at how greedily Audine was stuffing food into her mouth.

"So, darlin, are you going to tell me about your husband and why you're on this train alone?" he asked, staring into her eyes.

Walter's question nearly made Audine choke on her last difficult-to-chew steak. She quickly laughed and dabbed her lips with a white cloth napkin.

"I'm on this train alone because I left my husband. He was unfaithful and a thief; he stole money from me,

Walter. I was a wonderful wife to him. I never lied or gossiped. Do you want to know something else about him? His first wife was a common woman. Humph! She packed her bags and left him to be with some big-time criminal! Well, guess who comforted him? It was me, of course! I was there to keep him company when he had to go to New York to make funeral arrangements and bury her! And someone put over a thousand dollars in a sympathy card for him, hah! I was the one who told Wayne, now my ex-husband, to put the money in the bank. Did he listen to me? NO! He left it inside a dresser and accused me of robbing him; Humph! I told him I did not do such a thing, and then on Sunday, before we went to church, he accused me again of stealing the money. I told him I wouldn't dare do something so vile and evil, and that he's the one who's the liar, the one who's mixed-up! Well, I couldn't take it anymore, so I left him. I told him I'm through, and when I get to Chicago, I'm getting an annulment!" she said with clenched teeth. Then, on cue, Audine snatched up the white cloth napkin, pretended to sob uncontrollably, buried her face in the napkin, and rocked.

I'm going to pretend to keep crying so that Walter will eventually have time to feel sympathy for me and listen to more of my woes. Humph, by the time I'm done crying and batting my beautiful eyes at him, he'll have no choice but to fall in love with me, especially when he sees that the men in Chicago will be attracted to me! Wayne can kiss my juicy, beautiful ass now! Audine thought to herself, smiling, as she covered her face entirely with the napkin to hide her deceptive smile from Walter.

I know damn well Audine is lying! Her husband threw her out of the house because she stole money from him! Shit, does she think I'm a fool? By the time this train arrives in Chicago, she's going to be broke and fucked! Walter thought to himself as his full lips curled slowly into a smile. He rose from the bed, took the plate, and placed it on the table, covering it with the metal topper. Then, he sat beside Audine and wrapped his massive arm around her heaving shoulders.

"Shh, Wayne's gone, and I'm here. I'll stay with you to protect you until we get to Chicago tomorrow night. You have my word," he said, gently lifting the napkin from Audine's face.

Oh, she's good; she didn't cry one damned tear! She's just like the other woman I fucked a few months ago. Audine's nothing more than a got-damned liar! Walther thought to himself, amused.

Audine allowed him to remove the napkin without hesitation, but she kept her eyes lowered to her folded hands.

"Promise me that you'll watch only me, Walter. I don't have anyone who loves or cares about me anymore, and you- "

Just as Audine was speaking, she felt him draw her in, his tongue exploring the inside of her mouth. The kiss was slow and sensual, his lips soft and persuasive. As she opened her mouth, the kiss deepened, and Audine's entire body was consumed by pleasure.

Walter pulled Audine closer, and in one swift move, he managed to unzip her dress and pull it forward so that Audine's arms would slide out of the sleeves. Walter stopped kissing her long enough to gaze at her ample-sized caramel-colored breasts that were half covered by her bra. His eyes settled on her curvaceous figure.

"They're beautiful," he said, astonishment in his voice, smiling. He couldn't stop looking at her large breasts, which were surprisingly firm and not sagging.

"Thanks, Walter," she said, smiling back at him. "I like you, and with the short time we have together, I don't want to waste a moment of it." Her eyes fixed on him, Audine sat up straight and unhooked her bra with both hands. Both of her breasts spilled out, catching Walter off guard with a pleasant surprise.

"I know you've been waiting for this to happen between us because the moment I met you, I knew you wanted only me. I'm telling you the truth, Walter, when I say I like you very much. So, after I settle in Chicago and you show me around and introduce me to your friends and family, would you consider being more than my friend?" she asked, her voice husky but subdued.

"Shh, stop talking, Audine," said Walter, pressing his finger to her lips to silence her. "I'll figure that out later."

"But Walter, I–" Audine was cut off as he gently squeezed and caressed her breasts, then got rougher.

Audine's eyes fluttered shut, and she stretched her neck back, reaching for the hard mattress with her elbows for support. Walter's strong hands gripped her breasts, sending her into loud, deep moans as the old familiar shiver took over. For a brief moment, she thought of Wayne, but the thought was fleeting as Walter's mouth closed over her nipple, his fingers working the other. He sucked so deeply that the sound of his mouth echoed in the room. The frenzy consumed Audine.

As Walter pressed down on her chest to lay her on the bed, he paused to gently remove her dress and garter belt. He inched further up the bed, and Audine's eyes tracked him, her lips parting as she watched him unbutton his shirt and the rest of his uniform. She matched the intensity of his gaze with her own. Walter's erection was massive.

Imagine if I'd ended up with Walter instead of Wayne. I probably would've had four or five children for him. Humph, Wayne did me a favor, and if Maria could see the good life I have now, she'd be jealous green, especially with her rotten husband gone! Hah! She'd be jealous, all right, just like those funny green eyes of hers, hah! Audine thought, flashing a broad smile at Clarence's passing and Maria's widowhood.

"What are you smiling at, darlin?" he asked, taking pleasure in massaging his growing erection as she watched.

"You, Walter, and the reason is, I can count on you to do things for me, especially to take care of me. I've got no one else, and you're the one I'm counting on. Do you- "

As Audine opened up to this man, he moved quickly, mounting her and spreading her thighs apart with his strong knees, parting Audine's thighs as far as they would spread. Walter didn't waste any time. Their kiss was passionate, their breathing heavy as their bodies moved together, and Audine was eager for him to discover her.

Walter's thumbs spread apart the damp folds of her womanhood, and his long tongue slipped inside her. Audine let out a sharp, high-pitched scream, but Walter ignored her and thrust his tongue deeper, driving Audine to the brink of madness.

"Deeper, Walter, go deeper!" she groaned as she opened her legs wider to receive him.

Walter's tongue was doing new things as he pushed it deeper, circling slowly. He felt her hips writhing and knew this was the moment for his pleasure.

"Walter, please don't stop!" Audine pleaded, urging herself to focus on what he was doing.

Before Audine could say another word, Walter was completely erect. Gazing at his face, his look back at her was filled with lust, surpassing mere desire.

"Lie back, Audine; I want you to spread your legs wide open for me because I intend for you to be pleasured. Now do me a favor, darlin, stop talkin and try not to scream as I'm fucking you, okay?" he murmured as he crawled his way to be fully on top of her.

What I want is a tall, dark, and handsome man who's interested in me. I'm sure Walter will fall for me as soon as I settle in Chicago. I've given myself a year to be Mrs. Walter Pickman. I'm confident that Chicago has top-notch Black doctors who can help me have a child, because Walter and I both deserve a second chance at love and starting a family. Audine thought to herself as she and Walter kissed passionately.

Walter pushed his heavy erection inside Audine. He was so massive that Audine gasped. Walter pressed harder inside her, deeper, and began thrusting with intense urgency. As Audine wrapped her legs around Walter's narrow, tight waist, arching her hips, she met him thrust for thrust.

"Faster, Walter, faster," Audine said through gritted teeth, his voice rough with urgency.

"You sure you're ready for this? Because I don't want to hurt you, Audine,"

Audine could only arch her back, squeeze her eyes shut, and nod quickly in agreement.

Walter grasped her hips, pushing her tightly against him as he thrust one last time, unleashing his seed; he let out a cry of pleasure. Audine's frantic hands clutched his muscular shoulders as she reached her climax.

He knew Audine would cry out, so he silenced her

with his tongue in her mouth and made love to her in the darkness until they were both spent.

"Walter, that was the most wonderful time I have ever had. Not even my ex-husband could do the things you did for me. I know we just met, but once my marriage is over, we could maybe see each other in Chicago and start making plans," said Audine, snuggling close to Walter and closing her eyes.

"I've already made plans for myself," Walter said, smirking down at Audine, who was already asleep.

Audine didn't hear a word he said as she drifted into a deep sleep.

Four o'clock in the morning. The knock on the cabin door was soft but urgent.

"Hey, Pickman, wake up! The boss has been looking for you all night! He wants us all in front of the train in Berth number four in ten minutes! And another thing, make sure that round gal you were with all night is out there, too! Hurry up, man! Get out of there and tell her to make sure the berth is clean and doesn't smell like what you all did last night! The whole fucking train heard you two! Pussy-eating motherfucker," muttered Jimmy Lateman.

"Shit, got-dammit!" Walter hissed. "Tell him I'm on my way!"

Walter leapt out of the berth's bed, tripping over himself in his haste. Luckily, the uniform was already laid out by the time Audine drifted off into a deep sleep. They went at it again three more times before they collapsed in exhaustion. Audine urged him to do it a few more times, but Walter reminded her that he had to be up early for the line count and uniform inspection. If showing up late was a common occurrence, they'd lose five dollars from their pay. As soon as Audine fell asleep, Walter slipped out of her arms and headed to the small table beside the bed. He grabbed a pad of paper, scribbled a brief, detailed note, and addressed it to Audine.

Trying to get dressed on a speeding train heading to Chicago in the dark was quite a challenge. In his haste, Walter accidentally put both legs into the same pant leg, and when he heard a loud rip, he panicked. With little time left, he tore open his shirt, quickly put on his socks, slipped into them, tied his shoes, and then hopped, staggered, and stumbled to the floor. He got up, walked over to a sleeping Audine, and gave her a sharp nudge with his finger.

"Oww! That hurt!" a sleepy Audine cried out, her eyes fluttering open.

"Wake up! Time to get up and go back to where you were sitting. Hurry, Audine. Wake up now!" he whispered loudly, then opened the door and left.

Audine's eyes fluttered open. For a moment, she felt disoriented, but scanning her surroundings brought her back to reality. Her clothes were crumpled on the floor, and she could feel the train speeding along. Her thighs and the area between them ached—Yawning, Audine, a smile spread across her face.

I'm sore and a bit bruised, but if this is what it takes for Walter and me to grow closer when I settle in Chicago, then I'll endure a little discomfort, Audine thought to herself as she quickly got out of bed and dressed.

A quick wash in the small bathroom. As she

rummaged through her suitcase, Audine found a pair of clean underwear and, luckily, a pair of unused stockings. Glancing into the small mirror, she was mortified to see how messy and itchy her hair looked. Taking a brush, she scrubbed her scalp vigorously to remove dandruff and lint from her hair. With what was left in the jar of pomade, she put a dollop in her palm, oiled her scalp, and used the rest on her hair to restore shine. Afterwards, she took several bobby pins and secured her hair in a tight bun.

This looks much better, she thought as she fluffed and brushed away strands of hair.

Searching through her tattered suitcase, she discovered a crushed hat she had worn to church two days earlier. She squeezed her eyes shut at the memory of that Sunday morning when she and Wayne had fought in front of the church. Shaking her head, she reshaped the hat and carefully placed it on her head.

After changing the sheets, she left everything in the berth as if no one were there. Before leaving, she glanced at the berth again and noticed a small table with a folded piece of paper on it that had her name written on it.

"Ah! A note from Walter! He probably wanted to tell me how much he enjoyed last night and most likely wants to be together again and make plans for when I get settled in Chicago!" Audine whispered to herself.

As she opened the crisp, cream-colored lined paper, Audine began to read:

Dear Audine,

You looked beautiful last night, and I'm eager to see you again before we arrive in Chicago. About the food I've been serving you, here's what you owe for your food and for the use of this berth, which is for married White folks. I got it for us because an unfortunate incident happened to the previous couple staying here—the groom was murdered by his lover, a man he had been seeing for years. Thanks to that unfortunate news, I ended up with the berth. If you'd like breakfast with eggs, toast, and coffee, or a filling lunch, please give me twenty dollars.

I'll see you later, and I'll see you one more time before the train arrives in Chicago.

Sincerely yours,

Pullman Porter Walter Pickman

Audine gasped at the makeshift twenty-dollar bill. Grasping her chest, she crumpled the note into her fist.

"You fucking son-of-a-bitch, Walter! I don't have any money; you used me to get your way!" Audine cried out in anger as she threw the crumpled note to the floor.

Snatching up her belongings, Audine stormed off, slamming the berth's door. The train surged ahead, and Audine bounced back and forth against the heavy steel walls. As she inched closer to her seat in the Jim Crow section, Audine lost her footing and collided headfirst with the wall.

"Ouch! Oh my God, my head!" she shrieked. Cradling her throbbing head, Audine shuffled over to her seat.

"Excuse me, please," she said tersely as she stepped over two passengers sitting on the train's dirty floor.

"Humph, guess she had a good night, dinner, and getting fucked," whispered a female passenger to her friend.

"He must've been thick and long, because all that

hollering, she did woke us all up!" her friend replied, covering her mouth to restrain a laugh.

Audine whirled around to glance at the two women who pulled their hats down over their faces. She could see them smiling after the remarks were made. Ignoring them, Audine found her seat and plopped down across from Anais and Franklin, who didn't bother to greet her. Shoving her suitcase next to the one she had left behind last night, Audine sat back and tried to close her eyes. Rubbing her forehead, she felt it sore to the touch. She winced in pain.

"Oh my, I heard you take a nasty tumble. Does your head hurt, or does something between your legs hurt?" Anais said, leaning in close to Audine. "I saw you with that Pullman Porter. The entire train heard both of you! You're a nasty putain of a woman, and you're still married, you bon à rien putain!" she said, sneering at Audine.

"What did you just call me?" Audine asked, her voice laced with fury and rage. "Did you just say I'm a whore, you green-eyed French-speaking Creole? Let me tell you, I once knew a woman just like you! She was always treated like royalty! But guess what? Because of her husband, who put a baby in my daughter's belly, he's dead! So, who's the whore now, you Creole witch?" Audine said, mocking Anais's accent with a hint of sarcasm.

"That's enough! Don't you dare talk to my wife like that! You sit there and keep quiet! Your behavior on this entire train ride has been completely unacceptable! Until we get to Chicago, please don't say a word to my wife or me. Do you understand, Mrs. Collins?" Franklin said in a low, fierce voice that matched the hardness of his gaze. The entire train went silent.

Wrinkles of disdain spread across Audine's face as she snatched her hat down and turned, her eyes fixed on the window. For the next four hours, she sat in silence, gazing out the window amid the lively conversation that filled the train. Once again, Walter failed to show up with breakfast.

It was late afternoon when Audine woke up with a pounding headache. The loud chatter and laughter intensified her discomfort; she hadn't gone to the bathroom since her encounter with Walter the night before.

Where the hell is Walter? He promised me breakfast, and now it's past lunchtime, and he hasn't shown up! And he expects me to pay for that horrible food he's been bringing over - nothing but leftovers that were probably on someone else's plate! He's not getting a penny from me!" Audine fumed to herself, furious.

Audine rose from her seat to use the bathroom designated for colored people in the next car. As she tried to exit, Anais's foot obstructed her path to the aisle.

"Move!" Audine said through gritted teeth.

Anais flickered a devil-may-care look at Audine. She remained still, prompting Audine, furious, to huff in disgust, stepping over Anais's foot and narrowly missing her injured toe.

"Try not to be so noisy again back there," Anais said, annoyed.

Audine pressed her palms against one side of the train's wall and gradually moved sideways toward the bathroom.

Humph, I'm glad I grabbed plenty of toilet paper

from the bathroom's berth last night, Audine thought to herself as she headed to the bathroom.

"Good, no line!" she said gleefully as she grasped the doorknob. After turning the knob several times, it refused to budge. Audine began knocking on the door urgently.

"Please open the door! I need to use the toilet now!" she shouted.

After a moment, the doorknob turned, and the door swung open.

"Walter!" Audine seethed as she stepped back.

"Afternoon, darlin'. I guess you need to use the toilet. Welp, it's all yours," said Walter, zipping up his trousers.

"Oh, by the way, sweetheart, did you see the note I left for you? Sorry, I had to leave so quickly—had to get to work to serve those white folks. Damn, they wake up early! But about the money you owe me, sweet darlin, I need it now because the kitchen staff needs to be paid before we arrive in less than seven hours," said Walter, checking his pocket watch. He snapped it shut and slipped it into his trouser pocket.

"I need that money now, and if you want one more meal, I'll bring it to you again in the same berth. Oh, and dessert is chocolate cake," he said, licking his lips. Then, unzipping his pants, Walter took his hand and pulled out his erection, unashamed.

Audine gasped at its enormity. Walter quickly folded it back into his trousers. He grinned, his perfectly straight white teeth contrasting with his bronzed skin.

"I'm not giving you one got-damn cent! You should've told me the food you gave me would cost money! If I had to pay for food that tasted like shit, I would've accepted it!" she said through clenched teeth.

Walter took a step toward Audine and wrapped his arms tightly around her waist. Then, slowly, he pinned her against the wall.

"You son of a bit- "Audine started to protest, but Walter's massive body pushed her down and covered her mouth with his hand, cutting her off.

"Listen, sweet darlin'; I don't have time for your shit!

I owe the cooks money, and they owe the supplier who gives us the food. If you don't give me the money, I'll point you out to the cooks, who have some dangerous friends in Chicago. They'll follow you around, and let's say that pretty face of yours might get sliced from here to here with a straight razor," he said, tracing a line with his finger from her eye to her chin. Audine became so terrified that a trickle of pee wet the crotch of her panties. Audine had to cross her legs to keep from peeing.

"I only have eight dollars, and that's all I have!" Audine wailed in a low voice.

"That's all you have? Where's the rest supposed to come from?" Walter demanded loudly, his voice almost savage. Audine watched as Walter intently examined her gold wedding band and engagement ring, an evil smile lingering on his lips.

"Okay, sweet darlin'. I'll take all the money and those rings on your finger," he said.

"What? No! You can keep the money, but those rings are mine!" she replied, her voice trembling more.

"Okay, well, I'll let the cooks know that they ain't getting their money and have you follow as soon as you step off this fucker of a train when it arrives in Chicago," said Walter. He stepped back, tipped his hat to her, and started to leave.

"Wait! Here, take the money," Audine said in a choked voice. She opened her purse and grasped her last eight dollars: three from Wayne and five she had stolen from the abandoned baby in the toilet room. With trembling hands, she pushed the small wad of cash into Walter's hand.

Walter counted the wad and shoved the bills inside his trouser pocket.

"The rings, hand them over to me," he demanded.

"Walter, please don't make me; they're mine!" Audine replied, her voice becoming increasingly shaky.

Walter took Audine's hand and removed her rings. She grimaced, feeling Wayne's gift being lost forever. Watching intently, Walter examined the rings, then nodded approvingly. He tucked the jewels into his pocket and patted his stash of cash and jewelry.

"Thanks, sweet darlin'. Take care. I'll have that steak dinner ready for you at six o'clock, so be in the berth by five, okay, sweet darlin'?" he whispered in her ear. Leaning in, he kissed Audine on the forehead, gave her a playful smack on the behind, and then left.

Leaning against the door of the toilet, Audine folded down and silently cried.

At precisely five o'clock, Audine packed her suitcases. Before leaving, she observed that the passengers had put on heavy wool coats, hats, and gloves.

Humph, that's stupid. Why are these people so bundled up with heavy coats and hats as if they might freeze? At least I'll reach Chicago with a full stomach. I plan to persuade Walter to give back my money and rings, promising to pay him back twice as much once I'm settled in Chicago, Audine thought.

"Bon débarras, vulgaire pute ! Je ne souhaite que du mal ! C'est pour bientôt !" said Anaïs to Audine, smirking. She and Franklin smiled and waved at Audine, who didn't say a word, stepped over the seated passengers on the floor, and disappeared out of sight as if they knew she wasn't coming back; two passengers seated on the floor grabbed their suitcases and took Audine's seat, much to the relief of Anais and Franklin.

Upon arriving at the berth, Audine opened the door and was thrilled to see that the room had been dusted and polished, with a pitcher of water left on the small table. Audine sat on the edge of the bed, eagerly anticipating Walter's arrival with the steak dinner and hoping to have a reasonable conversation about getting her money and jewelry back.

Five hours passed, and Walter was still nowhere to be found. Frustration and hunger overwhelmed her, and exhaustion crept in. Audine's anger boiled over, and she tore off all her clothes, leaving herself completely naked. Crawling under the thick wool blanket, Audine curled up and closed her eyes, trying to stay hopeful. She imagined having a meaningful conversation with Walter over a steak dinner, getting her money and jewelry back, and then making love and making plans together. This thought made her smile briefly. The train's speed and silence lulled her into a deep sleep.

CHAPTER ELEVEN

It was completely dark in the berth, and the train stood still. Audine woke up alone, unclothed, feeling very disoriented. The silence felt strange. As she looked around, she saw no signs that Walter had been there—no indication of the hot meal he promised, and Walter was missing.

Panic-stricken, Audine threw off the blanket and quickly got dressed.

I don't give a got-damn if I leave this room a mess! Where the hell are you, Walter? Audine thought angrily.

After donning her coat and smashing her hat onto her head, Audine lifted the suitcases, carrying them in each hand along with her purse, which was empty of cash. She gasped at what she saw: the train was completely dark and passengerless! Panic set in as she hurried to find out where everyone had gone. Suddenly, she heard voices and laughter from the front of the "For Colored Only" section. Audine moved toward the section. When the six Pullman Porters in heavy wool coats saw her, they all paused their conversation. The cold night air shocked Audine, and she had to steady herself to avoid falling down the train stairs.

"Let me help you with your belongings, ma'am," said the stocky porter.

"Thank you," said Audine, handing him her suitcases. Another porter ran up and helped her down the short, narrow stairs.

"Is anyone going to meet you, ma'am? Because it's getting mighty cold out here!" the stocky porter asked.

"Well, I was supposed to meet Walter Pickman earlier this evening, but he never came to see me. Do you know where he is?" inquired Audine, flipping up her coat collar against the howling wind.

All the Pullman Porters averted their gaze from Audine, except for the stocky porter.

"He's over there," he said, nodding toward a blue 1932 Ford Model B.

"Oh, thank you!" Audine exclaimed, hurrying

away without tipping the porter for his help.

Ignoring the cold and swirling wind, Audine hurried toward the car. As soon as she saw Walter, she began waving, but then stopped abruptly. She watched with a mix of envy and horror as Walter Pickman assisted a tall, slender woman in a luxurious full-length coat out of the driver's side. The woman squealed with delight as Walter effortlessly lifted her from the ground. They shared a passionate kiss, and Walter embraced her again, lifting her once more before kissing her again. He then escorted her to the passenger side, helped her get in, and then got into the driver's seat, driving away without looking back.

As Walter's car disappeared into the distance, she felt cold without a warm hat, gloves, or thick stockings to protect her from the Chicago wind. She tightly grabbed the collar of her thin coat, trying to stay warm. Wandering down an unfamiliar street with her two worn suitcases, she was overwhelmed with humiliation. She started crying loudly and cursed Walter Pickman for making her feel like a total fool.

CHAPTER TWELVE

Walter Pickman

He glanced out the window at his new blue 1932 Ford Model B Deluxe four-door car parked outside his house. Working every day, saving tips, and tricking gullible women like Audine Collins into paying for meals was simple—tell them that the cooks are involved with dangerous people who want their money and that they'll be waiting at the train station dressed in black coats, hats, gloves, and with hidden knives.

Walter thought that last year's Christmas gift to Winifred Henson was the luckiest break he'd ever experienced as he lit a cigarette. He inhaled deeply, then gradually exhaled a cloud of smoke, his thoughts drifting back to the year before.

A Pullman employee reported sick for a double journey, leaving New York for Chicago, then returning to New York after a two-day layover before heading back to Chicago.

A tall, red-haired, white woman, mean and drunk, boarded the train alone right after leaving New York.

"I want you, boy, to serve me until I get to Chicago," she drunkenly slurred.

"Yes, ma'am. Anything you need, I'm at your service, ma'am," Walter said with a smile as he tipped his hat to her. The woman, a New York socialite, was twenty-six-year-old Norma Uppercliff, married to millionaire Alexandre Uppercliff. She was assigned to travel in Berth Number Twenty-One; a private and luxurious compartment heated for winter. It included a bathroom and meals served by Pullman Porters.

The maid assigned to Uppercliff tidied up the mess she left, styled her hair, and ensured she had plenty of magazines, books, candy, hot meals, and liquor throughout the day.

Uppercliff sent the housekeeper to find Walter the night before arriving in Chicago.

"That White lady in berth number twenty-one is asking for you," said the maid.

"What does she want?" asked Walter, brushing off

his jacket.

The housekeeper smirked at Walter and shrugged her shoulders before hurrying away.

Ever since that woman boarded the train, things have been messy! She keeps barking orders at us: 'Get me this,' 'Get me that,' and 'I need more whiskey!' Walter thought, irritated, as he grabbed his jacket to prepare for her next demand.

After draining the last drop of the piping-hot coffee, Walter left to find out what Mrs. Uppercliff needed from him again. Standing before her door, he straightened his posture, took a deep breath, and rapped gently on the door three times.

There was no answer. After three more short knocks, Uppercliff finally responded.

"C'mon in!" she said, her words slurred from the booze.

Walter turned the doorknob and stepped inside, his eyes widening in shock at what he saw. The berth was a mess. More than a dozen empty liquor bottles lay scattered across the floor, newspapers and torn magazine pages were strewn everywhere, and Uppercliff was sitting there, completely naked, with an unlit cigarette in her mouth and clutching an empty whiskey bottle.

"Ever seen a naked white woman as beautiful as me?" a drunk Uppercliff slurred.

"Uh, no, ma'am, I never have, but I think you should put some clothes on," said Pickman, his hands shaking.

"Put something on? What the hell for when I've got a tall, hot-blooded mass of a man standing right in front of me! Shit, I bet you have a poker curled up inside of those pants about this long!" she said, spreading her arms wide, bursting into laughter. "Come on, let me see how long your poker is!" she added.

"Ma'am, you know I can't do that; I can lose my job and get arrested. You know as well as I do that the law will find me guilty and have me executed by hanging. Please, let me leave now," he pleaded, looking horror-stricken. "I have a woman in Chicago that I love."

"What a lucky woman! Just think, having that long, thick black stick inside her every night! Shit, I'd love to see it for myself! And I can't wait to have it inside me," Uppercliff said, laughing drunkenly.

Walter stared, his frown deepening, as he shook his head and whispered a firm "no" to her.

"And if you don't do as I say, I have no choice but to call the conductor, who will call the police. Here's how it works: if you refuse me, I'll contact the conductor and tell him you attacked me. Then he'll call the cops. I'll let them know you forced me into doing something lewd, and you'll end up in prison. And then they'll hang you. So, please lock the door, turn off this got-damn light, take off your clothes, and show me that thing between your legs. Then you can fuck me until I can't take it anymore, got that?" she demanded.

Terrified she would carry out her malicious act, Walter reluctantly nodded in agreement, feeling he had no choice but to comply or face a noose around his neck.

"I hear all sorts of stories about you, colored men! How long and thick you all are! I've even heard from a few Chicago whores who work on Wabash say they were so sore down there they had to lie up in bed for a week! Hah! Can you imagine that? So, does that mean you're going to pound your long, thick black fire hook inside me?" Norma asked, tilting her head back to finish off the bottle of whiskey she was drinking.

"I'll try not to hurt you, ma'am, but we need to be quiet or else everyone will hear us," Walter said, unzipping his pants and taking off his glasses.

"I swear I'll be quiet. The only sound you'll hear is the train wheels rolling on the tracks. Hurry up, I'm getting pretty drunk and wet; shit, hurry up!" she demanded, a wicked smile spreading across her face.

Walter was completely unclothed. His erection was at full length, and it made Norma's eyes widen, and she held a flash of shock as she stared. She gave a breathless laugh.

"You ready for me, ma'am? I'll give you what you're asking for, but I'm warning you," Walter said, standing with his long, muscular legs spread wide, his hand massaging his growing erection.

Norma, drunk, was convinced she saw his erection grow.

"Before I push myself inside of you, let's share a drink to celebrate this moment," said Walter as he quietly walked over to the bed and sat down beside Norma.

"What are we celebrating?" she slurred.

"Why, you, of course. It'll be your first time with a Black man and mine with a White woman. But we must keep this as our special secret. You aren't to tell anyone about what happened. So, I'm going to pour you a drink first. Then, please relax and lie back; I'll take care of everything. Humph, by the time I get finished with you, you'll want more of me inside you," Walter whispered, his warm breath against her temple.

He looked to the side of the floor and saw an unopened bottle of whiskey and a dirty glass. He picked them up.

"Oh yeah, that's cause for celebration! Wow, I've never seen such a long fire hook in my life! Can I please touch it?" she asked, holding her breath in anticipation of his response.

Walter twisted the cap off the whiskey bottle and poured a generous amount into her glass, while he poured a splash for himself into the other.

"You can, of course, darlin'," he replied. "But first, let's raise a toast. To you, Mrs. Uppercliff, may you never forget what's about to happen for the rest of your life,"

"Hah! A toast from you is a real treat for me, like being with you!" she slurred. She laughed, tilted her head back, and drank the entire glass of whiskey. Walter held the dirty glass to his lips, tilted his head back, and faked drinking it, but he didn't let the liquid touch his lips.

"Are you gonna let me touch that?" Norma asked, pointing at Walter's erection.

"Here, let me take your glass," said Walter as he placed Norma's glass on the floor. Then, taking her trembling hand, he moved it to where she ached for him.

"Oh, this is as hard as a rock! Are you going to put that big thing inside me?" she asked, her eyes widening.

"Lie down and spread your legs nice and wide for

me," commanded Walter in a low tone.

Norma was too drunk to respond to his request, so she struggled to lie back. She shut her eyes and let Walter take her hands and grasp her knees. He easily spread her legs apart as far as they would go. Hovering above her, his eyes squeezed shut, he thrust his thick erection inside her wet opening.

"Oh, my goodness, I want this even more! Please go in deeper!" a drunk Norma pleaded.

"Yes, ma'am, if this is what you want, I'll do whatever you ask," Walter replied as his intense thrusts drove into Norma. His rugged, rough movements shook her body, and then, as she arched her hips, Norma matched him thrust for thrust. Norma was stretched and filled with his long, dark manhood, but suddenly Walter felt himself fighting for release.

Oh, no! I can't spill my seed into this drunk whore, shit! Walter thought to himself, terrified. He tried to slow down, but it was too late. His body tensed up and jerked; every muscle was rigid as he released his seed into her.

"Fuck!" he whispered through clenched teeth.

"I'm sorry this happened. I wasn't supposed to bust inside like that! Ma'am, ma'am?"

Norma did not respond, aside from her faint snoring that filled the berth.

What if she reports what just happened to the police? Shit! I'll end up in jail, and worse, what if I've already gotten her pregnant? Damn! But she was the one who wanted this, and besides, she's completely drunk! I need to get out of here now! Walter thought to himself, his panic growing.

Walter pulled himself out of Norma and looked at the time.

It was three o'clock in the morning. In two hours, all the Pullman Porters would need to be ready for the line inspection and serve breakfast to the early risers, as the train was due in at nine-thirty.

Once the two-hour cleanup was finished, the train staff would head home for a two-week break. The new train staff heading back to New Orleans would leave at 6:00 p.m.

After dressing, Walter covered Norma with a

blanket because she was completely passed out. He then took the dirty glass to the bathroom, rinsed it clean, and dried it thoroughly. Next, he took the glass Norma had been drinking from, gently placed it in her hand, and positioned the partially full whiskey bottle on her chest. He then crossed her right arm over the bottle.

When she wakes up, she'll probably think this was all just a dream, thanks to the drinking, Walther thought to himself, feeling pretty confident. As he turned to leave, one of her suitcases crashed to the floor with a loud thud, startling Walter as he tiptoed to the door.

"Damn it, shit!" he exclaimed out loud.

Norma stirred and then loudly expelled gas. Walter stood frozen, unable to move, as a foul, heavy odor filled the berth. He wrinkled his nose in disgust at Norma. He picked up the small, heavy suitcase that had fallen to the floor. Noticing that the latches were only partially unsnapped, he had to snap both latches closed, then open the suitcase to line it up with the bottom so the top would close evenly.

Walter unlatched the suitcase, opened it, and glanced inside. His eyes widened at the sight: stacks of cash, thousands of dollars.

"What the fuck?" he said, maintaining a low voice.

After scanning the cash wads, he noticed that each wad had a piece of paper tied to it, indicating the amount in denominations of two thousand dollars. Scanning the room, Walter spotted a soiled gunny sack on the floor, a perfect decoy. He pulled out twenty cash wads from inside the suitcase and meticulously placed them inside the sack. After securing the loot, he stood up and pushed the suitcase back to its original position. On the floor in a crumpled heap lay a fur coat. Walter peered closer for a better look. Hoisting it up, he discovered it was a full-length mink coat with deep cuffs and dark buttons.

"Damn!" he whispered, a smile spreading across his face.

Winifred's Christmas present had just arrived! He thought to himself with a smile. Reaching into the coat's deep pockets, he pulled out another stack of $180 in cash and a pair of brand-new tan gloves. Pickman folded and rolled the coat as tightly as he could, then *stuffed it into the sack and the cash into his pocket. The berth was pitch-black, except for the hum of the train and Norma's snoring; he slung the sack over his shoulder like Santa Claus.*

Your drunk white ass got an early Christmas gift: my long black cock, and in return, I got your money and a fur coat for my future wife. Now, who's the dumb boy, you red-headed whore, he thought to himself, smiling.

He glanced back at her one last time, tipped his hat to Norma, and smiled as if the thought of fucking a wealthy white socialite, earning forty thousand dollars, and a full-length fur coat for Winifred. It would be one of the best Christmases ever, especially for Winifred. He shut the berth door and left.

Later that morning, when the train pulled into Chicago, Norma needed help getting off the train from the train maid and a Pullman Porter who carried her luggage. She was wearing a cheap wool coat, a cloche hat, gloves, and Oxford shoes in the cold, blustery wind. Two black Model V cars, driven by one of Chicago's most notorious gangsters, escorted a hysterically drunk and brazen Norma Uppercliff into one of the vehicles. The Pullman Porter carefully loaded her four suitcases into the trunk. As he tipped his hat to the gangster in the back seat, he rolled down the window and handed the Porter a crisp, folded twenty-dollar bill.

With a nod, the gangster signaled both cars, and they took off in a hurry.

Walter gazed out the window of the "Colored Only" car on the train.

"You fucked her, didn't you, Walter?" a female voice from behind him demanded.

Walter spun around to see the train's housekeeper, holding a broom, a dustpan, and soiled cleaning rags.

"What did you just say to me?" he shot back at her.

"I heard you, Walter! I pretended to leave so I could wait for you, but when you didn't come out, I stood by the door and put my ear to it. Oh, my goodness, Walter, you fucked that white woman!" she wailed. "You can go to jail and- "

"Shut your fucking mouth!" Walter yelled furiously through clenched teeth.

"No, I won't shut up, Walter! For a full year, it's been just you and me! I've never had anyone like you, and you promised to fall in love with me! And now you turn around like I'm not here and go inside that white woman's berth and fuck her? I beg the question of why, Walter: Why? Why did you leave me for her?" she said, collapsing onto the train seat, crying.

"Shh! Be quiet before someone hears you!" Walter said in a low, enraged tone. "I told you I have someone else in Chicago I love, not you! I've already told you this over and over, and-"

"I'm having a baby, Walter. I've missed my monthly flow for two weeks now. We made the child at the colored hotel in New York. That cold night when we were in bed together, you climbed on top of me and told me to spread my legs for you. I did, and when you were getting close to unloading inside of me, I begged you to pull yourself out from inside of me. You told me not to worry, saying everything would be fine as long as I was near my flow time," she said, wiping away tears.

"What the fuck are you talking about? Are we, no, are *you*, having a child? Nope, I'm not sticking around for that, uh-uh! I won't lose the woman I love because of a mistake I made with you," Walter said, furious.

"Mistake? You sure as hell didn't think it was a got-damned mistake when you were pounding yourself inside me, calling out my name as you released your seed inside of me! No, uh-uh, Walter! You held me and kissed me like I was your wife! That night, I loved you so much, and I knew I had changed your mind about Winifred. She thinks she's better than us just because her father is a deacon at that church he serves at, and her whole family are church thieves! I also heard that she- "

Walter lifted her and slammed the back of her head against the train window, making her scream in pain.

"Don't you ever say another got-damn word about Winifred or her family? Do you understand? Answer me!" Walter said through gritted teeth, pressing the palm of his massive hand against her neck.

"Yes, yes, yes, I understand," she stammered, shaking like a leaf.

Walter eased his grip on her neck and gently brushed her shoulders.

"Here, take this," said Walter, reaching deep into his trouser pocket. As he pulled out his hand, he took the train's housekeeper's hand and pressed a crumpled fifty-dollar wad into her palm.

"What's this for?" she asked, her voice trembling.

"Get rid of it. Whatever is growing inside you, get rid of it tonight," Walter said. He bent down, kissed her on the cheek, patted her shoulder, turned around, and then left.

Mayola Barnwood, the train's housekeeper, stood frozen, staring at the bundle of cash in her hand. Her body trembled so violently that she burst into tears. Through the window, she watched Walter and Winifred, a strikingly beautiful, brown-skinned woman, share a passionate kiss. Walter, standing six feet four inches tall, towered over Winifred as he lifted her off the ground, spun her around in a circle, and set her back down. He then threw the gunny sack into his car and helped Winifred into the passenger seat. As Walter started the engine and drove away, Mayola was left in a state of shock and fury, her eyes filling with tears.

Two days afterward, a woman's body was found face down in an icy pond. The woman with red hair was identified as Norma Uppercliff, an American socialite and the estranged wife of fifty-seven-year-old English millionaire Alexandre Uppercliff, who was on holiday with his twenty-two-year-old mistress.

Mr. Uppercliff's wife, originally from New Orleans, was discovered with a gunshot wound to the head and fifty stab wounds. Her fingers and left ear had been severed, and during the autopsy, the coroner found them lodged in her throat. The coroner concluded that this was a brutal act of revenge, possibly a blood feud. After questioning Mr. Uppercliff, he confessed that he had sent his 26-year-old wife, carrying $50,000 in cash, to pay off a gambling debt to Chicago gangster Vincent Maretti, also known as "Vinnie the Pig" due to his poor table manners. Mr. Uppercliff stated that he had placed the cash in a suitcase for his wife to hand over to Mr. Maretti. He had also given his wife a new mink coat to keep her warm in the cold Chicago weather.

Norma Uppercliff arrived carrying just ten

thousand dollars in cash. The full-length mink coat was never found. When Chicago police questioned the train staff about the location of the suitcase and the missing coat, they all insisted they had not seen the suitcase with the cash or the full-length mink coat.

One Year Later. Walter exhaled a cloud of smoke through his nostrils, flicked the ashes, and stubbed out his cigarette in the ashtray until the embers went out. Then he pulled out his pocket watch to check the time.

Right on the dot, I leave at six o'clock to pick up Winifred at her parents' house. I'll have a short talk with her father, Deacon Wardell Henson. He'll give me his blessing, and he'll pay for everything. Shit, after that old coot is dead, I'll own two houses: the one I live in, thanks to that red-headed whore I fucked last year, and Wardell's. Got-damn, I'm so clever! Walter thought to himself, howling with laughter.

He put on his wool dress coat, snapped off the house lights, locked the door, and headed outside to start his car.

Later that evening, Walter proposed to Winifred Henson with the ring he had taken from Audine's finger, in front of her parents and visiting relatives. Six weeks later, on Saturday, December 31st, they were married at two o'clock on a sunny, windy afternoon in Chicago. They were pronounced husband and wife ten hours before ringing in the New Year.

CHAPTER THIRTEEN

The basement flat of Elizabeth "Betty" Coins, a tarot card and tea leaf reader.

"I searched all over Chicago for someone to operate on me. It was a cold day, and I wore only a maid's uniform and a cheap wool coat. Walter showed no concern for me. He told me to get rid of the baby growing inside. He said having children with Winifred was necessary because he intends to progress in his job and remain rich in Bronzeville. Then he left me on that train all alone," Mayola affirmed bitterly as she sipped the piping hot, bitter-tasting tea, with tea leaves floating on the surface of the porcelain cup.

She took a bite of the egg salad sandwich that Betty Coins had prepared every week for clients who came to have their cards read and learn about their future. For fifty years, sixty-eight-year-old Coins had read cards and tea leaves for a living. Her grandmother had taught her the ins and outs of shuffling, spreading, and reading tarot cards. She'd also shown Betty how to interpret tea leaves if a client requested a reading. As time went on, Betty started having dreams that would come true.

Every day, a huge older boy would punch Betty in the arm, both before and after school. When school let out, he'd run up to her and throw a bunch of punches at her upper body, almost knocking her out. Dazed, Coins had a clear vision that worried her grandmother.

"What did you see, Betty?' her grandmother queried.

"He was lying in a casket; nobody was there except his mother because everyone hated him," Betty said, her eyes fixed on the wall as if she were watching the scene unfold before her.

That was Thursday. By Saturday afternoon, a group of ten larger boys, as tall and tough as giants, brutally beat the boy to death. They attacked him fiercely, like a pack of savage wolves, in a horrific scene that no one, not even adults, could stop until he died. Afterward, they vanished without a trace, just as she had imagined. Unsurprisingly, no one attended Betty's tormentor's funeral except his bawling mother.

Over the years, Betty and her grandmother operated a thriving business until her grandmother died peacefully in her sleep.

"So, tell me what happened after you found someone to perform that operation, Mayola. Because the last few times you came to see me, you told me a completely different story. You keep changing your story," said Coins, shifting restlessly in her chair. This was Mayola's tenth visit in just four weeks, and she still hadn't paid for the previous nine card readings.

"I thought I told you what happened to me after I got off the train," Mayola said, laughing nervously.

"No, you did not, Mayola. Please start from the beginning again, because everything you've told me doesn't make sense," Coins said sharply.

"Okay, okay! Stop rushing me! You keep asking what happened, and I keep giving the same answer: I got off the train, wandered the streets until night, and then saw my best friend's house. She's a nurse at the city hospital. I knocked on her door, and her father answered, saying it was lovely to see me, but she wasn't home yet; she was on her way and would arrive any moment".

"He invited me in and offered me a bowl of stew and cornbread. It was so tasty that I ate two bowls!" Mayola exclaimed wistfully.

"Yes, go on," said Coins.

"Stop rushing me!" Mayola admonished. "Anyway, after we ate, my friend walked in. She looked so surprised to see me after all those years. Her father excused himself and went to his bedroom.

"Wait a moment," Coins interrupted. "Where was your friend's mother? I find it strange that your friend's father would cook stew and cornbread and still have time to clean up afterward. Didn't you mention she was a teacher? At least that is what you said the last time you were here." Coins frowned and pressed further.

"You're not listening to me! Be quiet and let me talk!" screeched Mayola, furious about Betty's nonstop interruptions and confusing questions.

Sensing her mood, Coins sighed, nodded, and

adjusted the tarot cards on the table.

"As I mentioned, I asked my friend if we could have a private talk. She agreed, and we went upstairs to her room. I shared with her how I met and fell in love with Walter Pickman, the Pullman Porter I told you about. I also told her about spending the night at the colored hotel in New York with Walter. He held me close, expressing his love and desire for me, even saying he wanted to marry me because I was the prettiest maid on the train! I warned him to be careful not to spill his seed inside me because my monthly flow had not come yet, and he could put a baby inside of me. He laughed and told me not to worry, that he'd be careful. Walter and I made love three more times until sunrise. After three weeks, I told my friend my monthly flow hadn't come. I told her that when I told Walter, he got angry and told me to get rid of it. I cried and told him I loved him and that we could marry and have the baby, but he didn't care. Do you know why, Miss Coins?" Mayola asked, wiping away tears of anger from her eyes.

"No, I do not, Mayola. Why don't you tell me?" Coins replied, laying down the cards and giving her undivided attention to Mayola, who nervously pulled at a loosened button on her tattered dress.

"Thanks to that woman, Winifred Henson! Her family is nothing but a bunch of church crooks!" Mayola burst out, slamming her fist on the table.

Coins stopped shuffling the cards and froze, her eyes widening at what she had heard.

"My friend mentioned she knew a nurse who worked with Black women and would call her immediately. She did, and the nurse said she could perform the procedure now for fifty dollars. Walter gave me fifty dollars, meaning I had thirty dollars left for myself after getting paid. There was no time to lose, so she told her father we were going shopping and later visiting another one of her nurse friends at the hospital. The nurse performing the operation instructed my friend to drop me off in front of the department store on Wabash and to look for a black car with two people inside: a Black man in the driver's seat wearing a brown hat, and a Black woman acting as the assistant, to collect the money. On the way, my friend asked if I had any relatives in case something happened to me. I said only my mama, who lives in Memphis," Mayola recounted softly.

"I told her to tell my mama that I loved her and that I was sorry."

I need to get Mayola out of here quickly because she's lost her mind, Coins thought as she sat, frowning and listening intently to every word that Mayola was saying.

"When, my friend, oh, and by the way, Miss Coins, I forgot to mention my friend's name," quipped Mayola.

"Oh, she does have a name?" asked Coins, pushing her gold spectacles down the bridge of her nose.

"Grace, Grace Mulberry. Anyway, Grace and I finally made it to the department store. She held my hand, telling me everything would be okay, when out of nowhere, a black car pulled up beside us. The driver rolled down the window.

"Are you Mayola Barnwood?" he asked.

"I said yes, I am."

"The woman in the front seat told me to get inside quickly, saying there were four more women needing operations. Grace hugged me and said she'd be waiting for my call to drive me back to her house. So, I climbed into the back seat of the car. The woman asked for the money, and before I could count it, she snatched the cash out of my hand and counted the wad three times to ensure it was all there. She handed me a long rag before the car pulled onto the street. I asked what it was for, and she told me to stop asking questions and to tie the rag across my eyes. I was scared, but I did as she said. Then I heard the driver tell the woman it was time to go. The car started moving slowly at first, then picked up speed. Nobody spoke while we were being driven; I could only think about Walter and what he had done to me. Sometimes, I hated him, but I couldn't because I still loved him," Mayola said in a low, pained voice.

"Even after how he treated you, left you all alone, went through that operation, and put you through all of that pain, you still love him, Mayola?" asked Coins in a deliberate voice.

Mayola nodded and continued her story.

"After thirty minutes, the car stopped. I heard both doors open, including the one I was sitting by. The cold air and wind almost made me want to stay inside, but the woman grabbed my arm and pulled me out. She told me to keep the rag tied over my eyes and not to say a word unless spoken to. I could hear men cursing, women laughing, the smell of whiskey and cigarettes, and the sound of them stepping on broken glass. She told me to stand still. I heard the woman knock on the door – four quick raps. I heard a woman answer, and she told the woman to bring me inside. The driver was given an address to pick up two more women who needed operations. But the woman in the car stayed behind before he left, and another one left with him. I was told to remove the rag from my eyes and coat. I did, and when I looked up, two women were standing before me," said Mayola.

"But why did the woman make you cover your eyes with the rag? I do not understand that at all," Coins said, confused by this information.

"Humph, I was told by Grace that, in case I had to be taken to the hospital if anything went wrong, the doctor would have to ask me who did the operation because if I told, the police would be called, and the person would be arrested! Then, I would have to testify in court as well as tell who put the baby inside me," replied Mayola.

"Walter put the baby inside of you," said Coins, whose voice sliced through Mayola's thoughts about what happened a year ago.

"Yes, and I'd have to tell the truth, but because I had the rag over my eyes, I could tell the truth that I didn't know who did the operation," said Mayola, smiling.

And she thinks this is funny? Coins wondered to herself as she shook her head in disgust. She continued shuffling the tarot cards.

"The other woman, who drove over there with me, handed me a blue shirt and pointed to a room for me to take off my clothes. She also told me to pee in the toilet room and then come back out to get ready for the operation. When I went into the room to change, it smelled terrible - like death. It was filthy, and I thought, Why was I doing this? I began to cry as I got undressed.

The room was freezing; I was shivering, and I wanted Walter to be with me. But then I remembered seeing him with Winifred," said Mayola, squeezing her eyes shut, rolling up her fists, and exhaling.

Noticing Mayola's gesture, Betty stood up and took Mayola's teacup. After pouring the cold tea down the sink and rinsing the cup, she poured hot water over a teaspoon of loose-leaf sassafras tea. Then she refreshed Mayola's plate with two more egg salad sandwiches cut into triangles.

"Why don't you have a sip of tea and another sandwich? My next customer doesn't come for another two hours," said Coins, sliding into the easy chair. She resumed shuffling the tarot cards while listening intently to Mayola's story, which was gaining steam.

"The toilet room was horrible. When I went to pee, the floor was filthy; it hadn't been scrubbed, and the toilet seat had old pee stains and dried blood. And then I saw this big pail in the corner with a large blood-stained rag over it. I walked over to it and lifted the rag, and I had to cover my mouth to keep from screaming!" she said in a strained voice.

"What was in the pail?" asked Coins, leaning in to listen.

"There's blood, lots of it, and the remains of the babies after the operations. I saw three, and I figure they'll be thrown in the sewer after my operation is done," Mayola said.

She paused to sip the steaming hot tea and take a bite of the egg salad sandwich.

"Oh, my sweet Jesus, those poor babies! Merciful God, have pity on their souls and the women who had to do those things!" Coins lamented. She sat back and shook her head in long, contemplative lines.

"Whelp, after I saw that, I almost changed my mind about going through with it," said Mayola, taking a bite of her sandwich.

"Why didn't you? What changed your mind?" Coins asked while taking short sips of her hot tea.

"Walter, I love him, but I don't think he loves me, at least not like he did when we made the baby in that hotel bed in New York, so I went into the kitchen where they were waiting for me. They had brown hospital gowns and aprons. They wore rags tied across their mouths. I was told to sit on this big, wide wooden slat with six legs. After I sat, the woman who had taken the money handed me back the rag I had worn in the car. She told me to put it on again and then lie back. And so, I did. The next thing that happened was when one of them asked me to open my legs as wide as possible," said Mayola as the events of that horrible time played back in her memory.

"Take a deep breath and hold it," said the woman on my left.

"Then I felt fingers opening me up down there," said Mayola, pointing to her crotch.

"Then, a long, cold piece of steel was suddenly shoved inside me. I screamed because it was extremely long, and then it opened wider and wider until it stretched me so far that it couldn't stretch me anymore. Oh God, it hurt so badly! One of the women told me to keep quiet or the police would hear me, so I bit my lip and tried. But the worst was yet to come because a wire was pushed up inside me; it felt like a coat hanger. Oh my God, she pushed it further inside me, and I couldn't help it; I screamed again! The pain, oh the pain!"

"Stop, please, this hurts!" screamed Mayola.

"It's too late to stop; shut up that screaming!" shouted one of the women.

"Then she told me to open my mouth wide. I did, and you know what she did to me? She shoved a washcloth inside my mouth! It was soaked in cheap wine that Walter and I used to drink before and after we made our baby. Then she put tape across my mouth. The other woman who was doing the operation kept whirling the wire until I felt a lot of blood gushing out. The one doing the operation said to hand me the gauze so I could fill her up! She started pushing so much of it inside me that I thought I would blow up! Then she told me that in the next fifteen minutes, I would want to push and push with all my might. Well, she wasn't lying about that one because, after fifteen minutes, my belly started to hurt, just like when I'd gotten my monthly flow; she asked me if I was ready to push. All I could do was nod yes. Then she said Push! I pushed with all my strength until I felt the worst pain in my belly, and the pain went between my legs," said Mayola, with tears spilling down her face.

Coins, sitting motionless, blinked back tears; her breath caught sharply in her throat, producing only more tears and sorrow so raw. Coins had not felt like this since she found her grandmother cold and dead. Betty took a handkerchief from her apron pocket, dabbed her eyes, and softly blew her nose.

"This is the saddest thing I've ever heard," she said, her eyes welling up with sadness. "So, tell me what happened to you after you started pushing."

Mayola's eyes were glazed and distant, captivated by another world. Betty was worried, but also felt a strong sense of discernment wash over her, urging her to get Mayola out of her flat.

"Mayola? You were telling me about what happened after you began to push," said Betty, speaking in a consoling tone. Betty's voice cut through Mayola's dark thoughts. She quickly regained her composure.

"Oh yes, I'm sorry, Mrs. Coins. My mind sometimes wanders off, and I get lost. Yes, I began to push, and then all of a sudden, something gushed out from inside me; it felt like a blob of jelly, and then I thought I was peeing on myself," Mayola said.

"Were you peeing on yourself?" Betty asked, confused.

"No, Mrs. Coins. It was blood because one of the women said to put the baby in the bucket and to get more gauze. After all, I was bleeding too much. To be truthful, I don't know if it was the wine-soaked cloth in my mouth that made me drunk, but I started falling asleep fast. That is when one of them shouted *that I was falling! Keep her awake; get that got-damned rag out of her mouth!* Then the rag was snatched out of my mouth, and I felt gauze, then two pads being shoved between my legs. I smelled alcohol, the kind used in the hospital. A damp cloth soaked in alcohol was rubbed on my legs and also between my legs," said Mayola.

"They, or whoever it was, were cleaning you up," Coins pointed out.

"Yes, one was doing one leg, and the other woman did the other. They even wiped the blood off my feet," Mayola said emotionlessly.

"Oh, dear God, Mayola, then what happened? What did those women do to you?" Betty asked in a soft tone.

"That was it. She told me the baby was gone, the bleeding had stopped, and I just needed a week of rest. The woman who operated gave me ten pain pills to take if needed. She said only to take one before bed or, if the pain was unbearable, to take one and wait until the next day. They helped me off the table and told me to look straight ahead and not back. I was supposed to go straight to the bathroom, get dressed, and leave. The driver was waiting to take me back to the store. Then, they removed the blindfold. I didn't see them because they were standing behind me. I did what I was told, rushing to the bathroom to get dressed and leave. When I walked in, I found my clothes in a pile and a brown paper bag. I opened it and saw about thirty pads for blood. They kindly included ten pairs of underwear and ten pain pills. But something didn't feel right about being in that bathroom," she said in a strained voice.

"What didn't feel right to you?" Coins asked as she raised the still-hot tea to her lips and took two quick sips.

Mayola's eyes filled with pain and remorse.

"I got dressed, and I smelled fresh blood. So, I walked over to the tin pail with the bloody rag, except there was a lid on it this time. When I lifted the lid and pulled the blood-soaked rag off, I saw what came out of me: our baby. Our baby was crammed in there with the others I'd seen earlier. I took a step back, spun around, and ran out of that hellhole. Oh God, oh Jesus, what did I do to Walter's baby, our baby!" Mayola wailed.

Betty Coins tightened her grip on the teacup, her body stiffening upon hearing the words.

This has to be the worst story I have ever heard! If my grandmother were alive, how would she feel? Would she ever feel pity for Mayola? Coins thought to herself as she firmly grasped her gold cross necklace, given to her by her grandmother before she passed away.

Coins handed Mayola a handkerchief, which she clutched in her trembling hands.

"Thank you," she said weakly as she blew her nose.

"You're welcome. Please tell me what happened

next, as it seems to have deeply hurt your soul. I can't imagine going through this," Coins said, taking a bite of her egg salad sandwich. After a quick sip of tea, she straightened her napkin on her lap and focused fully on Mayola, who appeared tired and worn out from crying.

"After the ride back to the store where I was first picked up, the driver let me out. I watched as he turned the corner and sped away. I was alone on that dark street, feeling scared because it was late. Suddenly, a car pulled up. It was Grace! She told me to get inside and that I could stay with her, promising she would look after me. When we reached her house, she explained that we had gone shopping and visited a nurse friend at the hospital. We were drinking coffee and talking when we realized how late it had become.

"But how did Grace know when and what time to pick you up in front of the store?" Coins asked.

Mayola responded, "Grace, when she called to make my appointment, asked exactly what time I would finish and made sure I had enough pads for the upcoming weeks."

"That was a very courageous thing for her to do

for you. She risked her safety being out so late, especially in that part of the city," said Coins as she gazed into Mayola's eyes.

"Yes. She is, and I'll always remember what she did for me that night as long as I live. I love her so much," said Mayola, dabbing away tears.

"After we arrived at her house, she took some shopping bags from the department store: four for me, three for herself, plus a bag full of pads, panties, and pills for me. We quickly went inside, carefully staying quiet. As we went upstairs to her room, I felt dizzy, and the cramps came back. Once we reached the top, she helped me out of my coat and told me to go to the bathroom because it was probably time to change my pad. But first, I needed to take a quick bath on my knees, just long enough to get clean, without staying in the warm water too long. When I entered the bathroom and turned on the lights, I couldn't believe how clean and beautiful it was! She was so kind. Grace had a pair of clean nightgowns and fresh panties on the radiator, warming them for me. On top of the linen trunks, there were fresh towels and a pile of paper bags," said Mayola.

"Paper bags, what for?" Coins probed. Mayola's account of what happened to her became more captivating. It's sad yet intriguing.

The voice of discernment spoke louder to Coins: "Get Mayola out of your flat now, or something horrible will happen!"

"The bags were meant for the soiled pads, and thank goodness, Grace had them for me because as soon as I undressed to bathe, blood was gushing everywhere. I made it just in time to get into the tub and wash the blood away. When I came out, the bag was gone. Grace was thoughtful enough to take the bag and exchange it for me in case I needed another. After I cleaned the tub and got dressed, I went to her room. She had two beds in there. Humph, I guess she knew I was coming; she gave me a cup of hot broth, another tablet for the cramps, a fresh tignon for my hair, and a hot water bottle. We said our prayers and hugged goodnight. We spoke in whispers for a while until I closed my eyes and went to sleep. I had a dream, though," said Mayola.

"Who did you dream about?" Betty asked.

"I dreamt about Walter all night until morning. When I woke up, the bed was soaked in blood, and the cramps were so bad that I couldn't move. I called Grace over and asked her to help me. When she woke up, she went into the bathroom and quickly ran to the shower to bathe. She helped me stand, but when I got up, I felt dizzy and almost threw up. We finally made it inside the bathroom. Oh my God, the pajama bottoms were bloody, and I started to cry. Grace told me to take them off and put everything inside the paper bag, even the soiled pad. Grace took care of everything. The hot shower made me feel much better, and the bleeding finally stopped. When I stepped out to dry off, Grace left me with another pair of pajamas, more pads, and fresh panties. She also left a glass of cold water and one pill for the cramps," said Mayola.

"Grace knew what would happen after your operation. She had everything ready for you," Coins said.

"Yes, she did. I spent the next few days getting better and stronger, and after five days, the bleeding and pain stopped. I spent Christmas alone, though;

"Grace had to work, her father was away with his church friends, and I felt sad. But Grace didn't forget me! She put a bag of presents on the dresser. There were so many presents when I opened the bag that it took me an hour to open them all! That made me happy! But my one wish was to be with Walter, to celebrate Christmas," Mayola reflected.

Betty's eyes widened in shock as she covered her mouth with her hand, gasping in disbelief at Mayola's confession that she missed Walter, considering everything she had been through.

"But Grace's father spoiled everything," lamented Mayola.

The voice of discernment spoke to Coins once more, this time with a sharp, shrill tone: "Get out; you need to go NOW!"

"What did he say?" Coins asked, furrowing her brow in a serious frown.

"On New Year's Day, Grace had to work again. I was feeling better, but I still experienced occasional cramps. The bleeding had stopped, though. Grace continued to ensure I was fed, warm, and comfortable. I didn't want to leave Grace or that beautiful house. She was my friend and looked after me during the worst time of my life. But her father? Humph! I despise that old man. It all began when I was sound asleep, then I felt someone shake me awake," Mayola explained.

"Grace's father?" asked Coins, bracing herself to hear the worst of Mayola's heartbreaking story.

"Yes, Grace's father," answered Mayola, shifting her position to cross her legs and take another bite of her egg salad sandwich.

"Whelp, he told me to wake up because he had made some collard greens, rice and beans, ham, potato salad, and smothered buttered biscuits. He laid a towel and a plate of food across my lap. I was so hungry that I forgot about the iced tea he had placed on the stool beside the bed. As I ate, he kept talking," said Mayola.

"And what did he say?" Coins asked, noticing Mayola tapping her foot loudly on the floor.

Mayola was visibly upset by the question.

"He sat on the bed's edge, watching me eat with his brown eyes that resembled walnuts," said Mayola.

Walnuts? That's an unusual color for a Black man's eyes, Coins thought to herself. She took another bite of her egg salad sandwich and brushed away the crumbs.

Coins inched closer to listen.

"After we talked and I finished the delicious meal he prepared, he stood up and took the plate and towel. Setting them aside, he sat right next to me," she said, looking away with a reflective expression.

"Mayola, I may not have paper schooling like you and Grace, but I ain't stupid," he said, a hint of mockery in his voice.

"I've seen all those blood-soaked pads that end up in the trash because they stink. The sour smell of blood is unmistakable, especially after a few days when the pads start to ferment. I know when Grace has her monthly flow. She had it last week, and she's seeing a young man, a church-going young man who's a doctor from the hospital where she works. So, you'd better know if I know where she's at with him! See, I know what happened to you, Mayola. My God, girl! You're going straight to hell for what you've done, letting Walter Pickman have his way with you and then letting him spill his seed inside you, and then having his baby grow inside you, hah! I heard what Grace told you about what those murderers do to their babies. They throw them down the sewer at midnight every Saturday, just like they're trash! But let me tell you, Mayola, I told this couple that my wife used to work for that you need a job. They're rich; he's an accountant for a law firm here in Chicago and recently took on a firm in New York. But see, he has a secret my wife found out about, and well, let's say he paid her to keep quiet. That's why we bought this house in Bronzeville; Grace didn't have to pay for nursing school, so she graduated at the top of her class. She and I both own our cars, and when that doctor asks Grace to marry him, she'll have the biggest wedding Chicago has ever seen! In the meantime, you'll meet them on Wednesday morning because they need you on Monday. His name is Paul, his wife is Elaine, and their daughter is Penelope, but they call her Penny. After two weeks of work, save your money and find somewhere else to live. I can't have a loose and sinful woman like you staying in my house, opening your legs to a man you haven't married! As soon as you can, get out of here and don't cha eh-vah call my precious Grace again!" retorted Grace's father,

Then he got up, took the plate, slammed the door, and left. I was so hurt that I cried until I fell asleep. On Wednesday, I took a taxi to the address her father had written on a piece of paper. I met Mr. and Mrs. Paul, Elaine Dellmar, and their daughter, Penelope. I instantly fell in love with Penny; she was such a beautiful little girl! By Monday, I was working for the Dellmars, and after saving two weeks' worth of my money, I said a tearful goodbye to my best friend, Grace. After that, I never saw her again," said Mayola, dabbing tears from the corners of her eyes.

"What was it like working for the Dellmars?" asked Coins.

"Secrets, Miss Coins. Paul Dellmar had many secrets," whispered Mayola, pressing her finger to her lips to hush Coins from speaking further.

Coins leaned in closer to catch every word Mayola was about to say. She motioned for her to continue.

"Whelp, as soon as I arrived on my first day, I started working around their home. I made breakfast for Paul, and Elaine made sure Penny was bathed, her hair combed, and dressed for school. Her mother walked her to school every day. After everyone was out of the house, I washed the dishes, scrubbed the floors, changed the bedding in Paul's room and Penny's room, and-

"Wait, you mean Paul and Elaine's bedroom?" interrupted Coins.

"No, I mean Paul's and Penny's bedrooms," said Mayola. "He was sleeping alone in his bed, and Elaine was sleeping in Penny's bed. Over time, he told me that he and Elaine weren't getting along and kept fighting. One night, when he rolled over to touch Elaine, she wasn't there. He was scared and ran into Penny's room to check she was still in the house. That's when he saw Elaine curled up holding Penny," Mayola explained.

"Oh my, what happened, and where did Elaine go after she took Penny to school?" Coins asked, her brow furrowed as she took another sip of her now lukewarm tea. The voice of discernment remained silent.

"Elaine would visit her friend's house, Mrs. Murchinson. She would walk to the hotel near Penny's school and take a taxi every day to Mrs. Murchinson's home. I became friends with the maids working in that ten-room house. Humph, Mrs. Murchinson would have breakfast ready for her friends, including Elaine, and after breakfast, they'd play a card game called, uh, Bridge, all eight of them. Then, around noon, they'd go shopping and have lunch at some fancy restaurants. The chauffeur would then drive them all home, except for Elaine, who told the chauffeur to drop her off at Penny's school so they could walk home together," said Mayola.

"I find that rather strange," Coins said. "Especially if it was cold outside. What would make her do that? Walk home with Penny when it's freezing out?"

"Well, for one thing, the more I looked at Paul and Elaine, the more I couldn't figure them out. Something was different about those two; Penny's nose was just like Paul's, and every time I washed Penny's hair, it would get very curly, just like lamb's wool. Humph, Elaine would get really ruffled because when Penny came home alone, the kids would walk behind her, throw rocks at her head, and make fun of her; the older ones were downright mean; they'd chase her home, throwing bigger rocks, calling her a high-yellow nigger. After four times when Penny came home crying and sometimes bleeding, Elaine finally had the sense to walk home with Penny. After that, I knew something was going on; Paul was keeping a secret about himself. When Paul came home early on Friday afternoons, I'd make him lunch, and then we'd talk. One day, after we ate and I washed the dishes, he sneaked up behind me and put his arms around my waist. When I turned around to face him, we kissed. Paul kissed me so deeply that he took my hand, and before I knew it, we rushed upstairs to his bedroom. Since that first time, we couldn't stay away from each other on Fridays. Oh, how I looked forward to our Fridays together!" she said, her eyes burning with excitement as she remembered every detail of Paul and their Friday afternoons. Coins stared at Mayola in disbelief.

"You know he was married, Mayola! It didn't matter that he slept alone in bed; he was still married!

What in God's name? What's wrong with you? Have you lost your senses?" she said, her eyes burning with disapproval.

Mayola erupted into uncontrollable laughter. Coin's eyes squinted as she scrutinized Mayola's tear-streaked face.

"No, Miss Coins, I haven't lost my sense, but you have! You couldn't figure out the answer about Paul," she said, with a half-joking tone.

"Oh my God, Mayola, what answer?" Coins demanded.

"That Paul is half-colored, and so is Penny, you silly woman! After the fifth time in his bed, he told me and showed me pictures of his Creole mother, who was passing for White, and another picture of his father, who was White! That's why Paul's and Penny's eyes are green, just like Paul's father!" shrieked Mayola.

Coins suddenly felt a chilling wave running through her, and her mind hurried to warn her. Mayola is entirely cracked and has lost her senses! Lord, forgive my wrongful thoughts about her. She's out of her mind!

"Oh, and by the way, that was the last time we were together. Elaine surprised us when she burst into Paul's bedroom and saw him between my legs; oh, my goodness, she grabbed one of his belts and beat his ass! I was screaming, and then she turned on me with that belt! Paul yelled for her to stop. I cried and quickly got dressed, knowing she would kick me out. Then I heard her shouting at Paul about the pictures she found. Paul told her that the man was his father and that his Creole mother was also partly of color. She backed away, ran into the bathroom, and threw up. She said we should leave before she calls the law on us. So, Paul packed his bags, and we left," said Mayola.

"So, what did you do, and what about Elaine and Penny? Oh, my goodness, that poor baby!" said Coins, shaking her head in disgust.

"Elaine told Paul to pack a suitcase for Penny, then head to the school to pick her up and take her with him. She said he was never to come back to her house again. Elaine couldn't believe she was living with a man who was half-colored, put himself between her legs, and had a child who was also half-colored. Elaine said she wasn't going to raise a girl who was a 'nigger.' She spat in my face, threw a wad of cash at me, calling me a common whore. Paul didn't say a word as he drove to Penny's school. He had me sit in the back seat. He stayed there for a long time, at Penny's school. When he finally came out, he was carrying an armful of papers and holding Penny, who was crying. I got out of the car and ran to them to comfort Penny, who got in the back seat with me and clung to me. She cried so hard that she eventually fell asleep. After driving around for an hour, Paul pulled up to a boarding house for Black women only. He handed me a stack of cash, saying it would last a month until I found a job. Paul helped me with my suitcase, squeezed my hand, and said he'd see me when he and Penny found a place to live. I never heard from Paul again," Mayola said, her eyes welling up with sorrow.

"It feels like I've had so many losses: first Walter, our baby, my best friend Grace, Penny, Paul, and both of my jobs. Still, I only crave more egg salad sandwiches and tea. Please add some cream and extra sugar to my cup, Miss Coins. The egg salad was delicious, and I'd like another card reading about Walter. I continue to love him dearly, Miss Coins," she said with a strained voice.

Coin's eyes widened in shock at Mayola's request.

"You what?" Coin's voice mirrored the intensity of her stare.

"I need to have another reading to find out if Walter loves me," said Mayola.

"Mayola, you've come here nine times for readings, and each time I finish, you keep telling me you'll pay! I want my money because you owe me forty-five dollars!" Coins retorted as she pulled out a wad of paper with dates, times, and the cost of each reading; at the bottom of the wad was the total amount owed, highlighted by a red circle around it.

"When will you pay?" asked Coins, tapping her finger on the amount owed.

"I've got the money right here, Miss Coins," Mayola said, opening her purse and pulling out a wad of cash, which she waved around with a smile.

Coins spotted a crisp new five-dollar bill on the outside of the wad, which looked thick with one-dollar bills inside. Mayola had the wad tightly bundled with twine.

"Please place the money in that bowl," Coins said, nodding toward an empty sugar bowl where customers usually paid after their reading.

A smiling Mayola nodded and placed the wad of cash into the bowl.

Coins pulled a deck of worn-out cards from her apron pocket.

Mayola will not be welcomed here again after this card reading ends, Coins thought to herself, feeling frustrated. This is the last reading I'll ever do for her.

Coins shuffled the cards for precisely one minute before slamming the deck onto the table. She then carefully spread fifty-five tarot cards across the surface and closed her eyes.

"Choose only three cards. After selecting them, give them to me without looking at them. Do you understand, Mayola?"

"Yes, Miss Coins, I understand," she said.

Mayola's voice trembled slightly, as if she anticipated the worst. She took deep, slow breaths.

On the left side, Mayola sat quietly and concentrated on the cards. Noticing one that was slightly frayed at the top edge, she picked it up and placed it in Coin's open hand.

"Two more," Coins said flatly.

Mayola nodded and selected a card from the center. Despite a small tear, she believed it could be a sign that something was about to happen.

Coins said curtly, "One more, then you're finished."

One final card. This will reveal if Walter loves me! I'll wait a year for him to propose, then find the best Black doctor in Chicago to help me have a child again for Walter. I believe he'll be thrilled at the idea of us having a child, and I hope it's a girl who resembles him! Mayola thought happily, beaming.

Mayola chose the final card, which appeared to have a grease stain in the middle, and gave it to Coins.

Opening her eyes, Coins immediately began the card reading. She spread the cards on the table and turned over the first one.

The Fool.

Coins' mouth tightened into a hard line. This isn't good news, she thought as she flipped over the second card.

The illustration on the card showed a man and a woman. The man was walking down the road with three decayed infants lying behind him. The woman, dressed as a bride, reached out her arms, inviting him to come to her.

Coin's mouth curled into a grimace. When she looked up, she saw Mayola, who was beaming and clueless about the cards that would bring a flood of sorrow, disappointment, and heartbreak. Coin flipped over the last card and gasped.

The broken hearts.

The image was disturbing. What looked like a harmless, chubby doll with overstuffed features had a leash attached to a heart split in two. The card was gray with black clouds, and instead of rain, hundreds of hearts of various sizes hung, divided in half. Those already on the ground were crushed. More disturbing about the card was that each heart had a long, sharp needle piercing it.

"What do the cards say, Miss Coins?" Mayola inquired. "Is there any good news you'd like to share with me?"

Coins looked at Mayola, selecting her words with caution. She had to uncover the truth.

"The news won't be good," Coins said slowly, avoiding Mayola's gaze.

"Whhaatt?" stammered Mayola.

"The first card you selected is the fool," Coins disclosed.

"The fool is a reckless, unthinking soul, much like you and Walter. Walter fits this description because he only thinks of himself. What's dangerous about him is that he believes common sense is for ordinary people. Walter doesn't follow anyone; he leads those who fall in line behind him and listens to what he says, especially someone like you. It was foolish to follow Walter into his selfish desires, Mayola. I could see both of you in a much larger city, further north. Umph, umph, umph! You are in a hotel room in your bed when you should have been alone! Humph! That's the night Walter pushed his seed between your- "

"That's enough!" Mayola yelled, covering her ears with her hands to shut out the troubling news Coins shared. "Stop it because I don't want to remember anymore!" she cried, distressed by the flood of memories from that night when she and Walter conceived their baby.

Coins was repulsed by Mayola's attempt to forget. At this point, she felt no compassion for Mayola's fragile state of mind and shook her head in disgust. Coins turned the card face down and read the second card.

A couple on a forked road to nowhere.

Mayola burst into tears, but Coins ignored Mayola's outburst and kept on reading.

"This card depicts an unfortunate scene. The couple is on a path from which they will soon part ways. The woman, alone, is pleading with the man to stay with her. Humph! He won't because of all his children.

However, all three of them are gone. That man is Walter! Coins said, pointing to the image of the man. "You aren't the first in a hopeful relationship with him, Mayola!" she added. "Hah! Walter has always been a crooked man with no morals! I hate to deliver bad news, but based on the three deceased babies found by the roadside, you aren't the first woman Walter messed around with. There were two more women before you! Humph, they were all good girls who were virgins, dreaming of Walter as their future husband. But they were deceived. All of them!" Coins snorted. "Look here," Coins said to Mayola, who was crying uncontrollably.

"Look at the two deceased babies over here," she said, tapping her finger on the illustration of two infants swathed in a dark-colored, tattered blanket.

"Humph, cities-big cities are dangerous places for young Black women like you, and the other two young women made some mistakes. You, along with those two, weren't under proper family supervision. The first woman came from a strong, hardworking, and God-fearing family. After Walter told her to get rid of the baby, she bled to death! Because of that shameful relationship, her family never found out about her, Walter, or the baby inside her. She's buried in a pauper's lot for colored folks. The other woman he got involved with did the same thing. Except when they took a two-day leave in New York, they stayed at a hotel in Harlem, the same one where you and Walter stayed. Whelp, again, that's where he planted his seed inside her! She waited until it was too late after missing her monthly flow. She had a dual visit," said Coins, rubbing her forehead.

"Lies! All lies you're telling me! Walter would never do such things! He made a terrible mistake; that's all! He-he-he's just a little mixed up!" Mayola stammered, her voice shaking in fury.

"I don't lie, Mayola, and neither do these cards. So far, you've been told that Walter is a no-good, filthy, self-centered man! Furthermore, the last woman he was with had his children!" Snapped Coins, again pointing to the two babies shrouded in the blanket.

"What did you say? Walter has two babies?" she asked, her voice trembling more and more.

"Had. That poor young woman bore him twins. They both died, and she risked losing her life to bring those poor babies into this world! My God, Mayola, aren't you listening to what I say and tell you? The woman trying to pull him over to herself is Winifred Henson," said Coins.

"No, no, no, not her! Walter loves ME! Do you understand? Walter loves ME, not her!" Mayola shrieked as she stood up, knocking the chair onto the floor.

"Get up and sit in that chair!" Coins commanded, her voice firm and unyielding.

Mayola bent down, grabbed the chair, and plopped into it like a spoiled child. She pressed her palm against her chest to hold back another scream about to escape as she swayed from side to side in the chair.

Right on cue, Coins shoved her hands into her apron pocket and pulled out a crumpled piece of newspaper that had been torn in half. She opened it and handed it to Mayola, who looked like she was on the verge of hysteria.

"To prove to you that Walter doesn't love you, read this!" admonished Coins, tapping the paper with her finger.

Mayola remained still, silent, and unresponsive.

"Read!" shouted Coins, slamming her hand on the table with such force that it shook. Mayola snapped to attention and carefully pulled the news clip from Coins' hands into her trembling grip. As soon as she held the news clip and began reading it, her eyes widened in shock. Dressed in a bridal gown and veil, decorated with an enormous cascade of flowers, was a stark black-and-white photo of Winifred Henson. Above her image, in large letters, was an announcement:

Winifred Olivia Henson wed Walter James Pickman on December 31st.

Mayola's hands trembled as she read the article, her lips moving silently as she absorbed how the wedding was one of the biggest ever held on New Year's Eve in the afternoon.

Guests enjoyed a lavish reception featuring a nationally renowned big band, a wedding gift from the groom to his wife after he saw them perform at one of Chicago's famous nightspots. Following the wedding ceremony, guests enjoyed a luncheon that included oven-roasted turkey, mashed potatoes with butter and gravy, green beans, Southern-style bread dressing, cranberry sauce, rolls, wedding cake, and fruit punch. Afterward, the happy couple will spend time close to home once Mrs. Pickman's husband finishes several more weeks at his job as a Pullman Porter for the Chicago Line Train, Inc. After that, they will head to New York for a week-long honeymoon. Mrs. Pickman works as a teacher at a high school in the Chicago community founded by Bishop Thomas Almonds, who presided over the couple's nuptials.

The article also provided Pickman's home address, in case anyone wished to visit and congratulate Mr. and Mrs. Pickman.

"No, no, no! This can't be right! Walter, why did you do this to me, to us? You made me do that horrible thing to our baby, and you're married to her?" she wailed, shaking her head violently back and forth.

Recognizing that Mayola was on the brink of hysterics, Coins hurried to finish the reading, count the money wad, and evacuate Mayola from her flat.

The last card.

"Mayola, this is the final card and reading I will do for you. This card here is your destiny, but there are several hidden messages in it," said Coins, tapping the card illustrated with broken hearts and needles raining from a dark sky. "Walter has been playing tricks and games on you. You've been lied to and bamboozled by him with many women. There are so many that it has been impossible to give an exact number. The card tells me that you also had no business going to bed with Paul because even if he had a bad spot in his lopsided marriage, you should have said no to him and left. Because you did that, you're the brunt of being hexed by his wife, who is going through insanity right now! You're in the corner of brokenheartedness, lies, and foolery. The child that you and Walter made cries for you. To make matters worse, Walter's wife is barren – just like you!" exclaimed Coins in a harsh tone.

Mayola, seemingly in a trance, finally spoke.

"What, what did you just say? That I'm never going to have any children at all?" she asked, her voice growing more and more shaky.

"Yes, that's right. You and Walter's wife Winifred

are both barren," answered Coins. She started putting the cards away in the wooden box and snapped it shut, effectively concluding Mayola's reading once and for all.

"Shut up about that fucking woman!" she snapped back, her eyes bulging with rage. "Open the box this instant, I want another reading! Those cards lied, and you know it! I'm demanding another reading right now! Do you hear me, Miss Coins? NOW!" she screamed, slamming her fist on the table, which overturned and crashed to the floor. The platter of egg salad sandwiches fell over, and a teapot passed down from Betty Coin's great-grandmother shattered, leaving a mess of tea and broken ceramic pieces.

Coins gazed at Mayola, who sat in the chair. Her lips quivered as though she were conversing with an invisible being.

"Get out!" screamed Coins. "Get your coat and get out of my home! You're cracked in the head, you crazy thing!"

Mayola didn't move from the chair until she saw Coins bending down to scoop up the wad of money scattered on the floor. Then, all of a sudden, Mayola stood up and dashed toward the chair, where her coat and purse lay crumpled in a heap.

Coins counted the wad, but after tallying up to a five-dollar bill and only five singles, the rest were scraps of newspaper cut to the exact shape and size of real money.

"Mayola, what is the meaning of this?" Coins demanded, furious at being taken for a fool.

Mayola already had her coat on, so she dashed to the door to evade Coins's wrath. She tried to open it, but it was locked and bolted.

"There are only ten dollars here; the rest are false bills of money cut to newspaper size! You owe me thirty dollars, you lying thief! Where's the rest of it?" Coins exploded in a furious tirade, tossing the cash and the wad of newspaper at Mayola, who was shaking the doorknob violently in her desperate attempt to escape.

"I'll pay you on Tuesday! I have to find Walter and tell him he's made a mistake and that he should divorce that bitch Winifred and marry me because I'll make him a much better wife! Now, let me get out of here before it's too late! Walter, Walter, I'm coming to save you from that ratchet woman!" wailed Mayola, sinking to her knees while gripping the doorknob.

"Since you want to be a deceitful, wicked woman, I'll tell you what: I'll call the law on you. Then you'll have your day in a Chicago court and end up in jail where you belong!" said Coins, rushing to her phone. With trembling hands, Coins dialed the operator to connect to the police.

"This is the operator; how may I assist you?"

"Operator, I need help right away! Let me speak to the police! I want to talk about a woman who won't pay me for a tarot card reading I did for her, and- "

Coins suddenly shrieked, and the phone's receiver slipped from her hand, crashing to the floor and causing the rest of the phone to fall and shatter.

At first, she felt a sharp tingling in her neck. It wasn't painful, but as she started to notice warm blood rushing out, panic took over, followed by a burning, searing pain unlike anything she had ever felt before.

This crazy woman just plunged a knife into my neck! Oh God, please, no, I don't want to die! Coins thought to herself as she felt her knees buckle and crumpled to the floor with a thud. The pain was indescribable, and warm blood spurted out of her neck.

"You shouldn't have made that phone call!" Mayola shrieked, hovering over Coin's glazed and lifeless eyes. There was hysteria, almost maniacal, in Mayola's tone, yet it seemed she found amusement in it.

Coins struggled to free her left arm as if trying to dislodge the knife, but the more she moved, the more blood flowed. Mayola stood, still looming over Coins. Then, all of a sudden, she pulled her leg back and repeatedly struck Coins' head.

"Grace was my best friend; she was like a sister to me," said Mayola as she delivered another blow to Coin's head, breaking her neck.

"While I was resting after my operation, I read her nursing books all day, especially the chapters on the neck and head. There is an artery in the neck called the carotid artery. If someone pushes a knife into that artery, they can bleed to death. Just like you are doing, Betty.

Oh, and by the way, I'm not as stupid as you think. See, while you were sitting, I noticed how you were rubbing the pocket of your apron. I figured it out; that is where the key to this damn door is! So, I'm going to see myself out so I can hurry to see Walter and that whore of a wife of his," said Mayola.

Squatting down, Mayola checked Coin's apron pocket and retrieved the front door key along with two cash bundles: one hundred dollars. She stood up and watched Coin, who was making gurgling noises as she choked on her blood. Coin's face was turning blue. Suddenly, a foul fishy smell filled the room as Coins urinated on herself uncontrollably. The gurgling ceased, and Betty Coins died.

Mayola crouched and gathered the remaining egg salad sandwiches from the floor near the overturned table. She opened her purse, slipped in the sandwiches, and tucked the leftover egg salad into her coat pocket. The news article about Walter and Winifred's wedding details also lay on the floor. Snatching it up, she read it once more, fingering each word until she found what she was searching for: their home address. Mayola reopened her purse and placed the news clipping inside. After securing her coat, hat, and gloves, she checked her purse once more to confirm the cash was safely deep inside. She then looked around at the room's chaos. Her gaze fell on Coin's unmoving body, lying in a pool of blood. She walked to the window, opened it wide enough for a breeze, drew the curtains, switched off the lights, and left through the door.

Discernment tried to warn Betty Coins since Mayola set foot inside her flat, but Coins didn't heed the warnings. Therefore, discernment floated out the window right next to Betty's sweet spirit.

Two weeks after their wedding, Walter came home with a bouquet and a surprise for Winifred: they had enough time for a prolonged honeymoon. He had planned to spend two weeks in New York with the band leader from their wedding and his wife, staying in their cozy two-bedroom brownstone. When Pickford hurried up the stairs to their house, he saw the front door slightly ajar. He called out for Winifred, but received no response. He searched the entire house and found her in the kitchen, lying in a pool of blood with fifty stab wounds - dead. After he stopped screaming, he noticed a tarot card depicting the fool nailed to Winifred's forehead between her eyes.

CHAPTER FOURTEEN

"Oh my God, have mercy on me, please!" cried Audine as she wandered through the deserted streets that led nowhere. People rushed past her, bundled up in heavy winter gear and boots to keep their feet warm. A thin wool coat, missing gloves and boots, shook uncontrollably. Every five minutes, she had to stop to warm her hands, which were in pain; the tips of her fingers had turned blue.

"Ya look lost; ya need sumptin? I'll pay ya two dollas if ya do sumptin for me," slurred a man's drunken voice close behind her.

Audine whirled around and spotted a drunken, toothless vagrant who swayed and stumbled. Unsteady, his legs buckled, and he fell onto the filthy ground, lying there motionless.

Twisting her face in disgust, Audine attempted to step over the tanked-up vagrant, but in a surprising move, he grabbed her ankle, sending her sprawling onto the ground.

"Help! Someone, please help me! Oh my God, I need help!" she screamed.

Suddenly, the vagrant seized Audine by her ankles and began pulling her into a dark, deserted field. Simultaneously, a group of intoxicated vagrants shoved and pushed each other, exchanging curses and insults as they rummaged through Audine's suitcases and took everything within reach. Two additional vagrants then arrived to assist in dragging Audine deeper into the field.

"Get off me, you stinking drunk! Leave me alone, I- "

Audine was interrupted when the larger vagrant, the one who had grabbed her by the ankles, punched her in the face.

"Shut up! Shut yoh got-damned mouf!" he hissed, swinging his fist and striking her in the mouth.

Audine shrieked in pain as warm blood poured from her mouth, and her lip split; she was bleeding heavily. Audine couldn't move, trapped in a semi-haze of drifting in and out of consciousness, but she felt a rush of cold air against her back. His hands roughly pulled up her coat and then her dress.

"Pull 'em offa her," growled one of the vagrants.

One of the vagrants tugged at Audine's panties, pulling them down to her ankles.

"Shit, I'm keeping these! I haven't smelled anything like this in over twenty years!" he said, closing his eyes, bringing Audine's panties to his nose, and taking a deep breath.

Audine could hear the loud rustling as he unzipped his worn-out, foul-smelling pants. He dropped to his knees, positioned himself behind Audine, and lifted her by the waist. She felt him place her so her ample backside was fully exposed. Then, he guided the tip of his ten-inch erection and pushed himself inside.

"No, no, no, Oww! Get out of me! You're hurting me, stop it!" she screamed.

Her high-pitched screams only fueled his excitement, driving him to frantic thrusts that pounded him into Audine even deeper. He was so far inside that the pressure amplified the pain to an unbearable level.

Then he erupted inside her.

"Shit! Got-damn! OH, but that was fine, oh that was mighty fine!" he said, gritting his teeth and squeezing his eyes so tightly that tears streamed down the corners of his bloodshot eyes.

He pulled back with a strain, as if he'd just sprinted several blocks through Chicago. His legs trembled fiercely, but he somehow stayed upright, towering over Audine, who was curled up in a fetal position, sobbing with a high-pitched wail.

"Shut up!" he said, delivering a sharp kick to her backside. "You're next, Charlie! Her ass is tight, so go deep and get it over with fast – I'm going in for seconds! Damn, that was good, really good!" he slurred.

As Audine slipped in and out of consciousness, she felt agony throughout her body: in her chest, stomach, mouth, lip, and the most private part of her, which was bleeding profusely. Then she heard the distinct sound of zippers being undone, and Charlie didn't waste any time. Just as strong as the first, he grabbed Audine by the waist, positioning her, and then WHAP! With his large, open hand, he repeatedly struck her backside, causing

Audine to yelp in pain. Despite the cold, he was utterly oblivious. Going inside Audine at a steady pace, he began muttering loudly.

"Damn, girl! I need more of this tight ass! I have to have more!" He shouted as his seed erupted inside Audine. Audine's eyes were fixed in the darkness; the cold Chicago night air froze her tears to her face, and her screams were silenced.

After two weeks, my marriage is over, and Wayne is never coming back to me. What have I done? Oh my God, Wayne, what have I done? Audine thought to herself as Charlie pounded into her.

Audine shut her eyes tightly and tried to scream once more, but no sound came out.

Mason wore his suit as he escorted her down the aisle to marry Wayne. Audine noticed Wayne's beaming face. It was their wedding day, and Violet looked beautiful in her dress, with plenty of food to take home.

Audine attempted to scream once more, but no sound came out. She was overwhelmed by pain and darkness, feeling hopeless about ever seeing them again.

CHAPTER FIFTEEN

BOOM, BOOM, BOOM! Even through the thick haze, the unmistakable sound of an extensive gun firing was clear. A flash of light lit up each shot. Cries for mercy went unheard as another shot was fired, followed by the thud of three bodies hitting the ground, then a deafening silence.

"Is she alive?" a female voice whispered.

"Yes, she's breathing," the other woman said.

"How do you know? I'm scared, and there's so much blood!" another said, her voice trembling and almost in tears.

"Hurry and slip that note into her pocketbook! Daddy's in the car, signaling us to come back now!" the first woman urged.

Then, the sound of boots rushing over freshly fallen snow quickly faded.

The haze struggled to keep Audine unconscious,

but it ultimately lost this fight, and Audine's will to live prevailed.

Audine's eyes fluttered open; her body was numb from pain, and her mind was foggy, unsure if this was a nightmare or if something terrible had happened.

"Oww! Those monsters hurt me!" she cried, tears welling as she touched her bare behind. She felt around and withdrew her hand, noticing bloody fingers.

A look of dread crossed her face as she suddenly recalled being terribly violated by three men. Nonetheless, there was no time to cry; it was pitch dark in this deserted wasteland, and cold.

Audine, aware of her surroundings, rose from the snow-covered ground and attempted to steady herself, but then stumbled into a dry, prickly shrub, which scratched her bare hand, worsening her pain.

Audine winced as she touched her still-bleeding lip, feeling a sharp sting. After the attack by three men, the pain in her legs made it difficult to bear weight on her left leg. She looked around, sighed, inhaled the cold air, and began searching for her belongings.

"Oh my God!" she shrieked.

On the ground, three bodies lay motionless. The men who had taken turns violating her were dead, each with a bullet hole between their eyes. Her suitcases, stacked nearby, seemed untouched, as if nothing out of the ordinary had happened.

"I need to get out of here!" she exclaimed.

Her pocketbook was easy to spot, lying beside the vagrant who had taken her panties. His bloodshot eyes, now dark and wide, still seemed to reflect something terrifying he'd seen.

"You son-of-a-bitch! You piece of shit!" Audine screamed. She lifted her foot and landed a series of savage, deliberate kicks to his bloodied head. Then, she raised her leg at the knee and pounded his nose repeatedly until it was utterly crushed.

Breathless and squatting beside his body, Audine rummaged through his pockets and pulled out a wad of cash: eight singles, a quarter, and two dimes. She took the money and coins, shoved the loot into her pocketbook, and snapped it shut.

She sprinted as fast as she could, ignoring the pain between her legs, towards the second body. When she reached it, she stopped and covered her mouth at what she saw. Lying in a pool of blood, the man's eye was shot out. The shooter had hit him twice, once in the eye and once in the groin. Audine cautiously sidestepped to a shuffle, getting closer to the body. Her legs trembling, she squatted beside him and slowly reached into his blood-soaked pockets. She pulled out a wad of cash, stained with blood. Audine rubbed twenty bills clean in the snow. Then, she opened her purse, stuffed the damp cash inside, and snapped it shut.

The last vagrant's body had identical gunshot wounds: one in the eye and the other in the groin. Without hesitation, Audine bent down, shoved her hand into his trousers, and pulled out cash: thirty dollars in single bills. Repeating her earlier actions, she washed the blood off with the snow until the bills were free of any blood traces. Audine stuffed the wet bills into her purse. Before snapping it shut, she checked to ensure the paper lay securely in the fold. Snapping her purse shut, Audine grabbed her suitcases and ran out of the vacant lot as fast as she could, despite her injuries and bleeding.

After running a mile, a taxi with a sign reading "For Colored Only" pulled up beside her. The driver honked the horn and rolled down the window.

"Ma'am, do you need a ride?" the handsome driver asked.

"Ye-ye-yes!!" she stammered.

"Where would you like me to take you?" he asked as she loaded her belongings into the taxi.

She didn't respond to the driver. All she wanted was to leave that hellhole where three hellions had assaulted her and left her for dead.

After Audine shoved her suitcases into the taxi, she sat in the back, shivering from the cold. The driver started the meter and sped up, causing the cab to lurch onto the road.

"Where are you taking me?" Audine asked, her voice barely above a whisper.

Looking at her through the rear-view mirror, the driver spoke to her in a soothing voice.

"Someplace where nobody will hurt you," he said.

Audine didn't hear him; her eyes were closed as she drifted into a dream of Wayne, Violet, and Mason. In her dream, they all faced away from her.

CHAPTER SIXTEEN

"Ma'am, ma'am? Can you wake up? We're here now. It's snowing pretty hard out here. I think I just got you in time - you wouldn't have made it otherwise. Are you okay?" he asked in a gentle, concerned voice.

With a firm hand gripping her arm, shaking her from a deep sleep. Her eyes flickered open as she took in the taxi's interior, unsure of where she was. But then, the memory of the three who had attacked her flooded back, and she felt the pain and wetness deep inside her.

"Where are we? What's this place?" she asked, taking in her surroundings.

"You've reached a safe place in Chicago, ma'am. We're in Bronzeville, on the South Side, where our community can work, worship, and get care if needed. When we're sick, we have a hospital nearby to take us in. But come on, the snow's getting worse, and the ice will start to freeze soon. I've got your luggage; hold my arm tight so you don't slip. By the way, my name is Ezra," he said, offering his arm to Audine.

With a sigh, Audine got back into the corner seat of the taxi and shook her head no.

"Ma'am, I promise you that nobody inside that house will hurt you, and I will not harm you. Judging by that busted lip, you need help. Come on now; it's getting cold out there, and I'm freezing!" he said, extending his hand. Audine heard the sincerity in his voice.

He wouldn't be able to harm me if that's what he wants, she thought to herself. I'm a mess, and I want to die.

As Ezra slid closer, he gave Audine a reassuring nod and a smile. Audine finally took his hand and let him draw her in until she slowly slipped off the seat and out of the car. He closed the door behind her and picked up her suitcases from the ground. As they started to make their way through the snow, Audine suddenly caught her breath at the sight of a massive house, complete with a circular porch, a yard, and a wrought-iron gate. Even in the snowy darkness, the house looked like a castle.

"I know, everyone who sees this house for the first time does that. Oh, sorry, I didn't catch your name, ma'am," he said.

"My name is Audine. Audine Collins, " she said, keeping her gaze fixed on the house.

THIS is exactly the kind of house I've always wanted to live in! I don't know who lives here, but I'll do my best to make it my home! Audine thought, feeling a pang of envy.

She attempted a smile, but the swelling and dried blood made her lip throb, so she managed a crooked grin and clutched Ezra's arm tightly.

As she finally reached the doorway, she stood in awe of the house's exterior, completely impressed by the large, inviting porch that stretched along the side of the house. She couldn't help but stare at the side door and window. The garage's exterior was massive; it was almost as big as a house, let alone a space for just one car.

"Did you see this?" Ezra asked.

"Huh, what do you mean?" Audine asked, refocusing on Ezra's question.

"Look what's on the door, Miss Collins. You should read it," said Ezra, pointing to a handwritten sign taped to the door.

She took a step closer to get a better view, and Audine read the sign:

Seeking a God-fearing Black woman who needs a room to stay!

Only God-fearing women should apply! If you need a room, step up to the door and, with all of God's strength, ball your hand into a fist. Knock on the door and shout 'Hallelujah' loudly! The Lord sent me here to this beautiful house!

Then ask to speak to God's anointed servant, the honorable Bishop Thomas Almonds, to receive you! God bless and keep you!

Audine scanned the ornate door with the sign once more. Audine followed the instructions carefully during the second reading while holding onto Ezra's arm. Audine heard footsteps padding across the floor. As the footsteps drew nearer, Audine noticed someone peering through the lace curtains of the small circular window. The doorknob turned, and Audine and Ezra stepped back. A young woman with brown skin opened the door.

"Good evening, may I help you?" she asked politely.

"Good evening. My name is Audine Collins, and I saw the sign on the door. I'm looking for a place to stay and wasn't sure who to talk to." Audine spoke through chattering teeth.

"Yes, yes, yes, of course, Miss Collins. Please come in so you can get warm," she motioned for Audine to come inside.

What hit Audine first was the aroma of rice, beans, and warm, freshly baked rolls, along with the unmistakable smell of chicken and dumplings. Audine couldn't help but notice the grandeur of the foyer: it was filled with family photos dating back to the days of slavery, a sturdy wooden table with a large, colorful vase overflowing with fresh flowers, and several neatly stacked Bibles.

My goodness, do Black people actually live here?

Audine wondered to herself as she took in the stunning interior of the house.

"Miss Collins, come with me to meet my family. By the way, my name is Ruthie Almonds," she said, smiling and revealing her perfectly straight white teeth.

"Wait, I have to pay Ezra, the taxi driver who brought me here," Audine said. She turned to pay the twenty-five cents she owed for the ride, but he was gone. He had left her suitcases next to the radiator to dry.

There was a puzzled look on her face.

"He's gone and was already paid. Ezra is going home, and you were his last stop for the night. Come, everybody is waiting to meet you," said Ruthie.

As Audine nodded and followed Ruthie, she took in the enormous, beautiful house. The scent of polished wood and soft lighting helped Audine relax. She tried to moisten her dry lips with her tongue, but the taste of dried blood made her wince. Passing a mirror on the wall, Audine gasped at her reflection. She looked like a monster- her lip was swollen, her eye was blackened, and the side of her face where she'd been punched was puffy. Her gait was slow and shuffling from the assault. Looking away, she covered her mouth, and for the first time in her adult life, she felt like a victim who didn't fit the mold of a confident woman. Audine wanted to turn around and flee this beautiful house, but where would she go? It was too late- Audine had stepped into a grand dining room that left her speechless.

Four people were already at the table, but now there were five, thanks to Ruthie joining them. At the head sat one of the most attractive men Audine had ever seen. Compared to the Creole men back in New Orleans, he seemed all the more impressive. He stood tall, with a long torso and long arms, but his skin was very fair, making him look almost White. On closer inspection, Audine noticed his hazel eyes and chiseled nose.

But the woman sitting at the other end of the table was a bit plain-looking. She had brown eyes, a lovely, rich skin tone, and her hair was neatly styled in a bun.

Strangely enough, the three young women sitting at the table were at different stages of pregnancy, especially Ruthie, whose belly was the most prominent.

Each wore a simple, thin gold wedding band. Audine gazed at them, wondering why their husbands weren't at the table.

Strange and unusual, Audine thought to herself. Her gaze shifted back to the attractive man sitting at the head of the table.

"Miss Collins, it's a pleasure to meet you," he said, rising from his seat to greet her.

Good Lord, he's tall! Audine thought to herself as the handsome man approached her, shook her hand, and kissed her on the cheek.

"My name is Bishop Thomas Almonds. I'm the head of Holy Vessel Church, and this lovely woman next to me is my wife, Sathronia. These two charming ladies beside us are our daughters, Lucinda and Delphine, and you've already met our oldest, Ruthie," he said, motioning with his hand.

"It's a pleasure to meet you, Miss Collins," their daughters said individually, except for Sathronia, who gave a curt nod without saying a word and glared icily at Audine with squinted eyes.

Audine couldn't help but notice how affectionately he gestured with his eyes and smiled while introducing his daughters.

Their last name is Almonds. Humph! What a strange last name! What are they, a bag of nuts? Audine wondered to herself.

"It's very nice to meet all of you," Audine said, averting her eyes and bowing her head low in shame at her appearance. "I-I guess by how I look, you can see I ran into a bit of trouble on the way here. Some men attacked me. And they- "

"We know, and I can see that something terrible happened to you," Almonds interrupted in a consoling voice. "I am so sorry as well as angry that that pack of wolves attacked you, but you rest assured, they're going to pay for what they did to you, dear sister. I promise they'll get what they deserve, but you need a roof over your head and a hot meal. Here, sit here next to me," said Almonds as he took Audine by the crook of her arm and led her to an ornate chair. Once seated, Audine didn't want to leave, as she had made herself at home.

"Delphine, would you please ladle some soup into

a bowl for Miss Collins?" asked Almonds.

"Yes, of course, Daddy," Delphine said.

Rising from her seat to fetch Audine's bowl of steaming hot soup, Audine's mouth watered at the sight of large dumplings at the edge of the cauldron. Unable to help but gaze at Delphine as she ladled the soup. Delphine was stunning, with a single braid that cascaded down to the middle of her back; the room brightened when she smiled. Strangely enough, she was just as pregnant as Ruthie, though her belly appeared much rounder.

Delphine placed the steaming bowl of soup in front of Audine and poured a goblet of cold water with lemon slices.

"Enjoy your soup, Miss Collins, but be careful because it's hot. Daddy says the best way to eat soup is when it's hot, right, Daddy?" Delphine asked, smiling at Almonds.

Almonds smiled back at her and motioned for her to come closer. As she approached, he wrapped her in a warm hug.

"Delphine, you, Ruthie, and Lucinda might want to head to bed for the night. Just be sure to gather around and have a prayer. Your mother will be up there soon to join in," Almonds said. Then, with outstretched arms, they all rushed to him, hugging him tight.

Sathronia sat, glaring at Audine. She hadn't touched her soup, which had grown cold, just like her gaze.

With great hunger, Audine grabbed the spoon that was already in the soup and ate it down.

"Ahem! In this household, we say a blessing over our food before eating, giving thanks for the nourishment it provides for our bodies. Do you know that many people go without even a single meal or a crumb of bread? And you professed to say that you're a woman of God before coming to our door? Unbeliever!" Sathronia shot back, rolling her eyes at Audine.

"Oh, goodness, I'm so sorry," Audine stammered, embarrassed. "I've been on a terrible train for days, and, well, I'm exhausted. Please forgive me for being rude, Sah-threw-nia."

After deliberately mispronouncing her name, Audine tried to stifle the smirk on her face.

"My name is Sathronia, Mrs. Sathronia Almonds, and you are to address me respectfully as Mrs. Almonds! Furthermore-"

"Let's bow our heads to bless the table, shall we?" Almonds interrupted, feeling embarrassed by Sathronia's outburst in front of Audine, who seemed overwhelmed by the attackers and was clearly anxious and hurt.

"Yes, let's pray," Sathronia replied, shooting a sharp glance at Audine, who smiled back at her despite the pain of her split lip.

Almonds shut his eyes, grabbing Audine's hand.

"By your grace, we come before you to thank you for the food before this lost soul who now sits before us in our home. Although broken in body, we thank you for letting her know that she is now safe and has food prepared for her and for us, which you graciously blessed us with. We thank you for the roof over our heads, this warm house we live in, the money that fills my pocket, and our friends and family. This we pray, amen."

"Amen," Audine said, her eyes opening. She was grateful for the warm bowl of soup in front of her.

Go to hell, Walter! I've got a decent meal and a warm bed to sleep in tonight! Fuck you and that woman you're with! Audine thought to herself as she shamelessly kept eating the thick chunks of chicken and creamy broth, soaking them up with the buttery dumpling.

It was the best meal she'd had since leaving New Orleans.

"So, Miss, or is it Mrs. Collins?" Almonds asked, looking at Audine's ring finger, which still bore the imprint of a wedding band, even though it was no longer there.

Does she think I'm stupid? How many women have taken off their wedding rings when I'm in their presence, changing their name from Mrs. to Miss? She's no different, Almond mused to himself.

The question caught Audine off guard, causing her to cough on the coffee she was sipping.

"Well, um, I'm Mrs. Collins, Mrs. Audine Collins," Audine said, stuttering.

"Humph, just as I thought. So, Mrs. Collins, what brings you to Chicago on a night like this? It's not only freezing outside, but it's dangerous! Why would your husband let you travel here alone?" implied Almonds as he dipped a thick slice of buttered bread into his soup.

"I was thinking the same thing," Sathronia said sharply. "And what's wrong with you? I hate to say it, but you look rough. You seem like you were in a brawl with some of those women who like to stay out all night in juke joints with men who spread those terrible diseases and-"

"Sathronia, that's enough! You seem to be finished! Would you kindly remove your plate from the table? When you head into the kitchen, please grab Audine and me some delicious apple pudding and two cups of coffee. Our daughters are waiting for you to form a prayer circle with them before we all go to bed for the evening. After you're done, please run a hot bath for Mrs. Collins. This poor soul has been through a lot." He said, motioning for Sathronia to leave.

"But—" interrupted Sathronia, alarmed by her husband's request.

"Now, Sathronia, do these things. As my wife, it's

your duty to serve me, your family, and our church. We all love and need you deeply, but as the Bishop of our church, the head of this household, and your husband, I need you to serve with joy and gladness, without me having to remind you of your place," Almonds said firmly.

With a glare at her husband, Sathronia spun around and shot Audine a look of disgust as she reached for a second helping of the still-steaming soup. Audine met Sathronia's gaze with a smile, then finished the water goblet and handed over the used utensils.

"Thanks, Sah-thew-nee-ah! I want my coffee piping hot, with sugar and cream. I like my coffee sweet, just like me!" quipped Audine.

Enraged, Sathronia grabbed them from Audine's hand and launched herself past Audine's chair, intentionally hitting her injured shoulder and slamming the door shut as she entered the kitchen.

Audine grimaced in pain yet finished her second helping of the soup.

That was delicious! Humph, for someone so

damned toffee-nosed, Sathronia cooks extremely well! Even the water with a lemon slice and a pinch of caster sugar tasted delightful; I've never had such a refreshing drink of water before! However, I must now answer Thomas's questions. If I have to lie about everything, it will be because I'm not leaving this house, but Sathronia will, in due time. Audine thought to herself, shifting in her chair.

"I have so many questions to ask you, Mrs. Collins. However, before I ask anything, I want to explain how I manage this household and the church I oversee. One rule is that there is no drinking, cursing, lying, fornication, or sloppiness. When we attend church services during the week, including Sunday, you're expected to join us because I won't cater to any heathens. The last woman who stayed here was everything I just described to you. The last straw came when I had to use the bathroom one night," disclosed Almonds.

"Oh my, what happened?" Audine asked, leaning in to catch every detail Almonds was about to share.

"I was heading to the bathroom one night when I

realized the woman who'd been staying there had already left the church. I told one of the ushers to let my wife know she needed to come back because she wasn't feeling well. When we got home, her door was closed, and I figured she was asleep, so I didn't want to wake her. As I walked past her room, I heard voices - hers and a man's. I pressed my ear to the door and overheard them doing things that only married people should do. I tried to open the door, but she'd locked it from the inside. So, I knelt and peeked in. I recognized a no-good, tall, brazen-faced man who'd been seen hanging around a vacant lot with two friends not far from our house. I saw my tenant on her knees, doing a lewd act on him. I quietly got up, did my business, and ran downstairs to call seven deacons to come right away. They arrived, and I let them in. We crept up the stairs, listened, and waited until they were done. When he came out of the room naked to use the bathroom, the deacons pounced on him, dragged him down the stairs, and threw him out. The other deacons took the tenant outside to be with that naked man. Then I had them pack her suitcases, and I even had the sheets they used burned."

Audine, her eyes wide as saucers, listened in horror to the detailed account of what had happened in that room and why there was now a vacancy.

"The tall man and his two friends! They were the ones who attacked me and left me for dead! But when I woke up, I found them all dead—each one had been shot in the head!" Audine said, fighting back tears.

"Oh? Humph. What a relief to know they're gone and getting what they deserve for doing such a terrible thing. I'm so sorry that happened to you, Mrs. Collins. If your husband had been with you, he would've protected you. But if you'd stayed in New Orleans, none of this would have happened to you," Almonds said.

Before she could protest his statement, Sathronia returned, balancing a tray with two bowls of warm apple pudding and two cups of coffee so hot that billows of steam swirled around, emitting the aroma of freshly ground coffee beans. She approached Almonds and served him first, then cleared away his used utensils.

"Thanks, dearest," Almonds said, nodding. He took a bite of the dessert, closed his eyes, and smiled as he chewed.

"You've outdone yourself, Sathronia. This is the next best thing to heaven. Mercy on me; umph, umph, umph!"

With a sideways glance, Sathronia shook her head, dismissing her husband's compliment.

Taking her time, she strode to Audine, removed her bowl, and carefully placed the cup and saucer of hot coffee in front of her. Making eye contact with Sathronia, she gave her an obnoxious smile. Sathronia took the pudding from the tray and slammed the bowl down onto the table.

"I see you're done with your soup, or would you like another bowl? That would be your third, Mrs. Collins. Tsk, tsk, tsk! It's amazing my daughters only had one bowl each, with babies on the way, and here you are having two! If you want more, there's none left because you ate it all!" She stormed off to the kitchen and started washing dishes as fast as she could, muttering curses under her breath and slamming pots back onto the shelves. After checking that the kitchen was spotless, she turned off the lights and headed upstairs to pray with her daughters.

Following the prayers, they kept holding hands, refusing to let go of Sathronia.

"Ma, are you okay? The moment Mrs. Collins walked into this house, everything changed. What's going on? We're all scared," Lucinda said, squeezing Sathronia's hand a little tighter.

"Yes, we heard you slamming dishes around, and we heard Daddy telling the story about what happened last week when Louise was staying here. We heard everything that night, Ma," said Delphine, nodding.

Sathronia gazed at each of her daughters, who were clearly concerned about her. She shut her eyes tightly and took a deep breath.

"I'm going to be perfectly truthful with you all. I have a bad feeling about this woman – she can't be trusted, and she won't tell the truth to any of us, not even your father. Her heart is filled with darkness, and she tells lies. A dark spirit entered this house just as we got rid of Louise." Sathronia seethed.

"What happened to her?" Delphine asked.

"Humph, dead. She turned up dead in a

flophouse on the other side of town. From what I was told, she was poisoned," said Sathronia, averting her eyes.

Ruthie and her sisters gasped in shock, covering their mouths.

"I've heard many things that come out of New Orleans, especially from those practitioners who read tarot cards and, well, do things," whispered Delphine, who now had her arms around Ruthie's protruding waist.

"Where did you hear such things, Delphine?" Sathronia asked in a hushed tone.

"My husband said he has a cousin in New Orleans who is a practitioner, and she's not one to mess with. Many people respect her, but they're terrified of her. He said he wanted to take me to New Orleans to meet her," answered Delphine, trembling like a leaf in the wind.

"You all listen to me. Be polite to Mrs. Collins because she's a border, and we're a church-raised family. I raised you girls to be obedient and kind, too. But do not go inside that room where she will be staying, and if you see anything that doesn't look or feel right, you come to me or your father, okay?" said Sathronia.

"Yes, ma'am, thank you," they all said, agreeing with Sathronia. They approached her and gave her a long, lingering hug before heading to their bedrooms.

"Delphine?"

"Yes, ma'am?" she replied.

"Come here, sweetheart," motioned Sathronia. Delphine walked into Sathronia's open arms and embraced her.

"You're not going," said Sathronia.

"Huh?"

"You're not visiting your husband's cousin in New Orleans. We don't believe in that sort of thing, and your father wouldn't let it happen, especially with your baby coming. He and I may have our differences, but we will not have anything happen to our grandchild or grandchildren coming soon," said Sathronia, inching away far enough to massage Delphine's protruding belly. "Don't worry about anything; I want you to go to bed and rest because we have early morning prayer," she said.

"Thank you, ma. I love you so much," said Delphine, reaching out to embrace Sathronia.

"I love you, too. I'll see you all in the morning," said Sathronia, hugging Delphine and slipping two vanilla cookies into her hand. She winked at her daughter, who smiled at receiving the surprise treat to eat before she went to sleep. She did the same for Ruthie and Lucinda. Delphine went to her room and quietly shut the door.

Creeping to the top rail of the stairs, Sathronia leaned over to catch snippets of Thomas and Audine's conversation, which was quiet but audible enough to hear.

There was something ominous about Audine being in the house, bringing lies, deceit, trouble, and chaos.

"I'll never have another dark spirit in this house again," Sathronia muttered to herself as she made her way into the bathroom.

She turned on the lights and cranked the hot water spigot to full blast, without mixing in any cold water. She made sure the water reached such a high temperature that the bathroom was completely shrouded in steam.

"Two must go, the dark spirit that came and Audine Collins," she said in a secretive hush.

Then, leaning against the tub's edge, Sathronia spat into the water to convey her wish for Audine to leave.

CHAPTER SEVENTEEN

Coffee, billowing cigar smoke, and notes of cocoa powder, pepper, cinnamon, and almond spices used in baking filled the dining room as Almonds drew the cigar between his lips and squinted his eyes in amusement, watching Audine scrape the bowl for her third helping of apple pudding. There was nothing left of the dessert.

Gluttony, sheer gluttony. That's what this woman's spirit is about, yet there's much more to her than I've not figured out, at least not yet. Almonds thought to himself as he sucked on the sweet-smelling cigar and blew another plume of smoke.

Unaware of Almonds watching her as she devoured the apple pudding, she finally looked up and met his gaze.

"Sorry about my manners, Bishop. I want you to know I just got off a long train ride with nothing to eat except food that was stale, burnt, or just plain awful. I didn't sleep at all, and after I got off the train, I told you what those men did to me. If it weren't for Ezra, I wouldn't be here. He was a lifesaver. Is he married?" Audine asked.

Almonds cleared his throat loudly and flicked the ashes from his cigar into a wooden ashtray.

"To be clear, Mrs. Collins, you've come to Chicago after taking a long train ride from New Orleans. Why is that? Because you still haven't told me anything," he said, rising. He strode over to where Audine sat. His six-foot-four-inch height towered over Audine. He stood behind her, placing his massive hands on her shoulders and gently squeezing them.

Umph, umph, umph! Please have mercy on me! I know he will take pity on me now, but if he accepts me as a boarder in his beautiful home and I attend his church, eventually becoming a faithful member, then I'll be humbled. Sathronia might as well pack her bags and leave! Audine thought to herself, smiling as she closed her eyes.

"Feel good?" whispered Almonds.

"Oh yes, what you're doing feels fine, Bishop! Mighty fine!" she cooed.

"So, if I'm standing here pleasing you in my living room and my wife is upstairs drawing a hot bath for you, after everything we've done to make you feel comfortable and safe, all you care about is whether Ezra is married?" Almonds asked, his grip on Audine's shoulders tightening.

Turning sharply in her chair, Audine stared up at him, stunned.

"What do you want from me?" she whispered, her eyes wide and filled with fear.

"For you to tell me the truth! So, tell me, Audine, what exactly are you doing in Chicago?" he asked, probing her further.

"I left my husband," she said, pausing. "I left him because I caught him with another woman! I begged him not to leave me, but he grabbed all my suitcases and told me to get out! He said he'd be getting our marriage annulled through the church we attended and would go to city hall on Monday to tell the clerk our marriage was over! We'd only been married for two months, and he had his eye on another woman! He took our savings, told me my son wasn't going with me, and my daughter, who was having a baby with a married man, took off to New York to live with my sister and her husband. So, you see, I've got nobody who cares or loves me! After all the wonderful things I've done for my husband, he's the one who ruined my life forever!" she cried, burying her face in the cloth napkin and pretending to sob, secretly hoping Almonds would believe her outrageous lie so she'd have a place to live.

Almonds observed and listened to Audine's wailing and weeping.

"Audine, stand up, dearest," he said, helping her out of the chair. He took the napkin from her hands and placed it on the table. "What you confessed is enough for me to accept you into our home. I'm sure that my wife will be more than pleased to help you. Regarding your condition, you'll need immediate medical attention. Therefore, I'll have my secretary at the church call one of our nurses in the morning to tend to your injuries. In the meantime, you and I will talk again because I have many more questions about your husband, son, and especially your daughter's circumstances. Until then, Mrs. Collins, have a restful night's sleep. Sathronia is at the top of the stairs, waiting to show you your room, the bathroom where you can bathe, and some fresh nightgowns. And just so you know, we're up and ready downstairs in the parlor at seven o'clock in the morning for early morning circle prayer. Breakfast is at eight. My daughters and I will be driven to the church, where they will help with church business. After the nurse sees you, Ezra will drop you off at the church for lunch and a tour. Sathronia will be here at home preparing dinner, and we'll all have six o'clock prayer," he said, smiling, showing his bone-white teeth.

Audine tried to hold back her tears, but this time, she couldn't help but let them flow.

"Thank you, Bishop. Thank you for letting me stay here to finally get a good night's rest, a hot meal, and a bath. I'm looking forward to everything you've got planned for me tomorrow. And please call me Audine. There's no need to call me Mrs. Collins anymore," she said.

Almonds pulled a crisp, white handkerchief from his trouser pocket and handed it to Audine. She dabbed at her eyes and nose.

"Thanks, Bishop," she said, nodding her appreciation.

Almonds smiled and nodded.

"Sathronia is waiting to help you, and Ezra is married. May I suggest something to you that I should have suggested to Louise, the woman we discussed who was here before you: keep your hands off and your legs closed around Ezra. We all love him, and so does his wife. Good night, Audine, and see you in the morning," he advised.

Too stunned to respond to his statement, Audine could only manage a goodnight and head to bed.

His eyes followed Audine as she walked up the stairs, where Sathronia stood seething, desperate for Audine to leave her house for good.

CHAPTER EIGHTEEN

Instead of showing this heathen to the guest room, I'll point her in the direction of where Louise stayed. And if she thinks I'll carry those ratty old suitcases of hers, think again! Sathronia thought to herself as she heard heavy footsteps coming up the stairs.

Audine finally pulled herself up onto the last step.

"Oh, my goodness, I didn't think I'd make it up here!" said Audine, gripping the handrail and struggling to catch her breath.

"Humph, maybe if you'd stop eating so much, you'd have little difficulty walking up two sets of stairs," Sathronia huffed under her breath.

"What did you just say to me?" Audine challenged.

"If you want me to be truthful, I will, Mrs. Collins! I saw you take three helpings of that dessert and two cups of coffee! My husband and I are especially watching out for our daughters, who are each about to have a baby, so I suggest that you control your mouth when it comes to eating food in this house! Now, it's the room next to the bathroom where you'll sleep. The Bishop's study is in the room on the left side at the end of the hallway. Stay out of it," snipped Sathronia.

Audine narrowed her eyes at the words.

"Sathronia, I need to see you now, please," Almond called from the bottom of the stairs.

"I'm coming, Thomas," she said, keeping her voice calm.

"Oh, and by the way, Mrs. Collins, you can grab your suitcases from the foyer downstairs tomorrow morning. Bishop, neither our daughters nor I will touch those smelly, old, broken-down things. They're being aired out in case of bugs," said Sathronia as she hurried down the stairs.

Sathronia left Audine standing on the stairs, blistering.

Who does she think she is, talking to me like that? Doesn't she realize what I've been through? The nerve of that heartless rat! All I need is six months in this house, and her daughters will call me their mother, Audine murmured in a low voice.

Finding the bedroom she would be staying in, Audine opened the door to reveal a reasonably large room featuring a neatly made bed with two heavy quilts and a stuffed chair accompanied by a matching embroidered ottoman near a window facing the street. A Perlina metal table lamp sat on a small wooden table draped with an off-white tablecloth. The light cast a soft shadow in the room, creating a cozy and comfortable atmosphere. The dresser in the corner boasted six drawers and a round mirror. Audine ran her fingers over the surface of the dresser and quietly gasped at its smoothness. Upon opening a drawer, she discovered several sheets, pillowcases, new nightgowns, bras, panties, underslips, slippers, and four frocks. At the foot of the bed on the floor lay two pairs of oxfords and one pair of gently worn dress heels, which were in better shape than the ones she had on her feet. Each pair of shoes was stuffed with heavy knit stockings. Walking to another door in the room, Audine opened it and was delighted to find two heavy wool coats and a pair of gently worn, almost-new boots. She clapped her hands together gleefully at the abundance of items she needed to survive the harsh winter in Chicago.

Rushing over to the dresser, she pulled open the drawer and took out a freshly laundered nightgown. As she unfolded it, she discovered a comb, hairbrush, bar of soap, washcloth, towel, honeysuckle-scented body cream, hair pomade, a scarf to tie around her head to cover her hair as a bun, rosewater face cream, toothbrush, and tooth powder to mix with water to create a paste.

Gathering everything in her arms, Audine walked past the mirror and gasped in horror at her reflection. Her face was gnarled, and her bottom lip appeared swollen and bruised. Audine touched the enormous bruise on the side of her face where she had been punched and slapped multiple times, a grotesque reminder of its black and blue hues. The scratches, cuts, and nicks on her legs were stained with dried blood. Feeling tears well up in her eyes, she inhaled deeply. Looking away from her reflection and wiping her tears away, she rushed to the bathroom. Closing and locking the door behind her, she caught a hint of the floral scent of Woodbury soap wafting through the bathroom. Flicking on the lights, Audine covered her mouth in shock at what she saw: a bathroom fit for someone wealthy. The pristine white bathtub rested on clawed feet and was enormous—no doubt to accommodate Thomas Almond's six-foot frame. There was a sink, a vanity, and a stool adorned with flowers. Various body creams, lotions, powders, and perfumes were arranged in neat rows, including three hair pomades: the Sathronia, her daughters, and the pomade for wave-textured hair.

"That's for Thomas," whispered Audine as she twisted open the pomade can and studied the creamy white concoction he used to slick down his hair, even though his hair seemed naturally straight, likely due to his Creole and Black background.

But what about his eyes? Where did the color of his eyes come from? Humph, if I were his wife and could have his children, they'd be beautiful! But how is it that the complexions of his daughters are different? Audine thought to herself as she quietly twisted the top back on the pomade can and hurriedly undressed, leaving behind her putrid-smelling garments, especially her undergarment, which was bloodied. Examining them, devastation flashed across her face as she began to recall the assault.

They're dead now and can never hurt me again, she thought as she tossed in the washcloth and soap bar before stepping into the tub.

As she dipped her body into the scorching water, her skin tingled. She winced in pain, gritting her teeth as she lowered herself in. It was as if she were starting anew, and she gently pressed the washcloth to her face. The intense heat of the cloth opened her pores, clearing away the crust in the corners of her eyes and making her bruised face throb with pain. She leaned back, her face covered by the fabric, and endured the heat until the cloth cooled. Then, she carefully scrubbed every inch of her body with the washcloth and soap, paying special attention to the area between her legs. Slowly standing up, she gripped the edge of the tub and continued scrubbing.

The pain, rawness, and tender areas where those

monsters had forcibly attacked her hours earlier brought her to uncontrollable weeping. Each time she wiped, more blood flowed. She didn't stop until the bleeding finally ceased, and the bath water became a mix of filthy liquid and congealed blood. The pain lessened. Turning on the water spigot, Audine rinsed herself. Searching around the front of the tub, she found the plug-stopper. Pulling the silver chain of the stopper, the water drained immediately. Hoisting herself out of the tub, Audine stood and watched the grime of two days and two hours disappear down the drain.

Locating the tub rag used to clean the tub, Audine scrubbed away the residue until the inside was spotless again. Padding over to the mirror in her bare feet, Audine studied her reflection. The facial cuts showed no signs of dried blood; the tiny scratches were still there, but less noticeable. After drying off, Audine used the honeysuckle-scented body cream tucked inside her nightgown, along with the face cream, being careful not to apply too much pressure. She brushed her hair up, applied pomade to her scalp, and brushed vigorously upward to detangle her hair and soothe her itchy, dry scalp.

I need to find a hairdresser as soon as possible, Audine thought, taking the fabric intended for her hair to use as a tignon for bedtime. *After slipping on the crisp-smelling, soft nightgown, she fell into the provided slippers and gathered the malodorous garments. Snapping off the lights, she opened the door to the bedroom and let out a shriek, dropping everything onto the floor.*

Standing in front of the door was Sathronia.

"You scared me, Sathronia!" she exclaimed, clutching her chest with a trembling hand.

"This is for you," said Sathronia, shoving a large brown bag at Audine. "Bishop said to put those rank-smelling garments you came dressed in inside this bag, and you're to leave it outside the door of your room."

Her voice reflected the intensity of her gaze.

"Why does he want me to do that? Can't they be washed?" she asked.

"He wants them taken away and burned. You'll get a few more decent-looking dresses to wear in this house and to church. If you don't like what Bishop requests, I suggest you leave in the morning. If you decide to obey him, don't forget that we have early morning prayers. You must wear one of these frocks, wrap your head in a tignon, and put on your slippers. Bishop doesn't want to hear loud noises in the morning," said Sathronia firmly.

Leaving Audine speechless once again, Sathronia whirled around, stormed off toward Thomas's bedroom, and slammed the door behind her.

Audine stood in disbelief at what had just occurred. Scooping up the items on the floor, she stuffed her clothes into the bag and stormed off toward Sathronia's bedroom, but stopped abruptly in front of the door. Thomas and Sathronia could be heard engaged in a heated discussion. Their voices quieted as she inched closer to listen to what they were saying. Taking a risk, Audine crept close enough to press her ear against the door. Suddenly, she heard what she thought was a loud slap, followed by footsteps pounding closer to the door.

She sprinted to her room, Audine dropped the

bag of clothes by the door, stepped inside, and quietly shut the door, snapping off the lights. As she tiptoed to the bed, Audine eased herself in from the hallway, trying to avoid making any noise; the sound of the door slamming was so loud it made the house tremble. Then everything fell silent. Audine slid under the covers, feeling exposed and vulnerable for the first time in her life, especially since she knew Sathronia would do whatever she said or be forced to go back out into the Chicago streets. Until a plan was devised, obedience to Sathronia was required.

Despite the pain, sleep arrived instantly, while outside lurked the spirits of covetousness and envy.

CHAPTER NINETEEN

Voices

"Are you sure she doesn't know about us?"

"Of course, I'm sure. I'm not going to let anything happen to my vessels. They've been planted, and I'm having the joyful pleasure of watching them grow!"

"May I ask you something?"

"Of course,"

"Will more be planted?"

"Oh, my dear, yes! And when the number reaches twelve, a new family shall begin, a pure one from a direct descendant, a bloodline that will endure even long after I'm gone!"

"No, don't say that! We need you, and I-I-I'm in love with you."

"And I'm in love with you more than anything, so much that another vessel will only be planted inside you after six months. The others will wait a year, but you've been chosen, and I expect you to carry another one. When the number reaches twelve, oh my love, that will be a grand day! The blessing of them all, and then the most important announcement will come."

"When and what will that be?"

The name of the family and having the name dedicated! It will feel just like a wedding, with everyone wearing white, and I expect it to start at sunrise on a Saturday and end at sunset. Oh my, the shouts of joy will be loud enough to hear as far as New Orleans!

"And then you'll tell everyone, right?"

"Yes, I will tell everyone".

Shameless kissing and soft moans gave way to the sounds of licking and sucking, escalating into passionate groans. Suddenly, a high-pitched, muffled scream jolted Audine awake, causing her to sit up and stare ahead, dazed and trembling.

Whose voices were those outside the door, and are they still there? What's happening in this house? Audine thought to herself, terrified.

Wiping the sleep from her eyes, Audine rolled back the blankets and quilts to get out of bed. The house that had been warm when she fell asleep was now icy; she had to resist the temptation to climb back in, where it was warm.

"Now I've got to pee and then I'll be getting up in a few hours," Audine mumbled, pushing away the blankets and sitting up in bed.

"OW!" she hissed, gritting her teeth.

She was in agony, her legs on fire and throbbing. Every step made things worse. The pressure on her bladder was unbearable, and she could feel urine trickling down her leg. She didn't care who was outside the door; Audine flung it open and sprinted to the bathroom as fast as she could. Slamming the door behind her, she rushed to the toilet and sat down. The relief of emptying her bladder was instant, like a weight lifted. Audine covered her mouth to stifle her screams, trying to push away the pain. After she was done, she grabbed the toilet paper and began wiping herself. The pain was excruciating, so she gently dabbed until she felt clean. Audine pulled the urine-soaked wad of toilet paper to examine the contents, her body shuddering. What she saw made her blood run cold: a thick, yellowish-green discharge with blood mixed in. Between her thighs, she noticed a cluster of angry-looking cherry-red spots, each the size of a raised pinhead. She was frozen in shock, her back prickling with fear. Distraught, she stood up and gazed into the toilet bowl, where a foul-smelling mixture of blood, urine, and feces oozed out of her body.

As she flushed the toilet, Audine wept softly about what was happening and said there was no one to talk to about it. However, it didn't take long to realize that this was caused by the three monsters that had assaulted her: when she turned on the sink faucet, a blast of hot water whooshed out; taking the bar of Woodbury soap, Audine lathered her hands up to her wrists, then rinsed them. While drying her hands, she glanced up at her reflection in the mirror and didn't recognize who she was or the circumstances.

She trembled with shame, switching off the light and stepping out of the bathroom. The hallway was dark and still, except for the loud, increasing howl of the wind.

Trudging to the bedroom, she opened the door and stepped inside with a heavy heart. Two weeks ago, she had been in bed with her husband, Wayne, and now it was over, as suddenly as Wayne would never return. Her heart ached, her stomach twisted in knots, and memories flooded in faster than she could process. She began to wish to be with Wayne, to be married and held by him, especially on a cold night like this.

Despite her debilitation, Audine wept until she closed her eyes and drifted back to sleep, pondering Wayne, questioning what those red spots between her legs were that caused her all that pain, and still wondering whether the voices heard outside the door were real or merely figments of her dreams.

CHAPTER TWENTY

New Orleans

Maria St. Laurent

Midnight. Everyone thought I was visiting Clarence's grave, especially since my good friend Eucharista accompanied me to the cemetery. Mr. Bristol and his wife, Zenobia, who owned the "For Colored Only" taxi service, were incredibly kind and drove us to the cemetery, waiting for us without charging a dime. Zenobia was quite happy to drive us there so she could visit her grandmother's resting place. She brought tools to clean the site of excess leaves, cut weeds, and collect and dispose of any animal waste near her grandmother's headstone. Was I visiting Clarence? Of course not! As I passed by his grave, I spat on it, just as he had done to our marriage, Maria thought to herself while she sewed the final details of the poppet that resembled Audine Collins. The innermost part of the poppet was filled with a mixture of recently taken dirt from Doctor Ellman "El" Shillings' grave and a discreetly placed lace handkerchief that Audine left behind at the last event of her life, her wedding day. The handkerchief would serve as a tag lock.

The dirt from his grave could either heal or cause illness, so Audine had to pay for everything she did to my family and me. Maria thought to herself as she began her work.

She used the handkerchief, mixed with the grave dirt, as the stuffing. Working late nights in the shed for four days straight to create and dress the poppet had become a routine.

"This is all your fault, Clarence! Especially you! I just found out you left a huge debt on this farm and the home of our children. You son-of-a-bitch! Violet, for the rest of your days, you'll have that cough until it kills you. And that bastard child Clarence planted in your belly will grow up lying to people, especially men. As for you, Audine, you selfish, bitter, jealous, and boastful liar, if any man puts his manhood in you and pulls it out, it'll shrivel up like a dead twig. Like you, it'll be infected and have red spots, a burning pain that feels like it'll never go away. When it does, it'll come back, and it'll be worse, with more spots. Those three men were nothing more than vicious dogs after their prey, and guess what? You were the one they chose! You were chewed up, infected, and now you're cursed. But I've learned one last lesson: when my powerful friend takes over, you'll meet Mrs. Lillian Moore," she seethed as she finished stitching the poppet that looked like Audine.

Propping it against the wooden box, Maria stood and admired her work as she took another deep draw from the new cigar mailed to her from Lillian Moore, who said everyone, especially practitioners, was smoking them because of the smooth and creamy smoke. Maria took in another draw and savored the undertones of chocolate, cinnamon, and nutmeg.

Blowing the smoke directly into the face of the poppet, Maria took pleasure in the naked poppet, which symbolized leaving Audine cold, miserable, and exposed to the winter elements. To further instill confusion in Audine, especially as she heard voices, small question marks were drawn on the forehead and the chest cavity, along with grave dirt and snipped pieces of Audine's handkerchief that were mixed with shards of black onyx from a piece of jewelry found in Clarence's suit pocket, creating a mystery regarding how it got there. This would lead to a breakup in Audine's marriage and any man she slept with for just one night.

"She'll turn into a one-night whore, just like her daughter Violet," Maria seethed, taking another long drag from the sweet and savory-tasting cigar and blowing a cloud of smoke at the poppet. And between its thighs were pins; the pin heads were red, meant to resemble the red spots that would later turn into painful blisters, break open, and ooze out infection.

They'll vanish just as quickly as they appear, but come back even more vicious than before, Maria thought, as she added more pins to the poppet's inner thighs, up to its knees.

"When she'll least expect it," Maria said aloud. Taking in one more draw, she tilted her head back and blew the sweet-smelling smoke in the air to purify the atmosphere. Then, grabbing the poppet, she tucked it inside the wooden box and put it on the top shelf where nobody would find it. Snuffing out the remains of the cigar embers on the bottom of her shoe, Maria gently put it in between the folds of the other unused cigars in a simple wooden box. Snapping it shut, Maria ran her fingers over the smooth box, a gift from Lillian Moore, who resided in Chicago.

Maria pondered as she turned off the lights. I need to send Mrs. Moore a letter of thanks for those cigars.

At that moment, the baby inside Maria's belly kicked as if to agree.

CHAPTER TWENTY-ONE

"I missed having you in our bed every night, and I cried myself to sleep, missing you like a child misses its mom. I shouldn't have let you leave and pushed for us to work things out. I was a fool for letting you walk out on us, but I promise you, things will be different this time. We'll fill this house with our own kids, Audine. I knew the doctor who said you couldn't have kids was wrong! Do me a favor, sweetheart?" Wayne asked as he made love to Audine.

A loud knock echoed on the door.

"Someone's at the door, Wayne; it could be Mason or Violet," Audine said, breathless.

Wayne ignored her, penetrating Audine more intensely, sending her to a loud climax.

The knocking on the door intensified and became more urgent.

"Wayne, the door, it may be Violet!" said Audine,

struggling to get from under Wayne, but her legs were locked around his waist, and she couldn't move.

"They're all gone, Audine, because of you! Violet, Mason, and our unborn child! Because of you, my family is gone forever!" seethed Wayne before he released a powerful climax.

"What, what the hell are those things between your legs? Those red spots: what are they?" he screamed, pointing at the thousands of red spots between her thighs.

Audine looked down between her legs; hundreds of angry red spots ran from where Wayne was inside her down to her knees. Everything down there felt like a raging fire, and Wayne, gripping his manhood, which was bright red and covered in thousands of red spots, was crying out in pain and cursing Audine.

The knocking at the door grew more urgent, and the voice behind it grew louder.

"Mrs. Collins, Mrs. Collins! Wake up right now! Early morning prayer will start in forty-five minutes!" the female voice outside the door whispered loudly.

Audine sat straight up, disoriented and confused about her surroundings. Wiping her eyes, she swung her legs over the side of the bed and slipped her feet into the slippers beside it. Scurrying across the room, Audine twisted the doorknob and flung it open. It was Delphine Almonds, the youngest daughter.

Even at this early hour, she had a beautiful glow. Her belly protruded as though she was going to give birth at any moment. Envy welled up within Audine.

"Good morning, Mrs. Collins," she whispered. "It's five, and we're gathering in the parlor for prayer at six o'clock. It would be best to make your bed, wash, and dress quickly. And don't forget that you're seeing the nurse from our church today. Daddy said she'd meet you at the hospital, and Ezra would drive you. Please hurry, because Daddy has a lot to do today, so don't be late! He hates it when people are late for his time!"

"Hospital? What for? I feel fine," said Audine, wincing at the pain between her legs and touching her bruised face.

"I don't mean to show bad manners, Mrs. Collins, but I heard you crying out last night," she said, feeling embarrassed.

"You heard me? What do you mean you heard me?" Audine said, her voice deliberate, as she crossed her arms over her chest.

"Mrs. Collins, I had to pass your room to go to the bathroom due to my condition. As I got closer, I heard you moaning and crying out for a man named Wayne and two other people named Violet and Mason.

"I was going to knock on your door to check if you were okay and then have a prayer with you, but my baby, who's growing inside me, needed to go to the bathroom, so we did. I hope you're feeling better. Just get ready now because Daddy starts morning prayers on time, and he can get pretty upset if we're late! I have to go now because my sisters and I don't get to spend much time with our husbands, who'll be joining us," Delphine said, smiling widely and making circular motions on her belly with her palm.

"You heard me call out the names of Wayne and my child; I mean, two people named Mason and Violet?"

Delphine nodded and maintained Audine's gaze.

"Delphine, could you please come downstairs? Your husband is here, and he's eagerly waiting for you. We're about to start soon!" requested Sathronia.

"Yes, Ma, coming!" Delphine's delight rang warmly when she heard that her husband had arrived and was waiting for her.

"I'll see you downstairs, Mrs. Collins," Delphine said. She rounded the corner and made her way down the stairway, holding onto the handrail with one hand and cradling her belly with the other. Audine could hear the joyous chatter and laughter of everyone, even Sathronia.

With a slam of the door, Audine hurriedly made the bed. Hurling the pillows to the floor, she pulled the sheets and blankets so tightly that there wasn't a wrinkle left on the bedding. All the while, tears welled in Audine's eyes as she angrily wiped them away.

Why couldn't that dream have come true, especially when Wayne was willing to give our marriage another chance? Oh, my goodness, Wayne, why did you leave me? Was it someone else, maybe Etta? It should have been me, not Violet, having a baby! That was supposed to be my chance to start a new family! Audine thought bitterly as she opened the drawer filled with dresses.

She yanked the first brassiere out of the drawer, slammed it shut, and grabbed a fresh one from underneath. After tossing the used panty into the pile, Audine rushed to the bathroom and turned on the faucet to brush her teeth. She mixed the tooth powder into a paste in her palm, then scooped it up with the toothbrush and brushed quickly. Looking in the mirror, Audine blinked in shock. The side of her face where the attackers had slammed her was a gruesome blue and purple, and her nose was flattened, swollen, and oozing a bit of blood from a deep gash.

Overwhelmed, Audine fought the urge to scream as she spat the creamy paste into the sink. She cupped her hands together, filled them with cold water, and rinsed her mouth, then spit it out again. Rushing to the tub, Audine turned on the hot water faucet and plugged the drain with the rubber stopper. As she pulled her nightgown over her head, Audine glanced down in horror, covering her mouth at what she saw: hundreds of red spots, many of them filled with infection.

"Oh no, what are these!" she softly wailed.

She spread her legs to get a closer look; a cluster of spots had already burst and oozed a mixture of infection and watery blood.

There wasn't a moment to dwell on the gruesome scene. Bishop Almonds and the entire family were waiting.

Tossing a bar of soap and a washcloth into the tub, Audine turned on the cold water to temper the ankle-deep water. Stepping in and kneeling, she splashed water on her face. She grabbed the washcloth and soap, scrubbing the bar against the cloth to create a creamy lather. The pain between her thighs was unbearable, especially when in contact with the hot water. Audine covered her mouth once again to muffle her wails of pain; the spots felt like thousands of needles pricking, and the ones that had already blistered and broken open stung. The pain made her feel nauseous.

As she carefully rose, Audine let out a whimper of pain and noticed new spots spreading to her kneecaps.

Her eyes welled up with tears.

There was no time to cry again as Audine wiped away her tears, pulled out the stopper from the tub, and quickly rinsed it out.

After drying herself, Audine sprinted back to her room. She applied lotion to her body using the provided toiletries and got dressed. Audine removed the tignon she wore to bed and tossed it aside. To her surprise, the pomade from the previous night added a shine to her hair and relieved the itchiness on her scalp. She brushed her hair and tied on a fresh tignon that matched her dress. Slipping on her slippers, she rushed to the door, shutting it carefully to prevent a loud thud.

Audine glanced at the clock—it was six o'clock on the dot.

Padding down the stairs, Audine lowered her head to see who was gathered in the parlor, which now looked breathtakingly beautiful with the natural sunlight illuminating it. A couch, large enough to seat only one person, was occupied by Almonds. What made it eye-catching was the customized footstool, which was red with a gold braided fringe. The chairs were arranged in pairs so that his daughters and their husbands could sit close together, while an additional chair was placed a few feet away from where Almonds sat. That chair was designated for Sathronia, and another chair, positioned in front of the doorway, was for Audine.

"You're late! Bishop is ready to start morning prayer, and we've been waiting for you!" Sathronia hissed into Audine's ear.

Without thinking, Audine spun around to face Sathronia, who wore a look of disdain.

I arrived on time! I came here at six o'clock. I was also having a bad nightmare and-

"Audine, finally, you're here! Please join us. You made it exactly at six o'clock, and you're on time!" boomed Almonds, who stood up and strode toward the stairs. Standing at the bottom, he stood tall, smiling, and extended his hand. Almonds looked grand in Audine's eyes as she sauntered down the stairs. She felt a quick jab from a finger on her back. Audine turned her head

only to see Sathronia cutting her a glare.

"He's waiting for me, not you, Sathronia; I'm here as a boarder, so you'd better get used to my being here," sneered Audine.

Almonds beamed up at Audine as she bounded down the stairs, and he took Audine's hand to escort her down the final three steps.

Audine couldn't help but stare at Almonds.

He ensured he stood out from everyone with his attire. Adorned in a tailored navy-blue pastoral vestment trimmed with gold piping, an embroidered design ran from his wrist to his elbow. The gold braided cincture, a knotted rope tightened and form-fitting at his waist, highlighted his physique. He wore no shoes or socks; his long, narrow feet were perfectly manicured.

Humiliated by his gesture toward Audine, Sathronia trailed behind them before taking her seat and glaring at Audine.

My beloveds, before we begin, I want you all to welcome Mrs. Audine Collins, who answered my prayers for a God-fearing woman to stay here in this house, especially after the last woman who was here. Nothing but evil filled that room, and to our joy, she's gone, along with that scoundrel of a man she was keeping company with, doing offensive things with him in the bedroom of this house! Well, thanks to the deacons, both of them are gone! He preached with an authoritative tone.

Shouts of "Amen!" and loud hand-clapping echoed in the parlor.

"Preach, Daddy!" Ruthie shouted.

"It's unfortunate how Mrs. Collins arrived here. You see, she was attacked by three men who were a pack of wild dogs out to slaughter an innocent lamb! But I tell you the truth, my loved ones; thanks be to the almighty, she was spared, saved, and brought here!" he proclaimed loudly.

"Amen! Preach, Daddy, preach!" Ruthie, Lucinda, Delphine, and their husbands all stood up, shouting, "Glory and thanks be!"

Everyone except Sathronia stared at Audine, who continued to smile at Almonds with her gaze fixed.

Audine couldn't help but admire how tall and

strikingly handsome their husbands were. They dressed alike in what seemed to be military-style uniforms similar to those worn by U.S. Army soldiers. The colors of Almond's sons-in-law were navy blue, featuring eight gold buttons running from the wrist to the base of their elbows. Their trousers were simple and cuffed, paired with cream-colored shirts, coordinated ties, and black shoes. Outside the door, they had a similar style. They were barefoot, while the women in the group covered their heads with a tignon, wore floor-length frocks, and slippers.

Seated with her legs and arms crossed, Sathronia was furious about the attention Audine was getting, especially from her husband, who still hadn't let go of Audine's hand.

"Do you have anything to say, Mrs. Collins?" asked Almonds, gesturing for her to speak.

Sathronia rolled her eyes upward.

Scared out of her mind, Audine attempted to stand up, but her legs shook, the room spun, and she felt like she was about to faint. Her stomach was in a knot, so she took a deep breath, grabbed the chair's arms, and pulled herself up. The room was silent, everyone waiting for her to say something or pass out from fear.

"Thank you for your kindness," she sputtered, clearing her throat. "I'm blessed to be here after being beaten by those cruel devils who almost killed me! If it hadn't been for an angel by the name of Ezra, I-I," Audine broke down weeping, covering her face with her hands to hide her smile as she felt Almond squeeze her hand, then, in an unexpected move, encircle her around the waist, firmly embracing her. Everyone, except Sathronia, burst into applause, clapping and shouting Amen.

Sathronia sat, glowering.

Yes, indeed, it's working in my favor with Thomas! The mere fact that I'm already in his arms is lovely! It's only a matter of time before Thomas and I are together once I get well. This is my day, my time, and my joy! Audine thought to herself as she buried her head into his chest, inhaled the scent of his freshly showered body, and embraced Thomas tightly.

Then, a loud hand-held bell rang out.

"It's going on five past the hour, and we need to start!" snapped an annoyed Sathronia, who slammed the bell on the side table.

What a waste of time with that whore, mumbled Sathronia under her breath, shaking her head in fury.

Thomas gently pulled away from the embrace and motioned for Audine to go back to her seat and continue serving.

As he walked to his chair, Almonds glanced over at Sathronia's seat, a hint of irritation and impatience flashing in his eyes.

There was a hint of a smile on Sathronia's lips as she chuckled to herself.

"Let us all stand and join hands as we bow our heads in prayer," announced Almonds.

Everyone stood with joined hands and bowed their heads low.

"By God's grace, we say good morning to you, and once again, we thank you, Father, for this wonderful morning."

"Yes, Lord, we thank you," murmured Almond's daughters and their husbands.

"We thank you for watching over us as we slept through the winds of danger; we thank you for keeping our house safe from any hurt, harm, or risk, especially from break-ins, robberies, thieves, and the enemy with his threats of darkness that come to search and destroy us. We thank you for the blessing of mercy on this poor soul who stands here in fellowship with us; we thank you for intervention, angels on assignment sent by you to protect Audine from being killed! It was you who kept her safe! She came out bruised and beaten, but you sent your servant Ezra to deliver her, and you sent retribution to those who beat her senseless! Thank you for bringing her to this holy house!" Boomed Almonds.

Shouts and cries of "amen" and "hallelujah" were heightened by loud hand-clapping; Ruthie's husband broke rank, jumping and shouting while fervently speaking in tongues.

Just in time, Audine snapped her head up and saw everyone with their arms raised high above their heads, praising and worshiping.

Almonds had stood up from his chair and was now standing in the center of the circle, entirely in control of the room.

"My beloveds, I ask you, what is your purpose? Is it merely to seek out what is best for your soul? Is it to worship every day, including Sundays? I'll answer that for you! It's to serve, help those in need, be humble and grateful, and have a roof over your head! For the food you eat, especially the food the church serves our brethren! My goodness, there's a depression going on in this country, but are you worried about it?" he asked, preaching fervently.

"No, we aren't worried because you take care of us and our church! You make sure we all have food on our tables and a warm bed to sleep in! Thank you, Bishop, for everything! Thank you, thank you, thank you!" Ruthie exclaimed, then fell to her knees in front of her chair, praying out loud. Meanwhile, Lucinda, the second eldest, was being supported by her husband, both with their eyes squeezed shut, their necks stretched back, as they shouted praise and wept. Delphine and her husband were in a corner, holding hands and praying together. During the intense praise and bursts of song, Sathronia crossed her arms tightly over her chest and shot Audine a glare.

Audine sat upright, her ankles crossed, oblivious to Sathronia's knifing looks. Audine was fascinated by what she saw at this hour of the day.

I have to get used to all this shouting and waking up early if I'm going to be Thomas's wife someday. My goodness, look at all of them, hah! It's no wonder that everyone goes to bed so early! All I need is two weeks to heal, and I'll do everything that everyone else is doing in this room so that Thomas notices me, and only me. Audine thought, scooching to the edge of her chair to observe what everyone was doing.

Looking up at Sathronia, Audine flashed a grin and, out of the blue, shot to her feet, unleashing an ear-splitting scream.

"Hallelujah!" The chair toppled over.

Everyone was caught off guard, except for Sathronia, whose face twisted into a frown.

CHAPTER TWENTY-TWO

"Bishop Almonds, that had to be the most beautiful time I ever had in an early morning prayer! I've never seen or done anything like this before! I'm looking forward to doing this tomorrow morning! But, umm, if you don't mind sharing, where are your daughters, and what do their husbands do? "Asked Audine as she shoved a mouthful of fluffy scrambled eggs mixed with creamy grits and melted butter into her mouth.

Umph, umph, umph! These are the best eggs and buttered grits I've ever had! The ham has a fiery flavor, and the biscuits are perfect. I'll be sure to try to make friends with Sathronia so that I can watch her cook the food that Thomas enjoys, Audine thought to herself as she took another bite of the ham and washed it down with another cup of coffee mixed with the special cream made of cream, cinnamon, nutmeg, and sugar.

"Why do you want to know?" asked Sathronia, cutting her eyes at Audine.

"Sathronia, dearest, why don't you get us some more of those delightful biscuits because our daughters will be here any moment after they bid farewell to their husbands? I must say that God is wonderful! They will have their babies two months apart, making this a very blessed family! Humph, Ruthie is already talking about having four more!" he said, grinning and flashing his perfectly straight white teeth.

"I think I hear them," he said, pushing back his chair and standing up.

"And would you mind bringing more grits? They're delicious! And bring a few more eggs? Your husband got me to jump and praise this morning!" exclaimed Audine, grinning and raising her coffee cup with sarcastic intention.

"You listen to me; you are a temporary guest here, and I'm not your maid! I happen to be the wife of Bishop Thomas Almonds, and from here on, you'll address me as Mrs. Almonds, not Sathronia, do you understand me?" she whispered through clenched teeth into Audine's ear.

She stormed off, spinning toward the kitchen and

slamming the door behind her with such force that it felt like the entire house shook.

Audine glanced at Thomas, who looked furious at Sathronia's outburst. His fists were clenched next to his breakfast plate, and his nostrils flared.

Audine turned her head away from him and buried her face in her napkin, smiling.

Hah! I must've really gotten under her ashy, dried-up skin! Hah! Keep throwing those tantrums in front of Thomas and me, Sathronia, because the more you do, the closer I'll get to gaining on Thomas! You're doing me a big favor! Audine thought to herself, trying to stifle a loud burst of laughter.

Thomas cleared his throat.

"Are you all right, Audine? Because that explosion of Sathronia's temper isn't acceptable, I want to apologize and seek your forgiveness for her outburst. She's acted strangely since our daughters got married and immediately expected children, with each pregnancy occurring two months apart. They're happy; their husbands are too, and I, humph! I'm overjoyed that this family will grow; let them be fruitful and multiply! Isn't that right?" he said, taking a short sip of his coffee.

"I suppose so, Bishop. I'm happy about your daughters. Humph, I wish I could've had the same experience, at least. My husband and I lost our baby just after we got married, which is why he left me," Audine said, slowly lowering the napkin from her face so she could hide her smile and look suitably disappointed.

"And on top of that terrible attack that happened to me, I have to say I've never seen so much anger just for a few bites of food, especially after what I've been through in the past few days, not having a proper meal on that awful train ride from New Orleans to get here. Sah-threw-neh-ah... sorry, Bishop, I beg your pardon. Your wife insisted I call her Mrs. Almonds. She's a wonderful cook! But please forgive me for being so rude while eating all this delicious food. Have mercy on me, sir!" Audine wailed softly, bowing her head low and slumping her shoulders in shame.

Thomas dropped his napkin on the table and walked over to Audine. He stood towering over her, his hand resting on her shoulder.

Audine could feel his warm fingers coiling around her shoulder. Inhaling the fresh scent of his hair pomade and the aroma of his just-out-of-the-shower fragrance, Audine scrunched her eyes shut and took another deep breath.

Ohhh, have mercy! How good his touch feels, and he smells wonderful! Oh, Sathronia, you dried-up fool! Can't you see what you're doing? You're making this so easy for me! Thank you, you dried-up prune; thank you so much! You remind me of a woman I once knew named Lena, another fool like you! And guess what? I ended up marrying her weak-minded husband, just like I'm going to get a second chance at becoming a wife by marrying your husband, gaining three beautiful daughters, and becoming a grandmother! Audine thought to herself, giddy, as she placed her hand over Thomas's hand, giving a firm squeeze.

"Audine, I've met many torn and broken women like you. Each has a different story, filled with lies or truths. It all comes down to this: They all come to me for love, comfort, and reassurance because I am their light and the only path to their salvation," he said, keeping his voice low.

"Look at me," he said as he walked back to his seat and sat down.

As Thomas took a bite of the warm eggs, Audine's eyes widened in amazement. He sprinkled on more pepper, took another bite, and nodded with satisfaction.

"Audine, look at my beautiful colored eyes. I've got good hair, and my skin is the color of coffee mixed with extra cream. This is why everyone *loves me*, but they can't figure out what I am in terms of whether I'm White, Black, or otherwise. Humph! I'll keep them all guessing! Don't you agree with me?" he asked, smiling.

Despite her cracked and sore lip, Audine couldn't hide her excitement after being touched by him just moments ago. Audine held his gaze and nodded emphatically, agreeing with every word he said. Audine felt smitten.

He and I think so much alike; I've got to do everything I can to get this man to focus his attention on me and earn that second chance at being a wife.

Humph, Wayne doesn't count; he was too weak for me, she thought, smiling as she sipped her coffee.

She didn't realize that Thomas fixed her with an unwavering, deadly stare.

The brief silence was broken by footsteps coming toward the dining room.

"Ah, welcome back, Ruthie, Lucinda, and Delphine! You ladies and the babies inside you must be hungry!" exclaimed Thomas as he quickly got up from his seat.

Each of them rushed to embrace him. Audine watched, fascinated by something she had never seen before.

After hugging Ruthie, he undid the last eight buttons on her dress and spread the panels open, revealing her swollen belly. He pulled out a small, ornate flask from his vest and twisted off the dome-shaped top. The scent wafted out of the bottle. Audine closed her eyes and took a deep breath. When she opened them again, she saw Thomas drizzle several drops of fragrant oil onto the palm of his hand. He knelt and massaged the oil, which smelled like a mix of roasted roses and exotic spices she'd never smelled before, onto Ruthie's belly.

He was uttering words that made no sense, but in an instant, Lucinda and Delphine stood behind her, their hands pressed against her back as if to protect her if she fell. Ruthie's arms were raised high, her eyes tightly shut as she, too, was uttering an incomprehensible language. When Thomas finished, he cradled Ruthie's pregnant belly and kissed it several times. He repeated the same to Lucinda and Delphine before standing up. After resuming his seat, he continued his conversation.

"Are you all feeling better about your husbands being away for the next six months?" he asked.

He signaled for Audine to pass the salt and pepper to season his eggs, and his daughters also went to their seats. Delphine took a seat next to Audine.

"Irving said that he's looking forward to serving our church, doing missionary work, preaching, and helping to baptize and save souls! He said he's sad he won't be here for the baby's birth, but he'll write to me every day and call once a month. When his missionary work is finished, he'll be back," said Ruthie as she massaged her belly and took a forkful of the buttery grits. She closed her eyes and savored the flavor.

"And what about you, Delphine, and Lucinda?" Thomas asked.

"Clayton and Mark said the same thing, Daddy, except they're going further south, and honestly, we're scared for them. We've heard terrible things about what goes on there. We want them back home in Chicago, sitting beside us at church to hear you preach, Daddy," Lucinda said, pushing her plate away.

"May I ask you all something?" inquired Audine, who appeared intrigued.

"Yes, go ahead and ask," said Thomas, rising. "While you ladies talk, I'm going into the kitchen to help Sathronia. She's taking too long with the rest of the breakfast. When we're done, I'm going to the church, and Audine, you'll be coming with me to meet Beatrice Huggs, a nurse who works at the hospital.

She's called to tend to your wounds. "Now, if you'll excuse me," he said, standing up from his chair and heading to the kitchen.

"Yes, Daddy," his daughters replied in unison.

Audine took another sip of coffee while gazing at Thomas's daughters. They seemed happy as they ate and chatted about their husbands and the names they would choose for their babies after they were born. Even Lucinda's mood shifted.

"So, where did your husbands go? Are you all excited about having your babies?" inquired Audine as she set her coffee cup down onto the saucer.

The three of them stopped talking and focused their gazes intently on her.

Why are they staring at me like that? Audine wondered as she shifted uncomfortably in her seat.

"My husband Irving wants to preach and is already good at it. He's not as good as Daddy, but he's learning. Daddy said Irving has to humble himself and do mission work for a year," said Ruthie. Lucinda and Delphine nodded in agreement.

"A year? Why so long? Can't he do missionary work here in Chicago? And shouldn't he stay here long enough to learn what he can from your father? I'm sure your husband will make a perfect minister, just like your father, but I still don't understand why he has to be away for so long. Wouldn't you want to have Irving here to help you?" Audine probed as she drained her coffee cup.

I wish Sathronia would hurry up with that coffee! That ashy prune is taking too long! Audine thought as she tapped her foot impatiently.

"To serve in our church, especially if any of the men are called to preach like Daddy, they must prove to him that they are truthful in their word. They must do many tasks to humble themselves," said Ruthie, taking another spoonful of eggs and grits.

"Humble themselves? How and why? I don't understand that at all," quipped Audine, expressing her confusion.

All eyes from Ruthie, Lucinda, and Delphine were fixed upon Audine, aghast at Audine's statement and lack of common church knowledge.

"Mrs. Collins, I don't mean to be impolite, but

when you came here, didn't you tell my father that you were a church-going woman?" quizzed Ruthie, her eyes narrowing at Audine, who was squirming in her chair.

"If you know anything about being a follower of our Father in Heaven, He requires us to be humble, not prideful, but truthful in everything, and most importantly," remarked Lucinda before being interrupted.

"Sacrifice. What our husbands are doing for our family and church is a sacrifice. Their time away not being with us, even missing out when I have my baby in June," echoed Delphine, who seemed particularly troubled by the issue of her husband, Mark, being away for a six-month missionary work assignment, as tears welled up in her eyes.

"Oh my, please excuse my inexperience in all this! I-I had no idea that you all were blessed with brave husbands who were willing to serve your father's church and wanted to be like him. You all need to know that this is all new to me; I-I never saw anything like what your father was doing to you all earlier. And Delphine, you have nothing to worry about. If you'd like to be friends,

I'll be here to help you, and you can tell me anything, especially about your husband Mark," she remarked sympathetically, grasping Delphine's hand, and Audine smiled.

Delphine felt an ice-cold chill run through her hand and up her arm. Remembering her mother's words, Delphine snatched her hand away from Audine's grasp and resumed eating breakfast.

"Ladies, we've got fresh, hot, buttered biscuits, hot creamy grits, a few morsels of ham, and plenty of scrambled eggs!" boomed Thomas, bursting through the door while holding a tray of piping hot food, with Sathronia trailing behind him.

The daughters squealed in delight, each bowing their heads for a quick blessing of gratitude for the breakfast overflowing on their plates. Their lively chatter resumed, and at times during the conversations, even Thomas threw his head back, howling with laughter between bites of ham and eggs. Audine joined in the clamor, casting constant glances of admiration toward Thomas, who seemed oblivious to Audine's ogling.

However, Sathronia, engaged in a deep

conversation with Delphine, glared at Audine when she noticed her staring at Thomas.

CHAPTER TWENTY-THREE

"Mrs. Collins, are you ready? Ezra arrived, and we're ready to go! Be sure to dress warmly; it's freezing outside!" called Thomas from the bottom of the stairwell. He paced, glancing at his pocket watch every few seconds since Ezra's arrival.

After breakfast, Audine helped clean up by taking the dishes from the dining room table. Ruthie and Thomas seemed to be engaged in a deep, whispered conversation. At times, her head was bowed as they clasped hands. They didn't leave the table until it was cleared, and Sathronia walked in with a broom, dustpan, dusting rags, and a vial of oil for the furniture.

"Thank you for breakfast! I enjoyed the food, the coffee with that special cream you make, and the eggs were delicious! I had second helpings of everything!" exclaimed Audine.

"You had three helpings of everything, Mrs. Collins; let me remind you that Bishop and I have three daughters with babies growing inside them, and they need every scrap of nourishment they can get so those babies will be born whole. Do you understand? And another thing, keep your hands off Delphine." Sathronia's voice was suddenly as hard as steel, matching the hardness of her gaze.

"Oh, I understand just fine. It's just that your cooking is delightful, and well, maybe you can be a maid and cook. That way, if you're a cook, there'll be extra food for us all. I have to go now; Thomas said I need to be ready in one hour to meet Nurse Beatrice Huggs so that she can care for me. Humph, I'll need as much nourishment as your daughters with everything I've gone through. Take good care, and enjoy your housework, Sathronia!" she stated squarely, then left, leaving a fuming Sathronia who clamped her tongue between her teeth to keep herself from starting a quarrel with her unwelcome guest.

"Coming, Bishop! I'm almost ready!" exclaimed Audine. Her delight rang warmly in her voice as she fluffed her hair as best she could.

It will only get mashed up inside this hat, humph. Whelp, once I'm healed from everything, including this worsening rash between my legs, my happiness today was that I got closer to Bishop Almonds. But why was Delphine acting rudely towards me, snatching her hand away when I was only trying to be friendly? Humph! The nerve of that brat! She acts just like that ashy, wrinkled prune, Sathronia! Audine thought as she folded her new wool coat over the crook of her arm and grabbed her purse to meet Thomas, who was waiting impatiently at the foot of the stairs, tapping his pocket watch as Audine strolled down the stairs.

"You look lovely, Mrs. Collins. Your boots are in the corner; we will leave when you put them on," he said hurriedly.

"Thank you, Bishop; I-I was wondering if you'd help me put them on because my leg is badly bruised and hurts," Audine said, stammering.

Almonds shot Audine a sly glance, holding up the boots with a sweet smile.

"Mrs. Collins, we're running short on time, and I don't have patience for this. When my daughters were little, they'd sit on the floor and put their boots on. You're a grown woman who doesn't need help like that. Just sit at the bottom of the steps and put your boots on," he said, exasperated.

Startled by the snappiness, Audine sat down on the bottom stairs and slipped on the boots with ease.

"Ready? Ezra is going to drop me off first at the church with my daughters, who are already waiting inside his car, and you'll be meeting Beatrice at the hospital," said Almonds, adjusting his hat.

"But I thought we were going to ride together so I'd have a proper introduction," Audine said.

"So did I, but because you took so long, Bee had to rush off to the hospital to be on time, not late like you seem to be. So please, let's go; we're already running behind," said Thomas, flipping out his pocket watch again to glance at the time.

Audine remained silent in response.

As Thomas made his way to the door and opened

it, a gust of wind nearly knocked them all back into the corridor. The frigid wind whipped into Audine's face, prompting her to adjust her neck scarf closer to her neck. Not accustomed to the icy ground, Audine nearly slipped but managed to reach the car, where Ezra helped Audine into the back seat with Thomas's daughters, who huddled close together, blankets on their laps to keep warm.

After a polite greeting, Ruthie and her sisters handed Audine a plaid wool blanket to keep her legs warm. Then they continued talking among themselves, steering clear of any conversation with her.

After ensuring everyone was covered and comfortable, Ezra shifted the car into drive and drove off carefully.

Peering through the lace curtains, Sathronia watched until Ezra's car had disappeared from view.

CHAPTER TWENTY-FOUR

Beatrice "Bee" Huggs

Nine-fifteen. They're running late, and so will I when I'm on duty at ten-thirty, Bee thought as she paced in front of the large window that allowed her to watch for Ezra's Cadillac, which he would be driving to bring Bishop Almonds to the church.

Thomas called late to let Bee know that a new border would be staying at his house. However, he also mentioned that she had been beaten and needed to tend to her wounds right away before attending church service, which was scheduled for five days later.

Bee felt proud of herself as a Registered Nurse for two years when she paused to glance at her reflection in the window. She couldn't help but slowly nod; she wore a perfectly starched and ironed white nurse's uniform, matching stockings, pearl white oxfords, and the crown jewel on her head: the nurse's cap. Her hair was styled in a perfectly coiffed, tight bun secured with bobby pins. Not a hair was out of place, not even a wisp. The uniform, which complemented her coffee bean skin tone, made her feel beautiful, enhancing the slant of her dark brown eyes. Many couldn't figure out who or what she was.

"Let them all keep guessing," she whispered, stifling a throaty little laugh.

Casting a keen eye at her ring finger brought a broad smile to her face. Isaiah Wellman was the epitome of every woman's dream. He was handsome, stood six feet tall, had a cinnamon complexion, and possessed a sparkling personality. He served as the principal of the first through eighth-grade school that Bishop Thomas Almonds founded and built, which served the Black community until students transitioned to the high school that Almonds also established. His identical twin brother Harris was a vice principal at that high school.

Isaiah served as a trustee and ushered every Sunday. When he told Almonds that he compulsively watched Bee, he knew she would be the one to become his wife and the mother of his future children.

After a year-long courtship, he proposed to her in front of their families, including Almonds, who appeared overjoyed for both of them.

Bee's thoughts were interrupted when she saw a familiar Cadillac slowly pull into the hospital's winding driveway for admitting patients. The hospital corridor was lively with the sounds of crying children, distant loud moans from patients in pain, and four pregnant women walking in with their husbands. All four women were there to deliver their babies in the fourth-floor maternity ward. Bee smiled and waved at them, as they were all members of the church where Almond preached. Almond officiated their weddings, and when it became clear that the wives had difficulty conceiving, they individually sought healing advice from Almond. Within two months, all four were expectant mothers.

Bee glanced up at the clock again. Nine-twenty. Ezra got out of the driver's side of the car, scrambled around to the other side, and opened the door. Reaching inside, he took the gloved hand of a woman whose face was bruised. Her eyes and cheeks were a grotesque mix of black, blue, and purple. Cuts and abrasions covered her face, especially a noticeable busted lip.

"So, this must be the woman Bishop spoke to me about. Have mercy; whoever beat her up like that is horrible," she murmured to herself.

Almond's mouth was pulled to one side in a grimace, Bee noticed. She took a deep breath and rushed out the door to meet them.

"Good morning, Bee! Sorry, we're running late. I want to introduce you to Mrs. Audine Collins, the new boarder staying with Bishop and his family. Mrs. Collins, this is Beatrice Huggs," said Ezra.

"Good morning, Mrs. Collins. I'm Beatrice Huggs, but everyone calls me Bee," she said, extending her hand to shake hands with Audine.

"Nice to meet you, Bee. I'm sure you know why I'm here," Audine said, shaking Bee's hand.

"Yes, she knows why you're here, Mrs. Collins, and Bee is going to take good care of you, and I'll guess that Bee will have you healed by Sunday, won't you, sweet Bee?" boomed Thomas as he glided effortlessly out of the car.

"I certainly will. After all, I graduated from the top of my class. Good morning, Ruthine, Delphine, and Lucinda," she said, waving to Almonds' three daughters. "You all look beautiful! Each of you is going to become a mother, and you and your wife will be grandparents!" exclaimed Bee, moving towards Thomas, who wrapped her in a warm hug.

"And after you and your fiancée are married, it'll be your turn!" he said.

He took her hand and pressed a wad of cash into her palm.

"That's for Mrs. Collins's care. If she needs any medicine, take it out of what's there. Anything that is left, you keep. You deserve it, and it's my way of thanking you for taking time out of your busy day to care for her," said Thomas as she stuffed the wad inside her uniform pocket.

"Thank you, Bishop Almonds. I just saw Deacons Van, Willman, Earl, and Tipperman arriving. It looks like their wives are due to give birth today! What a wonderful blessing of a day for them, don't you think?" Bee said excitedly.

"My, my, my, oh my! What a joyful morning for me!" he exclaimed, clapping his hands gleefully. "When you're finished with Mrs. Collins's care, call the church so I can let Ezra know to pick her up and bring her back to my house. Mrs. Collins, we're all praying for your recovery. Bee, please don't forget to let me know what our deacons' wives had to say. As you can see, I'm excited to know!" said Thomas.

Ezra opened and then closed the car door for Thomas. He climbed inside and signaled to Ezra that he was ready to go, prompting him to drive off. Ezra quickly moved to the driver's side, got in, and drove away.

"Let's get you out of this bitter cold, Mrs. Collins! I need to do a full examination on you, take care of your wounds, and have you out by ten-thirty because that's when my shift starts," said Bee, smiling. She took Audine by the arm, and the two women walked briskly down the brightly lit corridor.

Bee observed Audine's painful grimace with every step she took.

"I used to work at a hospital in New Orleans," said Audine.

"You did?" Bee exclaimed, beaming as they turned right down another corridor.

Why did I have to bring that up? And why does she need to know about it? Audine wondered to herself as she focused on the sounds of doctors being summoned, the whir of a hand crank, the bed being adjusted, and the distinct smell of alcohol used to prep a patient for an injection. What struck her as beautiful was the sight of numerous Black doctors and nurses rushing up and down the corridors to help the afflicted.

"Mrs. Collins?" Bee asked.

"Oh, oh, yes? I'm speechless about how big this hospital is and how beautiful it is. It's well kept and clean", acknowledged Audine, who was ogling at the activity taking place on the left and right sides of the corridor.

"Yes, we are all proud of this hospital. Bishop and Mrs. Almond have contributed a lot of money. Thanks to them, many of our patients have a place to come when they fall ill, and many women, especially from the church, have been giving birth to their children here for many years. Almost all the nurses and several doctors belong to the church." She said, motioning for Audine to go inside the private exam room.

"By the way, what did you do at the hospital in New Orleans?" Bee asked again.

"I, uh, was a nurse, just like you. I cared for so many people that, even on my days off, they would often ask me to continue taking care of them. I was up for a big promotion at that hospital," Audine said, sitting on the exam table.

"Oh, really? What level of nurse are you? Where did you study nursing, and did you get that promotion? I'm interested in knowing this, especially from a fellow nurse," remarked Bee.

"Well, uh, I am a top-level nurse, you know, the ones who are the leaders who tell the other nurses what to do, you know what I'm talking about, the top nurse. Yes, that's what I was!" beamed Audine, squaring her shoulders.

"I've never heard of a top-level nurse before. May I ask where you studied nursing?" she asked inquisitively.

"I studied nursing at the hospital where I worked. I even graduated first in my class and spoke at the graduation ceremony! The teachers were so impressed that they hired me to work the following week. As for that promotion, they gave it to someone else. Humph! At first, I felt sad, but after thinking about it, I realized I wouldn't want to work all those long hours. So, I put on a brave face and wished the other woman good luck. She's probably still there trying to keep up with her work. In my opinion, it was for the best. Humph, I don't need to go crazy working long hours like her. She's probably up and working right now from yesterday," responded Audine.

That should keep her quiet from asking me any more questions. The nerve of her asking all those ridiculous questions! I need to set her straight if she asks me anything else! Audine thought to herself evasively.

"That's, um, quite impressive, Mrs. Collins. I'm sure you made a wonderful nurse and guided many of the others to do well just as you have," said Bee in an amused tone.

Just wait until Bishop hears about this nonsense, hah! Top nurse? There's no such title as a top nurse! Bee thought to herself, smiling.

"Okay, Mrs. Collins, I will ask you to remove everything and put on this hospital gown. Since it's cold today, you may want to drape the sheet over your legs. I'll wait outside the curtain; let me know when you're ready," said Bee as she pulled the heavy white curtain along the rod.

"Thank you, Bee. It won't take me long to undress. Um, do you have any idea how long this appointment will take? I have many questions that I'd like to ask you about Bishop Almonds and his church, especially the members, how many attend, and what kind of church it is," said Audine as she began to undress quickly, removing her chilled outerwear.

"You want to know about Bishop Almonds? Why is that?" queried Bee, leaning closer to the drawn curtain so she wouldn't miss a word Audine was saying.

"Well, during early morning prayer. Bishop and his daughters were doing some very peculiar things. His wife, Sathronia, also seems strange to me. She always appears angry, and her behavior towards me has been rude. Humph! She doesn't act like a bishop's wife. She's very distant, and I've never seen her kiss or hug him once. He was delightful towards his daughters, the way he hugged them, and here's where it got pretty peculiar. When each of his daughters approached him after their hugs, he stepped back, unbuttoned the last several buttons on their frocks, took a flask out of his pocket, and poured oil onto his hand. Then he rubbed the oil onto each of their bellies. He started praying at first in a language I couldn't understand, then began speaking gibberish. I couldn't grasp his words because the louder he spoke, the louder his daughters did! They were muttering the same things, and when it was over, they all appeared exhausted! Another thing I'd like to know is why the husbands of his daughters left for their missionary work in such a hurry. Why, they didn't even stay for breakfast, which was dee-lish-us! Humph, as mean-spirited as Sathronia is, she sure can cook! Her cooking reminds me of my good friend's cooking. Her name is Maria St. Laurent," sighed Audine as she snapped off the garters, holding up her stockings and carefully sliding them off to her ankles so they'd puddle down into her shoes.

Wiggling out of her girdle, Audine looked down and gasped at what she saw. The cluster of angry, red lesions had increased in size and now resembled miniature pinheads, engorged with infection. Several had already broken, and oozed thick, creamy pus mixed with blood. Audine winced in pain as she climbed onto the exam table and covered her legs, feeling ashamed.

Disgusted at the cross-examination and premature gossip that Audine was blasting out, Bee stood silent and hardened.

She couldn't handle the comments, followed by tough questions. Adding Bishop Almonds to the mix made her question her motives and intentions, which she knew weren't entirely pure. However, if there were inquiries about the church and how Sunday services were conducted, she was willing to respond. Any questions about Bishop Almonds or his wife were off-limits, though.

And since when did her first name become a nickname for Bishop Almond's wife? Bee thought to herself, a frown creasing her forehead. The lack of respect was evident in crossing a dangerous roadway and, therefore, didn't provide any answers to the questions Audine asked.

"Mrs. Collins, are you ready for me?" asked Bee, adjusting her stethoscope.

"Yes," Audine said, her voice faltering.

Hmm, I wonder why she suddenly became timid when, just a while ago, she wouldn't shut her mouth, Bee thought to herself as she flicked the curtain back with a sweep of her hand.

As the curtain slid open, Audine flinched back. She clutched the hospital blanket tighter around her neck, taking in a series of quick breaths to calm down and get her bearings.

"Are you okay, Mrs. Collins?" Bee asked, edging closer to Audine, who looked visibly shaken about something. She appeared to have seen a ghost.

"I'm really nervous, especially after getting beaten up by those awful men and then seeing all three of them shot dead! Oh my God, it was terrible! Did the police or anyone else take their bodies away?" Audine said in a quiet voice.

"As far as I know, they were all found dead. Each one had been shot, but the killer remains a mystery. The whole town is relieved to hear that all three of them are gone because they were nothing but trouble and drunkards."

"Their families didn't want anything to do with them, so they were laid to rest in plots for unknown people. You don't have to worry about that anymore," Bee said, putting a reassuring hand on Audine's shaking shoulder.

"Thank you," Audine said softly, her voice barely above a whisper.

"I want you to lie down so I can listen to your heart," said Bee.

Audine lay down, and Bee took out her stethoscope, placing it directly over Audine's heart. It was racing and pounding, like she'd taken two spins around a city block.

Bee reached into her pocket and pulled out her

scribble pad to record her notes.

"Could you please hold out your right arm toward me?" Bee asked.

"Why? Is there something wrong?" asked Audine, who was now clearly panicked by the request.

"I'm going to measure your blood pressure. I thought you said you're a top nurse because if you are, you should know that every patient has their blood pressure taken," Bee said in a curious tone.

"But of course I do, don't be silly! I just wanted to know what you'll do with me with that thing you're holding!" Audine blurted out.

"Mrs. Collins, I need to use the blood pressure device to see how high or low your blood pressure is. You should know this. Now, please extend your arm towards me," said Bee.

As Audine watched Bee closely, she felt the blood pressure cuff tighten around her arm. The black bulb at the end of the hose was also squeezed, and the sensation was like a snake wrapping itself around her, causing her to cry out in pain.

"Ouch! This hurts! Do you hurt people like that using that thing? Are *patients* like that all the time because you hurt me?" exclaimed Audine.

"Shh, please be quiet, Mrs. Collins. I need to concentrate on the numbers to see if you have high or low blood pressure," said Bee, motioning for Audine to keep quiet.

This woman is a liar! Every nurse alive knows that blood pressure is taken on every patient and understands what the device is and its purpose. Bee thought to herself as she watched the numbers on the aneroid gauge drop. After reciting the numbers out loud, Bee flipped open her notepad again and scribbled the results. Bee opened and released the cuff on Audine's arm, removed it, folded the cuff neatly, and placed the sphygmomanometer back on the counter beside the exam table.

Quietly padding to the table, Bee took out a thermometer. She shook it a few times and held it up to the light to ensure the red mercury read zero.

"Open your mouth and place this under your tongue. As I take your temperature, I'll also check your pulse. Next, I'll clean the cuts on your face and legs," Bee said, placing the thermometer under Audine's tongue and starting the one-minute timer with a glance at her watch to get the temperature reading.

Audine opened her mouth wide, revealing several tonsil stones and a slightly salty breath, which made Bee wrinkle her nose slightly at the odor.

Audine caught Bee's facial expression and became annoyed.

Something's wrong with her because, one, she's a liar, and two, her physical symptoms concern me. Her blood pressure is elevated, her heart and pulse are racing, and her temperature is high, indicating that an infection is present somewhere in her body. These lies and inconsistencies are alarming. The more she talks, the more information I need to provide to Bishop Almonds. But first, I'm a nurse, and I must care for her, even when she's intrusive, Bee thought to herself as she jotted down additional notes in her notepad. After the one-minute timer went off, she took the oral thermometer out of Audine's mouth and checked the reading.

"One hundred two," she said out loud.

Bee quickly jotted the finding in her notepad, a slight frown on her brow. An infection is present in her body. Now, she needs to track it down.

"Am I okay? What's wrong with me, and why are you frowning like that?" pressed Audine as she lifted herself to sit on the exam table and talk with Bee.

"Mrs. Collins, a few things are going on with you; I discovered that your temperature is elevated, your blood pressure is high, your heart and your pulse are beating rapidly, and I've only begun my examination. A doctor isn't here because several doctors are running late due to the snow and ice. However, after I examine you more thoroughly, I'll share all my findings with the doctor I work with. For now, though, I need to examine your cuts and bruises and take cultures of everything that may be infected," said Bee.

"What do you mean by my blood pressure and temperature? What are you saying to me? Am I sick? What's going on?" Audine inquired, alarmed.

"You have an infection somewhere in or outside of your body. It may be caused by wounds on your face, particularly your lip, or the infection could be a result of scratches and cuts on your legs. Please lie back down so I can examine your legs. But before I do, Mrs. Collins, have you been experiencing pain anywhere else inside or outside of your body?" Bee questioned.

Audine pulled back from Bee's stare, her head downcast, as urgent knocking at the door continued.

"I'm sorry for the interruption; wait right here; I'll be back," said Bee, gently squeezing Audine's hand.

Audine could only offer a curt nod as she wiped away a tear that spilled from the corner of her eye.

Leaning closer to the doorway, Audine saw that the exam space curtain was still closed. Audine heard another female whispering to Bee, accompanied by soft laughter. After the brief exchange, Audine quickly straightened up. Bee pulled the curtain back to tend to Audine.

"I apologize for the interruption. The head nurse informed me that an error occurred during my shift. It won't start until eleven thirty, so I'll stay until eight this evening. The good news is that I'll be paid for my hours here. Now I can take my time, run some tests on you, and see what's happening with you. So, as I was asking you earlier, are you having any pain in your body before I examine your legs?" inquired Bee.

Audine's head lifted and locked eyes with Bee's.

"I do have pain down there," she muttered miserably.

Those three devils tore into my privates until they were raw and bloody," Audine said, her eyes welling up with tears.

"I'm so sorry about that. What happened to you shouldn't happen to any woman or girl," Bee said, her voice filled with heartbreak.

"Young girl? What are you talking about? Did something happen to a young girl?" Audine asked, baffled by what she'd just heard.

"Yes," Bee replied softly. "It happened to two girls who disobeyed their parents. They snuck out of their homes while everyone was asleep to meet their boyfriends. They took a shortcut through the area where you were beaten. According to the story, when they arrived at the hospital, the two girls were walking when they were suddenly grabbed and dragged into the field by the same men. Each one took turns with the girls. The men threatened to kill their families, especially their younger siblings, if they told anyone. To make matters worse, they told the girls to return every Saturday night at the same time, or they'd come to their homes and slit the throats of their parents. So, they kept going until they couldn't anymore," Bee said.

"They hurt those girls? Oh, no, no, no! What happened?" Audine asked, her voice filled with horror.

"It was regrettable. They both ended up taking their own lives," said Bee, shaking her head. "They each left a note to their families, telling them the terrible truth about where they were on that horrible night, that it wasn't any of the boys they knew, and that they were sorry for their disobedience. The most awful thing is that after their bodies were brought to the county office for an autopsy—

"A-who?" Audine interrupted, her expression puzzled. "What is an autopsy?"

"It's when the medical examiner takes apart the entire body to determine the cause of death. I found that each of the girls had multiple old scars and broken bones. Those monsters crushed their last chance at a normal life. But everything I'm telling you, you should already know as a nurse!" Bee scolded. "Are you a nurse?"

Audine knew at that moment that Bee had been cornered, and there was no way out of that line of questioning.

"I'm so sorry to hear about what happened to those two girls! Well, those devils got what they had coming. I hope all three of them are suffering in hell," said Audine, quickly changing the subject.

Bee found Audine's behavior and her lack of basic nursing knowledge bizarre, which made her suspicious of the questions Audine asked about an autopsy, a topic well understood by the medical community.

She's definitely hiding something, and she's a liar, Bee thought to herself. I'll keep asking her about basic nursing knowledge and see how she reacts.

"I didn't mean to upset you, Mrs. Collins. That

wasn't my plan for you at all. My job is to get you well again. So, let me look at what is going on with you, okay?" asked Bee.

Audine nodded, but seemed genuinely terrified.

As Bee rolled up the sheet, she noticed the tiny red lesions and swelling on Audine's thighs. However, when she pulled the sheet higher, Bee gasped at the sight of raised lesions, which were a deep crimson. Some had burst open, oozing watery, putrid pus, prompting Bee to cover her nose.

Audine wept.

"Oh, my goodness, I've never seen anything like this. I can see why you're in pain, Mrs. Collins. When did these lesions appear?" inquired Bee. Given their appearance, this is likely why you're running a fever".

"Those things appeared hours after I was taken to Bishop Almond's home. When I was getting ready to take a bath, there were a few, but they worsened throughout the night, and it hurt so much when I went to the bathroom, and there was also blood," Audine spoke the words in a barely audible voice.

"Did those men make you roll over on your stomach and then push themselves inside you?" Bee asked, her forehead creased with concern.

Audine went silent; flashbacks of that night stole her voice. All she could do was shake her head back and forth.

"Oh my God, Mrs. Collins, this is the most ungodly thing I've ever seen, but I assure you that I will help you," said Bee.

Drawing the curtain back, Bee rushed to the medical supply room. Pulling a stainless-steel tray from the supply stack, she began selecting the necessary tools: a syringe to inject penicillin for the apparent lesions that were infected, a small acropathy jar containing wads of cotton to swab Audine's buttocks with alcohol before the injection, and a vial holding the dose of penicillin. Hurrying down the supply aisle, she selected gauze, swab sticks to take samples for a Petri dish for the lab, peroxide, and ointment for the deep gash on her lip.

My goodness, I've never seen such a horrific sight! Her lips are mangled, and some of those lesions are as big as grapes, ready to burst! I need to have her see the doctor in a week for an examination. As much as I want to help her, this is something the doctor must see—not only to treat her but also to witness it with his own eyes. Bee thought as she silently counted the medical tools needed to treat Audine. After signing out the tools she had selected, she handed the check-off slip to the supply nurse and rushed back to the exam room.

"Mrs. Collins, I've returned, and I'm going to explain to you what I'm going to do," said Bee as she yanked the curtain open. "Mrs. Collins?"

Audine sat at the edge of the exam table, shaking uncontrollably and weeping.

Bee set the tray of medical supplies on the table beside the exam table and hurried over to Audine to comfort her.

"Mrs. Collins, please listen to me. I need to be honest with you – I've never seen lesions like those on a woman's private parts before. But what I'm going to do is take care of them, along with the cuts and bruises on your body. I know it'll be uncomfortable, but I'll do it as quickly as possible. Once I'm done, it'll be over, and you'll be ready to go back to Bishop Almond's home for some rest," Bee said, wrapping her arm around Audine's shoulders.

Fearing what might occur during the exam, Audine spoke up.

"I'm scared, alone, in pain, and mixed up - especially these terrible things that look like knots between my legs and inside when I have to use the bathroom! It hurts so badly and burns! Why is this happening to me?" Audine burst into tears again.

"That's what I will do to help you find the answers. Lie back down," Bee said, assisting Audine as she settled back onto the exam bed.

"What I need you to do is open your legs as wide as possible. I'll be taking several samples from the lesions that are oozing pus. I'll also be taking samples from your private areas where those men attacked you, including your buttocks. I want to be upfront with you – this will be uncomfortable, but I promise to be gentle and quick," Bee reassured her.

With her eyes closed, Audine clasped Bee's hand and put her trust in Bee to handle the procedure.

Taking the cotton swab, Bee searched for a lesion and found a large, angry-looking one that was already draining. However, upon gently pressing it, it burst, oozing yellow-green pus. Audine yelped in pain and covered her face with her hands. Collecting the infection by gently twirling, she saturated the swab and carefully smeared the contents on a glass slide for the lab to examine. She wrote the words "Infection-Urgent" on the outside of the cardboard into which the slide was inserted. Then she sealed it and wrote Audine's information. Pulling her notepad from her pocket, she scribbled additional notes about the procedure and moved on to the next task.

"Stay with me, Mrs. Collins; I'm almost done. I'm going to take one more sample, and then I'll tend to your wounds," said Bee. "I'm going to ask you to open your legs so that you can—"

"Open my legs for what? I'm in so much pain right now! Can't you give me medicine to make this all go away?" questioned Audine, horror-stricken.

"Not until I get one more sample for our lab, so the doctor can figure out how to treat what you have. I promise to do this quickly, and then we can grab some coffee while you wait to pick up your medication. Now, please, bend your knees and spread your legs", said Bee, keeping her voice down.

Audine complied with the request, hesitantly took deep breaths, and spread her legs apart.

As she pulled the bright lamp closer to investigate, Bee had to do a double-take at what she saw. The lesions on Audine's inner thighs were massive, angry-looking, and filled with infection, and they were huge and grotesque.

Bee was mortified.

Reaching for the sterile gloves that surgeons use, Bee first saturated a sterile cloth with alcohol and scrubbed her hands. The strong scent wafted into her nostrils, causing her eyes to sting. Blinking rapidly to refocus, she pulled the gloves from the package, slipped them on, and arranged several slides and swabs to collect the samples. She then began the procedure.

A foul-smelling, green discharge oozed out continuously. Gathering the specimen tools, Bee used two swabs to collect the unusual infection.

Audine let out a deep, painful moan. The strain from her abdomen caused the discharge to ooze out so quickly that it puddled and spread on the sheeted exam table.

"Please, stop! This hurts, and I feel like I'm going to wet myself! I'm so ashamed right now, please stop!" Audine said, sobbing in agony.

"I'm done. As soon as I bag the slides, I'm going to wash my hands and treat your wounds," said Bee.

Taking a damp cloth, Bee strategically wiped the excess infection from Audine's orifice, which continued to flow.

I'll be sure to send her back with a bag full of sanitary pads; her underwear must be completely soaked with this flow of infection, Bee thought to herself as she slid a towel under Audine's bottom.

After bagging the lab specimens, Bee removed her gloves and disposed of them in the trash can. She sanitized her hands again by washing them with soap and hot water, then set aside the bag containing

Audine's specimens and gathered the tools to treat Audine's legs and the gash on her lip. Pushing the tray to the foot of the exam table, she examined the abrasions.

"Mrs. Collins, the gashes on your legs are not as deep as they appear. The good news is that you bathed in a tub, which was good because that cleaned up any dirt that may have been in the snow," said Bee as she took a large wad of cotton and clamped it with the pickups. Taking iodine, she poured a small amount and mixed it with hydrogen peroxide, then applied it to the wound.

"What is that? What are you doing? Owwweee!" screamed Audine. The stinging and fizzing sensation was beyond anything that could be described as pain.

Audine's fingers curled into fists, her eyes scrunched shut, and her teeth clenched tightly.

Oh God, when will this pain end? Audine wondered to herself.

The pain intensified as Bee repeated the process on the lesions, particularly the broken ones and those with oozing infections. Bee disregarded Audine's cries and instructed her to stop. It was only after the final application of the salve that it felt remarkably cool and numbed the pain.

After the final peroxide application, a clear salve was applied to the cut on her lip. The examination and treatment of her wounds were finally complete.

"Mrs. Collins, I've completed my examination and treated your wounds. I will take the samples to the lab to drop off and then retrieve clean underwear from our supply closet for you. The ones you wore are soiled, so I want you to wait in here while I get you a bag of undergarments and sanitary napkins to wear," said Bee as she parted the curtain to exit.

"Sanitary napkins, what for? I don't have my monthly flow," said Audine, sitting and pulling the sheet to cover herself.

"I know, but the lesions that you have are draining, and you are discharging rapidly as if you're on a monthly flow. The sanitary napkins will absorb the infection, and you'll need to change them often to prevent reinfection. I'm going to ask Dr. Walker to sign off on your medicine. He's late today and therefore busy, which is why I can only do minor things besides prescribing medicines. He'll have to review the notes I wrote about you during your examination. Get dressed, but don't wear your underwear because it's soiled. Wait until my return with fresh underthings," said Bee as she hurried out of the exam room and disappeared behind the curtain and out the door.

As Audine sat on the exam table, she tried to piece together the events of the past forty-eight hours. The end of her marriage and the loss of her baby in New York replayed in her mind. Meanwhile, Maria St. Laurent's life was in stark contrast. Despite losing her husband, Clarence, Maria had her children, a farm, and another baby on the way. She also had a supportive network of friends and still looked radiant, even with another child on the way.

My saving grace in this is Bishop Thomas Almonds, and I'll make myself look so beautiful that Sathronia will have no choice but to surrender and leave. Audine thought to herself, forcing a weak smile through the tears that spilled onto her face, quickly wiping them away.

She pushed herself off the table and looked back

over her shoulder.

"What the heck is this mess? This stuff came out of me?" she said, clutching her chest.

Stepping back, Audine stared at the filthy exam table. Inching closer, she saw a substantial greenish-yellow circle mixed with blood and infection that had pooled where Bee was taking specimens. The odor was putrid, making her turn away, and she covered her nose. Ambling backward, she bumped into the stainless-steel table. Whirling around, she gasped at what she saw. Bee's tools were daunting; the pick-ups still had a wad of bloody gauze used to absorb the infection.

Struggling to process everything that had happened, she shook her head until she felt dizzy. Once she had composed herself, she quickly dressed, except for the soiled underwear, which she balled up and tossed into the trash bin. Then, she felt a gush between her legs. Pulling up her dress, she watched in horror as dark yellow pus tinged with green oozed down her thigh onto her leg.

"Hello?" a woman's voice from behind the door, followed by two quick, sharp knocks.

"Bee, is that you? Come in, please! I-I've had an accident! Did you get me the sanitary napkins and fresh underwear? I can't go out like this; can you help me? Oh, no!" Audine burst into tears, sobbing.

The curtain was pulled open, and a woman with the most immense brown eyes locked gazes with Audine in an implacable stare. She was dressed in a brown uniform trimmed with beige edges. On her upper right sleeve was the hospital's emblem, which all staff, from medical personnel to cleaning crew, wore. Her hair was pulled back into a tight bun secured with bobby pins. Behind her was a mop bucket filled with hot water, and the deep pockets of her uniform held several filthy rags. She carried a faint odor of sweat. Audine wrinkled her nose in disgust at the woman.

"I thought you were my nurse, Bee," said Audine dryly. "Why are you here?"

"Well, I'm here to clean this room for the next patient, ma'am, and your nurse, Miss Huggs, is on her way back. She went next door to the pharmacy to get medicine; excuse me, but you seem to have had an accident. Here, let me help you. I will get a towel for you," said the woman.

She walked over to a shelf, grabbed a towel from the tidy rack of hospital towels, and handed it to Audine.

"Here you go," she said, handing it to Audine.

Instead of showing humility and gratitude, Audine grabbed it from her hand. She shamelessly lifted her dress, spread her legs, and pressed the towel between her gaped legs just in time before she felt another gush. Tilting her head back, Audine squeezed her eyes shut and strained as if she were giving birth. Finally, the gushing stopped. Carefully pulling the towel out, Audine tilted her head downward to examine the contents. The contents on the towel shocked Audine; the infection was thick and a deep, almost greenish yellow, with an olive hue. Audine glanced up to see that she had an audience of one; the woman's eyes were wide with shock as she stared at the lesions. Audine glared at her.

"What are you staring at, huh? Why, you nosy piece of nothing! Do you like what you see? Answer me!" she demanded, her voice fierce.

"Ma'am, I meant no harm; I'm very sorry if I was

staring at you. I didn't mean it, and I can take that towel and hand you another one- "

They were interrupted when the door opened.

"What's going on here?" Bee asked.

As the curtain parted, Audine and the cleaning woman looked over to see Bee holding a large brown bag and a smaller one containing Audine's medication.

"I-I came here to clean this room and prepare it for the next patient, Nurse Huggs. It's gotten busy, and some doctors are still running late. I didn't know anyone was still in this room, but that proved to be a blessing because look at what happened here; your patient had an accident and- "

"She was watching me! I hardly had any clothes on, and she-she-she just burst into this room without knocking to see who I was; what a nerve! Toilet scrubbers, hah! They never have any sense!" snorted Audine.

"Nurse Huggs, that's not true!" the cleaning woman said, her patience fraying as she stood firm. Her shoulders were stiff with determination.

"Don't worry; I know it's your policy to knock on the door and announce yourself. As soon as Mrs. Collins is dressed, you may go ahead and clean this room, Amalie," said Bee. "Give Mrs. Collins five more minutes to get ready," said Bee.

"Thank you, Nurse Huggs," said Amalie, shaken. As she stepped outside, she took a deep breath and let out a sigh.

Amalie? Hah! What a ridiculous name! What's it supposed to mean, anyway? Maybe a janitor or something? Oh, wait, a toilet scrubber! Audine thought to herself, a smirk creeping onto one side of her face.

Bee observed Audine's exchange with utter disgust and shook her head.

"Mrs. Collins, I have a few things to give you. I'll go over how and when to take your medications. Inside this bag is a month's supply of your prescriptions, as well as twenty extra sanitary pads, so you won't have to worry about staining your underwear during your period. You should have enough to last until you start earning money to pay for your supplies. After you get dressed, we can grab coffee, and by the time we're finished talking, Ezra will be here to pick you up," Bee said, placing the bag at the foot of the exam table.

"Thank you, I'll be ready in a moment, and thank you for the clean underwear and sanitary napkins and for getting that toilet scrubber. Amalie soothing? Humph, if you ask me, it's a very silly name," said Audine.

"You're right, Mrs. Collins, I *didn't* ask you. Please hurry because I now have fifty-five minutes before my shift starts, and it's getting busy," she added firmly. Bee closed the exam curtain to give Audine privacy and waited outside the door.

Just as Audine was about to give her a glare, Bee vanished.

I wanted to ask her if Bishop Almonds would be with Ezra. Hmph! I guess I'll have to ask her when we grab coffee, which I know she'll be paying for, Audine thought to herself as she pulled out a clean pair of underwear from the bag, which was packed with sanitary napkins and six more pairs of underwear.

After smoothing her dress, fixing her hair as best she could, and snapping the garters once more to ensure they were secure, Audine carried her purse in the crook of her arm and draped her coat over it. Pulling open the curtain to the exam room, Audine whirled around to glance at the chaotic mess on the soiled exam table.

"Let the toilet scrubber clean up the mess," Audine muttered.

As Audine stepped out of the room and into the hallway, she felt like she'd entered a different world – one that existed just an hour ago. The hallway was packed with people: women cradling their crying babies, doctors being called to various rooms, and a man being supported by two friends because he couldn't walk. Up close, Audine noticed that his foot was badly mangled and bleeding through the rags wrapped around it. He cried out in pain; four women whose husbands were in rooms were wailing in agony, waiting to give birth. Bee peeked into their rooms to offer encouragement and let them know she'd help the doctor with the delivery. Their husbands were in a shared waiting room with other men pacing back and forth, whose wives were also in labor.

"It's gotten busier than expected. I'll likely be here until eleven this evening, but that's fine with me; I love being a nurse at this hospital," declared Bee.

"Oh, I can see that, especially when the women who are having their babies seem to know you," said Audine, captivated by the organized chaos unfolding around her.

"They're all members of Bishop Almond's church. They're the wives of the deacons who oversee every dollar and cent that comes in and out of the church," said Bee.

As they turned the corner, a loud flush came from the ladies' bathroom, startling Audine. Amalie stepped out, holding a mop and bucket that overflowed with foul-smelling water, reeking of vomit.

"Hello again, Amalie. How's your pace this morning?" asked Bee, pausing to chat with Amalie.

"So far, three of the four expectant women vomited, they wet themselves in the bathroom, and two others had a bad case of diarrhea. They didn't make it on time and got it all over the toilet seat. I've had a busy morning, but I'm on my way to clean your patient's room," Amalie answered. Amalie shot Audine an explosive glare. Audine shrank back from her gaze, a smirk forced on one side of her face.

"Despite everything, you do your best to keep this hospital clean. I'm sorry you had to do it alone after several workers called out today due to the bad weather a few days ago," said Bee.

"I'll manage; it may take longer, but at the end of the day, all the rooms, including the bathrooms, will be clean as if nothing happened. I'd better go now because I need to clean the room where you did your examination," said Amalie.

"Thanks for everything," Bee said with appreciation.

"Yes, thanks, especially for your help. Amalie, you seem like the perfect toilet scrubber. I tossed my soiled underwear in the trash. I wasn't sure where to put them. But I figured you'd know what to do," said Audine, letting out a sarcastic laugh.

Amalie, who was striding away, stopped suddenly

after hearing the obnoxious tone in Audine's voice and slammed the bucket down, spilling some of its contents on the pristine corridor floor. Turning to face her, she quickly advanced toward Audine, her hands curled into fists on her hips.

Audine tried to back away, but it was too late. Amalie's face was inches from Audine's, their noses almost touching.

"I may be a toilet scrubber and worker in Chicago's only hospital for the colored, and I love what this hospital is doing for our people, which is saving many lives! Your remarks and how you treated me show that you're a woman with no proper concern for your own!" she expressed, pointing to her skin color by sliding her hand across her arm. "Perhaps one day you'll work here as a toilet scrubber to humble your big-headed ass!" snorted Amaline, delivering Audine a smile full of knives and needles.

"Good day to you, Mrs. Collins!" she snapped.

With her hand over her mouth, Audine was struck into shameful silence by the sharp rebuke. She glanced over at Bee, hoping Amalie's comment would be her defense.

She glanced at her watch, avoiding eye contact with Audine.

Amalie pulled out a fresh rag from her pocket. She walked over to the small, smelly puddle near the bucket, took out a small vial of alcohol, and sprinkled several drops onto the cloth until the odor filled the corridor. She squatted down, scrubbed the area, and it was soon free of the puddle and any spills. Standing up, she folded the rag into a neat square, put it back in her pocket, picked up the bucket and mop, and walked away, blending in with the busy corridor.

Bee pulled out her handkerchief and pretended to cough, laughing so hard that tears spilled down the sides of her eyes.

Audine's mouth was agape in disbelief as she watched Amalie proudly stride down the bustling corridor until the head of the mop vanished.

"Did-did you hear what she said to me?" I hope this gets reported to your superior!" protested Audine, visibly shaken by the unexpected admonishment from a toilet scrubber!

"Mrs. Collins, the cafeteria is around the corner, so let's go for coffee so that I can explain how to use the medication prescribed for you," interrupted Bee, who was not in the mood to hear any of Audine's protests.

Audine didn't respond to anything further as they rounded the corner. Already, the aroma of freshly brewed coffee perked up her nostrils. As soon as they walked into the hospital cafeteria, Audine noticed that it was significantly more extensive than the one she had worked at while living in New Orleans. The cafeteria was preparing lunch, but the coffee was plentiful.

Audine and Bee headed to the counter.

"Mrs. Collins, how do you take your coffee?" inquired Bee.

Hmm, I'll take mine with cream and sugar," said Audine.

The faint aroma of bacon and ham made Audine's mouth water, despite having demolished a hearty breakfast, much to the disdain of Sathronia. The thought of it brought a smile to Audine's face.

Bees handed the coffee order to the clerk and paid a dime for two cups.

"Let's sit over here," Bee said, guiding them to a corner table for some privacy.

After they had taken their seats, Audine carefully picked up the cup and blew on it several times before savoring the first sip of the brew.

She closed her eyes and savored the rich flavor of the slightly strong brew that she would enjoy for the rest of the morning.

"Let's discuss the medication you'll be taking," Bee said. She took a quick sip of coffee and glanced at her watch.

"It looks like you have a cut on your lip and some bruising on your face," she said, reaching into the brown bag and pulling out a glass bottle filled with clear liquid.

"Twice a day, you must apply the peroxide to your lips. Do that after you've brushed your teeth. At first, it may sting, and you'll see a lot of tiny bubbles. Don't be concerned about that, as it's a normal part of the process of eliminating the infection. I also packed another smaller box of cotton for you to use on your lips," said Bee, who demonstrated how to use the cotton and peroxide.

For the lesions, discharge, and pain, I can provide a salve. Apply a small amount, about the size of a nickel, to each leg. This should help ease the pain and, over time, reduce the lesions. As for your fever, it's best to rest and stay in bed for a week. Take a spoonful of the tincture each evening before bedtime, and keep taking it until the bottle is finished," she said, holding up a bottle with a thick red syrup and tiny black specks.

"What's that stuff?" Audine asked in a defiant tone. "I've never seen anything like that before! I'm too scared to take it! I'm not taking that horrible-looking—"

"Oh, you will take this tincture," interrupted Bee, steadily losing patience with Audine. "You'll take this tincture because it was created by one of our beloved doctors who's been using this on colored children when he was visiting those children going door-to-door. The number of sick babies and children he saved is nothing short of a God-sent miracle! We don't dare share the information with the white hospitals about this medicine;

several children who survived into adulthood were so grateful that they went to medical school to become doctors and nurses. Ten of them work in this hospital!" she said, tapping the table.

"Oh, I didn't know that. So why won't the medicine and tincture be given to white hospitals? I would think the doctor would get rich by selling it," Audine said, sipping her coffee, but she was interrupted again by Bee, who was infuriated by Audine's comments.

"Money? Selling a tincture that saved hundreds of colored children in our community? Either you're not paying attention or completely ignorant!" seethed Bee. "First of all, if white hospital officials found out about this tincture, we'd all be out of our jobs! They'd shut down this hospital, and the doctor who discovered this tincture could end up in prison for life! Then what would happen is the white hospitals would take the tincture and have their laws claim *that they* invented the formula, using it to save their own, while our people wither and eventually die! And one more thing, Mrs. Collins, I was one of those ten children who survived, and I have since dedicated my life to becoming a nurse! And another thing: If it hadn't been for Bishop Almonds, I wouldn't be the nurse I am today!" snapped Bee.

Audine froze, her coffee cup suspended in mid-air, as she was taken aback by the revelation from Bee and the firm tone in her voice.

Amalie sat in a dimly lit corner near an exit, remaining quiet and keeping a low profile as she absorbed every word Bee spilled to Audine. After Amalie finished her coffee and the last bite of hot buttered cornbread, she quietly slipped out of her chair and carefully opened the exit door, closing it behind her to avoid the loud "clack" noise it made when swinging shut. She departed secretly, wishing to be a fly on the wall to hear Bee tear down Audine Collins. The thought made her smile widely, and she worked quickly and efficiently for the rest of the day. "Use-ter the rooster doesn't crow no mo!" she thought, laughing out loud.

CHAPTER TWENTY-FIVE

Things were getting chaotic with the nonstop sound of the cash register and hearing the clerk say "thank you, doctor" or "thank you, nurse" as they took payments.

"Thanks, ma'am, I hope you enjoy your coffee," the clerk said with a smile as Bee and Audine chatted on their way back for another round of coffee.

Audine did a double-take at the beautiful young woman.

Violet. Sweet Jesus, she was the spitting image of her.

Audine's eyes widened, and she felt a tingling in her chest. Memories of that horrible day came flooding back like a tidal wave: the screaming, the sight of suitcases by the door, hearing Mason's announcement about seeing Clarence on top of Violet, her legs spread wide open as Clarence deposited his filthy seed into her and made a child. Audine couldn't help but blink back tears that swelled and spilled from her eyes. She felt someone's hand on her shoulder, making her cringe and causing her to spill coffee onto the saucer.

"Mrs. Collins, are you okay?"

Audine jerked her head around to the voice. It was Bee who had a worried expression.

"She looks like my daughter, Violet, the woman I paid. I-I-I'm feeling sick right now," she sputtered in a low, pained whisper.

"Come with me, Mrs. Collins, and sit down. Let's discuss what's going on. I still have another half hour, and Ezra will be on his way soon," said Bee as she took the coffee cup from Audine's trembling hand.

"Grab my arm," said Bee, offering the crook of her arm for Audine to steady herself.

"Thank you," whispered Audine. A tear slipped down the side of her nose. The walk felt like three yards and a cloud of dust.

With caution, Bee balanced the steaming hot coffee and set it down on the table, then helped Audine lower herself into her seat.

Audine's tears flowed freely. Bee reached into her uniform pocket and pulled out a handkerchief.

"Thanks, Bee," Audine said, wiping away her tears and gently blowing her nose.

"I'm sorry, Mrs. Collins," Bee said, taking a quick sip of coffee.

"About what?" she asked, her voice suddenly flat.

"What you've been through and what happened when you paid the clerk - did something about her remind you of your daughter?" Bee asked.

Audine set her coffee cup down on the saucer, and her dismay was clear on her face.

"How-how, did you know?" stammered Audine.

"I saw it in your eyes, that look of disbelief as if you'd seen a ghost. My mother gave me the same look when I showed up at Bishop Almond's church a few years ago," said Bee.

Audine suddenly became captivated by Bee's story. Thoughts of Violet, Clarence, Mason, and Wayne vanished. Audine wiped her tears and focused entirely on Bee.

"I was alone and lost," Bee started.

"Lost? What do you mean by that?" Audine asked, giving her a tilted look.

Bee released a stifled breath to begin her bittersweet story to Audine, a stranger.

"Before joining Bishop Almond's church, I felt alone and lost. I was engaged to a man whom I believed had honorable intentions. He was tall and handsome, with a steady job that allowed him to afford a car and a room in a boarding house for working men. He always drove me to my nursing classes when I was a student, and I was doing very well in my studies. It seemed that whenever we got close to doing things that married folks do, I'd have to stop him because I didn't want to have an accident," she said, trying to keep her voice steady.

Audine suddenly became intrigued and sat up straight, forgetting the scene that had just unfolded moments before.

Oh-ho! So, Miss Perfect Nurse has problems, hah!

Audine thought to herself, amused, sporting a crooked half-smile. Pretending to cough, Audine suppressed her wickedness with a few sips of her coffee, then slowly set the cup down on the saucer and dabbed the corners of her lips with her napkin.

"I'm sorry to hear about the story you're going to tell me, but it'll help to hear it and ease my pain," Audine said. "Please tell me everything," she coaxed, waving her hand.

"I only let him do a little, like squeeze and kiss my breasts, but that was it. After a while, he stopped calling me, and he even missed picking me up from class a few times. My mom warned me he wasn't good for me and to stop seeing him. I told her he was probably busy at work and didn't have time. So, I focused even more on my studies. When it was time for my pre-practice at the hospital, I wasn't hiding my excitement about being assigned to the maternity floor. I was going to observe how they prepared women for surgery and how they took them to the operating room for delivery. One day, as I was reviewing my charts, a young woman walked in who couldn't have been more than twenty. I asked if she needed any help," Bee said.

"My water broke, and my husband had to go to the toilet room. This is our first baby; we got married a week ago," the twenty-year-old girl said to Bee, smiling broadly as she circled her protruding belly with the palm of her hand and cupped her lower back with the other.

I smiled back and congratulated her. I asked for her name and asked her to wait while I pulled out her file. I informed her that I would call the doctor to let him know she was there. Then I heard a man's familiar voice. I spun around, and it was him, Patrick, my suitor, with whom I was deeply in love! He stood there, shocked to see me. All I could do was gaze at his left hand," said Bee.

"His left hand? Why were you looking at his left hand?" Audine questioned.

Raising her cup of coffee to her lips, Bee took a few short sips before setting the cup down on the saucer.

"Since he was wearing a gold wedding ring, just like the woman who locked her arm into his, Patrick was married to her," she said, gazing into her coffee cup with her head down.

"Humph, it seems your mother was right all along; you should've listened to her," Audine snapped, having a brief flash of Violet's affair with Clarence and the shock of her pregnancy. Audine squeezed her eyes shut for a moment, trying to shake off the memory, but all she could visualize was Clarence's baby growing inside Violet's belly. "So, what did you do?" Audine asked.

"All I remember was the clipboard crashing to the floor and everything turning black. When I woke up, I was lying on a hospital bed. The nurse was checking my blood pressure and pulse, and I had a cold, damp towel across my head. When I tried to get out of bed, everything spun around, and my head hurt. Suddenly, I realized why Patrick had stopped calling me. He was seeing that girl all the time!" exclaimed Bee, taking another quick sip of coffee.

Audine's eyes widened as she leaned in closer to hear Bee's sorrowful story. Yet, deep down, Audine felt giddy, realizing that someone as smart as Bee could be so stupid, exactly like Violet. They were like two dumb flies caught in a venomous spider's web of lies.

"So, then what happened?" Audine asked.

"Humph, I didn't attend class for a week. I failed all the basic tests and didn't care about anything anymore. All I know is that I cried all the time. Patrick broke my heart. After a week, my mother burst into my room. She told me to get up, clean my room, change the bed sheets, and then take a bath. She went to the window and opened it as far as it could go."

"Why did she open the window?" Audine asked.

"At that moment, she fell to her knees and began praying loudly and intensely, speaking in tongues until the spirit of hurt and pain left our house, my room, and me. When she finished, I found myself sitting on the floor beside my mother, holding me tightly until her prayer ended. After we cleaned up my room and got it back in order, I took a hot bath, put on some makeup, and headed to my room to get dressed. To my surprise, my mother had already laid out a dress, polished my shoes, set out fresh underthings, and placed my purse on my bed".

"Hurry up and get dressed, Bee. Our ride's arriving in ten minutes; let's go!" her mother called from the bottom of the stairs.

"Humph, I never dressed so fast in my life! As soon as I ran down the stairs, she shoved a warm jelly biscuit into my hand. I heard a car horn, and Mother almost pushed me out the door, hah! I shoved the biscuit in my mouth and went outside. As Mother locked the door, the car driver rushed over to open the door for me. His name was Ezra, and he was dressed in a gray suit and wore a small pin on his lapel," said Bee, smiling at her memory.

"Why was Ezra wearing a pin?" Audine asked, raising her eyebrows.

"Because he was and still is a deacon. All of them wear a pin in the shape of the cross on their suit lapel," Bee answered, taking another quick slurp of coffee.

"Humph. Never heard of such a thing," Audine muttered to herself, loud enough for Bee to overhear.

Bee dismissed Audine's comment and continued her story, ignoring her altogether.

"We rode for half an hour. Ezra and my mother

talked while I sat in the back seat, next to the window, gazing outside. Suddenly, as we approached the church, I heard drums, trumpets, trombones, and cymbals clanging. I looked around to see if there was a parade, but there wasn't. As Ezra gradually moved closer to the roadside, the sounds of the instruments came from the most beautiful church I'd ever seen in my life, and it was glorious! We had to walk up many stairs, so Mother and I took Ezra by the crook of his elbows; Mother was on the right, and I was on the left. When we finally reached the door, he opened it for us to walk through. He took Mother by the arm, and I followed behind them. As soon as we walked through another set of doors, I couldn't believe what I saw and heard! People were on their feet shouting the Lord's name, jumping, clapping, singing, and beating tambourines! Standing at the front, on the left side of the church, were men in black pants, white shirts, and black ties, blowing their horns so loudly that it felt as if heaven and God were rushing down from the sky! We were escorted to the third row while Ezra went to the other side to sit with his wife. We prayed, sang, and jumped to the music for the rest of the evening, and then Bishop Almonds began to preach. It was as if he was a man whose spirit and speaking in holy tongues were overpowered by the holy spirit," said Bee as she gently swayed from side to side in her chair.

"Wait, you went to a church with drums, horns, and tambourines? Humph, I've never heard of anything like that! It must have been a total mess!" Audine said, bursting into laughter.

Bee, clearly mortified by Audine's failure to observe protocol by keeping her mouth shut and listening, reacted by shooting a glare at Audine, then shook her head and continued.

"Bishop Almonds then started prophesying to us. He had four deacons, and their wives stand up first. He told their wives that their days of being childless would be over and that within two months, each of them would be expecting a baby. Then he went to each of their wives and gently pressed on their stomachs. Each one fell into the arms of their husbands, who were openly crying tears of joy. Then he came over to where I was sitting," Bee said, wiping away tears and gently blowing her nose.

"What did he say to you?" Audine asked.

"Bishop said that no good, wayward man would ever marry you, daughter. He knew all along that he would never be with a crown jewel! You will marry a man who'll be worthy, live a holy life, and be a true man without a wayward eye and dishonest intent, and a hard-working man a year from now! Consider this prophecy done; I declared it, and it will be done! That man who went behind your back will reap what he has sown, and his punishment, so be exceedingly glad because he did you a favor, daughter, so your blessing will be unblocked!" said Bee, her swaying in the chair picking up speed.

Audine glanced around to see if anyone was watching them, especially Bee, who was getting increasingly excited as she shared her story.

She thought to herself, if she even thinks about getting the Holy Ghost in this cafeteria, I'm out of here in a flash! Audine stared wide-eyed at Bee.

"What happened to me was nothing short of remarkable because Bishop snatched my left hand into his and squeezed it so hard that I was screaming!" said

Bee.

"What? He squeezed your left hand? Why'd he do that to you?" Audine asked, unable to take another sip of her coffee without losing track of what Bee was saying.

"It got to the point when I found myself bending down at my waist; I mean, I was bent down so low that two of the female ushers were behind me with a sheet just in case I fell to the floor. But I was trying to yank my hand from his tight grip. The more I resisted, the more he squeezed. Well, I finally felt something come out of my body," said Bee.

"What came out?" asked Audine, sitting on the edge of her chair.

"I opened my mouth and let out a scream so loud that I fell backward into the arms of my mother and the two women holding the sheet to break my fall. As they lowered me to the floor, I remember Bishop Almond commanding that spirit to leave me and set me free from Patrick's trickery and lies. After that, everything went black, and I woke up in the arms of those women and my mother. Bishop lifted me and hugged me for a long time. I couldn't move even if I tried. Then he bent down to my ear and whispered:

"That spirit that held you back is gone. I made a prophecy that you would meet someone, fall in love, get married within a year, and graduate at the top of your class, landing a job as one of the best nurses in the hospital where you would work. Four seeds will be planted in your belly, one for each of the next four years," Bee said, wiping away tears with a napkin.

Audine sat there, speechless and stunned by what she was hearing.

So, Bishop Almonds is a prophet? Oh my goodness! This changes everything for me! I'll stand right by his side. A man who can preach, bring in money for the church, and prophesy! As soon as I'm healed, take these medicines, get rid of Sathronia, and join his church. Then, I'll become a leader, and he'll have no choice but to pay attention to me and only me! And before I get rid of Sathronia, I need to figure out how she makes that delicious coffee cream I love. Humph, I could use some now because this coffee tastes worse than the Mississippi River! Audine thought to herself as she took a sip of the still-hot coffee.

"So, what happened to you after Bishop did his prophesying? Did anything come true for you?" Audine asked.

Bee's gaze was fixed on Audine with a look of horror.

As Audine reached for the coffee cup and took another sip, Bee's annoyance at Audine's casual remarks became more apparent. Nevertheless, Bee continued telling her story.

"No, as a matter of fact, Bishop home-visited with me several times after I attended that service; he encouraged me to forget Patrick, that wayward man, as he'd called him. But there was one thing Bishop said about Patrick that did come true," said Bee.

"Oh, and what was that?" Audine joked.

"That Patrick would reap what he's sown. Patrick turned out to be a good-for-nothing man. I found out from one of my friends who knew his aunt. She said that soon after he and his twenty-year-old wife took the baby home, all hell broke loose in their house," she said, smirking.

"Their house went up in flames?" Audine asked.

"No, that's an expression Bishop likes to use when bad things happen to people who do bad things to God-fearing people like me," said Bee. "Patrick had to take on a new job driving for rich people, and he ended up losing his room at the boarding house because he now had a wife and baby. So, he and his twenty-year-old wife had to move to a one-bedroom flat. To pay the bills and keep what little scraps of food he could buy for his wife, the baby, and himself, he'd drive early in the morning until late at night. One day, his boss told him he could go home early since he had been working late for the last two weeks, driving. Patrick went home, and when he entered the house, everything was gone. A note was on the pillow from his wife, and she said that she couldn't hide the lie about the baby anymore; that it wasn't his. She'd been seeing a man named Peter Norman, a fifty-six-year-old wealthy man whose mother was half Black and father was White. He owns several flats from which he collects rent. Norman and Patrick's wife had a big fight, and he told her to leave. But she didn't realize she already had a baby growing inside her. So, after being with Patrick for only a few weeks, she lied and said the baby was his! After seeing Mr. Norman again and telling him about the baby, he counted the times they'd been together, told her to pack her things, and said he'd get her marriage to Patrick annulled, which he did for her. And that's not all. When Patrick got paid the day before all this happened, he tucked all his cash inside a wooden box under his bed. He'd already saved over five hundred dollars, a year's worth of money! From what I was told, she went into the box and scooped up every last dollar! Patrick had no money and had to pay rent to the woman who collected the money for the flat he stayed in! And guess what?" said Bee.

"What, tell me!" Audine exclaimed, perched on the edge of the chair, poised to slide right off.

"Mr. Norman owned the flat and had Patrick thrown out because he couldn't pay! Hah! Served him right, especially after what he did to me! So, Bishop was right; Patrick got what he deserved," said Bee, sipping her coffee.

Shivers nipped at Audine's spine as she listened to

Bee's story. She briefly closed her eyes, and memories of Wayne flooded back, hitting her with a sense of dread. She remembered consoling him when he got home to find the money and Lena gone. The irony was that Wayne had ultimately come out on top.

And I was told to leave, Audine thought to herself, her grief over the loss of her marriage welling up inside her as she swallowed hard.

"Mrs. Collins, are you alright?" Bee asked, his gaze fixed on Audine.

Audine, realizing she had become lost in thought, snapped to attention.

Uh, yes. I'm okay, Bee. I was thinking of getting another cup of coffee. But go ahead and tell me what happened. If you don't mind, I'd love to hear more about Bishop Almonds and the church," Audine said.

"Why do you want to know about the church, especially anything about Bishop Almonds?" Bee asked, suspiciously.

Audine fidgeted in her seat, clearly uneasy.

"Uh, uh, whelp, I'm new here, and uh, Bishop

Almonds and his wife are such wonderful people! I thought that if I stayed there for a while, I should try to get to know them, just like I did with you. I feel like I've already made a new friend with you," Audine said.

Audine's behavior is questionable, but why not if she needs a friend? However, being friends with Audine Collins would require constant vigilance. Keep your eyes looking straight ahead, Bee thought, smiling sweetly at Audine.

"After hearing what happened to Patrick, I immediately called Bishop. He said it didn't surprise him because one of the deacons at the church had spotted Patrick with two suitcases heading to the train station. But enough talk about Patrick. Bishop Almonds invited me to return to church. Each Sunday I attended, I felt happiness again. Because of Bishop, I've become more accomplished at reading the Bible. I got baptized and started attending other services during the week. Bishop encouraged me to read the Bible for an hour each day to keep my mind off Patrick and focus on returning to nursing school. I joined several auxiliaries at his suggestion, and he helped me get back into nursing school! A month before Easter, I was at one of the auxiliary meetings. Bishop came in, walked directly up to the leader, and slipped a note into her hand; she opened it and read it. After nodding in agreement and folding the note, she walked over to me and whispered that Bishop wanted me to go to his office immediately. So, I gathered my belongings and dashed to his office. I gave his office door two short taps and heard him say, 'Come inside.' I opened the door and went in, and he and another man stood up as soon as I entered. Bishop is very tall, but so is the man in his office. I couldn't keep my eyes off him. His complexion resembled Bishop's; it was more like a roasted cashew. They could pass as brothers! Anyway, Bishop introduced me to him. His name was Isaiah Ford, and he was a schoolteacher," said Bee.

"Was? I don't understand. He was a schoolteacher?" Why did he come here to Chicago? Was he looking for work?" inquired Audine, who wished Bee would stop blabbering so much. Hurry up and get to the point!

"Quite the opposite. I learned that he had taken

the job as the high school's principal here in Bronzeville! He came from Washington, D.C., and taught school for fifteen years. The high school's principal was not liked at all. As it happens, he went missing for three weeks. Then, one day, he was found dead in the flat he lived in," said Bee.

"Dead? Oh my goodness, what happened to him?" Audine asked with a sudden surge of interest.

"Psst, move in closer so that people won't hear us," said Bee as she gestured for Audine to come closer.

Audine scooched in as close as she could to hear this juicy morsel of information.

"His name was Mr. Reys. He was a real piece of work - mean-spirited and unfair to the students. Whenever a male student misbehaved or caused trouble in class, he'd drag them to his office. From what I heard, he'd make them drop their pants to their underwear and sit in a chair. Reys would motion the student to come over and bend across his lap. He'd tape their mouth shut, then rub their bare behind, kiss it, and give them twenty hard whacks with a heavy wooden paddle. After that, he'd take his hand and squeeze so hard that the student would scream through the tape. Then he'd give them another ten whacks until they stopped screaming. Next, he'd pick the student up and unzip his pants, making the student fondle him until he came. After ripping off the tape, he'd tell the student to keep quiet and ask if they'd be good in class for him. If the student said yes, he'd be over the moon and warn them not to tell anyone what happened in his office, or he'd find their parents and kill them. It was always the same thing, no matter how minor the offense. One day, the same boy who was Rey's favorite became fed up and paid him a visit with a loaded gun. Reys was thrilled to see him and invited him to his bedroom. When the boy walked in, he spotted a chair, a paddle, and a rag to tie his mouth. Reys ordered him to undress, this time telling him to take off all his clothes and lie across his lap. After tying the rag across the boy's mouth, Reys sat down and motioned for him to bend across his lap. He rubbed the boy's behind, then grabbed the paddle and gave him a beating. But here's the thing - Reys did something different. He told the boy not to get dressed. Reys, with his back to the boy, continued undressing, and that's when the boy aimed the gun at the back of

Reys' head and pulled the trigger. I hate to admit it, but he got exactly what he deserved," Bee said.

"So, what's the boy's current situation, and how did you find out all these details about the story?" Audine interrupted.

Bee cast a sharp gaze at Audine before she responded.

"Word gets around here, Mrs. Collins. Chicago is indeed a big city, and as Black people, we stick together when things like this happen to the innocent. Regarding the student Reys was attacking, he's no longer in Chicago. He's someplace safe where nobody will ever hurt him again. That's when Bishop came in. He got in touch with Isaiah and informed him of what had happened. He was on the first train leaving Philadelphia. Thanks to Bishop, he had a longstanding meeting with the school board and the teachers. He introduced Isaiah and persuaded the board to install Isaiah as their new principal," said Bee.

"So why did Isaiah come to visit Bishop, and why did he ask you to come to his office?" Audine asked, raising her eyebrows.

"Do you remember when I told you what Bishop said to me, that Patrick did me a favor? Whelp, he did because after meeting Isaiah, it was love at first sight for us. When we were introduced, Bishop said he had several meetings to attend and asked if I would please show Isaiah around the church and bring him to the fellowship hall kitchen for a bowl of soup and sweet potato pie. Mmm, we talked for hours about everything. Isaiah also attended church service that same Sunday, and Bishop invited him, my mother, and me to his home for Sunday dinner. I must say, Bishop's wife Sathronia made a feast! It wasn't long before Isaiah asked my mother and Bishop for permission to court me. I was thrilled that they said yes, and on Christmas Day last year, we all went to the bishop's home for dinner. In front of everyone, Isaiah asked me to marry him!" she said, beaming. Thrusting her left hand in Audine's face, Audine was taken aback by the exquisite engagement ring.

"Isaiah and I are planning to marry in July, and of course, Bishop will be doing the ceremony," she said, admiring her ring.

"I'm so happy for you, Bee!" exclaimed Audine. Rising from her seat, she approached her, and the two women embraced. Yet deep down, Audine harbored jealousy and envy, secretly hoping Bee's engagement would end before the first wedding invitation arrived in the mail.

Humph, you'll never get married, at least not before me. After everything I've been through, I'm the one who deserves happiness, not you! Audine thought to herself bitterly.

"Can you tell me a bit more about the church and Bishop Almonds?" Audine asked, leaning back in her chair.

Bee sat in silence, calculating how to respond to Audine's persistent questioning about Thomas and Sathronia Almonds. She inhaled deeply, shook her head, and smiled.

"Healing is just one reason so many people flock to his church, as well as the loud and lively step music! Umph, umph, umph! Yes, ma'am, when that music starts, you'd better be ready!" she said, full of excitement.

"Ready, ready for what?" Audine asked, frowning in confusion.

"Oh my goodness, the music is like thunder! Everything goes boom, boom, boom! There are so many drums, trombones, trumpets, and tambourines, and the whole congregation is going all out! We've got at least twenty trombone players, ten trumpeters, two drummers, and two rows of men and women, all pounding tambourines as loud as they can! It gets so loud that we all just want to shout out God's praises! And when Bishop takes his seat, everything—music, people, everything—gets even louder! Then we all shout even louder, and some people are dancing in the aisles in holy dance, and when he stands to preach, some rush to the altar to seek blessings or healing. Some members fall out, and when that happens—especially to the women—the ushers have big blankets and white sheets ready," Bee said.

"Sheets and blankets? During church service? What for and why are sheets needed?" mused Audine with a knowing smirk.

"When the Holy Spirit touches the women of our

congregation, we want to stop any immodesty, especially when they're wearing stockings and garters that are exposed. We want to preserve their modesty. Going to the altar to be blessed or healed by the bishop means that the Holy Spirit came down and worked through him. That's why, after he touches or prophesies over those needing healing, people will start falling, doing a holy dance step, and speaking in tongues more intensely than before, as if their lives depend on it. Some are so overcome that they'll start walking on the benches," Bee said in a serious tone.

"So, what is walking on the benches? Who would stand up and walk on the church's benches? Are they crazy? Humph, it sounds like a foolish and downright dangerous idea to me. Hah! I wouldn't do something so stupid!" cajoled Audine, trying not to burst out laughing.

With a poisonous glare, Bee shot Audine a look, who appeared to find everything hilarious. After taking a deep breath and closing her eyes, Bee continued.

"On top of that, we gather at church for an hour every Friday evening to rehearse high-stepping to the music, so we're all set."

"Ready and set for what? Because you just told me about the shouting, music, Holy dancing in the aisles, and so much added stuff that makes no sense to me! Now, the church where I used to attend and was an outstanding member just had an organ, and we sang quiet hymnals; that was enough. We didn't do all that wild performing that you're telling me, humph! Sounds like it's a place full of people acting like they don't have a lick of good sense!" Audine cackled, rudely interrupting Bee.

She made a conscious effort to remain professionally composed, but her hands had balled up into tight fists in her lap. For a brief instant, the fierce, unstoppable twelve-year-old girl inside her surged to the surface, and a long-repressed thought suddenly emerged: Bee wanted to drop-kick, punch, and beat the shit out of Audine's disgusting, disease-ridden ass. But that was out of the question, especially right then.

Go back inside, little girl. This is nothing more than a dark demon in front of us. In due time. This regurgitation of nonsense will make her regret what she's been saying! How dare this shameful piece of shit! Bee thought to herself, infuriated.

"Mrs. Collins, you shouldn't laugh or make fun of what Bishop Almonds is doing, nor should you think it's funny what goes on in the church I attend, and my future husband and the children we'll have. This has been the way we praise in that church for years. It saved many souls, as well as my life! If you ever have the privilege to attend service, you'll see why I joined. If I hadn't gone to church the night Bishop prophesied over me, I'd still be in front of the Peephole Watering Hole on the south side, getting myself drunk with a lot of lost and wayward women who already lost their souls on their way to hell!" declared Bee.

"Oh, so you used to be a drunk and a honky-tonk girl? I knew a woman like that back home in New Orleans! Her name was Maydell. That woman died in a pool of her piss and blood, hah!" said Audine, smirking.

"Perhaps I was a loose drunk, Mrs. Collins, because I was so broken and busted up over the fact that the man I was in love with didn't love me! Patrick hurt, humiliated, and made me lose my mind! So yes, I did drink a lot and got so drunk that I left nursing school. I was always a customer at the Peephole joint! I let men touch me, put their tongues inside my mouth, calling that kissing, and put their hands up my dress while they pressed me against the wall with the zipper of their pants down! And yes, I was on my knees on filthy ground, allowing myself to open my mouth wide and letting them put their manhood inside my mouth for two lousy dollars! So yes, Mrs. Collins, I guess that made me a honkey-tonk woman, a dirty woman with no shame! But by God's grace and mercy, Bishop Almonds hoisted me out of that foul-smelling, dirty muck, saving and forgiving me! It was grace! When I pass by those fallen women I once was, I dare not judge them!" exploded Bee.

Several people in the small cafeteria line paused and glanced over at Audine and Bee, trying to make out what all the commotion was about.

Audine sat still, her eyes widened in horror at Bee's tone and her revelation. Audine recalled the events that unfolded when she was finally with Wayne, but under different circumstances in New York, as she had planned Lena's funeral and judged her when Wayne learned that Lena had lived with the infamous gambler, High

Roller Gunn.

Humph, I'm sticking to my opinion that Lena Collins was a good-for-nothing whore who did me a favor. At least I had a lovely wedding, though. But who does Bee think she's talking to, especially in that tone of voice to ME like that? Just because she's educated, works as a nurse, and is engaged to a principal? Pfft! Who cares! Audine thought to herself as she crossed her legs and leaned back, drained from the last of her coffee and forgetting how she'd been insulted.

"Mrs. Collins, it's going on eleven-fifteen, and I need to be at the nurse's station to take attendance and disperse the nurses to the assigned patients they'll be caring for the rest of the week," said Bee, tapping on her watch and rising from her chair. "You do remember how you did that when you were a nurse in New Orleans, don't you?"

"Of course I do; after all, I'd have the nurses all lined up and listening to *me*. I was a wonderful nurse and an expert, and I saved many lives, so yes, those nurses all followed my instructions." Audine said as she stood up from her chair.

"I'll walk you back to the waiting area, where you'll wait for Ezra. His instructions are to take you to the church to meet with Bishop Almonds," interrupted Bee impatiently, who was disgusted and fed up with Audine's apparent lies and rude behavior.

With purposeful speed, Audine snatched up her belongings and fell in behind Bee.

After the five-minute walk-in and the awkward silence, they stepped into the brightly lit waiting area, which was crowded with people dealing with a range of illnesses.

Deep, loud hock-ups punctuated low whispers, throat clearing, wheezing, and fits of coughing. Women leaned on their husbands' shoulders, some crying in pain as they spat out blood-tinged mucus into handkerchiefs. In a corner, a disheveled man in a tattered coat sat alone. He'd suddenly start coughing, spitting blood into a bloody rag, then wipe his nose with it and tuck it into his back pocket. Unaware of the others in the room, he repeatedly let out loud, long farts, ignoring the stares, dirty looks, and disapproving glances from those around him.

He crossed his mangled leg, let out another loud, long crack, and looked out the window.

Poor fellow. The only chair left in the room is next to him, and that is exactly where Bee planned to send Audine to sit, amused by the thought.

She smiled to herself and walked straight over to the empty chair.

"Alright, Mrs. Collins, you can take a seat right here; it's a perfect place because you'll be next to the window and can keep an eye out for Ezra's car. I'll give you a call in a few days to check in and set up a follow-up visit to make sure everything is okay. Just one more thing: please read the instructions carefully on when to take your medication," Bee said, checking her watch again and tapping it a bit impatiently.

Audine didn't hear a word Bee was saying to her. Instead, she stood glaring at the disheveled man who seemed to reek of body odor and the sharp scent of recently expelled gas.

"Why are you doing this to me?" Audine spat, jerking her head to the side, her face twisted into a fierce scowl.

He let out another explosion of gas as he kept staring out the window.

"Will someone please get this son-of-a-bitch out of here! I've been waiting here for over an hour, and I'm sick! That brittle son-of-a-bitch is making my stomach go into knots and making me even sicker! Get this fucker out of here now, or I will!" bellowed a frail, dark-complexioned man as his wife tried to pull him down. He plopped down in the chair, snatched a handkerchief from his wife, and covered his nose.

"What's wrong, Mrs. Collins? Honestly, if you're a nurse, as you claim to be, you should be used to dealing with people who are impatient and in pain. This man is no exception. Plus, this is the only chair left in the waiting room unless you want to stand," Bee said.

"Look at him! He stinks, he's filthy, and I don't want to sit near him! So, find me a different chair to sit in!" demanded Audine, her voice rising to the edge of hysteria.

"Mrs. Collins, take a seat! Ezra is on his way. As I

mentioned, you can either stand for the next fifteen minutes while Ezra arrives, or you can sit and remain quiet. It's your choice. Honestly, I didn't think a nurse would have trouble with that. Just take care of yourself and follow your medication instructions. I'll check in with you in a few days."

And just like that, Bee returned to a bustling corridor filled with medical staff and walked a short distance to a group of eager nurses who were prepared to care for sick patients, hold the hand of a dying patient, or be in the delivery room to assist with bringing a new life into the world.

Enraged, Audine clenched her teeth. Wiping the tears that spilled from the corners of her eyes, Audine opened her purse and rummaged for a fresh handkerchief. Suddenly, a filthy rag appeared before her. Taken aback, the disheveled man sitting next to her smiled, revealing a mouthful of decaying teeth, and offered her his snot-filled, bloody rag to dry her tears.

"Get that damn thing away from me, you worthless piece of shit!" she snarled in a cold tone.

He shrugged, his face expressionless. Shifting his

thin frame, he crossed his legs and tucked the rag into the back pocket of his dirty pants, exposing the stained area on his backside. There were streaks of old, dried feces and a makeshift hole where he would squat to do his toilet business. Audine's eyes widened, and sensing what was about to happen, he expelled gas again, as loose, bloody feces sprayed out, landing in the chair and forming a puddle.

Too late.

Audine yelped and jumped out of the chair. At the last moment, Audine saw a black Cadillac, driven by Ezra, pull up to the doorway. On cue, Audine bolted out of the waiting room, opened the car door, and let herself in without waiting for Ezra to open it for her. He got inside, started the car, and sped off.

CHAPTER TWENTY-SIX

Bee dialed the seven numbers on the rotary phone during her hour-long break from dinner to talk to Isaiah, her future husband.

The doctor she worked with had to leave for another delivery; the last of the four women from the church was finally giving birth after being in labor for seven hours. Therefore, his office and the telephone were available for only fifteen minutes to keep his phone lines open for incoming calls.

Isaiah always appeared happy, especially when the conversation turned to their upcoming nuptials, which were just a few months away.

But the conversation suddenly turned to Audine.

"Honey, she's not a nurse. She's a professional liar! You should call the only hospital in New Orleans that serves our people and ask about her," Isaiah said with suspicion.

"That's a good idea because our hospital really needs more staff, including nurses and doctors. I'm checking out the job postings, and there are twenty openings!" Bee exclaimed, taking another bite of the leftover ham she'd turned into a sandwich.

Call them right away before they get too busy. When you get the information, tell Bishop everything, then give me a call. I want to hear everything, okay, sweetheart?" he advised.

"Yes, as soon as I get off the phone, I'll call that hospital and talk to the office that handles all its workers. I'll call you tonight after dinner. I've decided to stay at work until eight o'clock," said Bee.

"All right, then. Hey, one more thing, Bee," he said, his voice husky.

"Yes, sweetheart?" she said.

"I love you so much. I can't wait to see you walk down the aisle on our wedding day, especially when I put that gold wedding ring on your finger and hear you say 'I do,'" he said.

Bee sensed the smile in his voice.

"I love you, too, Isaiah. I'm looking forward to our wedding day, but I'm even more excited about our wedding night. I can't wait to make you my husband. I know that sounds shameless to you, but I don't care!" she said, trying to hold back her laughter.

"Why, Miss Huggs, I do declare that if I were there, I'd have to bend you over my knee, pull up your uniform, pull down those panties, and give that round, chocolate, bon-bon candy-shaped ass of yours a good spankin'!" he growled.

As Bee thought about being over Isaiah's knees, with his open palm slapping her bare behind, she started to feel a wetness between her legs.

But until now, she had been holding onto a promise that would finally be kept on their wedding night. Her mind was filled with memories of her past as she closed her eyes, reliving what had happened over a year ago when she had given herself freely to all those men at the Peephole – the only exception being a man named Percy Gateman.

"I don't mean to rush off, but I'm going to make that call to New Orleans now," Bee said.

After saying their goodbyes, Bee hung up and opened the desk file drawer. She flipped through the files, which included the names, addresses, phone numbers, key contacts, and departments of all the Black hospitals nationwide. The files proved particularly useful for travelers in the Deep South.

"Ah, found it!" said Bee.

She pulled out the file with the contact information for the only Black hospital in New Orleans.

Bee dialed the telephone number, and after two rings, the switchboard operator picked up.

May I speak to Mr. Arthur Mecks? I'm Beatrice Huggs, head nurse at Brownsville Hospital in Chicago. Yes, I'll hold for Mr. Mecks, thank you.

After waiting for just a few minutes, Mecks came on the line.

"Good afternoon, Miss Huggs, Mecks here. How can I assist you?" he inquired.

Good afternoon, Mr. Mecks. I'm doing well. I know you're busy so that I won't take up much of your time. Are you familiar with a woman named Mrs. Audine

Collins? She's in Chicago and was brought to the hospital for a medical emergency. She claims to have worked as a nurse at your hospital, saying she was a top nurse. Could you confirm her employment as a nurse?

"Oh my," sighed Mecks. "Yes, Mrs. Collins went under the name Audine Booker. She married a hospital worker named Wayne Collins. He's a wonderful man, the salt-of-the-earth kind of person. Everyone in this hospital loves Wayne. He's still working here and caring for Mrs. Collins's son."

"Her son? Wait, Mrs. Collins has a son?" inquired Bee as she scribbled notes in her notepad.

"The fact of the matter is that Audine has a son and a daughter. Her daughter had an affair with a married man and got pregnant. Her daughter's name is Violet. When Audine found out, she brutally beat her daughter, and it took Wayne and her son, Mason, to pull her off. After that, Violet was sent to live with Audine's sister and her husband. A few weeks later, Wayne kicked Audine out on a Sunday, and on Monday morning, he went to City Hall and met with his pastor. By the end of the week, the marriage was annulled, and Audine was on a train heading somewhere. And to be clear, Audine telling you she was a nurse at this hospital is not true," Mecks said.

"What?" said Bee, dropping her pencil.

"There's no doubt about it; Audine is a liar. She was the one who changed beds and emptied the trash, and if a patient passed away, she'd often help wash the deceased. That stopped when family members complained that everything from cash to wedding bands was going missing. Once we stopped her from doing that task, the items remained in place. And one more thing I forgot to mention: she was caught stealing almost a thousand dollars from Wayne," he said firmly.

"Oh my God! So, what happened after that?" Bee asked as she scribbled additional notes in her notepad.

"As I mentioned earlier, Wayne insisted on keeping Mason, and she was banished from the home. All I can say is, if you do hire Audine, keep a close eye on her. From what I've heard about her, she's a liar, a thief, a gossipmonger, and a troublemaker. Do you have any more questions for me?"

"No, sir, Mr. Mecks. You've been wonderful, and I appreciate your time. Don't worry, sir. I'll keep an eye on her if she works here," said Bee.

Then she hung up the phone.

Once Bee finished her notes, she twisted the pencil between her fingers. Then she tapped it down on the desk and glanced at her watch.

She thought to herself, just fifteen more minutes, as she picked up the phone and dialed as fast as she could.

There was a pause, and then the voice on the other end said, "Hello?"

"Isaiah, I know you only have a few minutes left before school lets out for the day, but I need you to pick me up from the hospital tonight," Bee said.

"Of course I will. Everything okay with you? What's going on, Bee? You sound like you've run around the hospital and back to your office," he joked.

"Hah, I wish it were. Soon after we spoke, I called the hospital, as you suggested," said Bee.

"The one in New Orleans?" Isaiah asked.

"Exactly. I spoke with a man who handles hiring for that hospital, and boy, did he give me an earful about that woman! By the time he got to the part where her daughter was with a married man and he put a baby inside her, I was shaking. There's too much to cover over the phone, so how about you come to the hospital, meet me in the cafeteria, and I'll fill you in on everything?" she said.

"Geeze," Isaiah whistled in a low tone, "If I hear you right, there's much more to this woman than you've learned. She may appear harmless, but watch her every move, sweetheart. I also advise that you tell Bishop Almonds what you've learned about her. In the meantime, I've got to go. I'll meet you later this evening in the cafeteria; we'll have some coffee and share a slice of cake, okay?" he said.

"Yes, I look forward to seeing you," said Bee, glancing at her watch.

They ended the call.

Bee gathered her stethoscope, tucked her

notepad into her uniform pocket, adjusted the laces on her pristine nursing shoes, fluffed her hair, and returned the file. After snapping off the lights, she approached the door, pushed it open, and found the corridor in chaos. Running toward the waiting room, she navigated through the massive crowd of onlookers to gain a clearer understanding of what was happening.

She let out a loud gasp and covered her mouth in horror. There, on the floor, lay the disheveled man face down in a pool of blood, with a long bloody knife protruding from his ass. Standing over him was the frail older man with bloodied hands.

"I told that guy if he didn't stop stinking up the room, I'd plug his ass to shut him up! As you can see, he won't be stinking up this room again!" he said.

He calmly walked to the chair he had been sitting on earlier, crossed his legs, and sat down.

CHAPTER TWENTY-SEVEN

Ezra parked the car in front of a towering building with ornate doors, stained-glass windows, and three crosses. The central one was a massive replica, while the two on the left and right were more minor yet still significant. Several steeples gave the entire structure a storybook-like appearance. If the sun were shining, the twenty-eight steps leading to the church doors would perfectly complement the beige exterior.

It was a magnificent building, and Audine's mouth hung slightly open in disbelief that this was the church where Thomas Almond had preached, taught, saved, baptized, married, and conducted funerals.

"We've arrived, Mrs. Collins," said Ezra.

"Before you open the door for me, tell me something. How many people can fit inside this church?

I've never seen anything like this before in my life! It looks like a castle, it's so big!" stammered Audine in awe as she peered out the car door window.

"This is the most well-known Black church in Chicago. My grandfather and father helped build this church when I was a child. My grandfather, formerly enslaved, did the masonry work. When my father was older, he learned, so together with over one hundred of us, we worked day and night until every brick was laid out," said Ezra as he slid out of the driver's seat and opened the door for Audine. She had forgotten how cold it was, and a blustery wind caught her off guard. Audine rummaged through her purse, pulled out a pair of gloves, and slipped them on. Shivering, she pulled up her coat collar and blinked away the tears in her eyes caused by the cold air.

"Hold on to my arm, just in case the stairs are still a bit slick, and grab the railing," Ezra said, offering the crook of his arm to Audine. For a moment, Audine thought of how Wayne used to make that same gesture whenever they went out in public, and how proud she felt of keeping pace with his stride. For a fleeting moment, Ezra was Wayne.

Ezra was right when he said the stairs felt like a sheet of ice!

"Hold on tight and take your time, because if you walk too fast, we'll both end up tumbling down these stairs!" said Ezra.

"Oh, my goodness, Ezra, how do you manage in this freezing weather? My teeth are chattering, I'm having trouble breathing, and the wind is too much!" moaned Audine.

"I've been doing this my whole life, so don't worry too much – you'll get used to it in time," Ezra said.

Finally! The stairs were manageable, and Ezra's stride carried them both safely to the door. Gripping his arm tighter, he grasped the door handle with his gloved hand.

Swoosh!

Audine yelped as the door swung open, dragging her into the church vestibule.

"Oh, my goodness," she gasped at the sight before

her.

The woodwork was beautiful; two large portraits hung on the walls, one depicting an older man and the other, unmistakably, a much younger Thomas. Drawings illustrating stories from the Gospels were clustered together beside each edge of the stained-glass windows. The entire vestibule was filled with a warm sandalwood scent. The thud of the heavy wood door brought Audine back to her senses.

"Come, let me take you to Bishop Almond's office," said Ezra as he opened another set of doors leading to the sanctuary. Audine caught her breath, shocked by what she saw. Hundreds of neatly arranged wooden pews held fifty or more women, some very still with their eyes squeezed tightly and arms outstretched. In contrast, others boldly stood and prayed fervently in the holy language of tongues. Moving closer to the front, a curved wooden railing came into view. At its base was a thick, plush, red tufted cushion. Several people knelt on the cushion in prayer, while others prostrated themselves on the floor in worship. In the corners on the left and right, stairs led up to a balcony with twenty-five pews. At the center of the floor was an enormous, ornate, button-tufted high-back chair with mahogany arms that resembled a throne. At this point, Ezra guided Audine further along the altar, where a side door mysteriously blended into the wall. A small, hooked door handle opened the massive door, which made no sound as it swung open, revealing a longer hallway. Several women dressed in aprons over their clothing and tignons greeted Ezra with smiles and nods.

"Good afternoon, Brother Ezra," whispered a woman carrying a large pot and a soup ladle.

"Good afternoon, Sister Posey; it's a pleasure to see you," whispered Ezra.

"Sister Posey, I'd like to introduce you to the new boarder at Bishop's home. This is Mrs. Audine Collins. Mrs. Collins, this is June Posey, the head of our kitchen staff, and oh my, can she cook!" gushed Ezra.

"Pleased to meet you, Audine!" greeted Posey as she tiptoed towards Audine to shake hands.

"Nice to meet you, June. But please call *me* Mrs. Collins," Audine said firmly, reaching out to Posey for a brief, limp handshake.

Posey stiffened at the abrupt, curt gesture and tone in Audine's voice.

"Oh, I see. I hope you all have lunch in the dining hall. I'm making something simple: apple-and-cheese sandwiches and hot soup. For dessert, Bishop's favorite is peach pie," she said, giving Ezra a sideways glance.

He smiled as though he were reading Posely's thoughts.

"See you later, and thanks for letting us know what's on the menu for later. I'm looking forward to it," he said.

Posey nodded and rushed down the hallway to the kitchen.

"Uh, Mrs. Collins, why did you talk to Sister Posey like that? I thought you were being rude to her, especially since you just met her," Ezra said.

Audine's stride suddenly halted as they walked toward Almond's office.

"Rude? I wasn't rude to that woman at all! I simply

corrected her on how to address me and my title as a married woman; humph! Besides, she's just a kitchen cook who isn't getting paid, so she should respect me as Mrs. Audine Collins!" she shot back.

Ezra glared at Audine, speechless at what he had just heard.

"I never thought I'd live to see the day when a Black woman like you would say something so hurtful to another Black woman! My goodness, Mrs. Collins, our people are already constantly mistreated by White people who hate us! You should be ashamed of yourself! I thought you were a decent person. Come on, let's go. Bishop's office is just down the hall," said Ezra, clearly shocked and shaking his head.

Audine shrugged her shoulders and yawned.

Bristling, Ezra scooted ahead of Audine, who lagged due to the pain between her legs.

As soon as I can, I'm going to take whatever medicine Bee put in this bag to relieve the pain! Audine thought to herself.

They paused briefly at a heavy wooden door with

a gold brass ball-shaped handle. Ezra knocked on the door.

"Take off your boots and shoes and place them over here," said Ezra, motioning to a crate that had a neatly written sign that read:

Put your shoes and boots inside this crate.

"What for?" Audine asked, sounding annoyed.

"Because the Bishop's office is sacred, Mrs. Collins. Bishop does not want the nonsense, bad spirits, or haints on the ground we walk on tracked into his office. So please honor his request," he replied.

"Spirits? What kind of spirit, Ezra? Please don't tell me Bishop believes in that mumbo-jumbo silliness! I will say this, though: when I lived in New Orleans, a woman who used to be my friend was all into that craziness, humph! That explains why her husband left her!" Audine said, laughing loudly.

Ezra glared at Audine with disgust and dismissed her flippant comments.

He said, "Please remove your boots and shoes, and keep your voice down to a whisper, as Bishop is finishing up his afternoon prayers."

Done with the hassle, Audine removed her boots and shoes and stowed them in the wooden crate. On closer inspection, she spotted neatly stacked knitted socks. She selected the brown ones, put them on, and waited at the door with Ezra to head into Bishop Almond's office.

After fifteen minutes of silence between Ezra and Audine, the door to Bishop Almond's office swung open.

Good afternoon, Mrs. Collins and Brother Ezra! Please come in. Sorry for the wait—I've just received some exciting yet urgent news. All four deacons and their wives gave birth on the same day! Can you believe it? Truly wonderful—our creator's mysterious ways. Please, come into my office, especially you, Mrs. Collins; I have plenty to show you around the church".

"I'm honored, Bishop. As soon as Ezra pulled up in front of this church, I couldn't believe it was yours! And when dear Ezra helped me up those stairs, I thought I would fall apart, let alone be in your presence in one piece! But as soon as I stepped inside, I was taken by the windows, the striking photos of you and your father, and the interior of this glorious house of worship! It's now clear to me why you and your lovely wife and daughters are working so hard to help those who come to this church, including the woman I just met – what's her name? Oh, June Posey, that's it!" exclaimed Audine, snapping her fingers to remember June, whom she had met only minutes before.

"She seems like a wonderful person! I can already tell she and I will become wonderful friends!" said Audine, edging closer to Almonds and beaming.

With no hesitation, and to her pleasant surprise, Almonds wrapped her in his arms, holding her in a tight embrace.

"Receiving a compliment like that from you is a true gift! Oh, yes, my dear Mrs. Collins!"

Almonds caught Ezra's eye, and he shook his head, rolling his eyes in response. Almonds saw the flash of irritation and impatience in his gaze.

Call me tonight, Almonds silently mouthed to Ezra.

Agreeing, Ezra pulled his cap low and slipped out without a sound.

Got him! I'm all alone with Bishop; his arms wrapped around me. Oh, mercy, he smells so good! Umph, umph, umph! I'm completely smitten with this man! Audine thought to herself, snuggling her head against his chest and closing her eyes. Her heart was racing.

Sensing her need and desire for him, Almonds played along with Audine's exaggerated acting, as though she were a young girl infatuated with a boy across the playground. With a sly smile, he pulled her closer, their bodies pressing together, until his gentle massage on her back slid down, stopping just a few inches from her curvy backside. Squeezing her right side, he drew Audine in even tighter. To his surprise, Almonds felt himself becoming aroused, and could sense it growing through her coat.

The phone rang.

"Dammit!" Audine growled to herself as she felt Almond's arms loosen. She watched him stride over to his desk.

"Hello? Oh yes, how are you, my dear? Just a moment, can you hold on?" he said to the person on the line.

"Mrs. Collins, I need to take this urgent call. It'll only be a moment," he said, covering the phone with his hand.

"Of course, Bishop. I need to use the toilet room; where is it, please?" she asked.

"When you go out the door, take a right, then head down the hallway, past the kitchen, and into the fellowship hall of grace. It will be on the left side," he whispered.

"Thanks," she said, a hint of flirtation in her tone. She unbuttoned her coat, slipped it off, and dropped it quickly onto the small brown tufted couch before hurrying off to find the toilet room.

Why does he have a couch in his office? I've never known a minister to have a couch inside their office. Humph, who cares because his arms were wrapped around me, and that's all that matters! She thought to herself, giddy, as she searched for the toilet room.

"Hello, dearest. Sorry about that. I've got a meeting with a church member. So, how did everything go this morning? I'm curious to hear what happened. What?" he said, sitting up straight.

"Bishop, what I need to tell you will take me over an hour. After meeting Mrs. Collins and gathering more information, I want to say something my grandmother would say when something didn't feel right: Something in the cream ain't clean! Have Ezra pick me up tomorrow morning at ten o'clock, and I'll tell you everything over coffee at the church. He can drop me off at the hospital because I'm on duty from eleven o'clock in the morning to eight-thirty in the evening," Bee said, her voice quiet and tense.

After confirming, she hung up and went back to attending to her patients.

CHAPTER TWENTY-EIGHT

Finally! Audine let out a sigh of relief as she found the door with the scripted sign that read "Ladies' Toilet Room." As she walked down the long, narrow corridor, she noticed that each door had a sign: Sunday School, Music, Elders and Deacons, and Auxiliary Rooms. Each room was designated for a specific group, with Auxiliary Room One for children, Auxiliary Room Two for women, and Auxiliary Room Three for men. The other rooms had signs that read "Ushers," "Choir," "Nurses' Prayer," "The Kitchen," and one that piqued her curiosity: "Treasury." That room was locked with two heavy locks. Passing the kitchen, she saw a group of busy women in blue long-sleeved uniforms with colorful aprons and white Oxford shoes, and white tignons on their heads. The scent of hearty chicken soup, baking bread, and peach pie filled the air, and Audine's mouth watered. But she didn't have time to waste; the sudden urgency to use the toilet and the pain returning between her legs made her want to rush in. She quickly grasped the gold brass doorknob and entered the pitch-black space. Even in the darkness, she could make out the silhouette of a mirror and a shaded lamp. Feeling her way along the wall, she moved sideways until the lamp was within reach. When she tugged on the braided cord, the light flickered to life. Audine gasped at the sight of the bathroom. It was huge, with twelve stalls: six in front and the rest divided by a wall. The floor was spotless, with black-and-white tiles, and featured six sinks, each with a bar of soap, a towel basket, mirrors, and two tufted chairs. The bathroom felt like a fancy living room! Audine thought as she strolled to the other side of the bathroom, which held the last six stalls. She chose the one near a window and stepped inside. She set her brown bag on the floor, hoisted up her dress, and pulled down her panties. The blisters had worsened, and some had broken and dried out, especially where Bee had applied the salve. Carefully removing the sanitary napkin, she wrinkled her nose at the stench of pus and rotten sardines. She reached into her bag and pulled out the salve. Scanning the directions, she nodded in understanding: use it three times a day for pain and infection. At night, take a hot bath, gently dry the area, and then apply the salve to clean, dry skin. Bringing the jar to her nose, she was hit with a fresh citrus scent, a far cry from the sardine-scented sanitary napkin. She applied the salve, grimacing in pain as it stung. "Ouch!" she whispered, massaging the creamy mixture into her thighs until it was absorbed. She returned the salve to her bag, sat on the pristine toilet seat, and relieved herself. The stream of urine burned, and the pain left her breathless. After the stream slowed, Audine rolled up some toilet paper and wiped. It burned so badly that she let out a yelp of pain. She turned to face the toilet chain, pulled it, and watched the contents swirling down. She unlocked the stall door, discarded the used sanitary napkin in the ash can, washed her hands with the fresh-smelling soap, and dried them. Looking at herself in the mirror, Audine sighed. Her once-neat hair was a frazzled mess, and dark circles had formed under her eyes. The bruise on her face and lip made her look like one of those vagrant women who stood stooped under a lamppost. "Humph, I wonder what Thomas thinks of me and how I look!"

Audine thought, disgusted, as she shook her head. "I need to make friends to get help and get better. If I want to get noticed, I can't look like this."

"Oh, I forgot to take this tablet for pain. Bee said to take the syrup medicine at night to help me fall asleep and the tablet during the day," Audine mumbled to herself as she returned to the stall to retrieve the bag.

Two women walked into the bathroom.

Audine quietly grabbed the bag and held it to her chest. She returned to the far corner of the restroom, standing silently to catch snippets of their conversation.

"Shh, is anyone in here? It looks like we're finally alone. Lock the door, though. God, I've missed seeing you, but right now, I'm just so grateful you could spare a few minutes with me, sweetheart. Last Sunday, I watched you the whole time during the early morning service. You looked beautiful in your dress and shoes! And as always, your hair is perfect. My cousin Geneva isn't just a great cook in the church's kitchen – she's got half of Chicago's women looking good!" the woman said.

I'm happy to see you too! I've missed you a lot, especially with the cold and all the bad snowstorms we've had lately. But things have been tough at home, and I'll fill you in later. For now, I want to talk only about us. Being apart for so long was really hard on me, no question. But I promise you, things are about to change because I'm planning to leave him and be with you for the rest of our lives. We'll need to work hard, save up, and get out of here," the other woman said.

Drawn in by their hushed conversations, Audine leaned in closer to the stall wall, straining to hear what they were saying.

But are you sure you'll leave him, sweetheart?"

"Of course I am! Why are you asking me like that?"

Because you seemed so happy at first when you got married, you glowed on your wedding day. What happened? Tell me!

"He wanted children immediately."

"Oh my, how many?"

"Five! He wanted me to have five children, one every two years. Can you imagine that? I told him NO, that I didn't want any more children. Every night, he'd keep pawing at me until I'd give him a hard kick, which he thought was funny. Well, one night when I was asleep, I started to feel his long fingers going inside me, and I knew he was waiting that particular night to do what he did to me because my flow ended the week before."

That was when he must have counted the days from when your flow started until it ended. That's when he counted!

"Yes, exactly!"

"That son-of-a-sneaky bitch! That fucking snake!"

Then came the sound of muffled crying.

"Shhh! Sweetheart, please don't swear in this holy house!"

"I'm sorry, I didn't mean it; it just makes me so damn mad what you're telling me, what he did to you. This is the first time you've shared all of this with me. Come here and let me hold you."

"Hold onto me tighter, please. You have no idea how much I've missed your touch, and you smell so good.",

Audine pressed her ear closer to the stall door and could hear passionate kissing between the two women, along with deep moans and soft weeping. Her mouth dropped open.

"Don't cry, oh please don't cry, sweetheart! I love you so much, and I hate seeing you this unhappy. Here, let me dry your tears".

The woman could be heard gently blowing her nose, and the other woman comforted her.

"Finish telling me what happened, what that son-of-a-bitch did to you," the woman snapped.

She could be heard taking deep breaths to clear her nerves, and then she began.

"He knows exactly when to touch me because that's when we'd start trying for a child. He's powerful because when I woke up fully, he was already on top of me, spreading my legs wide open with his knees and covering my mouth with his big hand. He kept telling me it would please him if we did it this way and didn't scream, and that once he was inside me, I'd enjoy it.

Then he thrust his long thickness inside me all night until he spilled his seed. Oh my God, he did it again to me early the next morning and every night until the end of the month. Then my flow didn't come!"

"Oh my goodness, he did that to you every single night? He was determined to put a baby inside of you, and it broke my heart when you told me what he put a baby inside of you and what you had to do to make it go away".

Both women were now crying.

"It was horrible; oh God, it was horrible! That place on Wabash in that alley where criminals and whores roam about was frightening. When I arrived, the woman had me take off my panties, put a rag across my eyes so I wouldn't see anything, and then had me lie on a table. She seemed nice, but her assistant was a full-sized, mean woman. She was the one who opened my legs and kept them open while the other woman tied my mouth shut with a rag. So, you see, I couldn't see or say anything! Then the nice one said to relax, that she was going to open me up down there, and that I'd feel much pressure, much like when my husband would push himself deep inside me. That part didn't hurt much. Then, before I knew it, I felt her push something long and sharp inside me. I screamed until I passed out. Then it was over. I heard a loud *'Cathunk' noise and saw* the nice woman say to the mean one that I'd be fine and to take what came out of me and put everything inside the bucket. Then she took off the rags from my mouth and my eyes. She handed me pills for pain and helped me put my panties on, which were already lined with a sanitary napkin. I remember you taking me back home. He demanded to know where I was all day; he was mad! I told him that I had lost the baby and had to lie about where I was. All I wanted was to be left alone and be with you. You were the one I wanted to have care for me by my side. After a few months, he stopped touching me. I'd hear noises in my sleep, wake up, and he'd be gone. On Sundays, on the way to church, when we'd drive by Wabash, I always looked out the car window at the gutters and wondered which one it was dumped in," she said, weeping again.

"No, no, no! It's over, and so is your marriage to that horrible demon of a man you're married to. I will take care of you forever; hear me, sweetheart."

"Yes, I hear you. I love you more than you know".

"Not only do I love you, but I've fallen even more in love with you, and I'm not letting you go".

Creeping closer to the stall door, Audine carefully pried open the lock and slowly opened the door wide enough to watch June Posey and Sathronia Almonds passionately kissing and holding onto each other for dear life.

CHAPTER TWENTY-NINE

It was still early morning. The air outside was heavy, with a huge blanket of snow clouds looming, ready to unleash a few snowflakes at any moment. The sudden, sharp sound of a high-pitched wind howling cut through the morning stillness, making the house feel like it would rattle off its foundation. The scent of coffee, sizzling bacon, eggs, and freshly baked cinnamon rolls lured Audine out of bed.

Thanks to the prescribed syrup, the pain went away, and I slept through the night without any nightmares. Audine stretched, yawned, and smiled. My new goal for today is to become Sathronia's best friend. First, I'll catch her alone in the kitchen, apologize for being such a downer, and ask her how she makes that delicious coffee cream. If I play my cards right, she'll be mine by the end of the day. That way, she can focus on June, and I'll get to enjoy Thomas. Maybe I'll even get to meet his long and thick side, like Sathronia says. If I get myself healthy, I'll make sure to see a doctor here in Chicago who can help me. I might even be able to have a child with Thomas, despite his age. What a dream! Audine thought to herself as she brushed her hair.

As she glanced at the brush, she realized, to her dismay, that a considerable amount of her hair was falling out.

Glancing at the clock, it showed exactly four-thirty in the morning. She carefully made the bed, pulling the sheets tight to get rid of the musty smell. Then, she tucked in the sheets and blankets firmly, making sure the bed was neat and smooth. The pillows were fluffed and arranged just like in those fancy magazines. Taking a step back, awed by how well it turned out.

It'll be good practice for me once I'm Thomas's wife, she thought giddily, clapping her hands.

She opened the dresser drawer and pulled out a dress, fresh undergarments, and socks. With everything balanced in the crook of her arm, she grabbed the bag holding her prescribed medications and took one last glance around the room before closing the door and quietly making her way to the bathroom.

Tiptoeing down the corridor, she crept past the bathroom to Thomas's bedroom. Standing dangerously close to his door, she leaned in and pressed her ear against it to listen for any sounds of movement—the faint rustle of sheets, followed by the soft rhythmic squeaking of mattress coils.

Oh my goodness, did Sathronia change her mind? Audine thought to herself, panicking.

Inching closer, she pressed her ear against the door in a risky move.

"Are you sure you want me to do this for you?" she heard him whisper hoarsely.

Audine heard no response.

"We haven't loved each other like this in a long time, and I've missed you so much. I wanted to touch you, but I understand what you've been through. Sathronia, please come closer to me and take off that silly thing because I need to see your nakedness just as you need to see mine. I am your husband, after all! Let me help you back into bed; breakfast can wait. You turned off the fire from all those pans just as I asked you to, and you were obedient, returning to your husband's bed as I instructed you. In obedience, as your husband, I'm telling you to allow me to spill my seed inside you. Sathronia, answer me, honey, and say yes to your husband," he whispered.

"Yes, Thomas," Sathronia said softly.

More sounds of rustling sheets.

"I have to taste these; my goodness, Sathronia, your breasts are like luscious mounds of fruit!" His words turned into hungry grunts.

There were no more words, only the sound of passion, until Audine heard Thomas release a rough shout as he came.

Backing away from the door, Audine covered her mouth to stifle a cry of despair. Tears streamed down her cheeks; she could not believe what she had just heard: Thomas was spilling his seed into Sathronia! But how could that be when she kissed June yesterday? This isn't happening, and it isn't right!

Wiping her eyes with the back of her hand, Audine

turned back to the door and pressed her ear against it.

The sounds grew more intense - loud moaning and Thomas clapping Sathronia's behind with an open palm.

Shaking, Audine carefully lowered her bundle of items to the floor. Grimacing, she crouched low enough to peek one eye into the generously sized keyhole. Focusing her bruised eye, Audine could see that the room was magnificent. It cast a warm silhouette, and the low light from the table lamp enhanced the ambiance. Oh, there! She watched and listened as Thomas instructed Sathronia to come to where he sat on a simple wooden chair, bring the pillow from the bed, and lay it across his lap.

Sathronia did what he told her to do.

He asked her to recline over his knees and rest her face on the pillow.

"Do you know why I have to do this to you, Sathronia?" he asked.

"Yes, Thomas," she replied, nodding.

"And you understand that you were being disobedient by not letting me sow my holy seeds within you, for my pleasure and to bring forth fruit so that I won't be mocked and ridiculed. Do you agree?" he asked.

"Yes, Thomas. I was very disobedient," she whispered.

"I'll give you ten lashes. That's just a warning, a gentle reminder never to disobey me. Are you ready to take your punishment?" he asked.

Sathronia nodded and clenched the pillow.

Pulling out a leather strap, Thomas raised it and shut his eyes.

"In my name!" he said through gritted teeth.

Whap!

Audine saw Sathronia flinch and heard her muffled yelp when Thomas delivered the first lash to her buttocks.

"Four more, and for each lash I deliver, that's how many children you'll have for me, one each year for the next four years! You'll bear my children, and this family will grow for generations to come!"

Thomas raised the strap, closed his eyes once

again, and repeated the phrase just as he had when he delivered the first one.

Then it was over.

"Go back to bed now so I can finish this and do it right. If we get this done correctly, Lucinda, Delphine, and Ruthie will each have their baby, and you and I will announce that we're expecting ours!"

Before Sathronia could respond, Thomas was already on top, thrusting into her in a passionate rhythm, until he climaxed, letting out a high-pitched scream into the pillow as he spilled his seed.

Drained from exhaustion, Audine could hear his breath released in a slow, steady exhale.

"Thomas, please, can we lie here for just a minute so I can get ready?" Sathronia asked.

"Of course. Before you leave, do you love me, and will you continue to be obedient so we can start a family together?" Thomas asked.

Sathronia slid out of bed without responding to him. Then, she got dressed for the morning prayers.

Audine backed away, covering her mouth in horror after all that she had seen through the keyhole.

I heard her tell June yesterday that she hated him! Even though she was underneath him, I still couldn't believe that she was enjoying him! No, no, no! I need to work quickly now! Sathronia is not going to ruin everything for me, NO! Audine thought as she snatched up her things and tiptoed toward the bathroom to bathe and take her morning medications.

Quietly, she pried open the bathroom door and stepped inside, locking it behind her. Flicking on the lights, she removed her nightgown and examined what was between her legs. The infection was still present, but it wasn't as severe as when it first appeared, and she nodded to herself with a half-smile. Audine quickly prepared for her early morning time with Sathronia. In a rush, she turned the hot water knob, watching the steam rise. After tossing in a handful of Epsom salts, a bar of soap, and a clean washcloth, she sat on the toilet to relieve her urgent need to urinate. The burning sensation made her wince, and as she checked the sanitary pad, she noticed more traces of the infection mixed with blood. However, the thick fluid oozing from her panties wasn't as bad.

I still need a sanitary napkin as long as this mess is inside me," Audine *thought to herself, feeling repulsed.*

As she crumpled the soiled napkin into a tight wad, she dug through her medical bag for supplies. With a smile, she pulled out an old newspaper sleeve that Bee had tucked inside. She cut the sleeve into several long, wide strips to use as decoys for throwing away the soiled napkins without drawing attention. The talcum powder Bee had added to the bag would be lightly sprinkled onto the soiled pad to mask the smell of fermenting blood or, in this case, infection.

After the hurried hot bath, Audine got dressed, oiled her hair, and fastened her tignon. Giving the tub one final hot rinse, it shone as if it had never been used. Satisfied, Audine took the tablet in her mouth, turned on the icy water, and cupped her hands to catch it. She gulped down the water and swallowed the bitter tablet. Next, she applied the salve. Massaging it between her thighs, Audine ignored the sting. Looking in the mirror, she noticed that the bruising and split lip seemed to be healing slowly.

When I befriend Sathronia, I'll ask her where she gets her hair done, hah! After I'm done getting myself all dolled up, Thomas will have no choice but to stare at me, and once she sees us together, Sathronia won't be able to keep his interest if I'm around! Oh, wait until June finds out about this! Audine thought to herself.

After turning off the lights, she returned to her room and set the brown bag on the bed. Before going down the stairs, Audine paused to listen for any other sounds coming from Thomas's bedroom.

Silence.

Audine took a deep breath, grasped the stair railing, and strode down the stairs as if it were her parade to befriend Sathronia Almonds.

CHAPTER THIRTY

Sathronia

What did I do? How did I let Thomas kiss me on the forehead, go to bed, and before I knew it, he had me bent over his knee, facing a spanking with his hand on my bare behind, and then I went back to bed with him to let him plant his seed inside me? And then I let him punish me for disobeying him, and I agreed to have a child with him.

I promised June I'd never let Thomas touch me again, but after he kissed me, memories of when we first got married flooded my mind. Oh my, the fact that Thomas cared about me and my daughters a year after my husband Stokman's murder was precious. Too many women were chasing after Thomas, yet he chose to be with me and my daughters.

It's just this tiny fact that I couldn't have any more children for Thomas. I didn't want any more with him. How he held me last night into this morning has made me hate him even more! Sathronia thought, grimacing as she touched her behind, which was painful to the touch.

She ignored the soreness and broke a cinnamon stick in half, adding it to the warm cream for her hot oatmeal as part of breakfast.

I became attached and attracted to June almost immediately after we first met. We talked for hours after church and met for lunch and coffee every Wednesday at noon. It was then that she invited me to her place. We had a great time; we laughed, I teared up, and we enjoyed a delicious lunch of chicken salad sandwiches with tea. She surprised me by bringing out dessert —a golden pound cake so tender it melted in your mouth! Umph, umph, umph! She added a dollop of whipped cream and showed me how to sprinkle just a bit of nutmeg on top. While we were doing the dishes, we discussed Thomas's and my feelings about not wanting more children. She spun me around, placed her soft, Jergens-scented hands on my shoulders, looked me in the eye, and said:

"Don't feel like you have to do it if you're not

comfortable, Sathronia! Take extra care a few days before and after your period. I'll show you how to handle it. No worries, okay?"

I was thrilled to hear her say that! Ah! She made me feel strong, and we hugged for what felt like an eternity.

Then she and I gazed deeply into each other's eyes and kissed-no, not like friends do on the cheek, but full on the lips. June and I kissed like married couples do in private. June even showed me how to swirl my tongue around in her mouth. She told me to close my eyes, hold onto her tight, and imagine I was trying to lick peach ice cream off her tongue.

As June had asked, I tasted her tongue, stirring feelings within me that I had never experienced before. Not even my late husband, Noddington, had made me feel that way. Next, she took my hand and led me up the stairs to her bedroom. She helped me out of my dress, leaving me naked. She undressed as well and mentioned we needed to clean up. So, we headed into her bathroom, where we bathed together in her tub. As she washed me, she continued talking. Afterward, she dried me off and applied a thick, sweet-smelling cream to oil my skin.

"What's that, June? It smells beautiful!" I asked her.

"I made it myself with roses, lavender, and vanilla," June told me.

She made it herself! Ha, can you believe that? My June makes her soap!

She led me to her bedroom, and I lay down on her bed. As I watched, she opened a wooden box on the table beside her bed and pulled out a beautiful jar. Without a word, she climbed onto the bed next to me and spread a sweet, sticky concoction over my lips, breasts, belly, and the sensitive spot between my legs. After that, we kissed, and the flavor on my lips was just as sweet as I had imagined! I couldn't help but want more. June smiled at me.

She said, "I'm just getting started with you, my love."

She took me down, down, down, and spread my legs wide, telling me to push them as far apart as possible. I did, and then she asked me to close my eyes for a surprise. I smiled and shut them, expecting something. But then, I felt her tongue slip inside me. Oh, goodness! It was like Thomas was inside me, only it was June! She made me feel so good! June had me coming so hard that I thought I'd explode! She must've known, because she was pushing her tongue deeper and deeper. I was thrashing up and down like a fish out of water, and when I had one last climax, I screamed her name. Then, I told her I was in love with her, and she said she loved me too.

Then it was time for me to please her. She showed me how and where to spread the sweet, sticky, flavorful jelly. At first, I felt nervous, but she was lovely and patient with me. Before I knew it, I was doing the same thing for June; she loved it!

But now, I've done something I shouldn't have with Thomas. I wanted him, despite his hands being all over me. He kept asking and pleading to have a child, saying he wanted children of his own. Whenever I tried to say something, he'd cover my mouth with his hand. By then, he was already on top of me. This morning, he accused me of being disobedient and took a belt to my behind, lashing me ten times. Then he pushed his thick manhood inside me, going deeper and deeper until I did something unthinkable. I arched my hips and loved every minute of it. I even begged him to go faster, and he did, asking each time:

"Are you sure, Sathronia? Because once my seed spills inside you, there is no turning back!"

How could I say no to him? I didn't want him to stop when we kissed.

So now, what's next? What about my beloved June? Oh my goodness, what have I done to us?

Sathronia sensed someone in the kitchen and spun around, startled by the person who was just observing her without moving.

"Good morning, Sathronia. I was hoping we could talk for a bit. I'd love to help you out with breakfast, and I wanted to apologize if I've caused you any trouble – I'm hoping we can be friends," Audine said with a smile, her lips betraying her true intentions.

CHAPTER THIRTY-ONE

"Are you going to tell June what happened between you and your husband this morning? What did she say when you mentioned you and Thomas wouldn't be together that way?" Audine asked.

"Shh! Keep your voice down, Audine! Someone might hear you, especially Thomas—he's always sneaking around the house, listening at doors, I have no idea what he's up to!" Sathronia said, craning her neck to scan the kitchen to see if Thomas was lurking about.

Smirking, Audine sat watching Sathronia with amusement at her nervousness, behaving like a paranoid pecker-head.

"I want to help you and June because after everything you've shared, it's clear you two need to start planning for a life together. It's too dangerous for you to keep staying in Thomas's bed. What if he gets rough again and won't stop? What if he does it again tonight or next month, with no monthly flow? Then what,

Sathronia? What happens to June? Don't forget how much she loves you. If Thomas puts a baby inside you, it's over between you and June, and you'll have his babies for the next ten years." Audine whispered.

"I won't let that happen! I can't let it happen; he can't come between June and me! I need to think it over and talk to June about it. She and I get together every Thursday at her place to talk. Thomas thinks we're just discussing the kitchen menu and that I'm only there to enjoy whatever she cooks," she said.

"Ezra picks me up around four o'clock to go home, and then I prepare dinner. But now that you and I are friends, you can help me get ready for the Thursday evening meals in the kitchen, especially since June and I are spending more time together. I'll teach you how to season the vegetables the way Thomas likes and how my daughters enjoy them without making them feel sick. How does that sound to you?" Sathronia asked, looking worried.

"I think that's a smart idea. Let's talk about it more so you won't feel nervous or make any mistakes, okay?" Audine said.

With a nod of enthusiasm, Sathronia reached over to take Audine's hands.

"Thanks for talking to me. I'd been keeping this secret to myself for a long time, and I was worried about how Thomas would react to me if he found out I had feelings for June. I'm excited to share with her that you and I are friends and that you're trying to help us out. Oh, Audine, thanks for being my friend and asking me those difficult questions I wouldn't have asked myself!"

She rose and went to Audine, wrapping her in a hug.

Later that evening.

"Audine, I'm scared. I'm worried about going to bed and what might happen. We had such a wonderful day, but it flew by so quickly. I still can't believe we're doing dishes together and chatting. I'm counting down the hours until I see June. She'll be delighted to know you know everything about us!" Sathronia said, handing Audine another plate to dry.

"Are you sure that you want June to know that I know about both of you? I don't want to cause any trouble," said Audine, rising onto her toes to put away the last of the dishes in the cabinet.

"I am positive that June will be relieved to know that I spoke to you. Again, I beg of you to never let Thomas know about me and June, or else he'd kill me," said Sathronia.

Audine couldn't help but notice Sathronia's terrified expression when she revealed what Thomas might do to her, and she relished every moment of it.

The more scared she becomes, the more likely she is to act carelessly and mess things up, hah! This is going to be easier than I thought! Audine thought to herself, amused by Sathronia's potential demise, not necessarily at the hands of Thomas but by her own.

"The dishes are done, and I'm exhausted. Why don't I help you tidy up and then head to bed? The more you stay busy around the house and with June, the more drained you'll be, and Thomas won't want to bother you anyway," Audine suggested.

"You're right! I'll keep myself busy around the house and come up with a plan to add an extra day in June.

That way, she and I will have more time together, and I'll be too exhausted to want to spend time with him, obedience or not! And who knows, if he loses interest, maybe he'll find someone else to be with. By then, I'll file for divorce, which will free me up to be with June, and my daughters can be with their husbands and raise their new families!" Sathronia said, covering her mouth with her hand to stifle a burst of laughter.

"What a delightful plan, Sathronia! See, I like what you're thinking! C'mon, let's get everything done quickly so I can bathe and go to bed!" said Audine.

Once the last chair was dusted, Sathronia and Audine walked upstairs, embraced, said goodnight to each other, and parted ways.

As Sathronia walked down the corridor, Audine watched until she opened the door to her bedroom and stepped inside.

Audine went to her room, gathered her bathing supplies, and headed straight to the bathroom. As the bathwater ran from the faucet, she took the syrup medication that helped her sleep. While examining her inner upper thighs, she noticed that the red blisters had crusted over into itchy scabs, with some starting to disappear. Relieved, Audine quickly brushed and oiled her hair. After covering it with a tignon, she turned off the water and carefully eased herself into the hot, soapy tub.

Getting rid of Sathronia will be easier than I thought! It's about keeping her in June's arms, away from Thomas, and at the right moment when Sathronia believes everything is a secret. I'll plan something so that she and June will be surprised! Mused Audine as he rinsed off and climbed out of the bathtub.

"I just need to make myself more attractive to Thomas, and that starts with Sathronia taking me where she gets her hair done," she said to herself, gazing into the mirror and feeling rather disgusted with her appearance.

She let out a sigh, then cleaned the tub until it was pristine. Opening the salve, she scooped up a fingerful, massaged it in, and waited for the sting to fade. Wincing, she rubbed the mixture into her skin, and it was absorbed. She slipped on her night slip and robe, turned off the lights, and left the bathroom door open to air it out.

Gathering everything in her arms, she headed to her room and put away her bathing items.

Then, she anxiously tiptoed down the corridor straight to Thomas's bedroom. Pressing her ear against the door, she heard the familiar moans of Sathronia and the loud, rapid squeaking of their mattress. Audine clenched her fist in anger, feeling her fingernails dig into her palm. Then, she heard Thomas's guttural climax. He said, "I love you," and Sathronia echoed it back to him! In tears, Audine hurried back to her room and shut the door. Climbing into bed, Audine sobbed into her pillow until the prescribed syrup she had taken earlier worked its magic, lulling her into a deep sleep.

The sound of fire crackling and the searing heat intensified. Audine tried to move but felt paralyzed. The house is on fire, and I can't move! One, two, three, sit up and run out of this burning house! Audine thought to herself.

The heat was intense, and the acrid smell of smoke stung her nostrils, causing her nose to run. Whoosh! A massive fireball, followed by an explosion, rocked the house. Audine could hear Thomas shouting for his daughters to open their door because the house was engulfed in flames. When they woke up, their screams echoed as they raced down the stairs with Thomas.

Ruthie asked Thomas where their mother was.

"Sathronia is dead, and I failed to save her or our baby! She's gone!" He screamed.

"Help! Don't leave me, Thomas!" Audine screamed. But it was too late. The ceiling of the house crashed down near the window.

"My legs won't move! I've got to get out of here!" Audine screamed.

Counting aloud again, Audine sprinted upward after the count of three and ran toward the door. She threw it open and found the hallway pitch-black. There was no sign of fire or smoke. Thomas and Sathronia were in bed, their mattress creaking, while Ruthie, Lucinda, and Delphine were fast asleep behind their closed bedroom doors.

Confused, Audine returned to her room and

removed her wet nightgown. The bed was soaked with her sweat. Sighing, she stripped the sheets and remade the bed with fresh linens. Then, she climbed into the bed, completely naked, to cool off.

Sathronia can wash these tomorrow, she thought, dazed and frightened by a dream so surreal that she felt she still smelled smoke. Or was it?

As she fell asleep, the dream returned; this time, she dreamt of the home where she had lived before marrying Wayne. Smoke, fire, burning wood, and falling embers surrounded her until the house was reduced to a pile of ashes. Twenty-four hours after it caught fire, the smoldering remnants of her home were carried away by a mighty wind that lasted six hours. When it was all over, Audine Collins's house was gone, leaving not even a trace of the foundation.

CHAPTER THIRTY-TWO

New Orleans.

"I suppose you all heard the terrible news," remarked Alice Wade.

"Oh yes, we certainly did. Wayne didn't seem to care what happened to Audine's old home, which burned down. When he went to check it out, everything-every single thing-was gone! All that was left was a huge pile of ashes; I saw it with my own eyes! It was the most terrifying sight I'd ever seen," said Alice, pulling up a chair to the table and joining Maria and Eucharista. Maria poured Alice another cup of piping hot coffee.

"So, tell us what you saw that scared you so much," Eucharista said, leaning in close so she wouldn't miss a word of Alice's story.

"I was going to check on Mrs. Wenderson because she said she felt cramping and wanted me to look at her. After I confirmed that everything was fine with her and the baby, my husband picked me up so we could go home. While my husband was driving us home, he suddenly slammed on the brakes."

"Oh my God, Alice, look! It's Audine's house, and it's burned to the ground! But where's the house? It's just a pile of smoldering ashes! There's nothing left!" he exclaimed.

"I tell you, it's like the house disappeared!" said Alice as she sipped her coffee and enjoyed a piece of cake.

"Humph serves her and that tramp of a daughter of hers right. Audine's mouth has caused a lot of damage and hurt many people here and in our church. I'll never forget that day when the awards were given to the girls who won scholarships and what she said to Carol," said Maria.

"Oh, you mean Phyllis's daughter?" Eucharista said.

"Yes," said Maria, shoving a piece of pie into her mouth and rubbing her belly.

"Ohhh, yes! I heard she's doing very well in that women's college! I talked to Phyllis, and it sounds like

Carol is at the top of her class and getting all A's in everything! I knew she'd do well! And what about Audine's daughter, Violet? Humph! I heard a morsel about her!" quipped Alice, taking another sip of coffee.

"Oh, well, what are you waiting for, Alice? Tell us!" insisted Eucharista, slicing another piece of pie.

"Whelp, last week, I received a surprise phone call from a good friend of mine who's a doctor in a place called Harlem in New York. We were talking about old times when he suddenly told me about one of his patients having a child. He described her as rather troubled," she said.

"Yes, Alice, go on, and don't leave anything out," declared Eucharista.

Maria appeared unfazed by the chatter and kept eating, even managing to sneak in another slice of pie.

"Anyway, the woman complained about a cough that wouldn't go away. When my friend asked more questions about the whereabouts of the baby's father, she broke down and said he had died and that the coughing had been present for many months. But here's the part that almost made me fall out of my chair," said Alice, heaving a deep sigh.

"When I asked him where she was from, he said New Orleans. Then I became curious about who he was talking about, so I asked him what her name was," Alice said.

"He mentioned that her name was Violet Booker".

Eucharista almost spat out her coffee, and Maria halted, lifting a forkful of pie to her lips.

"What? Violet lives in New York. What's she doing there?" asked Eucharista, wiping the corners of her lips.

"She's living with her aunt and uncle. The aunt is Audine's sister. Violet told the doctor that when her mother found out that she was carrying a baby by a married man who was a neighbor, her mother beat her so badly that she busted up her lip. And there's much more to the New York story! It seems like little Miss Violet got herself tangled up with that high-stakes gambler visiting New Orleans, the one Maydell and Lena were mixed up with. That man, his name was uh, uh, High-Roller Gunn!" she said, snapping her fingers to remember.

"What, hold on, Alice. Are you telling me Audine's daughter was also involved with that gambler? Hah! She is a shameless hussy! Lord, have mercy! First, Maria's husband, then High-Roller Gunn?" Eucharista shook her head in disgust.

"So, what happened to Gunn? Is that whore still with him?" Maria asked, clearly disgusted by the news Alice was sharing.

"Nope, the gambling man's days of raking in everyone's money are over. He was found dead," Alice quipped.

"What? How?" asked Maria, giving Alice her full attention and hanging on to every word she said.

"Hasn't she ruined enough lives? My goodness!" snorted Eucharista, disgusted.

"According to what my doctor friend said, Gunn's body was found weeks later, rotting in his flat. The tenants complained about the bad smell, so they had to call the police to enter the premises. My doctor friend said that Gunn's flat was a mess! Rats the size of my husband's hands were chewing on Gunn's hands, and several were chewing on his eye, the one that was blown off when he was shot in the head! Cockroaches were everywhere, and thousands of white, wriggling maggots covered the uneaten food on his dinner table, the sink, and in the bedroom, where the police discovered more uneaten food. My doctor friend, whose name, by the way, is Dr. Fields, said the news was all over Harlem, with people talking about it after it made headlines in the Harlem newspaper. And it appears that Gunn killed himself," said Alice, shaking her head.

"How was that determined?" Maria asked, captivated by what she was hearing.

"A note was in his hand. It said that he was the one who killed his mother's lover, an old woman who was the washerwoman of that building, and the most upsetting news of all, he admitted to the murder of Lena," responded Alice.

Both Eucharista and Maria stared at each other, their faces registering shock.

Maria picked up her coffee cup and took a quick

sip.

"This Gunn monster, Violet, and especially Audine can all join Clarence in hell," Maria said softly, her voice filled with pain.

"Indeed," responded Eucharista, taking another quick bite of her pie.

"I've got one more piece of news that will tickle both of you; it certainly did me," Alice said with a smile.

"Tell us, please, because that bite of news that you told us shook us up," said Eucharista.

"Whelp, get ready to be shaken up in a good way," Alice exclaimed, her grin so wide it could split her face.

"Tell us!" said Maria and Eucharista in unison, bursting out in laughter.

"It's Etta and Wayne. Etta is expecting," said Alice.

"What? Are Wayne and Etta expecting? Are you joking, Alice? We thought Wayne was still married to Audine! Please don't tell us that our sweet Etta did something foolish like—"

"Violet, just like she did with my husband, that dead son-of-a-bitch Clarence," interrupted Maria.

"No, no, no! Etta would never do something awful like that, absolutely not! So, here's what happened. After Wayne got rid of Audine, he immediately had their marriage annulled and went to see our pastor at the church about it. Once Wayne had his marriage annulled, he and Etta got together pretty quickly. On Christmas Eve, he proposed to Etta, and they got married the Saturday after New Year's. From what Etta told me, only eight people were there - nothing like Audine's wedding. Etta mentioned that things between her and Wayne moved fast. She said she knew their child was conceived on their wedding night. Twelve days later, she and Wayne came to see me. After I examined her and asked the necessary questions, it all came down to the fact that our sweet Etta would be having a baby in late October! When I sat them down and concluded that she was having a baby, Wayne got up, went over to Etta, pulled her out of the chair she was sitting in, and hugged her for so long that I could hear him crying tears of joy," Alice reported.

"This is wonderful news! We need to figure out a way to get together with her!" Maria exclaimed, clapping her hands with excitement.

"Grand news as well as a blessing! I'm happy for Etta, but even happier for Wayne that he married the right woman God intended him to be with!" said Eucharista.

"I've got an idea! How about we throw a surprise lunch for Etta, Beryl, and Ricks? His wife is also expecting!"

'This is the happiest news I've ever heard, especially about them; they're our friends. All of them wanted to start a family, and now look, they're all being blessed! What about you, Maria? How do you feel about it?" asked Eucharista.

Maria looked lovingly at her two friends. Despite the terrible things that had happened to Violet, Clarence, and Audine since they first met, Maria felt a sense of hope for the first time, and things were slowly getting back to normal.

"Of course," she said, beaming with joy.

For the rest of the afternoon, the conversation centered on hosting a big lunch, while Alice and Eucharista secretly plotted a surprise for Maria.

CHAPTER THIRTY-THREE

Since taking control of various sections of the barn, farm, and smokehouse, Ricks and his team have become the driving force behind these operations. Their unwavering commitment and tireless efforts—a true testament to their dedication—have not only proven beneficial but have also resulted in the sales of vegetables and meat from the smokehouse surpassing all expectations. This remarkable achievement is something they all take immense pride in, serving as a source of inspiration for those around them.

Since Clarence's passing, people from outside the county have been arriving, particularly to purchase produce. Ricks and his team plowed the fields and harvested collard greens, white and sweet potatoes, tomatoes, and small corn patches the week before Thanksgiving.

Jean, a Haitian who had become an integral part of their lives, was a treasure in the smokehouse. He shared his knowledge with Sampson, not only about the art of cutting, gutting, and slowly smoking meats and curing bacon, but also in French Creole. Much to Maria's overwhelming joy, Sampson's rapid mastery of these skills became not just a source of delight but also a beacon of hope for everyone, filling them with anticipation for the future.

Ricks, the master of woodcutting for the wood-burning stoves, had left a pile of chunks. Maria, her belly gently cradled, noticed a stick the length of a magician's wand among the pile. She used it to carefully sift through the mound, taking precautions against any snakes that might be lurking within.

Two chunks of wood fell into the dirt, causing Maria to yelp and nearly slip.

"I almost fell over!" Maria exclaimed, her gaze dropping to her stomach. A sharp kick followed, as if the baby inside had heard her.

Brushing herself off, she noticed the two fallen chunks and crept in for a closer look.

"Oui, Oui!" she exclaimed gleefully, clapping her

hands. The two chunks of wood, seemingly shaped like houses, filled Maria with joy. Gathering them up, she brushed off the dirt and debris, examining them closely. One was slightly pocket-sized, shriveled, and crooked. The roof-like structure was jagged, splintered, uneven, and sloped as if it had been crushed. Maria's smile and enthusiastic nodding reflected a sense of wonder and delight at this extraordinary discovery, a moment that captivated her.

She whispered to the piece of wood, naming it Audine, a name that reflected its crooked shape, and slipped it into her apron pocket.

Carefully examining the other mid-sized piece of wood, Maria glided her finger across its sturdy surface. Although it was wood, its texture felt smooth, almost like silk to her touch. In comparison to the other piece, the top had a thick, durable finish that was strangely and hauntingly beautiful, though it was shaved at an angle. The wood stood out from the others because of its unique color.

"Wayne, my dear Wayne, despite our differences, has never inflicted the same heart-wrenching pain as

Violet and Audine. This house, this symbol of unity, will be for Wayne and Etta. It's no secret that they've finally found each other! If only he had chosen Etta instead of wasting time on that wretched beast Audine!" Maria muttered, her voice echoing in the empty barn as she walked toward the door to begin her chores.

Inside the shed, Maria flipped on the light. She pulled a wooden stool with four legs from the corner and moved it to the shelf, then carefully hoisted herself up to gather her tools. As she lifted a large wooden box, she held it steady to prevent a cascade of scattered supplies and tools used for the barn and her work. After setting the box down, she placed it on the table to improve her balance and slowly stepped off the stool. She opened the box and took out the tools she needed to get started, including matches, wood chips, charcoal, fine-tipped wood, a bell, and a leather pouch containing iron dust from the small pile of iron shavings near Clarence's work tools. He used these to sharpen everything from axes for chopping to knives and smaller axes for slaughtering hogs, chickens, and turkeys in the barn.

Rummaging deeper inside the wooden box, she pulled out a grease-stained brown piece of paper, small jars of honey, dried lavender leaves, a bottle of Four Thieves vinegar, dirt from the crossroad that led to Audine's former house, and a clay flowerpot. On the floor beneath the shelf was a cactus plant- a gift given two months ago by Jean, whom Ricks had assigned to work in the smokehouse. Jean sensed that Maria needed such a gift to "banish that woman who caused much trouble in her family," referring to Audine as that "Sal ki tout-bitch, ki moun ki merite mouri, filthy whore-bitch, who deserves to die."

With the last item, the heavy cast-iron cauldron, Maria squatted as low as she could, then tugged and dragged it to the shed's center. What was once a manageable twenty-five-pound cast-iron cauldron now felt like a burden, especially with Maria already dripping with sweat and panting. She held her hand protectively over her protruding belly, took a deep breath, and closed her eyes.

Phew! This took me way longer than I thought! This is the last piece of my work to keep Audine and her daughter, who's no better than a whore, away from me, my family, friends, and Louisiana forever," she said aloud, pulling the wood chunks from her apron pocket and throwing them to the ground.

A mason jar filled with cold lemon water rested on a shelf in the corner of the table.

Oh, what a thoughtful and considerate gesture from my daughters! I'm sure they knew I'd be spending time here! I'm so grateful to them, and to all my children! "And to you, too, mon Cheri!" she acknowledged, looking down at her belly.

After taking a few gulps of lemon water, Maria quickly gathered the tools. She tossed four handfuls of wood chips into the cauldron, ignited a fire, and fanned the smoke toward the open window until the wood was reduced to embers. The four extra handfuls were set aside for the final task.

Taking the splintered piece of wood, she carefully wrote the names Audine Booker Collins and Violet Booker Collins on the face of the house with the charcoal pencil. Then, she meticulously penned the words: disrupter, troublemaker, glutton, gossip-monger, prideful, envious, confrontational, deceitful, thief, and liar.

Once she finished writing, she grabbed the brown, grease-stained paper and wrote the names "Violet" and "Audine" on it.

"Humph, greasy, just like Audine's lying lips!" Maria muttered.

Setting the paper aside, Maria tossed two more handfuls of wood chips into the fire. After five minutes, she watched the cauldron blaze. Without saying a word, Maria rose from the stool. With the house bearing Audine and Violet's names, she looked at it resentfully. Then, she spoke in French Creole.

"Mwen banni tou de nan nou, yon sèl manman se deranjman an pwoblèm, glise, tripotay, tripotay-monger, fyète, anvye, konfwontasyon, mantè twonpe, vòlè, ak pitit fi ou Violet, ki moun ki pote timoun nan batay ki te plante nan mari m '! Se pou ou pa janm mete pye nan Louisiana tout tan ankò, pa men nan lanmò," intoned Maria.

She smeared a wad of putrid-smelling hog

manure with a stick and tossed both the stick and the house into the roaring fire. After adding the final handful of wood chips, she watched the house burn until it became a mound of ashes.

"And let it be so," she repeated three times.

With the grease-stained paper bearing Audine and Violet's names, Maria removed the top from the mason jar containing the Four Thieves vinegar and thoroughly soaked the paper in it. She then shook off the excess vinegar, replaced the lid, and set the jar aside.

She carefully folded the wad away from herself and placed it at the bottom of the clay flowerpot. Taking the jar of crossroad dirt, she poured three-quarters of it onto the paper wad. Then she began scooping dirt from the cactus into the prepared flowerpot, positioning it in the center, pouring the remaining dirt around the plant, and adding water.

She then spoke.

"*Epi se pou rasin plant sa a ki pral pwoteje m ',
fanmi mwen, ak zanmi toufe* **ou**, *Audine, osi byen ke sa
ki nan yon pitit fi nan ou,*"

"And let it be so," she repeated three times.

Wayne and Etta, who had been rumored to be seeing each other shortly after Audine left, were now married and starting a new family, as Maria dedicated the second wood chunk to them. Meanwhile, Rick's wife, Beryl, and her husband, Turner, were expecting a new baby.

Maria carved the names of Wayne and Etta into the wooden chunk. On the front of the house, she then wrote the words happiness, long life, joy, love, laughter, abundance, and the number "3" between their names.

"For the three daughters that you'll have, and though we aren't friends, I send you and Wayne happiness as well as for the rest of our friends," she said.

She dipped three fingers into the honey jar and smeared the honey over their names and acronyms on the wooden chunk. Then, she sprinkled a small handful of lavender leaves onto the honey.

Maria gently wrapped the wood chunk in an unused white linen cloth, tying it with a three-corner knot. She then lifted herself and stepped out of the shed, burying the piece deep in the soil where sweet honeysuckles would grow and bloom later in the spring.

After the ashes had cooled, Maria collected them into a metal bucket. She walked a quarter of a mile from her home, along the dirt road, carrying the bucket of ashes before pouring them into a pile.

As she walked home, a strong gust of wind nearly knocked her off balance. Straddling her legs to maintain stability, she turned her head, shielding her eyes to look back at the mound of ashes. To her shock, the wind scattered them into an abyss of nothingness.

When she returned to the shed, Maria put everything back in its place. Grabbing the cold glass of lemon water, she took several gulps, drained the glass, and let out a loud burp.

"Excuse me, little one!" she said, laughing.

She switched off the shed light, shut the door, and, before heading inside, grabbed the cactus plant, and placed it by the front door.

She then went inside her house for the rest of the night.

Sondra J. Hardy

CHAPTER THIRTY-FOUR

Two o'clock in the morning.

The thunderclap was so intense that it shook the whole house. Remarkably, Maria's family slept through it.

Maria pulled back the blankets and stood up, rubbing her eyes as she strolled over to the window. She gazed out, and a vast white lightning bolt flashed across the sky, lighting up the whole scene in a burst. Maria stepped away from the window as the thunder crashed out in two loud, violent bursts.

BOOM! BOOM!

Another bolt of lightning hit, followed by a loud explosion that rocked the house, making Maria jump and put a protective hand on her belly.

Looking out the window, Maria spotted thick gray smoke billowing up a quarter of a mile away. Then, another lightning bolt flashed across the sky, heading straight for the smoke and triggering yet another explosion. Maria kept her gaze fixed on the smoke, which grew thicker by the minute.

Then, out of nowhere, the thunder stopped, and so did the lightning. Everything came to a halt.

"The show's over, I guess," Maria said, yawning.

She climbed into bed, pulled back the covers, and drifted off to sleep peacefully.

News of the incident spread quickly across the county the next day: the house where Audine once lived had been hit by multiple lightning strikes and destroyed by fire. All that was left was a massive pile of ashes and smoldering debris. The fire still burned with bright orange embers, but it quickly died down into the ashes.

When Wayne Collins was notified and arrived at the scene, he looked around and shrugged.

"Good, now I can get back to my life in peace," he said.

Then he got into his car, with Etta in the passenger seat, and drove off.

According to what Alice Wade had told Maria and Eucharista, Etta and Wayne got married on a sunny Saturday morning in front of a small, intimate family gathering.

Alice did not reveal that Wayne and Etta were eager to consummate their marriage. Etta deeply adored Wayne, and when they were alone in his house that afternoon, having taken the day off from work, the joy of their enthusiastic lovemaking unfolded shamelessly for the first time.

Hours after county residents saw Audine's house turn to ashes, a violent wind swept through, causing people to scramble to their cars to drive away and seek refuge in their homes.

The wind scattered the ashes of Audine's home to the distant hills beyond New Orleans.

When the wind stopped, nothing was left of Audine's property except for traces of burnt grass.

CHAPTER THIRTY-FIVE

"This is a no-fuss cake my mother used to bake, Audine. She learned how to make it by watching my grandmother. It's an ugly-looking cake, but it makes up for the flavor!" laughed Sathronia, pouring the cake batter into a round pan.

Audine helped by opening the preheated oven as Sathronia placed the pan inside.

"One hour to bake! The mixing bowls are already washed and dried, so we can sit down and talk over coffee. One of us needs to keep an eye on the time. We certainly don't want a burnt cake!" exclaimed Sathronia as she opened the cabinet and selected two coffee cups and matching saucers.

"When Bishop and I first met, I was already married, but my husband and I would have him, the deacons, and their wives over for Sunday dinner monthly after service. Oh, how grand those days were! Every time it was our turn to host Sunday dinner, Bishop would take me aside a week beforehand and request the apple cake with sweet cream," said Sathronia, standing back with her eyes closed and a smile across her lips as she marveled at the memories and how the aroma was already permeating the entire kitchen.

"So, Bishop was alone when you and your husband got together for Sunday dinners? Oh, that sounds interesting. Tell me more. Now that we're friends, you can tell me everything, especially about Bishop," Audine said with a sly smile and a false expression of concern.

Humph, the more I know, the more I'll have to spill to Bishop about his wife's little romance with her girlfriend. Hah! Two of the nastiest fiends I have ever seen, kissing each other on the lips in the church bathroom, sticking their tongues inside each other's mouths! Ugh, how nasty! They probably have that nasty woman's disease in their mouths and everywhere else! Audine was appalled by what she had seen in the church bathroom.

"When my husband and I joined the church, Thomas's relationship with a woman from Georgia ended, and he was struggling. But it seems his mood shifted after he met me and my late husband," Sathronia said, looking wistfully into the distance.

"Thomas admired both of us as a couple and loved our daughters like his own. A year after my husband and I joined the church, Thomas ordained him as head Deacon because he excelled in managing money effectively, his education, and his sense of humor. Sometimes, those two would laugh so hard that Thomas had to delay the service by ten minutes to regain his composure! Oh, have mercy, Lord. They became such great friends that Thomas eventually forgot about that woman in Georgia. Thomas cherished and kept the Deacons close, but he remained especially close with my husband, especially after noticing the increase in church funds and my husband's advice on property purchases. Thomas thrived not only because of the money coming in, but also because he and my husband welcomed the homeless into the newly built flats, thanks to the church members who worked as carpenters and bricklayers. The residents kept those apartments spotless. Women soon worked as laundresses, caring for children whose mothers had to work, while their husbands served as drivers, cooks, plumbers, hospital workers, and clothing factory workers. Thanks to Thomas and my husband, many bricklayers and lumber workers built flats and the businesses where we shop for food, schools, live, go to school, and more. The older members of our church play music during the service. It's magnificent to hear them play!" exclaimed Sathronia, smiling.

"So, how much money do you think the church has, Sathronia? Just from what you're saying, it seems like a lot! And how can the church members afford to live in those lovely flats?" inquired Audine, eager to learn more about Thomas.

For a moment, Sathronia was hit with a sudden rush of nerves.

"Honey, are you alright? You don't have to say anything if you don't want to. I thought that as best friends, we could share anything – even secrets or personal stuff. But if you don't want to share, I understand," Audine said, giving Sathronia a tight hug.

Audine felt Sathronia melt into her arms as if she

had been waiting to do so for years —a trusted friend who would understand everything: her troubled marriage to Thomas, her daughters married to husbands on long missionary assignments, and her biggest secret, her love for June Posey.

"Audine, do you swear you won't tell anyone what I'm about to tell you?" she asked in a hushed, sad tone.

"Yes, of course, Sathronia. Honey, what's the matter? What's got you all ruffled up?" asked Audine.

"The money. Most of the money that paid for all those flats, businesses, even the church, came from my husband!" Sathronia said, wiping away tears that had gathered in the corners of her eyes.

Audine squeezed Sathronia's trembling hands.

"Shh, take a sip of coffee, then tell me everything," urged Audine, who was trying to hide a noticeable smirk.

She took a deep breath and sipped the hot coffee several times.

"Thinking my husband was working late, he was breaking into the houses of several wealthy white men while working as their chauffeur around the city. Late at night, he and some friends broke into their homes, located their money, and then robbed them. While one group ransacked the houses, others acted as lookouts at the stairways leading to the bedrooms of these men, where they slept with their wives or mistresses. Well, one night, according to my husband, a rich married man's wife and children were all out of town visiting, so he had his mistress at the house. But something went wrong that night. People were killed; each took a bullet to the head," said Sathronia, who trembled as if having spasms.

Audine grabbed Sathronia's coffee cup and refilled it with fresh coffee, sugar, and cream. She then set the cup down in front of her, and Audine pulled her chair closer.

"Drink that slow; it's boiling," Audine said.

She nodded and took a sip of the hot coffee, which helped calm her nerves. Closing her eyes, she took a deep breath.

"This is exactly what I needed," she said, feeling relaxed.

"So go on, finish telling me what happened," urged

Audine as she joined Sathronia for another cup of coffee.

Audine sat on the edge of her seat, her eyes wide as saucers, listening to this extraordinary tale of robbery and murder, which revealed how Thomas's church, along with the properties that supported the community's children in school, helped their families earn a living.

"It was truly remarkable because it was one of the best-kept secrets in the Black community, particularly during the Depression. It was way ahead of its time and would last for generations. Just the properties themselves are worth millions," she said.

With her eyes locked on the target, Audine's mouth watered like a predator about to strike.

"Go on," Audine said softly, her voice reassuring.

"Anyway, the gangster pulled out a gun on my husband, but my husband's friend was quicker on the draw. He shot the gangster in the neck, and the guy dropped dead instantly. After they found the toy box and stuffed the money into burlap sacks, they were about to take off when they heard footsteps coming down the stairs. My husband's friend stepped in front of him and pointed the gun toward the footsteps, then *boom!* He shot the person walking down the stairs", said Sathronia.

"Oh, my goodness, who was it?" Audine asked, covering her mouth with her hand.

"His mistress, who was hiding in the closet. She must've thought they all left," said Sathronia.

"And what about the other friends of your husband?" Audine asked.

"The gangster shot them all. He always kept a loaded gun under his pillow, so when they broke into his bedroom, he fired and killed them. With everyone dead in the house, my husband and his friend split the money – 15 years of savings in four bags. His friend took two, and my husband took the other two. Then they jumped into his friend's car. My husband said he drove like a madman, straight out of hell. He dropped my husband off at our home, and my husband ran to our bedroom, woke me up, and told me to pack up the girls because something terrible had happened. After I packed up our whole family, we were on our way. We drove for two days and ended up here in Chicago."

"Where exactly did all this take place?" Audine asked.

"New York. We're from Brooklyn, New York," Sathronia replied.

At the sound of New York, goosebumps erupted on Audine's arms and back.

Oh my God! My sister, Cee-Cee, and Hubert are in New York, taking care of Violet. But the money, all that money! Audine thought to herself.

"How much was in those sacks?" Audine asked, unabashedly curious.

"Each bag had ten thousand dollars in cash. My husband took off and ran with twenty thousand dollars. As soon as we got to Chicago, we moved into this house," Sathronia said, taking another sip of coffee.

"Hold on, I'm confused. This house was your husband's?" Audine asked.

"Yes, Thomas was living in a flat, which was very

nice, but nothing like this beautiful house. But then we began to hear people on the streets talking about a preacher named Thomas Almonds and the Full Trumpets of Heaven, a musical style consisting only of trombones and trumpets. One Sunday, we attended church service and heard him preach. After hearing his music, we indeed joined the following Sunday! Thomas baptized me and my entire family, and that's when all the wonderful things started to happen for us, thanks to my husband," said Sathronia proudly.

"After five years, my husband helped Thomas buy fifteen damaged apartments, rebuild them, and then purchase fifteen more, bringing the total to thirty. All twelve Deacons have homes, every church member is employed, and we even have *our own* grocery store, so we no longer have to rely on those whites who want nothing to do with us. As for the clothes and uniforms we wear to church, my husband and Thomas had the bricklayers build a structure where fifty women sew clothing from seven in the morning until three in the afternoon. From three to eleven in the evening, skilled men take over sewing and tailoring. So, as you can see, this community is never going down; it's going higher than ever! Thanks to my husband, who advised Thomas to always travel in style: a Packard driven by a church member, four guards, the Deacons, including my husband, the head Deacon, and his secretary, a retired English teacher," Sathronia said.

Oh my, Thomas has people who drive him around and protect him. His Deacons are always close by, and he even has a retired teacher acting as his secretary. With all these luxuries, including this magnificent house, and the fact that they're not going without food despite the Depression, this seems like a perfect opportunity for me to slip in and for Sathronia to escape! Audine thought to herself, taking another sip of coffee.

The aroma of the cake baking in the oven made Audine's mouth water as she cast furtive glances at the stove, hoping Sathronia would catch the hint that it was time to take the cake out, let it cool, and then indulge in it all for herself.

She must have caught the hint because, suddenly, Sathronia leaped out of the chair, removed the heavy towel from her shoulder, opened the oven, and took out the cake. She set it on the counter to cool and then returned to her seat.

"Audine? You okay?" Sathronia asked, shooting Audine a suspicious glance.

Audine could feel the blood rushing to her head and quickly snapped back to attention to what Sathronia was saying.

"Yes, Sathronia, I'm fine. I was thinking about how happy you were to have all of this, your church, your house, everything!" exclaimed Audine, gesturing with her arms.

"But I do have one question for you."

Out of nowhere, Sathronia started to feel queasy and uneasy, worried that too much information had been shared, especially with Audine, who was still a stranger to her.

"What's your question?" she asked.

Her voice trailed off suddenly. I'm done thinking about Audine, period. She's my new best friend, Sathronia reminded herself.

"So, what happened to your husband?" Audine asked bluntly, her lips curling into a sly smile.

Seated at the table, Sathronia winced at the question, completely taken aback. She dropped her head, looking down.

Oh, I think I hit a nerve! This information is going to be juicier than a ripe orange! Audine thought to herself, struggling to suppress a huge smile.

"What's wrong? This must be painful to talk about. I should know because I've suffered, too. Please talk to me about it as your dearest friend. Come, and you can tell me everything," Audine said convincingly as she clasped her hand around Sathronia's, which was curled into a trembling fist. Audine noticed silent tears rolling down her face.

"Sathronia, look up, look at me," cooed Audine as she gently lifted her chin.

When Audine's gaze met hers, she felt completely at ease and trusted Audine.

She's my friend, and I feel safe with her now. I can trust Audine, Sathronia thought to herself, feeling a sense of relief.

Her hands trembling, Sathronia grasped Audine's hands as if they were the only thing keeping her alive.

"My husband was murdered," Sathronia said, her hands covering her face. "He was stabbed over forty-eight times. What's even worse is that he had forgotten to bring Thomas the deed to another property they had just closed on. Thomas was excited about it because the second floor would be a beauty salon, and the first floor would be a large restaurant. He was late for the meeting and kept asking what was taking my husband so long to arrive. One of the other Deacons suggested they check outside, so Thomas and all the Deacons rushed out to look for him, heading towards where my husband's car was parked."

For a moment, Audine felt numb, almost feeling sorry for Sathronia, but unearthing the truth was crucial.

"Sathronia, what happened?" implored Audine.

"He-he-he was on the ground, lying dead in a pool of blood," Sathronia stammered.

"They all tried to help him, but he was already

gone. The Deacons tried to pry Thomas off my husband's body. Ezra told me that Thomas collapsed in grief. He was in hysterics and wasn't left alone for days following my husband's funeral. I had to be strong for my daughters, especially when they approached the casket and saw their father lying there. I had to tell them he was asleep and wouldn't wake up. When the lid was closed, the shrieking and screaming began. It took twenty ushers, along with Thomas, to calm them down. It was beyond my ability to describe that entire service without breaking down even now as I speak about it." Sathronia said, wiping away tears.

"Oh, my goodness, I'm so sorry, especially for your daughters," Audine said, squeezing her eyes shut and wiping away fake tears.

"I continued attending church, caring for my daughters, and managing the household. Thomas was wonderful, though. He started showing up every Wednesday and Friday, especially on Friday evenings," she said with a fond smile.

"What made Fridays so special?" Audine asked warily.

"Fish. This community has a special tradition on Fridays, calling them "Fish-Fry Fridays." There are two reasons behind it. First, we buy fish from a few men who are skilled at catching them. They take the fish home for an extra dollar, and their wives prepare it by scaling, gutting, cleaning, and wrapping it in that brown butcher paper. The husbands help clean up the mess and deliver the fish, and we also give them a little extra for gas. If they know of a family with cats, they even save the fish guts for them. Nothing goes to waste. We serve potato salad, green beans, and cornbread with fish. If the fish aren't biting, we have pancakes or biscuits with butter and homemade jam instead. The second reason for this tradition is that Thomas's mom was Catholic before she converted to the faith he practices now. He wants to honor that tradition as a tribute to her. So, when I make the fish, I make it extra crispy, which Thomas loved. I'd give at least two pieces and four biscuits for any leftover fish," she said.

"Why is that?" Audine asked.

"So that he could make himself fish sandwiches. He said that when he'd get home, he would unwrap everything, make the sandwiches, and have them the next day because the biscuits would soak up the grease," she said.

"Oh, I see," Audine said, her voice laced with jealousy.

"Thomas loved reading to my daughters and helping them with their schoolwork, especially Ruthie, who was still struggling with nightmares about her father's funeral. Although she was falling behind in school, once Thomas started coming over to help, she excelled and topped her class. Her teachers were amazed at how well she was doing, particularly in arithmetic. He also assisted me because, by the time I finished washing the dishes, cleaning the kitchen, and putting away leftover food, Thomas had already checked their homework, put the girls to bed, and read to them until they fell asleep. The biggest surprise was that he had all their school stuff ready for the next day, so they wouldn't have to rush to get ready on Mondays. On Fridays, they'd stay up late playing games outside until it was time for everyone to come in, giving the girls time to clean up and get ready for bed. When Thomas came down to check on me, I'd already finished cleaning the kitchen, and well, that was our time together," said Sathronia softly.

As Sathronia spoke, Audine's jaw clenched.

"Oh, and what did you two do together, especially being alone with a man as good-looking as he is?" Audine asked with a hint of envy.

Sathronia pressed her fingers to her lips to hush Audine.

"I let Thomas touch me. At first, we mostly talked about my daughters, the future, this house, and all that. You have to understand, as a Black woman who had just lost my husband to murder, I was alone in this world with three young daughters, aged ten, eleven, and twelve. That's when Thomas said he'd take care of me and my girls. Then he kissed my cheek, held my hands, and asked if I trusted him. I said yes, of course. He kissed my hands, my cheeks, and then my lips. I didn't stop him or say no. I didn't want Thomas to stop. Before I knew it, he was unbuttoning my blouse, pulling down my bra, and covering my breasts with his mouth. Oh, my goodness, his tongue was all over them, nipping each one, sucking them like a baby nursing. Thomas picked me up in his arms and took me to my bedroom, where we undressed and got into bed. Thomas is long and thick down there," Sathronia whispered, pointing between her legs.

"I enjoyed him more than my husband, which made me feel guilty. But Thomas reassured me that there was nothing to be ashamed of. My husband was gone, and we were alive. So, when Thomas entered me, his huge erection filling me up, I stretched so wide I cried out, not from pain, but because I wanted every inch of him inside me. He thrust deeper and faster until his groans grew louder, and then he emptied himself into me. We clung to each other, not wanting to let go, but it was getting late, and he had to leave. I was sad, but it gave me a sense of purpose. I spent hours keeping this house clean, ensuring that food was served on time and that everything was in order. My daughters were doing well in school, and Fridays couldn't come soon enough. Thomas was in my bed, inside me, every Friday until..."

"Until what? Until what, Sathronia?" interrupted Audine, who was seething with jealousy, enraged that it was Sathronia, not her, who was in bed with Thomas.

"Thomas had put a baby inside of me. I knew because every morning for a month, I was throwing up, and my monthly flow had stopped. It was so bad that the smell of fish made me sick. I had to tell Thomas what was happening."

"And what did Thomas say?" Audine probed.

"He was so happy, it was like he was giddy. Then he picked me up and started spinning around the bedroom. Next thing I knew, we were downstairs in the living room. When he sat me down on the couch, he told me to stay still, ran upstairs, and got my daughters, having them sit down beside me. Thomas asked them how they'd feel about having a new father," Sathronia said.

Audine shot Sathronia a glare, waiting to hear her response.

"They were all excited and said they'd love to have a new father. Me? Hah! I was completely confused! Then he stood up in front of me and asked me to stand up too. He stood up, took my left hand, and kissed my fingers. Then, reaching into his pocket, he pulled out a blue velvet box and opened it up. Inside was the most stunning engagement ring I'd ever seen! He asked me to marry him in front of my daughters, and they were over the moon! None of us got a wink of sleep that night. The next morning, after breakfast, I made sure my daughters and I got our hair done so we'd look our best for Sunday service. Then, on Sunday morning, it was announced that we were engaged and would be getting married on Thomas's birthday-his idea, not mine. We hadn't even discussed setting a date; he had chosen his birthday as the date. I didn't say a word; I just wanted to soak up the moment and the excitement of it all," Sathronia said, taking a sip of coffee.

In her jealous rage, Audine didn't respond. Without saying a word, she stood up and walked over to where the cake was cooling. Selecting a plate, fork, and knife, she cut an enormous slice, placed it on the plate, plopped down in her chair, and ravenously attacked the cake, shoveling in mouthfuls and remaining oblivious to Sathronia.

Memories of Wayne's proposal and their wedding flooded Audine's mind, and hearing Sathronia's tale of her engagement deepened Audine's envy.

"Go on, Sathronia. I couldn't stand waiting for this cake to cool down. It's delicious. Keep going with your story!" she said, shoveling another forkful of cake into her mouth and making a loud slurping noise as she drank her coffee.

Stunned, Sathronia watched as Audine shoved another forkful of cake into her mouth, following it with yet another cup of scalding hot coffee. She noticed how aggressively Audine handled the utensils, cutting and serving only for herself, without even offering to cut an extra slice for her.

What's wrong with her? All of a sudden, she flipped. Sathronia wondered.

"Anyway, birthday or not, the wedding was beautiful," Sathronia beamed at the memory.

"I was lucky to find a seamstress who could tailor my wedding dress to hide my growing belly, but just two weeks after our wedding, I woke up in the middle of the night with soaked sheets. Thomas and I had been intimate every night, and I thought it was due to the way he was doing me from behind, on his knees. I loved it, and he kept going deeper. He said that if we kept this up, he'd want me to have five more children after this one, one every year. However, the cramping started hours later. When I turned on the lights, the bed was soaked in blood. Thomas woke up the girls, and he drove us to the hospital," she said.

"What happened?" Audine asked, putting her fork down long enough to listen.

"We were told we lost the baby," Sathronia said, her voice barely above a whisper. Thomas and I cried for hours. He blamed himself for loving me in our bed every night and cried so much that he went into a coughing spell. The doctor had to calm him down and give him syrup to stop the vomiting long enough for him to drive home and watch our daughters. I was in the hospital for two days to halt the bleeding. Once I returned home, all Thomas would do was insist that we try for another baby again. Every time he put himself inside of me, I'd cringe and hope that nothing would happen. Then, suddenly, he stopped. As soon as we'd get into bed, it was just sleep, that's all. Thomas asked me one more time to please have a child with him," said Sathronia.

"And what did you say to him?" Audine asked, leaning in to hear Sathronia's response.

"I said no to him," answered Sathronia.

"What? You said no to Thomas? Why would you even say that?" Audine asked, her heart racing at Sathronia's response.

"I lost my love for Thomas, and his high expectations in our marriage were too much. Serving and being active in the church became too much for me to handle. I felt lonely and sad, crying all the time, especially after losing our child, whom I thought was a blessing. I tried to tell Thomas that my daughters were enough for us, and I also didn't want people to make fun of me for having three older girls. Plus, how would I appear to him with four or even five more babies, one every year? So, I made sure he didn't touch me at certain times of the month. But then something-or someone-else came into my life," Sathronia said with a smile.

"I don't even have to guess; it's June Posey," Audine replied.

"Yes, it's June, and I'm asking you again, as my friend, to keep this a secret. I have no one else to talk to, no real friends except one, and that's you, Audine. I love her so much it hurts - not in a bad way, but in a way that gives me an ache I can't shake off because I don't want it to fade from her and me. But I have secrets I haven't even shared with June," Sathronia whispered.

"Tell me, what haven't you spoken about to June?" Audine asked, leaning so far off the chair that she nearly toppled to the floor.

Even though I was weak when Thomas and I made love, and I told him I would give him a child this time, I haven't told June that I let Thomas touch me again. Things will only get worse if I find out I'm having a child with Thomas. Then June will be done with me for good unless I can encourage her to let me have the baby, and then we can plan to leave Chicago and start anew somewhere else. If she agrees to my plan, June and I will leave Chicago for good.

"How would you do that? How would you get away from Thomas?" Audine asked, becoming more interested in how this plan with June would play out if

Sathronia had a child with Thomas.

"I'm leaving him, that's a given. After that, I'll have the baby. Then, June and I will start fresh. My daughters are already married with their own families, and once we're settled, my new baby, June, my daughters, and their children will be a family again, without Thomas. So, promise me, Audine, that you won't tell anyone my secret," she whispered, clutching Audine's hands.

"As your friend, I promise I'll never tell anyone about you, June, or the baby you might have with Thomas. You can trust me with anything, including your life and your secrets," Audine said, smiling in a way that didn't quite ring true.

CHAPTER THIRTY-SIX

Sunday Morning.

I look awful. This dress is a mess, and my hair is terrible and itchy! How am I supposed to face Thomas today? Audine thought, staring at her reflection in disgust at her appearance.

She roughly ran her fingers through her scalp, scratching until she broke the skin. The gentle knock at the door brought her back to reality.

"Good morning. May I come in?" whispered Sathronia. She twisted the doorknob, tiptoed inside, and sat on the edge of the bed.

"Good morning, Sathronia. Oh, my goodness, don't you look glorious today! Just look at you; you look like an angel straight out of heaven, visiting me. I wish I could look half as good as you do, especially on my first day at church," said Audine, trying to hide her jealousy and envy.

Audine's eyes were fixated on the stunning navy blue button-down, six-gore, inverted pleated dress with long sleeves and a beige, rounded-edge collar. The shoes and basic oxfords fit Sathronia perfectly, and the form-fitting dress complemented the hat beautifully. Sathronia pulled her hair back into a tight bun, and her pearl earrings, undoubtedly a gift from Thomass, accentuated her chiseled face.

Why can't I look like her today? I'm supposed to look like that for Thomas, not HER! Audine thought bitterly, her teeth grinding with resentment.

Audine wiped away a tear that was rolling down her face.

"What's wrong, Audine? What's going on? What's bothering you?" Sathronia asked as she got out of bed to comfort her.

"I don't look as beautiful as you, Sathronia! Oh, my goodness, look at me! I look awful! My hair is an itchy, knotted, tangled mess, my dress is a rag, and I'm still wearing the same shoes from New Orleans – they're worn out and filthy! Everyone's going to laugh at me!" cried Audine, who was soon wrapped in a hug by

Sathronia.

"Listen to me. You've been through a lot in the past few weeks, and to be honest, most women wouldn't have made it out alive like you did. They'd be stuck in some dive, drinking every night, or standing around waiting for some wayward, no-good man to give them money after they'd put out for him. But not you, Audine. You need a fresh start. Tomorrow afternoon, when the factory opens, we'll be the first ones in, and I'll pick out some dresses for you to wear around the house and to church on Sundays. Don't worry anymore; I'll make sure you're an outstanding church member, and everyone will respect you," said Sathronia, wrapping Audine in her arms.

Is she shopping for dresses at the church-owned factory tomorrow? This means that Sathronia will pay for everything. I'll also make sure she pays for lunch unless we stop by the church for a meal there; however, that means she'll run into June, which might not be a bad idea after all! Audine thought to herself as she concealed her smiling lips with deception.

Audine took a deep breath.

"Please, we need to hurry! Ezra will be at the house any minute now. I can hear his car horn. Come on, Audine!" Sathronia's voice was laced with urgency as she rushed out of the room. With a final glance in the mirror, Audine adjusted her dress, smoothed her hair, and slipped on her coat. She tightened her boots securely on her feet, ensuring each strap was fastened to prevent her ankles from getting tired. Grabbing her purse and Bible, she hurried out the door and bounded downstairs, her heart racing with anticipation.

"Good morning, Mrs. Collins!" bubbled Ruthie, Lucinda, and Delphine, who were helping each other into their coats.

"Good morning! Oh my, don't the three of you look beautiful in those dresses! They certainly show how far along you are with the babies inside each of you! Are you all eating well?" Audine asked.

The sisters looked at one another and glanced at Sathronia, who was delighted that her grown daughters would soon be mothers. She would be a grandmother, but it was also possible that she might have a child growing inside her because she and Thomas were intimate every night, reminding her that he wouldn't stop until she announced that she was carrying his child. The thought of it all made her wince at the idea of being a grandmother while also having a baby.

Everyone will laugh at me, and June will leave me! *she thought, taking a deep breath and trying to hold back her tears.*

"All three of my daughters are eating well, but I think Ruthie is the one eating the most!" Sathronia exclaimed, her voice brimming with pride and joy, a smile lighting up her face.

Her daughters smiled and nodded at Sathronia, then linked their arms and headed out the door first, followed by Audine and Sathronia. She turned off the lights, locked the door with a key from her purse, and slipped it back inside. After giving the doorknob a final jiggle to double-check the lock, she was all set.

Audine watched Sathronia intently.

"Shall we?' a smiling Sathronia asked, extending the crook of her arm to Audine.

Audine forced a bright smile as she held onto the

crook of Sathronia's arm. As they descended the stairs, Audine glanced to her right and noticed the dashboard of a black Ford Model B peeking through the garage's glass window.

"Sathronia, whose car is that?" Audine inquired, pointing to the garage.

Without warning, Sathronia halted her walk.

"Noddington. That was Noddington's car. He was also known as Noddy, which was his nickname," she said, looking straight ahead.

"Noddington? What kind of name is that?" Audine asked, trying to hide her smirk by keeping her eyes on the car.

"Noddington was my husband, and he was killed in a car while trying to escape after being stabbed repeatedly. I mentioned that to you yesterday," Sathronia said, her voice flat and emotionless.

Audine already knew the story, but in her twisted, vindictive mind, she wanted to hear it again to throw Sathronia further into chaos and leave her so devastated that she'd have no choice but to keep seeking comfort from June and Audine, and in doing so, push herself into Thomas' arms. The thought of it all made Audine suppress a smile by pulling out a handkerchief and pretending to wipe her nose.

CHAPTER THIRTY-SEVEN

Something about the church felt different. Even on a bright, chilly, windy day, the parishioners hurried up the church stairs, not to escape the cold, but to eagerly await the powerful music and listen to Thomas preach and prophesy.

Audine gazed out the car window to see what was going on. The street was packed with cars on both sides, so many that more than fifty drivers had to park another two miles down the road.

"Is it always like this?" Audine asked.

"Like what?" Ezra asked, seeming slightly annoyed by Audine's curiosity and not apologizing for her reckless behavior at the church a few days ago.

"Look at all those people! My goodness, they're running up the stairs like crazy! What's going on?" Audine asked, craning her neck to get a better look at what the woman worshipper was wearing.

He disregarded her, turning away and rolling his eyes.

She couldn't help but think, 'This is more like a fashion show than a church service!" Her dry, brittle hair was driving her crazy, and she kept fidgeting with her hat, trying to scratch her itchy scalp without anyone noticing. But the dandruff flakes on her coat's shoulders gave her away. Everyone in Ezra's car took notice.

Audine felt Sathronia's grip on her wrist.

"It's time to go inside," Sathronia said.

Audine's heart swelled with mixed emotions as she noticed a glint of happiness in Sathronia's eyes. When it was her turn to be helped out of the car by Ezra, Sathronia took Audine's arm at the elbow, and they slowly ascended the stairs toward the church, with Sathronia's daughters following and being assisted by Ezra, who kept his eyes on Audine with a blend of disdain and distrust.

There's something about that woman that doesn't feel right. It's like every word out of her mouth is a calculated lie, Ezra thought to himself, with Ruthie holding his arm on one side and Lucinda on the other, while Delphine clutched Lucinda's hand and gripped the rail.

At the top of the stairs stood two imposing figures dressed in black wool coats, gloves, suits, and fedora hats pulled low to shield themselves from the cold wind. Each greeted Sathronia with a respectful nod before opening the massive wooden doors, revealing the sanctuary's grandeur. Inside the vestibule, over one hundred devout worshippers eagerly awaited entry, their anticipation enhancing the solemnity of the moment.

Audine was awestruck the moment she entered. She gazed up with excitement at the church's elaborate style surrounding her: men, after removing their hats and coats, wore tailored suits, while women donned beautifully styled wool dresses, complemented by stylish yet straightforward polished oxford shoes, modest purses, wool coats paired with matching gloves and hats, and perfectly coiffed hair, with not a single strand out of place, even secured with a hat pin.

Energy pulsed through the air, driven by the

sounds of trombones, sousaphones, and tambourines. The worshippers, already swept up in the Holy Spirit, made a breathtaking scene. Some were lost in bliss, their feet moving with a sense of divine joy, while others danced, pranced, or stood still in quiet corners, their arms raised in surrender and their eyes tightly closed in prayer.

From the ethereal mist, two women glided towards Sathronia, their figures draped in ankle-length white frocks and their heads entirely veiled in matching tignons. Audine looked at their feet and noticed they adorned heavy-knit white socks.

"Praise the Lord!" they said in unison.

"Praise the Lord on this glorious morning!" exclaimed Sathronia, smiling and nodding.

"Sisters of our highest Lord, this is my good friend, Mrs. Audine Collins, from New Orleans. She's the new boarder staying at my home. She's new to Chicago and settling in. Please ensure she's sitting directly behind me and my daughters. Oh, and please make sure my daughters are checked on and cared for, especially Ruthie, because she'll have her baby in February and will need to go to the bathroom more often."

As Sathronia turned to a smiling Ruthie, she saw her rubbing her belly through her coat. Ruthie shook her head and smiled.

Audine forced a smile, but at the same time, she felt a pang of jealousy and resentment toward the loving bond between Sathronia and her daughters.

Thinking of Violet only fueled the growing infuriation.

"I'll take the coats of Bishop Almond's wife, his daughters, Ezra, and, uh, my apology, but what was your name again, beloved?" asked the smiling woman dressed in white, glancing over at Audine.

"Audine Collins, Mrs. Audine Collins," Audine said, her voice quiet and ominous.

"Yes, ma'am. Just so you'll know, you'll be sitting behind Bishop Almond's family," she replied coolly.

As the coats were gathered, a formation took shape: Sathronia, a strong-willed woman with a commanding presence, would lead, followed by her daughters, and Audine, a quiet observer, would bring up the rear.

Ezra had already entered the sanctuary through the side door to join his wife and the other deacons.

Two women, their white robes glowing in the dim light, led the way to the door. They took their places on either side, grasping the ornate gold-plated handles. With a single, unified pull, they swung the doors open, revealing the sanctuary's grandeur.

Throbbing music, a deafening blend of sounds, filled the air, its volume and intensity stunning Audine. The high-pitched notes from over fifty trombones, two sousaphones, and tambourines reached a frenzy, echoing throughout the space. As they walked down the aisle, Audine's eyes widened, trying to take in the scene: worshipers lying prostrate at the altar, others on their knees in the middle aisle, their passion palpable in the air.

As Sathronia and her daughters took their seats in the center pews, the music intensified and sped up. The moment they were settled, her daughters jumped to their feet, arms raised, heads thrown back, and let out a loud, piercing shriek, bursting into a frenzy of speaking in tongues.

As Audine sat down at the end of the pew, right behind Sathronia, she noticed that Sathronia looked preoccupied, with her neck tense and a worried expression on her face. But then Sathronia's face suddenly changed.

Who was she looking at? Audine wondered to herself as she casually turned her head toward the direction Sathronia was casting her flirtatious gaze, accompanied by a wide smile.

June Posey.

Standing just a few feet away, June joined the rest of the congregation, pounding her tambourine so hard that it looked like she was sending a message of love to Sathronia. Now that she felt relieved, her beloved was just a few feet away. Sathronia stood up and began shouting and praising alongside the other worshippers.

Audine stood up to absorb the church's volume, and the music shifted from a chord to an even louder tune. This time, the aisle began to clear as people who had been lying on the floor rose. The ushers hurried to assist the women covered in sheets and lifted them to their feet.

"Make way for Bishop Thomas Almond's grand entrance!" Ezra's voice thundered, leading the deacons in a loud round of applause as they formed a semi-circle around him. The excitement in the air was palpable.

As the music started again, the congregation rose to their feet, facing the center aisle.

With a regal stride, Thomas entered, followed by a procession of twelve deacons whose presence commanded respect and awe.

Audine's eyes widened just in time to see Thomas, resplendent in his customary early morning prayer attire, now enhanced with a regal red trim that glimmered in the spotlight, serving as a testament to his elevated status.

At the forefront was the formidable group of twelve deacons, all wearing navy-blue tailored suits and ties. They were followed by the revered Elders of Eight, a select group of eight men who had become the backbone of the church. With roles ranging from founders to builders, they worked under Thomas's father, leaving a lasting legacy that would shape the church into one of Chicago's largest.

However, the ninth elder cast a dark shadow with a disturbing prophecy. He revealed a vision that served as a stark warning about Thomas. The prophecy stated that if Thomas gained power, he would lead a corrupt group of lies, false teachings, and a reckless attitude toward the church's women. This warning left the deacons feeling uncertain and anxious.

He would also commit a string of terrible crimes against his own family, causing so much turmoil within the church that it would take years to recover. However, Thomas would be exposed, humiliated, and forced to leave, and his life would ultimately end tragically, without ever reaching the age of forty-two.

Precisely a month after the prophecy was made, the ninth elder passed away.

As the church music filled the air, it brought back memories of New Orleans. For a brief moment, Audine got lost in the music, swaying with the others in the church, and then raising her arms and throwing her head back.

Thomas strutted up the aisle, approaching the spot where Audine was sitting, and flashed a smile.

Audine experienced immense joy from the small gesture.

He saw me! She thought, slowly inching her way into the middle aisle to do her wild, ecstatic dance for Thomas to notice. But he wasn't smiling at Audine; he was smiling at Sathronia and their daughters.

Audine's dance attempt was cut short as she abruptly changed her pace, sat down, and took deep, exasperated breaths. She felt like everyone was watching and probably laughing at her.

She cast her eyes down, shooting June a sly glance. June, who was staring daggers at Thomas and then Sathronia, felt her anger boil over as she saw Sathronia smile back at Thomas.

What's going on here? Why is Sathronia grinning at Thomas, and why the fuck is Audine, of all people, here? June fumed to herself, unaware that she was beating her tambourine so hard it broke.

CHAPTER THIRTY-EIGHT

"You're just as crooked as a road with no sense! There's a road that has two sides: my sisters and brothers. The left side features a beautiful, smooth surface with no unevenness, rocks, or deep cracks. Each side is lined with trees that sway in the wind, green grass, and people who seem kind and loving. Now I ask you all, how many of you desire to walk further down that road?" preached Thomas as he strolled down the aisle, his deep baritone voice resonating so loudly that it could be heard up in the balcony.

Congregants were already on their feet, surrounded by shrieks, howls, shouts of "amen," and waving large white handkerchiefs.

My brothers and sisters don't fall for it! Don't let the temptation of a road that will ultimately be filled with lies, deceit, destruction, and sin, among other things, draw you in. What will it lead to, beloveds?

"Death!" the worshippers shouted.

"Amen, yes! As you walk down the left side of the road, which at first seems beautiful, it suddenly becomes rocky. It's as if you're walking a road to hell! And the people you thought were kind and loving toward you start acting like two-headed serpents, with tongues that flicker in and out like fire. Their words turn into nasty gossip and offensive stories, and they're despicable! When they're done with you, my dear ones, you'll feel worthless, empty, and alone – like a beautiful bird with broken wings, beating its wings in vain. A bird can't fly with a broken wing; it eventually dies! After they're finished with you, you'll feel like you've been punched and stomped, and that hurts! It's painful! Please avoid them; they'll pretend to be your friend, but watch out for those backbiters! They're not your friends; they don't even like you! But I'll leave you with this, my dear ones: there's a lesson in every disappointment, just as there is in victory! Find the lesson in the holy word; uncover the lesson! Let's all commit to walking the path of truth and righteousness and be vigilant against the deceit and sin that may cross our paths!

A whirlwind of holy energy consumed every

corner of the church. As the spirit took hold, people were overcome with an intense, ecstatic worship. The music thundered, driving worshippers to burst into sacred dances. Audine noticed that many women took off their shoes and danced so quickly that their feet seemed to disappear. The air was filled with the sound of tongues, people collapsing to the ground, weeping, and wailing. Several women, including Sathronia, danced with such abandon that they lost their balance. Still, thankfully, the ushers were quick to catch them, removing Sathronia's hat and covering her legs with a sheet.

As she sat, Audine swayed back and forth, but she shot a sideways glance at June, who was crying and speaking in tongues in the corner. Her attention suddenly turned to the middle aisle, and Audine's eyes grew wide with shock as she saw Bee and Amalie lying on the floor, being tended to by the ushers, with their legs covered and their bodies prostrate on the ground.

"And if I can say one more thing to all of you, run to the right side of the road, which has no room for the liars, deceivers, and scorpions who inflict purposeful pain! Their tongues are like arrows on fire that speak deceit and death! No, no, no, brothers and sisters! Travel on the right side of the road and run as fast as your feet can carry you from those sinful gravediggers! They're murderous, and their weapons are their mouths and their evil deeds and desires!" boomed Thomas, whose eyes were fixed on Audine.

With her gloved hand, Audine covered her mouth, looking over at Thomas, who held her gaze until she looked away, then smirked.

Hah! I know exactly who Thomas was talking about, and it wasn't me! Audine thought, her smile hidden behind her gloved hand as she fixed her gaze on Sathronia and June.

Thomas kept his eyes on Audine, observing as she attempted to conceal her mischievous smile with her gloved hand.

He figured this would be way too easy; Audine was trying to get his attention. He glanced over at Sathronia, still face down on the floor. In another corner of the church, Ruthie, Lucinda, and Delphine were clustered in a tight circle, their arms wrapped around each other.

Thomas hurried over to join in their intense worship. They clung to him as if their lives depended on it.

Audine shot the four of them a glare, but before long, her gaze turned curious, wondering why they were receiving so much attention.

Wasn't that supposed to be the kind of attention their husbands would give them? Audine wondered to herself, lost in the music's intense din, as the entire church erupted into holy chaos once again.

CHAPTER THIRTY-NINE

Sunday Dinner.

"Sathronia, this meal was delicious! Even in tough times, we can still appreciate good food, right? I've got to say this: our church members truly care about us. It's clear from the fact that after the Trustee tallied up the offerings from all the auxiliaries this morning, we broke last week's total by over a thousand dollars. I think they took my sermon to heart when I reminded them that when we enjoy a good meal, our household gets blessed, and so does theirs!" boomed Thomas as he reached for a second slice of sweet potato pie.

"So, Audine, how did you like my sermon? Did you enjoy yourself?" he asked.

Placing her coffee cup on the table, Audine locked eyes with Thomas and took a deep breath.

"To be honest with you, I felt something about your sermon. It was so soul-stirring that it touched me in a way I've never felt before," she replied.

That's a flat-out lie, Thomas thought to himself as he straightened up in his chair.

"Tell me how it touched your heart. Was it the music, the singing, my sermon, or watching the saints fall out on the sacred floor? You have heard that the floor in *my* church has wonderful working powers! So, tell me what you liked and appreciated today."

"Your sermon on the road to take the left or right-side tore right into my heart. You reminded me of some people who were liars, deceitful gossipers, and downright disloyal. Humph, that's exactly what happened to me! When I was living in New Orleans, several people close to me were on the left side of the road, and being the proper, upright woman that I am, those people, including my husband and a woman who wanted to dig her dirty fingernails into my marriage, were those serpents! Hard-boiled pieces of liars and deceivers, hah! The hardest thing I had to do was ask my daughter to leave my house. She did a horrible, sinful thing that is shameful, especially for me," answered Audine, who was visibly shaken.

"Have mercy; I'm so sorry to hear that, Audine.

You must've been through a tough time," Sathronia said, taking Audine's hand.

Let me squeeze her hand a little tighter, so Thomas will feel so sorry for me that he'll melt and come closer to me, Audine thought as she dabbed at the corner of her eye to catch a fake tear.

"That's sad, Mrs. Collins. How's your daughter doing? What's her name, and how old is she?" Ruthie asked, just as curious as her dad. At that moment, she felt the baby inside her move. She smiled down at her belly, rubbed it gently, and glanced at Thomas.

So did her sisters, Lucinda and Delphine.

"Her name was- I mean, Violet. She's about your age, Ruthie. She-ah was supposed to be a teacher. Anyway, she decided to become a teacher and leave for France with a married man; now he's divorced, and they're happily living there. But it was my husband who betrayed me and left me for another woman, so I left, and, well, here I am," Audine replied.

Lies, lies, lies! I'm well aware of everything because Bee filled me in about your little tiff and how your husband, not you, chose to leave the marriage. And I've got more dirt on you that I'll be sharing soon! Umph, umph, umph! You can keep spilling lies, and I'll add them to my list! Thomas thought to himself, averting his gaze for another sip of coffee. Sathronia cleared her throat, eyeing Thomas with a smirk.

"Audine, the fact that you got the message from my sermon tells me you're ready to join my church and serve. I'd like to see this happen soon. What do you think, Sathronia? Do you feel she's ready to become a member?" he asked, looking over at Sathronia, who was still holding Audine's hand.

"I believe that would be a huge help, especially for me. Since I visit June Posey every Thursday, we can have Audine take me to June's home to discuss the menu for the church's soup kitchen, which serves struggling members. As you know, the menu changes every week. June also prepares many of the items at her home so we can taste them and adjust. We also do afternoon devotions, so it'll work out perfectly! That way, Ezra won't have to use his car, and Audine can handle the shopping".

"My dear, wait a minute. How will you get to June's if you don't have Ezra to drive you?" interrupted Thomas, who had Sathronia's full attention.

"Audine will drive me. She'll drive Noddington's car," she said, keeping her voice steady and firm.

Blindsided by the discussion, Audine sat in stunned silence.

"What?" She whispered, her eyes wide with astonishment.

"Noddington's car? Do you know that car hasn't been on the road for years? I'm not going to have that thing driven! What happened in that car and the circumstances are awful, and I think it's a bad idea. Plus, it probably won't even start anymore, and Audine can't drive!" Thomas shot up from his chair, his voice rising in anger.

"Yes, I can; I most certainly can drive a car, Bishop," Audine said, gripping Sathronia's hand even tighter.

"What? Can you drive a car?" Thomas asked, clearly stunned.

"Yes, I can drive. I drove if my husband was sick and I had to pick up my son from school on rainy days! Not many Black women living in New Orleans's countryside could drive. It was hard at first, but I was determined to learn," Audine replied, her head held high.

Thomas's green eyes seemed like they might pop out of his sockets. Ruthie, Lucinda, and Delphine proudly watched their mother as she stood her ground to receive transportation assistance from a woman.

"How long have you been driving?" he asked.

"Two years. My husband, Wayne, and I were good friends before we married, so he taught me. And Sathronia is right about me doing my part to help with shopping, and didn't you ask me—I mean, prophesy to me—about becoming a member of your church to serve? Well, I'm here to tell you that I'm ready to join and to serve," declared Audine.

With a gentle squeeze, Sathronia closed her eyes, while Audine reciprocated the gesture.

Thomas kept his gaze focused on the interaction

between Sathronia and Audine.

Something's off with these two women. Even my daughters are on board —like Audine just walked in and gave them some power—every woman rising against me, hah! We'll see who comes out on top because Audine's got a lot of baggage that needs to be flipped over. Humph!

"I need to see how you drive and make sure my wife will be safe when you take her to June's house. Additionally, I wanted to mention that if you continue staying with us, you'll need to earn your keep and contribute to expenses. Since you've been with us for 3 weeks, you owe us $5. Next Wednesday, you'll head to the hospital to meet with Bee. She's got a job lined up for you," said Thomas.

Audine stared at Thomas, her eyes wide with panic; Thomas noticed and smiled confidently.

"Are you alright, Audine? You looked like you were about to jump out of your skin when I said you need to work to stay here. To clear things up, I took you in out of the goodness of my heart. It was a miracle that Ezra found you in your condition - bruised, beaten, and hungry. I was the one who provided a roof over your head, a bed to sleep in, and paid for a nurse to treat your wounds. You got fed, took your medicine, and now you'll have a church to attend and serve. Plus, you're living in one of the nicest and safest houses in Bronzeville! Now, my dear, if you're going to stay, you'll have to pay the rent! As soon as you start earning a paycheck, I'll expect to see the money in this box right here," he said, heading towards a wooden box inside the cabinet where the Sunday dishes were kept. Thomas pulled out the box and carefully set it on the table.

"This box will be on the table every Friday. When you arrive at the house, head straight to this room, open the box, and put your money inside. If you miss a payment, you'll find your belongings outside the door," Thomas said, setting the box on the table.

Still holding Sathronia's hand, Audine stood up from her seat, reached into her pocket, and pulled out five crumpled dollar bills-the ones she had found in the monsters' pants pocket after they attacked her.

She let go of Sathronia's hand and made a bold move, lifting the box lid, dropping the crumpled wad of money inside, and closing the lid again. With a satisfied look, she went back to her seat. Sathronia, Ruthie, Lucinda, and Delphine stared in shock, realizing that Audine had already paid the whole five dollars.

Amusement sparkled in Thomas's eyes.

"Oh-ho! So, I see you were prepared, wonderful! Now that you know what's expected of you, I appreciate your willingness to follow through. Thanks for the money. As for next week, don't worry about it yet since you won't be paid until you work a full week. I'll be in touch with Bee about your weekly earnings," he said, wiping the corners of his mouth as he stood up.

"To all of you, goodnight, and I'll see you all for early morning prayer. Daughters, will you come with me for our prayer circle?" he added.

"Yes, Daddy, we'll be up as soon as we finish clearing the table," said Ruthie, rising from her chair.

Thomas beamed with pride as he watched his daughters collect the dishes and quickly organize the kitchen, giving Sathronia and Audine a chance to wash and dry them.

"Oh, and one more thing, Sathronia and Audine, dinner was delicious. I'm grateful my wife is sharing her cooking, but soon we'd love to get a taste of New Orleans-style cooking! I heard y'all can cook!" he exclaimed.

"Uh-huh, yes, Bishop, your wife is teaching me the Chicago way of cooking, and I certainly can cook some New Orleans-style dishes. I'm looking forward to cooking a New Orleans-style dinner," Audine said with a forced smile.

"Good! I'm looking forward to enjoying every bite you cook for me!" he said, clapping his hands together.

Thomas then stood up from his chair and headed up the stairs.

"I-I'm sorry. I can't believe how awful Thomas was treating you!" Sathronia sputtered. "Are you- "

"I need your help," interrupted Audine. If I'm going to meet Bee to start the job, I need clothes, a hair appointment, and some cash!"

"Don't worry about that," Sathronia whispered, beckoning Audine to lean in closer with a finger motion.

"Thomas has two meetings starting tomorrow morning, so he'll be tied up all day. We'll head to the church, and I'll grab some money from the treasury room for you to pick up dresses, one for your meeting with Bee about the job, and a few more for church. I'll also make sure you have matching gloves, hats, and Oxford shoes. We'll stop by the hair salon where I get my hair done. Willa, my hairdresser, will give you a wonderful hairstyle that's perfect for your meeting with Bee and church. After that, we'll head back here for a quick lunch, and then we'll start dinner. Thomas won't have any idea what we're up to."

Audine nodded and smiled.

"So, I get a new dress for the job meeting with Bee, new dresses for church, and a visit to the hairdresser to get my hair done?" she asked, running her fingers through her dry, matted hair.

"Yes, yes, and yes! As long as you're working, please take me to see June twice a week and keep our little secret. There will be plenty more dresses, shoes, and trips to the hairdresser. I promise you, me, and June will be the most stylish women in church!" Sathronia exclaimed, springing up from her chair. Audine's lips curved like flames.

Leaping from her seat, Audine embraced Sathronia tightly, unable to believe how her luck was finally changing and, deep within her deceptive heart and twisted mind, that these changes would bring her closer to Thomas.

CHAPTER FORTY

After the early morning prayer, Thomas appeared eager to leave. While eating breakfast and gulping down a hot cup of coffee, he animatedly talked about his meetings with the twelve deacons, as well as meeting the four wives of the deacons and their newborns. When he heard a knock at the front door, he rose from the table and kissed Ruthie, Lucinda, and Delphine goodbye for the day.

Audine couldn't help but notice how Sathronia rose onto her toes to wrap her arms around Thomas's neck, sending him off with a warm embrace, and how he kissed her on the forehead. He whispered something in her ear that delighted her, as shown by a crinkle of a smile forming on her face.

After staying up most of the night, Audine used her sleepiness to sneak into her slippers and tiptoe down the hallway to Thomas and Sathronia's bedroom. She pressed her ear against the door and heard Thomas groaning, followed by his declaration that he was about to release his seed. Sathronia seemed to be enjoying the moment, as Audine, her mouth open in shock, ducked down, peeked through the keyhole, and watched Sathronia straddle Thomas. Her neck was arched back, and she was guiding Thomas's hands over her breasts.

Audine kept watching as Thomas grasped Sathronia's hips and flipped her over onto her back, positioning himself on top of her. Her final word turned into a loud moan as he thrust himself inside her.

With her hand over her mouth muffling her cries, Audine quickly retreated to her room, slammed the door shut, and crawled into bed, furious that it was Sathronia sharing a bed with Thomas, not her.

"Audine, are you almost ready? It's nearly nine o'clock. Thomas should still be at his meeting, and we need to get that car out of the garage. Hurry, please!" she urged, knocking urgently on Audine's door.

"I'm ready. I'm putting on my boots so that I won't get too cold," Audine replied as she laced up her boots and opened the door.

"I've already let Ruthie know that you and I will be running some errands for the church and should be back by three o'clock. Our neighbor, Mrs. Preyer, will keep an eye on my daughters while we are away. Let's head to the garage and get the car started!" said Sathronia.

"I'm ready and excited for this shopping trip and finally getting my hair done at last! Does Thomas know you're doing all this for me?" Audine asked as they headed downstairs.

"He knows about me taking you to get your hair done, but when he asked how we were getting around for the day, I explained to him that you were driving," she said, slipping on her gloves after reaching the bottom of the stairs.

"Oh, I see, so Thomas doesn't know about the new clothes?" Audine asked, searching for answers.

"Nope, as far as he's concerned, those clothes you're getting are a gift from June, who I'm going to visit while you get your hair done. The hairdresser is just up the street from her house, so I'll walk over. After you finish getting your hair done, you can swing by to pick me up, and then we'll head home," Sathronia said, beaming at the prospect of seeing June again.

"Ruthie, Lucinda, Delphine, Mrs. Collins, and I will be back at three o'clock. Mrs. Preyer will be stopping by for lunch," Sathronia called out to them.

They came out of the kitchen, hugged their mother, and waved goodbye to Audine, who secretly wished they would do the same for her.

Both garage doors were heavy, so they had to use all their strength to pry them open. The stale, musty smell was overpowering, and Audine had to turn away to cough. Sathronia covered her nose with her gloved hand, but even the strong gusts of wind didn't help.

And there it was, the black Ford Model B - Noddington's car.

"This was your husband's car," Audine said, nodding toward the vehicle.

"Yes, this was my husband's car, Noddington, my heart, my love. I miss him so much sometimes. It's been years since I last saw this car inside the garage. He was always so careful with it, keeping it clean and smelling good," she said, with emotion welling up in her throat.

She ran her gloved hand along the car's front end, which still looked polished and clean. A speck of dust was all that marred it. Audine gently tapped the tires with her booted toe, a technique she'd learned from Wayne to ensure the tire was firm and not nobby, or else a flat tire might strike when least expected.

Sathronia gasped.

"What's wrong?" Audine asked, rushing to Sathronia, trembling, hand over her mouth. She pointed to the rear window.

Audine pulled the lever to open the door. In the back seat, a chauffeur's cap and black gloves, both belonging to Noddington, sat.

As Audine collected the cap and gloves to give Sathronia, she noticed dime-sized rust stains on the seat.

"Oh my God, those are bloodstains! Sathronia was right when she said that Noddington was murdered in this car!" Audine thought to herself as she pulled out his belongings with trembling hands.

She watched, tears streaming down her face.

"Shh. I'm here now, and I'll take care of you. I see

why you've been upset about this and haven't been able to talk about it. I'm your friend now, and I'm glad you shared everything about your husband and how you got this beautiful house. At least you have something of his to remember him by. When we get back, put these somewhere safe where only you know they are," advised Audine as she gently gathered a crying Sathronia into her arms in a protective embrace.

It appeared to soothe Sathronia, who looked at Audine with reddened, swollen eyes, while taking Noddington's hat and gloves.

"Thank you, Audine. These are precious, and you're right to advise me to put his things somewhere safe, which I'll do when we get back," Sathronia said with a quiver in her voice.

"Come on, we need to move before the day ends. Sit next to me. Where are the car keys, and do we have blankets to stay warm? I need one over my legs, and you can use one too," Audine said, scanning the car for essentials.

"Yes, I have the keys, and there might still be a few blankets in the corner on the back seat," Sathronia said, pulling out the key and handing it to Audine.

"You get in, and I'll find the blankets. Once I have them, I'll drive the car out so I can close the garage doors," she said.

Taking charge, Audine spotted three blankets on the car's floorboard. As she unfolded the first one, Audine wrinkled her nose at the musty smell. An enormous brown stain marred it, revealing an old bloodstain.

Oh no, this blanket must have been used to stop the bleeding or cover Noddington's body as he lay dying after being stabbed, Audine thought.

Her heart racing, Audine grabbed the blanket, wrapped it tightly under her arm, and hurried to the corner of the yard, where a lit ash can from that morning was now burning down to embers.

"They burn trash every Monday here in Chicago, like wash-day Monday in New Orleans," Audine muttered as she dropped the blood-stained blanket into the ash can. With a loud whoosh, it turned to ashes.

Even though I hate Sathronia, I couldn't be that

heartless and let her see her husband's blood on that blanket, Audine thought as she got into the car and handed the remaining blanket to Sathronia, who wrapped it around her legs and clutched Noddington's hat. She pulled his gloves over her own hands for warmth and hugged his hat tightly to her chest.

"Ready?" Audine asked excitedly as she started the car.

"As soon as you close the garage doors, let's go," said Sathronia, who looked a little happier, hugging Noddington's hat closer to her chest.

Carefully pressing the gas pedal to prepare the car for reverse, Audine remembered how Wayne had taught her to tread cautiously when backing out of a garage. This would be easier since it involved moving forward. Pulling a few more inches away from the doors, Audine shifted the gear into park, got out of the car, and closed the garage doors. Then she got back inside the car.

As you coast down the driveway, turn right. We're heading straight to the church first," Sathronia said.

"Yas, ma'am," Audine said, mimicking a deep Southern dialect.

They burst into laughter as Audine looked both ways and headed toward the church.

Since there were hardly any cars on the road, the drive to the church was quicker than expected. At Sathronia's request, Audine pulled over to the curb, just a few feet from the church, to remain discreet.

I'll be back soon. Thomas is still meeting with the deacons, which is a good thing. That means they'll go all morning before he sees the wives of the deacons who just had their babies. I don't understand why Thomas wanted everyone to come today to see the babies, especially since it's chilly out here," she said. "Oh, well, I'll be back in a bit."

"I'll be waiting for you. Just be quick and careful," said Audine, smiling broadly and nodding. *This is easier than I expected! I need new clothes and shoes, and I'm finally getting my hair done. A new job is waiting for me as a top nurse! All I have to do is convince Bee about that, watch, and do what the real nurses do every day, and get paid just as much as they do!* Audine said aloud, clapping her hands with one hot, gleeful snap.

Sathronia entered the church through the side door. Kitchen sounds included clattering pans, workers humming tunes from the previous day's service, running water, and the smell of coffee brewing in the percolator.

She tiptoed and moved closer, catching sight of June. The other woman was too busy to glance up from her work, probably preparing for the next two weeks. There was no time to stare at the woman she loved. Sathronia hurried as quickly as she could, heading straight for the door labeled Treasury Room - Trustees Only.

Sathronia pulled the key from her pocketbook to unlock the treasury room door. With a quiet click and a turn of the doorknob, she entered, turned on the light, shut the door, and hurried over to the table where more than thirty baskets from yesterday's offerings overflowed with cash.

This will be quick. Since the trustees haven't counted and tallied yet, it will be easy! I'll put whatever is left back as my offering on Sunday! Sathronia thought, elated.

She went over to the first basket.

"Fifteen dollars for hair, split three ways between me, Audine, and June, my sweetheart. Then there's fifty dollars for dresses, shoes, stockings, and new underwear for Audine, a new girdle for me, hats, gloves, pocketbooks for Audine, and some extra cash just in case." She quietly ran through the numbers in her head as she added them up.

As she neared the last basket, she reached in and pulled out a handful of cash, but then she heard a knock at the door.

It was June!

"Hello, is anyone in there? Trustee Saunders, if you are not, I'll need to remind you to turn off the lights when you leave, because electricity ain't cheap!" June joked. Then she could be heard walking away from the door and back into the kitchen.

Sathronia stayed frozen, terrified of getting caught, even when she saw a small mouse scamper across the room into its hole in the corner. The loud laughter from the kitchen was still echoing, and it was time to make her escape. With careful speed, Sathronia counted out the cash. Satisfied with the amount for shopping, hair, and extra expenses, she stuffed the bills into her pocketbook, tiptoed to the two lamps illuminating the room, and switched them off. Then, she cautiously opened the door, peeked both ways, and when the coast was clear, she quietly closed it. With lightning speed, Sathronia dashed out the side door, unaware that Trustee Saunders was watching her from the window in Thomas's office.

"Drive!" yelped Sathronia to Audine, who already had her hands on the steering wheel.

Without hesitation, Audine started the car and sped toward the clothing factory, which was a ten-minute drive from the church.

"We made it!" Sathronia exclaimed, panting. Audine smiled and pulled the car right up to the factory entrance. After parking and stashing the keys in her purse, she and Sathronia linked arms and headed inside to shop – a luxury most women in their community couldn't even dream of, let alone afford, not even a new pair of shoes.

As soon as she walked in, Sathronia knew exactly where to find what she needed - the section with the most formal suits for business or church. The staff welcomed her warmly and let her know that new dresses were on their way from the sewing rooms, but they wouldn't be ready for another few hours. They invited her to come back for the first pick. Sathronia agreed and handed one of the staff a dark blue business suit for Audine's meeting with Bee. "Please hold this for my friend; we'll be back for the new arrivals," she said.

"While they're putting the clothes on the racks, let's get our hair done, then head back to the factory to grab the clothes you'll need," Sathronia suggested as she and Audine hurried to the car.

As they headed to the hairdresser, the laughter and conversation had Audine in fits at times, especially when they started talking about the church members — particularly the women — who were all trying to get Thomas's attention.

"And when that didn't work, Geneva turned to the deacons," Sathronia said, her hand covering her mouth to stifle another burst of laughter.

"She did what?" Audine asked, pulling into a spot near the hair salon.

"Geneva went onto the deacons, but it seems like the only one who was interested in her was Deacon Clahvell, and he's way older than Geneva!" said Sathronia, bursting into laughter.

"How old is he?" Audine asked, pulling into the parking spot and turning off the engine.

"She's twenty-nine years old, and he's fifty-nine! She's one of the wives Thomas is meeting later this morning. She's the one who had her baby last out of the three who gave birth early that morning, the day you met Bee. She and Clahvell had been trying to have a baby for over a year. One day, she woke up feeling sick, so Clahvell took her to the hospital. Luckily, Bee was there. After some tests, she was sent home to rest. A week later, Bee called her and told her to sit down. She had a surprise to share – she was having a baby! Clahvell turned fifty-nine the day his daughter was born, and he told Thomas that in a year, he and Geneva would start trying for another one to grow their family," said

Sathronia.

"And what did Thomas say? What was Geneva's response?" Audine asked, anxious to hear the answer.

"Geneva wants to start right away, in six months. Thomas told Clahvell to wait for the good news," she said as she got out of the car. "Well, we're here, and it looks like only three customers are getting their hair done inside. Earlene and Ellaria are wrapping up, and no one else is waiting, so let's head in," said Sathronia, leading the way.

Audine followed suit. Sathronia still grasped Nodington's gloves, but Audine saw that his hat was gone and chose not to mention it.